The Weight of Swords

From the Sword Bearer Chronicles

By Lance Conrad

DAWNSTAR
PRESS

The Weight of Swords

For information about special discounts, bulk purchases,
or reproduction of content in this book, please contact
Dawn Star Press:
info@dawnstarpress.com

Cover art by Noel Sellon

ISBN: 978-0-9910230-7-3

Printed in the United States of America

To my parents,
who have the unfailing belief that
their children are capable of anything.

Prologue

The seething dragon crouched, quivering with pain and rage. His red-tinged eyes tried in vain to watch every figure moving around him. Another lance bit into his flesh and he twisted like an enraged cat, snapping at the offending object with jaws powerful enough to crimp the steel.

The attack stopped short as shining chains as thick as his legs jerked tight, halting his retribution. He roared with frustration, bloody froth dripping from his jaws. He had always been treated gently, talked to kindly, until this day. He was confused, frustrated, and enraged that he could be treated like this.

The two-legged demons circled him, lances carried at the ready, dark blood—his blood—staining the blades and the thick wooden handles. Each man wore a mask that covered everything but the eyes. The masks were useless as protection against his wrath, but they frustrated him.

He would always remember this experience, and he tried desperately to see something of his attackers that would allow him to hunt them down. He could not see their faces, and every whiff of his human attackers burned his sensitive nostrils with a stink that was obviously intentional. If he could find something to identify them, he would hunt them down if it took his entire lifetime. Such was the persistence of his species.

A sharp pain and a gush of warmth burst on his shoulder as another lance penetrated his young, soft armor plates. A small flood of steaming blood splashed down his scales and was immediately chewed into mud by his churning claws. If it weren't for the chains he could end the punishment. In mere seconds the mismatched fight would be over.

Then the command came. To him the words of the Master were a feeling more than a sound. They washed over his consciousness like a warm caress, calming the pain of his wounds and closing his gaping jaws. There was no question of his obedience; he did as the command said as quickly as if it had been his own thought. He stood calmly, his head bowed, his eyes closed, waiting for his Master's touch.

He waited, trying not to quiver in anticipation, until the touch came. The Master touched him on the shoulder, next to a deep lance wound that was still seeping blood.

Another command and he was lying on his stomach, his Master standing next to his horned head. He had already forgotten about his attackers, the frustration gone. His entire world was his Master and the spoken commands. In some corner of his mind he recognized that the attacks had ceased, but it was a trivial detail.

He heard a sound above him, but it was not a command, and while his Master stood near him only the commands mattered.

The saltwater mixture was too thick to splash, but the murky flood bathed his entire body with scalding, burning liquid. He wanted to roar, to scream in outrage and pain, but that was not allowed of him —the command was to lie still, not to react to pain. His muscles locked solid with pain, the pressure pushing more blood from dozens of wounds.

When the flood ceased, he lay shaking violently, dripping with blood and salt sludge. His entire body was burning, tearing with pain.

Another command brought him to his feet, and one more allowed him to rest his head against the breastplate of the Master himself. He felt a slow hand rub the side of his head, and he hummed with pleasure, a sound that rumbled out of his massive chest like distant thunder. His armor scales warmed from a solid, inky black to a dark red as he hummed in happiness.

The Master was smaller than he was, in fact the top of the Master's head would not have reached the top of his shoulder, but none of that mattered.

Human screams warned him of another man's approach a moment before the scream's owner landed on his back on the floor. The newcomer struggled to drag himself back toward the wall from which he had been thrown. The man's screams had stopped with the impact, whether from injury or terror, no one would ever know.

A mask, like the one his attackers wore, had been bolted in place seconds earlier.

The stroking stopped and the Master stepped away. The humming in the dragon's throat stopped. He knew not to question, not to be frustrated with the end of the Master's affection. Still, on this very trying day he wanted very much to stay with his Master. With the Master everything was always okay, always nice.

The man in the mask was talking from the ground, meaningless human mumbling. The Master responded with the same. The words were not commands, and therefore gibberish to him.

He stood waiting, watching the man in the mask and listening to the Master's voice. Then, a moment later, he heard the command he was hoping to hear.

With a baring of teeth that looked eerily like a smile, he launched his bulk forward with the speed and agility of a massive panther, and the first strike of his tail tore the man in the mask into two pieces.

Chapter 1

Artair traced a massive footprint with a gauntleted finger. The clawed print had been left in the mud next to where water had pooled during the rain the night before. The edges had only begun to dry, and the nearly continual wind had not yet blown any grass into it.

His men stood around him, blocking the wind and throwing shadows across the dragon tracks. The group was so perfectly camouflaged that anyone watching would have a hard time keeping track of them against the backdrop of the plains.

Then, as if talking to himself, he said, "The beast was here less than an hour ago. We'll catch up to him as he gets into the middle of those hills, I think. Shall we?" He grinned up at the men surrounding him and there were a couple laughs. They had been fighting since childhood, as their fathers had since their childhood. This day would be no different. As a farmer would go out to the field for a day of plowing, they went into combat.

Artair stood up, and with his foot deliberately scraped the footprint into a muddy smudge, then trotted off in the direction of the tracks. His men followed close behind, running in his footsteps in single file. The dragon slayers made no more sound running than the wind that rustled their green cloaks, playing the thick fabric across their scaled armor.

The broiling afternoon sun was beginning to fall toward the horizon as the warriors finished creeping into position on the brink of a hill a couple miles from their previous location. The knee-high grass afforded them some cover. It was still green enough to allow them to move through it without a sound. The hill was not truly a hill, but they were used to that.

Centuries ago this had been a smooth valley stretching between distant mountains. A series of rivers had supplied lush grasslands that stretched for miles. The ruins of innumerable wars had since scarred and marked the landscape far more than nature had ever intended or desired.

The grasslands were no longer smooth, no longer pristine. Instead, the land was pockmarked and hilly, ridged with stone brought from faraway quarries. The hill they were on had once been the outer wall of a fortress destroyed more than a century before. The final battle for control had continued for all of ten years, changing hands half a dozen times until there was nothing left to fight over.

They earned themselves a nickname during that time period, one which had no direct translation from the old language. The *vak-halhatatlanok.*. The closest they could come was the Blind Immortals. After another two years of fighting the nickname lost some of its appropriateness, as their mortality was proved beyond question. Few of them lived long enough to pass their bloodlines on to the current Helveti.

Over time, the mighty stones of the wall had loosened and fallen, crumbling until the ground reached up to reclaim them. After all its grandeur, now the only thing that was sure was that it had existed, and that it was once again a battlefield.

They heard the dragon long before they could have seen it, and smelled it not long after. They had taken great pains to ensure that it wouldn't see them before they were ready. For more than half an hour they had been flat on their stomachs, hoping to keep out of sight, silent, and away from the wind that could carry their scent to their prey.

Crawling in the heavy dragon plate armor was not something any man would do willingly, but for them it was essential. Their plan depended on surprise and coordination, and without either one they would be lucky to survive at all. A year did not go by without notice of a team that had been utterly decimated by a bungled ambush.

Men had been known to survive a solo fight with a dragon. There were two in the party who could boast such a thing if they chose to. None could say for sure that they would survive another such encounter, however.

The four archers had already taken their positions, in two sets of two, twenty yards from each other. A lancer lay next to each set of archers. The three Sword Bearers eased into their positions at intervals between the two groups. Still, none of them had seen the animal, but they could hear it growling and could smell its stench. Dragons always smelled like the rotten meat they favored; almost as if they were rotting while still alive. They smelled of death, and it was fitting.

When everyone was in place, Artair locked eyes with the swordsman closest to him. Calum, his best friend, returned his gaze and gave a short nod. Artair grinned at him through his visor and in one smooth motion rose to his feet, putting himself into view of the small valley below and its monstrous contents. The pocket was deep, a part of a moat at one point undoubtedly, and their quarry took up almost half the floor.

The dragon faced away from him, its head low to the ground as it rooted in the dirt, grunting loudly. Twice it flicked its tail into the hard-packed loam, slicing into the rock-like earth with movements so quick that only the practiced eye of the Sword Bearer could see that it was the tail doing the work.

A long-dead animal, a deer most likely, had drawn the beast. Only the bones remained, but the smell of death was irresistible to the large reptile. It had not noticed him and Artair had a moment to look at the magnificent creature.

As dangerous as they were, there was no one who would say they weren't beautiful. A rainbow of colors when not agitated, the dragon stretched nearly ten spans in length, and was over two spans tall at the shoulder. Very few were any taller than this one. He had seen one that had been much larger, but that was long ago.

The dragon's tail had a single fixed blade, like that of a sword though twice as wide, protruding from its tip. There were two other blades sheathed inside the tail that would appear only when the dragon decided to use them. This three-pronged weapon, at the end of a whip-like tail, was one of the most dangerous parts of the monster.

A half dozen curved blades at the top of the dragon's neck worked the same way, turning the massive head into a spiked battering ram that moved as fast as a man could blink. Artair had seen a dragon battle for several minutes with a man hanging from those horns. In the end neither man nor beast had survived. Artair had taken the dragon's head home to his friend's widow. She hadn't appreciated the gesture as much as he had hoped.

There was not a soul amongst them that was not afraid of what the dragons could do. No man who could claim sanity would say he was not, but for Artair there was a stronger emotion at work.

A wicked smile growing on his face, the swordsman's armored hand reached up to his helmet, moving slowly in order to remain undetected. The oiled links in the armored gloves flexed and moved without a sound. Ignoring Calum's hissed protest, he delicately removed his headpiece and, after holding it a moment, drew his arm back and threw it at the dragon's scaled back.

The creature whipped around, alerted by the sudden motion. The helmet missed and landed on the ground with a puff of dust. The triple-bladed tail curled, cat-like, in front of him. The murderous red eyes bored into Artair's face as he slid and jumped his way down to the floor of the pocket and stood to face his opponent. Staring back at the dragon, he spread his arms and roared at the creature. When he finished he was smiling, realizing how ridiculous he must look to the monster.

Not another muscle in the massive animal moved as the blades around the dragon's head slowly slid from their hiding places, locking into place soundlessly. It was as obvious a mismatch as could be imagined. Artair, formidable though he was by human standards, could not compare by strength or size with even the smallest of the dragon's four legs. He was prey, not a fellow predator.

A terse half second later the dragon leapt soundlessly toward him, the gleaming eyes never leaving its intended victim. For the dragon, this was a simple decision: another animal was within sight, and that meant that it had to die. There was no hesitation, no deliberation, and no doubt of its success. The largest animals known to exist, the dragons were nonetheless as quick as animals a twentieth their size. It was their speed, above all else, that made them so dangerous.

As the creature's back legs left the ground, Artair's sword slid from its sheath across his back, the steel scraping musically as it came free. The dragon's jump took it straight at him, and the beast uttered a frightful scream as razor teeth and claws prepared to meet human flesh.

A ringing clang of steel on armored scale met the dragon's premature victory cry. Artair, rolling under the leaping creature, slashed upward at the animal's belly as its bulk sailed over him. The Sword Bearer rolled to the right and lay still, his face in the dust. The tail blades pounded a trench in the hard ground an inch from the end of his nose, filling his face with dirt.

As the dragon whipped around to find its lost prey, Calum leapt from the hillside and, airborne, swung his sword at the spiked head. The animal ducked, dodging the blow, and he landed in a crouch right in front of it. Spinning as he landed, the warrior sliced at the animal's chest as the scythe-like tail cut the air directly above him. The blow of the sword rang like a hammer on steel, armor plates of the dragon withstood the attack without damage.

Calum rolled forward under the huge beast as arrows filled the air above him. The first arrow bounced off the back of the dragon, but the second lodged itself deeply into the beast's heaving flank. The monster roared in anger and, leapt at the source of this new attack. The archers dropped down out of sight and the lancer stationed next to them stood.

Not once had a lancer ever been solely credited with killing a dragon, but many times they had saved their archers from certain death, often sacrificing their own. The lances they carried were heavy and long enough to allow the tip to contact the dragon before the deadly jaws were able to reach the holder. Their effectiveness, though not their survival, depended on them being able to hold their stance even though they died in it.

The beast's lunge carried it over Artair, who thrust upwards at the dragon's belly as it passed over him. The sword penetrated the weaker armor on the underbelly but the speed of the attacking reptile tore the weapon from his hands. Spinning once more, the creature roared in pain and frustration.

This was a new and unpleasant experience for it. Its prey always ran from it for the brief period of time before it was ripped down by tooth and claw, and for a dragon there was nothing that moved that wasn't prey. That these insignificant creatures would dare to act the way they did was confusing.

Lying motionless at the dragon's feet, Artair's searching eyes found his sword, now lying between the back legs of the enraged beast. He had no illusions about his chances if the dragon spotted him. He was wearing armor, of course, but that would only protect him against glancing blows, not a full attack.

Dragons had one flaw that made fighting them possible. Probably due to the fact that all creatures ran from them, the dragons couldn't see what was holding still. Whether it was their eyesight or simply a lack of attention span or memory, a still form was safe from everything but being stepped on. Artair needed his sword to continue the attack, but could not move without being seen and likely killed.

At that moment, one of the archers positioned in front of the dragon stood and fired his shaft at the enraged creature. The archer was new, and if he didn't learn patience he would not live to become experienced. Until the dragon was turned away from them, they were supposed to leave it to the Sword Bearers. That was their job.

The gleaming, horned head caught the arrow in its jaws and crushed it to splinters. The beast leapt to run along the upper edge of the hill, closing on the standing archer, obviously deciding that the bottom of the trench had become too dangerous. Its clawed feet dug into the side of the hill, giving it purchase on the steep slope.

The third Sword Bearer, Moray, exploded from the hillside with an inhuman roar and rammed his sword to the hilt between the monster's ribs. The hilt tore upward as the force of the powerful attack and the surprise of the dragon sent both man and beast rolling together down the hill.

A human scream joined the roar of the reptile as Moray was pulled from his perch on the monster's side and torn by razor claws. True to his craft, he pulled the sword a sideways down the side of the monster as he went, leaving a gaping wound that fountained steaming blood.

As they hit the bottom of the hill, the dragon threw Moray to the ground, its bloody claws still gripping the wounded man as Calum rushed in. With a metallic clang the Sword Bearer flew back as the heavy tail blade caught him in the chest, tearing away his breastplate. He hit rolling, but dazed, his breath coming in ragged gasps.

The dragon's head whipped down to strike Moray's writhing body, but halfway down the dragon's lethal jaws closed on the blade of a sword. Their tumble had brought them within reach of Altair, who had used the moment of distraction to roll over and regain his sword.

From the ground, he drove his heel into the dragon's eye while ripping his sword back out of the monster's mouth. Grunting at the blow, it swung its head around to glare at its attacker through its uninjured eye as teeth and blood dropped from his injured jaws.

Jumping to his feet, Artair watched the beast from just outside the reach of its jaws. He could smell the fetid breath of the predator as it struggled for breath. It desperately wanted to hold on to the one enemy it had succeeded in capturing, but hatred burned in its eyes for the men who encircled him. Moray's sword, meanwhile, remained buried in its side, promising to bleed the animal to death.

For the Sword Bearers the fight had now changed. The task of killing the dragon had been accomplished, it was as good as dead. Now they were fighting to get Moray out of its grasp. If they could get him free, they could retreat until the sword had finished its work.

Without taking his eyes off the beast, Artair nodded, using a slow, exaggerated motion. As his head lowered, the four archers fired simultaneously, striking the dragon on both sides. Roaring, it reared up on its hind legs, releasing Moray. The wounded man rolled out of the way as Artair rushed in close to the creature and drove his sword up into its underbelly.

The silver blade disappeared through the scaled armor and Artair angled it upward and shoved again. The stench of the animal made him want to retch as a flood of dark crimson blood gushed from the wound, covering the sword and splashing onto his hands.

A pinprick of pain turned his head as Calum's thrown sword sank deep into the body of the monster, slicing the top of his ear as it flew past. The dragon screamed a shrill cry, its back legs buckled, and it started to fall.

Artair continued to shove at the huge animal as it toppled, trying without real effect to push it farther from his wounded comrade. The impact of the fall shook the ground, causing dirt and rocks to cascade down the crumbled wall.

Rolling away from the thrashing creature, Artair tore his sword free from its body and retreated from the beast's death throes. The amount of blood pouring from the mammoth monster had already turned the dirt at the bottom of the pocket into reeking mud.

The dragon's roars weakened, and the claws stopped tearing at the bloodstained ground. With one last, futile effort, the great beast collected its legs under itself and, amazingly, lifted its bulk off the ground almost a foot before falling back down into the growing lake of its own blood.

"Stay down, old man. You're done!" Artair growled. Slowly circling his dying opponent, he finally stood next to the monster's great head. The animal was done thrashing, but its one good eye still glared at him from the ground as the horns around its head retracted into its skull. Swinging his heavy weapon, the Sword Bearer severed the dragon's head from its body. The huge animal convulsed once more and then went limp.

Artair stared at the dragon, and then watched as the red stain of blood on his sword spread to the rest of the blade, turning it to a dark crimson. The blade would stay that color for about an hour, at which point it would slowly return to its original silver sheen.

They had no idea why the swords did that, but all weapons from the Olden Times did. They also did not know how they were made, only that they could not make them anymore. Nor could they even scratch them, no matter what tool they used or how they tried to heat them. Whatever they were made of, they were the only weapons that could consistently penetrate the dragon armor, and that meant that everything else about them was unimportant.

Artair returned his weapon to its sheath and looked around as silence descended on the battlefield. Calum stood a few feet from him, blood dripping from a cut on his chin. He was breathing hard and stood holding his ribs. The archers and lancers jumped and slid down the steep walls of the pocket, and though he could see them coming, the sound of the rolling rocks and sliding dirt did not reach his ears. He was still in the light state of shock that always came after a battle.

Turning, he gaze landed on Moray, who lay motionless where his roll had taken him. He was alive, but even from a distance it was clear that he would not be for long.

The rest of the team gathered around as the two Sword Bearers took off their friend's helmet and breastplate. Moray's hair was wet with sweat and there was a bloody froth on his lips. The pain was clear on his face, but he was trying to keep from showing it.

Watching him struggle was harder for the team surrounding him than fighting the dragon had been. As the armor came free Calum and Artair exchanged a glance over their blood-soaked friend. The lethal claws had caught Moray in the side between the armor plates, almost as if the animal had known how the armor was made.

"Well, that doesn't look so bad, does it?" murmured Moray with a small smile. Even weak as he was, he could see the blood spreading across the front of his shirt and soaking the ground beneath him.

"You never could resist a good wrestling match, could you Moray? You always want to get in close and grapple these big things!" Calum said. The wounded warrior winced as he tried to laugh at the comment. The three men had been together for almost fifteen years and had seen many men and dragons die. Death was always with them, they lived it in an irony they continually tried to forget. Every time they left home they knew that death would be with them all the way. It was their purpose, and the goal of their training. There were times, though, when death decided to take one of them along with the dragon.

"I had him right where I wanted him until you guys came barging in!" The dying man's smile was weak, but sincere. Artair squeezed his hand as best he could through the gauntlet.

"Well fought, old friend, well fought." Calum spoke softly in farewell.

Moray nodded weakly at the statement. "Ahala'l." *Until death.* The rest of the team repeated the sentiment softly.

The group watched in silence as the Sword Bearer gradually relaxed and was gone.

Chapter 2

Artair laid the man's arm down across his chest as Calum stood. Walking around the dragon, he retrieved his own sword and sheathed it. Then he wrenched Moray's from the monster's flank and returned to the group, carrying their friend's weapon in his hands. Taking it by the blade, he handed it across Moray's body to Artair, who stood and reverently accepted the now-crimson sword.

He studied the blade sadly for a moment, wiped it clean on his cloak, then bent down and picked up the sheath from beside its former owner. He strapped it to his back, crossing it over his own.

As the leader of the attack, it was his responsibility to carry his friend's sword until he could find someone to take Moray's place as a Sword Bearer. There were many who would be willing to take the sword, but none he knew of who were ready.

Most of his memories were of battle, of swords and shields and painful mistakes. All Helvetians were warriors, trained to fight from their infancy, but the Sword Bearers were a full measure above their countrymen—they had to be.

Moray's body, wrapped in his own cloak, bounced along behind Calum in a makeshift litter made of two lances and a couple of the green cloaks. The litter had taken only minutes to assemble, and no words were necessary. Sadly, they had a lot of practice.

The group was quiet during the first leg of their return journey. If they had not lost a man there would have been exuberance and lighthearted laughter. The death of a dragon was to be celebrated.

The death of a Bearer was a tragedy, however, and Moray had been one of the best. His strength had gained him a kill, but it had not saved him. He had been with them almost from the beginning and had saved the lives of his comrades on countless occasions. He was the most recent casualty in a war that seemed to have no end, or at least no end they wished to contemplate.

The dragons were coming more often now. They all knew it, and it haunted them. As far back as their history reached, the Helveti had been warriors, ferocious fighters that had battled all takers as quickly as they would come, and each other when there was no one else.

All of the men were old enough to remember the time when dragons were only a myth and a scary story to tell small children. That had all changed not long ago, and the great beasts had proved to be a nightmare to more than children.

They were too far out to make it back to the city before dark, so Artair stopped the group at dusk and the men made camp next to the ruins of a stone tower. This one had been used as recently as fifty years before, and had fallen from natural causes. None of the tribes had claimed it and it had fallen during a fierce winter storm.

There had been talk, by one tribe or another, of rebuilding it, but the dragons had put a stop to that. Now anything beyond the line of walled cities that had repelled the initial wave of dragons had been abandoned.

After a scant trail dinner, they lounged around their small fire and tried to relax. Dragons were attracted to fire, they had learned that. So they kept their fires small and found ways to hide them whenever possible. Most likely it was the smell that drew them, as that was their best sense, but there was no way to tell for sure. Fire was also extremely dangerous for dragons, though it was difficult to create a fire big enough to catch them.

"So, Artair," Calum began, "why can't you be satisfied to leave your helmet on when you're fighting? That's why it's there you know!" He was lying on his side next to the fire, a small twig rolling in his calloused fingers. Handsome by anyone's standards, still there was something about him that kept women away.

In Helveti it was the women who initiated relationships, and yet none had ever dared approach him. Some had said it was the sense that he was continually fighting, whether he was physically in a battle or not. There was simply no way to distance him from the cause he was committed to.

Artair smiled and shrugged. "I don't know, I guess that I just want to even the odds a little. I mean, one of me, one of him, the poor creatures don't really stand a chance." He grinned and Calum threw the twig at him from across the fire.

"You're one to talk! What's with that sword you threw at me today? It was sheer luck that it missed and hit that dragon!" Artair's tone was serious, but his eyes twinkled as he spoke. His hand touched his ear for emphasis. The cut the sword had left there was no more than a scratch, but he planned to remind his friend of it for as long as possible.

Calum rolled his eyes. "Wear your helmet and you wouldn't have to worry about it. This is a good example of how little you know about the higher skills of battle, Artair. My blade did as much damage as yours, and I didn't have to be hugging the beast to get the job done!" Calum's voice was a model of mock superiority.

"Sure, you just try throwing that thing when I'm not around to distract the dragon with my hugging, and you'll get nothing but a good chance to practice your rolling after you lose your sword!" Artair said.

Calum laughed.

"Real funny, you two, but I don't see the humor in any of this."
The speaker's name was Iain, one of the archers. "To you this is all
funny, but we lost a man today."

Artair's smile disappeared, and he stared thoughtfully into the
coals of the fire. When he looked up, the archer was glaring at him. No
one else around the fire spoke. They all knew what would happen if the
Sword Bearer decided to take offense at the statement. They knew their
leader and the limits of his self-control.

"You don't need to spout your bitterness at us, Iain, especially
not at me. We're all fighting the same fight, and some of us have been
fighting it for a lot longer than you. If we choose to keep our sense of
humor, that is our right.

"With luck," at this he paused and smiled with all the warmth
of a dragon baring its teeth, "and the help of our swords, you may live
long enough to learn that not everything has to be as serious as combat.
However, if you would like to experience a different kind of battle, I
will gladly provide it." In an instant, almost too fast to separate the start
of his movement from the conclusion, Artair was standing.

Artair's words left no room for further conversation and Iain
finally dropped his gaze to the flames of the campfire. Rash in speaking
he might be, but he was no fool. Everyone at the fire, and possibly
everyone in the empire, knew the story behind the first two Sword
Bearers. They were the first, the best, and their only real hope for a
future.

"Douse the fire, spread out. May the sun rise." Artair said over
his shoulder as he left the fire's light.

"May the sun rise." Each of the men repeated as they faded into
the darkness of the woods.

Chapter 3

Artair wrapped his cloak around him and settled back against the trunk of a large tree. The team didn't sleep around the campfire anymore, ever since the mate of a dragon they had killed tracked them back to their camp.

They'd lost several men that night before driving the animal away,. Now they slept apart and in the dark. They all agreed that they preferred the cold to fighting dragons in the dark. Artair's fingers traced the hilt of his sword for a few short moments, pondering the strange nature of the weapon. Each of the ancient swords was unique, beautifully crafted as if for display instead of use. Upon first seeing one, you had to assume that a master craftsman had once presented each of the swords as his crowning achievement. Just by looking at them, you would never guess their true potential and power.

Most Helvetians knew about the sharpness of the swords, their durability that bordered on invincibility. Very few, however, knew how unique the blades really were. He had tried to explain it every time a new Sword Bearer was brought onto the team, but in the end it worked out better to let the newcomer discover for himself.

The swords were, at very least, temperamental. It started there, to be sure, and sometimes would graduate to something more complex. Nearly all of them seemed lighter or heavier depending on the person. His own sword, for example, was as heavy as three regular swords to almost any other man. It was heavy enough to be almost unusable, except to him. To him it was as light as a practice foil, the kind given to children when they were first taught swordsmanship.

That was where it began, but some of them had other attributes. One was said to actually hum while in combat, especially after a killing blow was dealt. The blade hummed loud enough to be heard two paces away.

What was more troubling is that everyone agreed it sounded like a happy humming, almost a purring. Other swords seemed to have either a moral compass or a lazy streak, and would suddenly become heavy to even their masters when the cause was suspect or it was early in the morning.

His own sword was never stubborn, and did not hum, but it had its ways of telling him when it was pleased or disturbed. It warmed in his hands when in combat, and cooled to an icy frost if he stayed too long in town, even in the heat of summer. In essence, his sword enjoyed the heat of battle, and was displeased if kept from it.

His fingers continued to stroke the handle of his sword as sleep slowly overtook him.

…two dragons stood side by side, watching the men run at them. Although they had never seen such creatures before, it was obvious what they were. The animals were motionless as they were surrounded except for the catlike twitching of their tails.

On signal, the men surrounding them attacked. Their actions were smooth and fluid, displaying long practice and instinctual obedience to training. For several seconds, dust clouded everything except a general sense of violent movement, but the roars of the dragons and the screams of the men reached and terrified the watching youth.

The battle stopped suddenly, and the dust slowly settled. At least half the attackers now lay on the ground, crumpled heaps of

blood and dust. The remaining men huddled in a small group several
yards from the beasts. Fear marked them plainly, and several were
already bleeding from gaping wounds as they struggled to stay
standing.

The reptiles again stood still, waiting for the men's next move.
The group moved abruptly as they ran in pairs straight at the big
creatures and then broke away to either side as they came within reach
of them. The maneuver was designed to pull the animals away from
each other and allow the men to get in close to the dragons' flanks.

It worked.

The creatures spun in opposite directions, tearing the first two
men down with tail and claw. The town's blacksmith ran in beside the
bigger of the two monsters and thrust his sword up into the belly of the
reptile.

Or, at least, he tried. The blacksmith's sword bounced off the
dragon's armor and skidded across its pebbled skin, barely scratching
the great beast. The dragon whipped around and cleaved the man off
his feet with one slicing swing of a paw.

The surviving men gave up and ran desperately for their
homes, but this time the reptiles attacked, running down the fleeing
villagers with dumbfounding speed. The last man screamed as he died,
and then there was no sound. The dragon's bloodstained jaws gaped
wide as it roared…

Artair awoke with a jerk, sweat beading on his forehead. He
was breathing heavily, the sound of it loud in the night air. The Sword
Bearer switched from panting to holding his breath as he realized that,
other than the noise he was making, the night was silent. He had fallen
asleep to the sound of insects and other noises of the night. All those
were now still. He rose to a crouch, his eyes probing the darkness.
Brutally awakened by the dream, all sleep had fled from him.

A twig crunched a few feet to his left and Artair pivoted toward the sound. Motionless, the Helvetian was close to invisible to the man who walked into his sight and stopped within a few feet of him. The stranger was dressed in dark greens and browns, like the Sword Bearers themselves, but not in dragon plate armor. The clothing was not that of a Helvetian. He was looking toward the long-cold site of the campfire. It seemed that he had not yet seen Artair as he took another slow step in his direction.

The warrior stayed perfectly still, both swords still in their sheaths, waiting. He knew exactly what he would do when he decided to attack. He would try to disarm the stranger, but would kill him if necessary. Above all, he would keep the man from raising any alarm. No matter who he was, he wasn't likely to be alone. He did not worry about his own men. As skilled as they were, fighting men was not a challenge.

Another step and the man stood almost within arm's reach of the Sword Bearer. The stranger took another half step toward Artair and then pivoted to face him and yelled a word in a strange language. The Helvetian could see the shine of the other man's eyes as he reached for his sword. The other man's shout meant he was truly not alone, and he no longer had the choice of holding back.

Artair's sword was half out of its sheath when a heavy, shapeless force hit him from above and to the side. The weight of the net staggered him and forced his sword back into its sheath. The stranger dove at the Sword Bearer and hit him in the stomach with his shoulder.

Artair fell back and instinctively rolled to the side, gasping for breath while further tangling his arms and legs in the net. As he attempted to stand, his attacker jumped onto his back, forcing him to the ground with his knees on his shoulder blades.

Hearing someone else rush from the trees, he turned his head in hopes that it was a member of his team only to see the newcomer swing something in the darkness. Then bright lights exploded in his head and he saw nothing…

*

Calum's eyes opened at the sound of the foreign yell, and he rose to a crouch. The sound had come from the other side of the campfire, where Artair had headed to sleep. There were sounds of a brief struggle, and then silence.

He started moving, skirting the edge of the clearing as he came closer to where the sound had originated. He was sure that it had awakened the others, but he did not expect to see or hear the practiced woodsmen in the dark. They were all alive at least in part because of their ability to move without making noise—even in the dark.

The men running from the trees were almost as quiet as the Sword Bearers until they got close. Calum stopped short, his sword in his hand without a thought. He didn't have time to shout before the first stranger swung a heavy weapon at his head. He diverted the blow, stepped back, and barked orders to his unseen men. There were clangs of steel as the Sword Bearers engaged their attackers all around him. His attacker swung again, a ponderous blow that had no hope of connecting.

Then, as quickly as they had come, the strangers were gone, melting away into the forest.

*

"Who were they?" Calum demanded, the light of the fire dancing off the hard planes of his face. They had chased the strangers into the trees, the trained warriors instinctively trying to finish the fight.

When there was no answer, Calum looked around for Artair. Not finding him, he looked again.

"Where's Artair?"

The rest of the men looked around them, puzzled.

"Wh-where's Iain?" Another man asked. Without another word, the men faded into the trees, searching for their friends. They found Artair's helmet, and Iain's bow, but nothing else.

The rising sun found the Sword Bearers still searching, trying to track the strange attackers—but to no avail. As the sun was setting the next evening, the team finally conceded defeat and headed for home. This was to be a somber day in Greenock. Two Sword Bearers were gone, but even worse was the fact that they had lost two of the swords. New men could be trained, but the weapons were irreplaceable.

Calum's head bowed low as he pulled Moray's litter, and the team traveled in silence.

Chapter 4

Artair's head throbbed him awake as the sun pried at his closed eyes. When he tried to open them, he found that his right eye wouldn't open. His left he opened slowly, and then closed it again, his mind racing. As he had been trained, up until this point only his eyes had moved, and he didn't think that anyone had noticed that he was awake.

Several times he had been knocked unconscious or senseless in a fight and had woken up underneath a dragon. Not moving when he woke had kept him alive on more than one occasion. His mind raced from what he had seen. He was still in his armor, but he was in a cage of some kind that was sitting on the ground.

There was dried blood on his arm, and he expected that it was his own. The memory of the night before rushed back and he struggled to keep control of his anger. He had been captured, and not only captured but captured easily, like a young fool, new to the field.

The cage he was in faced a large campfire. Around it he had counted seven men in the time he had been looking. He did not recognize any of them. They looked to be waiting for something, or someone. Artair opened his eye again, slowly, and noted that their clothes were different from any he had seen in the empire. Their weapons were also foreign. They wore short swords around their waists and a dagger was strapped, handle down, to each man's left arm at the bicep. They were armed to fight men, not dragons. They had the uniform look of soldiers.

However, these men were not from Helveti, and that meant that he was in serious trouble. Raiders from the west sometimes attacked outlying villages, but not in a century had they ever come against the eastern borders. If they were not raiders, though, who could they be?

Artair closed his eye again and lay motionless. He didn't know what to think about his current situation, but he knew that his predicament was far more dangerous than the battle with the dragon the previous day. In that fight he had known his enemy. Here, he did not. He would need to get out of this cage, obviously, and then he would need a weapon.

He grunted with surprise and sat up as cold water splashed through the bars of his cage, drenching him. The men around the fire laughed but did not rise as Artair glared at a man he hadn't seen before. He stood next to the cage with a dripping bucket in his hands and an amused grin on his face.

"I knew you were awake, just playing dead there for a minute, and I figured it was time for us to get to know each other."

Artair stared at him. He spoke Helvetian well, but his accent betrayed the fact that it was not his native tongue. It was said that Helvetians learned pronunciation during the time spent in the womb.

"Go ahead and say something, friend. You've been asleep for so long we started wondering whether we'd struck you too hard and broken that head of yours. Aside from the headache, how are you feeling?" The man was still smiling as he set the bucket down on the ground.

Artair looked him up and down appraisingly. He looked to be able to handle himself well, and stood with an air that belied confidence. He could not be sure, but he would have wagered that this was the man he had first seen the night before. He met the stranger's eyes and held them until the other man grinned even wider, blinked, and shook his head.

"Friend, you stare a lot better than you talk so far, so how about giving me your name to work with?" Rather than feeling challenged by Altair's icy glare, the man seemed amused.

Artair looked away from him and glanced at the others gathered around the fire. A couple of them were watching the one-sided conversation, but most acted entirely uninterested in the affair. Worse than that, they looked bored, like they'd seen all this before.

His gaze darted back to the first man as he pulled another bucketful of water from a short barrel next to the cage. The man chuckled at the way his prisoner glared at the bucket, then walked over and set the water in front of Artair, right up against the bars.

"If you're not going to talk to me you'd better wash your head off a little bit; you'll be in a lot better mood as soon as you can glare at all of us with both eyes." With that he turned and joined the others at the fire, seeming to forget all about his prisoner.

Artair waited for a minute and then reached up to explore the wound on the side of his head. From the feel of it, the blow had only split the skin when it rendered him unconscious, but head wounds always bleed well and the blood had run down and cemented his eye closed as it dried.

Scooping handfuls of water from the bucket, he washed his eye until he could open it again and bathed his head until he could work on the wound itself. The cut was not deep, for that he could be thankful, and was mostly hidden by his hair. It would heal quickly.

Then he checked for his weapons. He had already seen his two swords lying beside the fire, but as he searched he found that they had not discovered his dagger, hidden underneath his breastplate right up against his chest.

The armor had been made to accommodate the small blade, and it was almost impossible to find unless one knew that it was there. Many times he had wanted to remove the blade, as it was too small and of the wrong steel to be used against dragons, but the breastplate didn't feel right without it and now he was glad that he had kept it. Against these men it would work very well.

He left the weapon where it was as the stranger came back, took the water away, and dumped it. Setting the bucket down, the man returned to Artair's cage.

"So, what's your name then?" he asked.

This time the Helvetian answered. "Artair. Is the captive allowed to know the name of his captor?"

The man nodded, as if acknowledging the statement and then stepped closer and extended his hand toward him. "My name is Artimus, and I am the leader of these men."

Artair eyed the gesture warily and then stuck his arm through the bars to shake it. As they gripped hands, he peered into Artimus' face. "For me to have to reach through bars to introduce myself is a hard way to get to know someone."

The other man nodded as he dropped his arm to his side. "That's true, but without those bars I would have stood in danger of losing my hand, and that also would have proved interesting!" The grin never left the man's face. "What's the rest of your name?"

Artair felt a flash of annoyance even while reminding himself that this man was not Helvetian. "My second name is not your concern, nor is it polite to ask for it."

"From last night you should have guessed that it is not my goal to be polite. What is the rest of your name?"

Among the Helveti, a man's second name was given to him by his father when he was of age, or by the general consensus of those in his city if his father did not live to see his son grown. It was given as a token of respect or as a description of how they lived their life.

Artair had never told anyone his second name, for that was something they would learn of through those who knew him, if they cared. To speak one's own second name would be akin to bragging. Calum and he had the same second name, and it would not likely change even though some did. Neither of their fathers had lived to give them a second name. Orphaned by dragons, their lives now directed by their war with them, the people had named them the Dragonbane.

Artair was saved from answering as a new group came through the trees to their left. His glimmer of hope disappeared when he saw that the newcomers were dressed just like the strangers around the fire. Two of them were carrying the body of a man between them on a kind of stretcher.

The group moved immediately through the camp and disappeared into the trees. A moment later they were back, one man carrying an empty stretcher. As he watched them return, he noticed the other cage.

Like Artair's own, the cage was long enough to lie down in, and tall enough to sit up in with a little room to spare. There was a man lying in this cage as well. As he looked the man stirred, rolled over, and looked across the camp at him. It was Iain.

"How did everything go?" asked Artimus in Helvetian as another of his men approached the Artair's cage. Artair noted the use of his language and wondered if he was trying to be polite or if he wanted him to understand what they were saying.

The newcomer seemed to not hear the question as he squatted down to look at Artair, his gaze the same as if he were appraising an animal.

"As well as could be expected. He was dead by the time we got back to him, like you said he would be. He's now in the ground and I,

30

for one, have already started to forget the man." He answered slowly and with a thick accent. It was obvious that he was speaking in Helvetian because his leader was, but he shaped each word and spat it out like bile.

The big man crouched next to Artair's cage and squinted in at him, his mouth held in a way that made him look as though he smelled something incredibly unpleasant.

"You know," continued the big stranger, "you said these men were warriors. Are you sure they can even fight?"

Artair slowly bared his teeth at the big man in a type of smile.

The crouching man peered quizzically at him, confused at the prisoner's response. In the next instant the Sword Bearer's right hand slipped the hidden blade from underneath his breastplate and lashed out at the man's scarred face.

The razor edge sliced a clean six inch cut along the scar already on the big man's face as he threw himself backward. One of the other men rushed in and thrust a short sword through the bars at Artair's chest, intending to avenge the injury. Twisting, Artair caught the darting blade and pulled it past him, jerking the attacker forward and off balance. He grabbed the man's hand as it entered the cage and broke the wrist against the bars. He heard the crunch of breaking bone over the man's shrill scream and felt the hand go limp in his grip.

Bringing his feet up underneath himself, he exploded upward, striking the ceiling of the cage with the back plates of his armor. The hinges burst and the top swung up and open with the cry of rusty metal.

Artair parried one thrust with his newly acquired sword, and then ducked as another attacker swung at his head. He knocked the blade from a weak hand, and then jumped up and back, clearing the back of the cage and landing on his feet.

A flood of men surged toward him and he took several quick steps away from them. The first of the strangers to reach him attacked with his sword held up over his head. Artair dropped to his belly in front of him, thrusting forward and up into the man's thigh. The warrior rolled to the left and onto his feet as the wounded stranger fell. Swinging as he stood, he sliced backhanded at the next attacker, but his hand stopped halfway to its intended target.

From behind, Artimus's right hand clasped Artair's wrist, while his left hand slid the point of a thin sword up to his throat. The Helvetian's eyes met the other man's and he let the short sword drop to the ground. The look in his eyes left no room for misunderstanding. The rest of the soldiers stopped and stood staring at the two men.

"Let that other blade drop too. Do it or I will kill you." the kidnapper said. There was no anger in his voice, only cool assurance. He would do what he promised, and he would do it without hesitation or regret.

Artair decided it was better not to doubt the other's words and let the dagger fall. The small blade sank partway into the soft earth. Artimus's sword did not move as the large scarred man came walking up. Blood streamed down his face from the long gash made by Artair's knife. The cut had opened up, spilling blood in thin rivulets down his throat and under his collar. In spite of all this, the man was smiling!

He stopped a few feet from the Helvetian and Artimus and once again looked the prisoner up and down, this time with a touch of respect in his gaze. Then, nodding, he turned to the rest of the men.

"We are going to get rich on this one!" he shouted, wincing from the fresh pain it caused his wound.

Artair stared dumbfounded as even the wounded men cheered, nodded, and began talking excitedly to each other in their own language. When he finally turned back to Artimus there was pure wonder in his eyes. The other man just grinned.

"No, we're not crazy, but you are going to make us rich, Artair, very rich. Well done, very well done."

Artimus's sword never moved from its assigned place at the captive's throat until the door on his cage swung closed on him. This time the hatch was reinforced with chains at each corner, and for the rest of the day the strangers kept a respectful distance from their dangerous prisoner as they tended to their wounded.

For Artair it was a time of careful reflection. Fighting the strangers had been easy, almost too easy. Had he wanted to he could have killed at least three, maybe more. The knowledge was at the same time unsettling and reassuring.

He was not one who enjoyed the thought of killing anyone, but if it meant escaping these people he might have to and now he knew that he could.

Chapter 5

Artair's thoughts of home and the day's strange turn of events were interrupted as Artimus once again approached his cage. The grin on his face seemed to shine in the failing light of dusk, but the plate of food he had in his hand was what captured his prisoner's attention. He had not eaten the night before after Moray's death, and nothing earlier that day either. Artair raised an eyebrow when his captor set the plate right up against the bars and placed a crude wooden fork inside his cage.

"Usually I open the top and hand prisoners their food, but due to your earlier display the boys decided that it would be better if we left those chains locked." Artimus smiled to himself and then turned his back on him and returned to the fire.

Artair's stomach complained about how long it had been since he'd eaten, but he eyed the food with extreme suspicion. Even he knew ways to poison someone, and if he had learned anything in the fight earlier it was that this man was not one he should underestimate.

On the other side of camp, the scarred man tossed food to Iain like he would have thrown it to an animal, the chunks of meat and vegetable bouncing to a stop on the dusty floor in front of the sitting warrior.

Artair looked up as Artimus came walking back to his cage, this time carrying the two Helvetian blades, one in each hand. Calmly seating himself opposite the plate, he pulled the two swords from their sheaths and set them across his lap, studying them each in turn.

Artair felt a small twinge as he saw the way Artimus carried the two swords. He did not strain or shift his grip as he would if he found them to be extraordinarily heavy. Was it possible that both swords had warmed to the stranger? Moray's sword had been light when it was handed to him after its owner's death, but that was not abnormal considering how long he had fought beside him.

"So, since you don't seem to be too hungry, why don't we talk a little? You haven't said a word since we put you back in there. Usually our prisoners are yelling by now, demanding we let them free or some such. Tell me about these swords." With the last sentence, Artimus's voice seemed to harden slightly--the statement was more of a command than a request.

Artair simply looked at him. The request amused him. "Why are you so curious?" he asked. He had a grudging respect for Artimus as a fighter because of the skirmish earlier, but that didn't mean that he would give up vital tactical information easily.

The other man chuckled and shrugged his shoulders. "Oh, I don't know, I've found that weapons usually have more interesting histories than the people who carry them. People have simple stories, they are born, they grow, then they die. Weapons last longer, they span lifetimes. I'm sure these two would have some stories to tell, am I right?" His attempt at nonchalance was not successful. ·

Artimus returned Artair's steady gaze.

"Yes, they would." Artair struggled to keep a straight face at the obvious annoyance on the other man's face. "Tell you what, you eat some of that food for me and I'll talk about where those swords came from." Artair's eyes challenged the other man to refuse, but Artimus only shrugged.

"You've got yourself a deal, big man, so tell me a story," Artimus said as he reached forward, picked up a piece of meat off of the plate and popped it into his mouth.

Artair had thought that he would refuse, but now he was stuck. He sat back against the bars of his cage and looked at the two swords resting in the other man's lap, their silver blades gleaming dully in the failing sunlight.

"To begin with, the sword closest to me is not mine. I inherited the other one from my father. He got it from his father, who got it from his father, and so on back as far as we know."

"But you don't know…?" Artimus cut in.

"Who the first owner was? No, we don't. There is writing on the handle that we can't read anymore. Our records only go back so far. Why do you care?" Artair asked, annoyed by the questions.

"Because I'm curious, how about that?"

"I'm afraid satisfying your curiosity happens to fall into the category of things I don't care about."

Artimus smiled abruptly. "I interrupted you, please continue."

"Back then, according to legend, or history if you want to call it that, my people found a boulder that was made up of solid steel. They melted it down and made a variety of things out of it. Swords, apparently, and a few other trinkets." The Sword Bearer intentionally left out the fact that, along with the swords, many other types of weapons had been forged from the material. Whole suits of armor had been made at one point, although they had been lost during the passing centuries.

"These swords are still here because they were made family heirlooms and passed on from generation to generation.

"There aren't very many of them around. In fact, the weapons we use now are not too different from the swords your men use, just better." Artair had to suppress a chuckle as Artimus raised an eyebrow at the slighting comment. "However, to remain loyal to my father I still use his sword, and it does well for all I use it for."

"Oh, and what do you use it for these days?" questioned Artimus. "There aren't any wars among your people right now, and it's a little big to be a hunting knife."

"Just because we are not at war with anyone doesn't mean that we don't train, does it?" He felt no obligation to tell his captor what he did or about the capabilities of his swords, and the less he knew the better anyway.

Artimus searched Artair's eyes for several seconds before averting his gaze. The Helvetian felt hope surge through his body. The other man seemed to be accepting his tale as truth. If the strangers knew nothing of the steel's true purpose, that meant that there was hope for escape.

If they ever allowed him access to his swords he could easily fight his way free. Also, if they had no such swords with them there was no way they would survive if a dragon attacked them. With the number of reptiles that infested the area, there was a good chance of such an attack occurring.

"Now it's my turn to eat, and your turn to talk. How about telling me about your sword, that thing looks too thin to be a real weapon. Or even better tell me where we're headed and what you plan to do with me!" he said bitterly. Artimus chuckled again, dismissing his prisoner's bitterness.

"I'll return the favor and tell you about my sword, and then I'll tell you what we're doing tomorrow. After that I'm headed off to bed, unless you want some more food by then," the head kidnapper responded.

Artair showed his agreement by reaching forward and picking up the fork. Artimus waited until he began eating before he started talking.

"My sword is really nothing special. I had it made for me back home by a blacksmith who thinks of himself as a master of the craft.

It's thinner for reasons of weight, but it's still as strong as one of those short swords you proved so proficient with earlier. Of course, I get ceaseless ribbing about it since it looks funny. Probably for that reason, you won't see many swords of this design.

"Tomorrow we are going to pack up camp, conceal the fact that we were here, and head due east toward the mountains. Any other questions you have will have to wait because I'm getting tired. For reasons that don't need to be explained, we didn't get much sleep last night."

Artimus stood up, taking a sword in each hand as he rose. "By the way, the next time we talk, you should try telling me the truth when I ask questions. I will not always be so amused by lies."

Artair stared up at Artimus, the fork halfway back to the plate. "If you're so smart, why don't you tell me what I'm lying about, and while you're at it you can tell me why a man who kidnaps people for a living has anything to say about morals?"

"These swords are not what you claim, I know that much. You want to try the truth this time?"

"It's a sword, Artimus, passed on to me by my father, and I know no more about where it came from than what I know about you."

"Just a sword, Artair?" Artimus asked, pulling Moray's sword from its sheath and weighing it in his hand. Glancing back at the men around the fire to make sure they were not watching, he set the edge of the sword against the skin on his arm.

The razor edge sank into the skin as if it were no boundary at all and a thin line of blood appeared. Like blood running on flesh the color ran up the blade in rivulets until it reached the hilt and then started back down. Soon the entire blade was covered, and in the near darkness the red steel shone as if it contained a light of its own.

Artair watched, both curious and dismayed that Artimus knew more about the swords than he had portrayed.

"This is no mere sword. Would you want to tell me the truth now?" Artimus asked, sheathing the red blade with a snap of his wrist.

Artair said nothing, returning the glare from the other man.

"Who does this sword belong to, if you say it isn't yours?" He asked, shaking the sword in its sheath.

"It belonged to a friend."

"Oh, did you kill him for it?" Artimus asked icily, though his tone made it clear it was more of a taunt than an accusation.

Artair jerked forward and grabbed the bars that stood between him and his captor. "Open this cage, Artimus. Face me like a man if you are going to talk to me like that."

Artimus laughed, a sound that made several of the men at the fire turn to look. "Good night, Artair. You'll know tomorrow why I won't take you up on that offer!"

Without another word he picked up the plate and walked back to the fire where the other men were cleaning up from dinner. Artair, puzzled, meant to stay awake longer, but his eyes grew heavier by the second and his world soon receded into darkness.

Chapter 6

...the dragon roared and clamped its blood-stained jaws shut with a metallic snap. Artair stood still, paralyzed by the spectacle in front of him, his mind racing. The animal charged, its head and long neck coming through the open window at the terrified boy as its body crashed into the house. The youth threw himself back as the monster's jaws snapped shut on the air in front of his face.

The house shuddered from the impact of the charge, and then shook again as the dragon pounded the front wall with its chest, trying to get at its prey within.

Artair pushed himself against the back wall, his eyes riveted to the dragon's head as it snapped and roared at him. The monster stopped pushing and pulled its head out of the window. It let out a high-pitched squeal and then shoved its head back in through the opening.

A couple seconds later the wall to Artair's left shook as the beast's companion threw itself into the house's framework. The blow knocked everything off the shelves on the inside and showered the boy with various tools, articles of clothing, and kitchen utensils.

Artair scanned the room desperately for some way to escape, for it was only a matter of time before the two enormous animals pushed their way into the house, and then there would be only death.

The door in the small cottage was in the corner by the window, right next to the snarling dragon. To run for it would put him within reach of the beast's jaws that were now snapping and tearing at everything within their range. The reptile continued to throw its weight into the structure of the house.

The boy's eyes landed on the sheathed sword hanging on the wall to his left, the wall that was now cracking due to the repeated attacks by the enraged animal outside. Even as his eyes lit on the weapon Artair was on his feet and heading for it. Reaching it, he yanked the heavy sword from its cracked leather sheath with both hands and turned to face the dragon's snapping head. The handle warmed in his hands, startling him.

The wall behind him exploded inward, knocking him across the room. He landed underneath the first dragon's dripping jaws. The animal had been distracted as pieces of wood and plaster from the wall struck it, but now looked down at the terrified human tidbit its mate had supplied for it.

Artair desperately jerked the sword free from the debris covering his right arm as the dragon growled and snapped its jaws down at him with blinding speed.

Every joint in his arm wrenched as the dragon's head impacted on the sword. Screaming as the dragon's hot, stinking breath bathed his face and neck, he felt the sword jerk from his hand as the monster threw its head up, smashing into the low-hanging rafters.

Then the beast paused and a tremor passed through its body. Artair watched, unable to take his eyes from the sight above him as the animal relaxed suddenly, its head crashing to the ground next to him and the huge body slumping against the house.

In a daze, he saw the red tip of his sword protruding from the top of the dragon's head. The creature's bloody jaws enclosed most of the blade, and the hilt now lay only a foot from Artair's outstretched hand. Taking a deep breath, he let it out slowly, looking at the fallen beast. Tentatively, scared that it was somehow going to wake up, he reached out and took hold of the sword's hilt.

The youth's eyes jerked to the far wall as a low growl rumbled through the house. The other dragon had forced its head and shoulders through the hole it had created in the wall and was now glaring into Artair's eyes, its jaws opening and closing in a chewing motion. The beast growled again and snapped its jaws at the space in front of the blood-spattered youth. Then it drew back and slammed its shoulder into the half-broken wall.

Before the boy knew what he was doing, he stood, ripped the sword from the carcass of the first dragon, and charged its mate. Throwing itself forward into the hole in the wall, the dragon strained toward the youth as he drew near. Artair ran at the animal and then dropped to his haunches as the beast's jaws whipped forward and its teeth snapped shut on empty air.

Exploding from the ground, Artair swung the heavy sword at the dragon's huge head like the hammers he had used in his father's shop. The shock of the blow knocked the sword out of his grasp and numbed his hands. The blade cut into the dragon's skull, destroying its left eye and shattering the terrible jaw. Artair was showered by the monster's blood as it tore its head out of the house with a terrible, slurred roar of pain and rage.

His numb hands fumbled at the sword and he drew it to him, then ducked under the table and lay down, covering himself with clothing and other debris that had been knocked off the shelves by the raging animals.

A second later the surviving dragon shoved its wounded head in through the window and roared again, a hideous sound of pain and fury slurred by the animal's broken jaw. The boy began to tremble and tried not to look at the animal as it roared again, the sound amplified in the small room...

Artair's eyes opened slowly, and his mind struggled to comprehend where he was, and why the earth was moving. He rolled

42

over and slowly sat up, turning his head to the side. His sluggish brain finally worked out that the earth was not moving, but that the cage he was in was being carried up a small hill.

Long wooden poles had been run through rings on the sides of the cage, and four men carried them on their shoulders. The bearers seemed to be well accustomed to the burden and walked with speed and ease.

Raising his hand to rub his eyes, Artair was startled to see that his armor was missing! He was wearing his breeches and undershirt, but every strip of armor had been taken. How had they removed it without waking him?

Shaking his head to clear his mind, he turned to look behind him and found himself staring right into Artimus's smiling face. He was walking behind the men carrying his cage. He was visibly pleased to see that Artair was awake. The Sword Bearer's eyes narrowed as he looked at the man.

Motioning to him, he said, "Artimus! Get up here and wipe that grin off your face!" His voice was hoarse and lacked the commanding tone he had hoped for.

Still, the other man stepped around the poles holding the cage and came to walk beside it, out of arm's reach.

"Good morning Artair! Sleep well?" asked Artimus.

The Sword Bearer gripped the bars of his cage, clenching and unclenching his fists trying to get rid of the numbness and weakness that came from unnatural sleep.

"Yes, I slept well. In fact, I slept far better than I should have. What did you put in that food last night and why weren't you affected by it? Also, why couldn't you guys have picked something that doesn't make my head feel like it's stuffed with wood chips?"

Artimus waited a moment before answering, to Artair's distinct displeasure. "I think I'll keep the secret of what that was, but I have long since become mostly immune to its effects. I also didn't have as much as you did. Still, I slept very well last night, thank you for asking. As for your head, I'm not sure that it wasn't already filled with wood chips." Artimus laughed out loud at the anger in the other man's face, and then continued.

"Anyway, Artair, we couldn't afford to have you pulling any more knives out of your sleeves on us, and we couldn't trust you to behave if we opened that cage and tried to take off your armor while you were still conscious, so you really gave us no other choice. Don't worry, though, I don't think we'll have any reason to do it again, so long as you behave yourself."

His prisoner glared at him. "How much good am I going to be to all of you if I decide not to eat on this little trip?" Artair released the bars and sat back, folding his arms across his chest.

Artimus shook his head. "Oh, don't give me that. You'll eat all you can and do everything possible to keep your strength up, even if you do risk getting poisoned in the process."

"Oh really, and how do you know that? Do you read minds as well as mix potions?" Artair retorted.

"No," Artimus replied calmly, "you'll do all you can to stay healthy in preparation for that one chance to escape that you're so sure we're going to give you. The only flaw in that plan is that we've been doing this for years and no one has succeeded in escaping yet. Believe me, they've tried to before and either turned up dead for their troubles, or really didn't get that far."

Artair coolly looked into the other man's eyes and replied. "You've already seen that I am not like your other prisoners, Artimus. The only way to keep me from escaping from you people would be to kill me, and you don't seem too willing to take that step."

Artimus's sword whipped from its sheath and pressed its needle-like point against Artair's throat. The Helvetian didn't move, but the men carrying his cage noticed and slowed to a stop.

"You and I need to get one thing straight, Artair," Artimus said. "I am perfectly willing and able to kill you at any time. The only thing, and let me repeat that it was the only thing, that kept me from killing you back there at camp was the fact that you're worth a lot of money to us. That saved you once; it will not save you again." Artimus held the sword point at Artair's throat for a moment longer, then returned the blade to its sheath and signaled to his men to continue on.

The prisoner waited for a couple of minutes before reaching up to wipe away the single drop of blood that Artimus's sword had left on his throat.

Chapter 7

The team of men continued on through the day, pausing only briefly for lunch, then stopped for the night in a clearing next to a small lake surrounded by trees. Artair doubted that the lake would have survived a dry year, but right now it was full from the wet spring. The site showed signs of having been used before, and camp was quickly set up.

Artair idly wondered why they had stopped so early since there were still a couple of hours of daylight left. If he were traveling this road, which he wouldn't have without a full Bearer team, he would have taken advantage of every minute of daylight. It was obvious to him that his captors had a different agenda. What it was he did not know. He stopped wondering, however, when Artimus and several of the men approached Iain's cage.

The Sword Bearer watched as the man was pulled out of his cage and chains were clamped to his ankles. At the end of the chains were large balls of iron that, judging by their appearance, weighed a great deal. The rest of the men gathered around Artimus and the prisoner, blocking Artair's view of whatever was going on, but not before he saw Artimus hand his countryman a short sword.

The attitude and yelling of the men in the circle told him that a fight was taking place. He had no doubts as to who would come out victorious. All Helvetians were warriors, but Iain was an archer by trade and would not likely be able to match Artimus.

The shouting and the match lasted only a couple of minutes. Then the crowd broke to allow Iain to be escorted back to his cage and deposited inside. Artair had not yet had a chance to talk to the man, and unless he was wrong they would not let them speak to each other any time soon, if ever.

Artair looked up as Artimus and the others walked up to his cage. He smiled as he noticed that most of the men were carrying swords. They hadn't been so careful with Iain, but then he had already proven himself a greater danger than what they were used to.

Artimus smiled back at him. "Your turn, Artair. It's time for you to get a little exercise."

The warrior looked around him with an amused expression. "Are you sure you all want a rematch? In case you don't remember, the last one didn't turn out too well." The Sword Bearer chuckled as the men around his cage stiffened angrily.

"As I recall, the last two matches we've fought have ended up with you in that cage," Artimus retorted as he stepped forward, unhooked the chains, and flipped the top open.

Artair stood slowly, surrounded by a forest of short swords, and calmly stepped over the side to stand in front of his captors. Artimus bent down, hooked the chains onto his ankles, and then stepped back. Some of the men sheathed their swords and moved the cage out of the way, the rest of them stood where they were, weapons at the ready.

Turning, Artimus took Artair's swords from a man standing behind him and stuck them into the ground in front of the prisoner, who still hadn't moved from his previous position. The Helvetian had to keep from smiling when he saw the weapons.

The chains on his legs gave him about two feet of motion in either direction as long as he didn't trip himself, and they were heavy enough that he could not easily move them. This was not exactly the chance he could have dreamed, but it might have to do. Every day took him farther from home and deeper into dragon territory.

The entire group took a couple of steps back as Artair reached down and picked up one of his weapons. He swung it a couple of times, two-handed, and then picked up the other one and stood with both swords up, facing his opponent.

Artimus studied him for a moment and then attacked, his blade passing through his prisoner's defense to snag his shirt above his heart. The Helvetian's response was ponderous, knocking the kidnapper's sword down only on its reverse trip.

Artair glanced down at the neat slit in his shirt and whistled in wonder. Then he swung at his captor with the sword in his right hand. It was a powerful sweeping arc at the other man's head that didn't come close to making contact.

Artimus ducked under it easily, and laid the blade of his own sword against his opponent's neck until he could recover and knock it away. Artair thrust with both swords at once, but the swordsman slid to the side and parried the blow easily with his thin, darting blade. The men surrounding them who had started cheering at the first attack were now quickly quieting. This was not the fight they had expected to see.

The exercise went on for another couple of minutes. The ponderous movement of the heavy ancient weapons was contrasted and defeated by the thin, flicking sword of the other man. After only a few minutes it was clear that the Helvetian had no endurance for a long fight. He was breathing heavily, and his reactions had already begun to slow down. The handle of his sword had cooled from warm at the beginning of the fight to a nearly painful cold. His sword wanted a fight, and was not amused with this ruse.

After another minute he heaved a heavy sigh and stuck the tips of both swords down into the ground and stood leaning on them. The men around him were markedly confused. They had expected much more from the man who had defied them all the day before. None of them would have ever doubted their leader, but they expected that even he would have some trouble with the tall warrior.

"Somebody give him a smaller sword, he's no good with those big things. I mean, look at him! They're wearing him out." The suggestion came from somewhere in the crowd, but several others voiced approval of the action. Artimus stood silently, his sword still out, watching the heavy panting of his prisoner.

A man standing to Artair's right pulled his sword from its sheath and, taking it by the blade, cautiously extended it to the Helvetian. The weary warrior didn't acknowledge the proffered weapon for several seconds, and then looked up at the man holding it. After another deep breath, he straightened and reached for the sword with a shaky hand.

Artimus snapped a warning in the same moment as Artair clasped the handle of the short sword. The Helvetian pulled the weapon six inches back toward himself, and then flicked it forward into the extended hand of its owner. The wounded man screamed in pain and surprise and threw himself back into his comrades.

Artimus leapt toward him as Artair swept both of his swords free of the ground and swung them forward. The two heavy blades caught the other man's weapon between them and the smaller blade shattered. The kidnapper jumped back as shards of the metal flew in his face.

Artair's swords completed a graceful arc through the air, swinging down along his sides and connecting with the chains attached to his ankles. There was a metallic clang as the ancient steel cut through the soft iron and the chains fell to the ground. Had he wanted to he could have cut the iron balls into slices with his sword and it wouldn't have come close to the feat of piercing a dragon's armor.

Everything paused in the clearing as Artair stood breathing evenly with his two swords held easily in his hands, his captors stunned and paralyzed by the transformation. Smiling, the Helvetian warrior looked around at the men surrounding him. His sword burned almost to the point of pain in his hand, now excited for the coming combat.

He attacked. The two heavy blades that had seemed so ponderous a minute earlier now blurred in the eyes of the people standing near. The first man fell clutching his arm and Artair moved past him, stabbing a second in the thigh while knocking yet another unconscious with the flat of his sword.

Throwing his shoulder into one man who was struggling to draw his weapon, he gained the outside of the ring of spectators and ran. He could hear the men behind him crying out in pain while others raced after him. He sprinted twenty yards before he dropped to a knee and swept both swords back in an arc behind him. Two of his pursuers fell as his swords cut into their legs while a third tripped over Artair's back and sprawled in front of him.

Swinging both swords around him as he stood, Artair drove his heel into the chest of the man on the ground at his feet. He felt the crunch of a breaking bone and heard the fellow scream, curling into a ball in response to the pain. He parried another man's thrusting blade and smashed the attacker in the chin with the haft of his other sword.

Grabbing his enemy's falling body, he shoved it at the group that ran toward him. The large man with the scarred face jumped over his comrade's limp body and thrust his sword at the warrior. Moving slightly, Artair felt the other man's blade slide between his left arm and his chest. Twisting toward the weapon, he tore it from the other man's grasp. Swinging around, he slapped the scarred fighter on the side of the head with the flat of his sword. The kidnapper disappeared from his vision like a fly slapped out of the air.

Artair looked up at the remaining men. All those who could still stand had gathered behind Artimus. Armed with two short swords, the head kidnapper bled from a collection of cuts on his face.

"Come on, Artair. Let's try this for real," Artimus said.

In response, the warrior slid his left-hand sword onto the blade of the sword in his right hand, and relaxed his free arm. He caught the handle of the short sword as it fell and threw it, side-armed, at his captors. The men around the head man jumped back as the lethal object sliced through the air toward them. Their leader didn't so much as blink until the weapon came within arm's reach, and then he slapped it out of the air like an annoying insect, sending it spinning into the ground.

As soon as he had thrown the sword, Artair caught his own as it began to fall from its precarious perch on the other blade and darted back a few paces, distancing himself from his enemies and the unconscious forms of the men who had fallen.

Artimus advanced slowly for a few steps, his men keeping their distance, and then he rushed at the Helvetian. The swordsman's blades moved independently, as if they had taken on a life of their own. Artair parried, and then thrust only to have his own darting attack parried away.

The two swordsmen moved as if dancing as their weapons clashed without pause. They moved continuously up and down a ten yard space, trampling the grass to pulp as they battled. Both men fought with the confidence that came from years of countless victories, and yet neither could gain an advantage.

When the two finally backed a step away from each other blood ran from the prisoner's arm, and his captor bled from a slash across the top of his thigh. Both wounds were superficial and represented mistakes neither man would make again.

Artair lunged toward Artimus, then crouched and swung one sword at his opponent's legs while thrusting upwards with the other. Artimus jumped straight in the air, dodging the stroke meant for his legs while deftly parrying the blade aimed for his stomach.

He swung both swords down at the other man's unprotected head as he descended through the air. One of Artair's swords swung up, knocking away the two blades while kicking his adversary's legs out from under him as they touched the ground.

Artimus rolled away as he hit, then suddenly changed direction and rolled back into his prisoner's legs as he began to chase after him. The dragon fighter fell forward into a somersault and rolled to his feet, turning to face Artimus.

He found the tip of the other man's sword pressed against the skin under his chin. The other short sword point rested against the side of his neck. The Helvetian stood still for half a second and then arched straight back away from the blades, sweeping up to parry with one blade while the other thrust forward.

Artimus's blade ripped a gash in Artair's chin, while the prisoner's sword sliced into the other man's body. Seemingly oblivious to the pain, the wounded man kicked him in the midsection, knocking him onto his back.

A half-second later the two swordsmen closed the distance separating them and the sound of steel on steel rang in the evening air. The two men moved with serpent-like fluidity, several times dodging the other's blade by only a hair's breadth. The rest of the kidnappers stood watching breathlessly, knowing that the skill level of the two combatants was far beyond them.

The captor began to give ground as his swords were pounded and cut by the superior steel of the Helvetian. Artair pressed his opponent harder, his weapons assaulting the other man's blades. A gasp rose from the watching men as one of Artimus's swords shattered under the onslaught.

Spinning, Artair slapped his opponent's remaining weapon down with one blade and set the tip of his other sword against his captor's throat. Stomping down on the short sword with his foot, he jerked it out of his adversary's hand and heard it hit the ground.

"You lose, Artimus." Artair said hoarsely as he set his other blade against the side of his neck. The other man glared at him over the shining steel.

"Not a chance." the swordsman hissed.

The Sword Bearer sensed the approach a split second before the scarred man's full weight crashed into him. Artimus arched back, away from the blades at his throat. He straightened back up as one of his men threw him another sword.

Artair dropped both swords to the ground as he was born to his knees by the force of the attack. Twisting as they hit, he broke the other man's vice-like grip and pulled himself erect.

Slamming both fists into the bigger man's midsection, the Sword Bearer butted his opponent in the face with the top of his head. As the kidnapper reeled back from the blow, Artair jumped into the air and kicked both feet into the other man's scarred face. Twisting as he fell, the dragon fighter's hands hit the ground first.

The seasoned warrior could see Artimus coming as his feet reached the ground. Without bothering to rise, he rolled forward, under the sweeping blade of his captor, and came up with one of his swords. As he spun to face the swordsman, he caught sight of several men running toward him from the campfire. They were carrying crossbows.

It was likely he would lose this fight in a matter of seconds, no matter what he did. His opportunity to escape was gone now, replaced with only a faint hope for survival.

"Give it up, Artair, you can't win." Artimus demanded. The Helvetian didn't bother to acknowledge the comment as he attacked the other man, swiftly circling around to put the head man between him and the deadly crossbows. The long fight was beginning to tell on the Sword Bearer as he again crossed swords with his captor.

Artimus pressed his prisoner back, taking advantage of his opponent's fatigue. The Helvetian, recognizing his own weakness, gave ground and concentrated on the kidnapper's darting blade.

Artimus recognized too late the other man's strategy. Artair, knowing that his time was running out had been cutting his way through the weaker short sword--always hitting the edge in the same place. The realization came as the head man's weapon splintered and broke halfway up the blade.

Artair attacked viciously, hoping to end the fight, but Artimus surprised him. Instead of retreating, the swordsman parried once with his splintered weapon and then stepped in close, driving a knee into the other man's crotch and then jumping to catch him in the chest with a powerful kick.

The Sword Bearer grunted and took a step back as pain from his groin rolled up into his abdomen. From behind him, the scarred kidnapper exploded from the ground, hitting Artair at the back of the knees and lifting him off his feet.

The Sword Bearer landed flat on his back and immediately tried to rise. He failed as the scarred man grabbed and held both his feet in a death grip. An instant later Artimus landed on his chest, pinning his arms to the ground and placing the jagged tip of his broken sword against the weary combatant's throat.

The last thing the Helvetian saw before a club was laid across his skull was a small smile on Artimus's face.

Chapter 8

An hour after the dragon fighters returned home, runners were dispatched to all of the surrounding villages bearing both the news of Artair's capture, and a call to all Sword Bearers to gather at Greenock in two days' time.

The message was passed from village to village and, at the prescribed time, over a hundred men stood in the city center to answer the call of the only remaining original Sword Bearer.

The hum of conversation ceased as Calum strode toward the group. He was in full battle armor, his sword swinging in his right hand, and the side of his face painted black in mourning. They had all heard about Artair's capture. That news had traveled faster than the messengers that had brought them together.

He stopped ten yards from the front lines and looked out over the assembled men. There was something in the big man's demeanor that caused any who locked eyes with him to look down. There was intensity there, tinged with anger and sadness. It was a gaze that could not be held unless one had the same intensity burning within himself. Calum reached up, pulled off his helmet and dropped it to the ground in front of him.

"Comrades, we have had enough." His words, though he did not shout, reached each man in the silent group.

"On our last hunt, we lost two Sword Bearers. One to a dragon, and the unseen forces that have plagued us for close to fifteen years took the other. It was a clear message to me, and it should be to all of you. What the dragons do not take from us will be torn away by enemies we cannot even see. We have had enough of fighting those monsters on their own terms and convenience, and we have had enough of seeing our people drug away in the night by we know not what."

"I called you together as the guardians of our society to see if you all truly desire to see our people safe in their homes. Do you have the courage to end the war we have been fighting for the last fifteen years? Any who lack that desire or that courage, leave this company now, for what I have to say is only for the ears of true Sword Bearers."

Calum paused, and realized that his sword was now raised in his clenched fist, pointing at the men in front of him. No one moved, though several could now meet the head man's gaze. The warrior nodded and lowered his sword to his side.

"What I propose is simple. We will leave two days from today, and we will head for the Spine. On the way, we will search out once and for all where our people are being taken, for we know that they are being taken in that direction.

"We will hunt down and slaughter any of those cursed reptiles we find until we reach the base of the peak that our fathers named the Bleeding Tooth. There, at the place where we first met the dragons we will finally have an end to this war. Whatever portal was opened, whatever pass was cleared to allow those demons to reach us will be closed. We will destroy all that are left on this side."

"The time has come, my brothers, for us to conquer or be destroyed. I, for one, will not wait for death to find me here. If death is to meet me I would have it be during a struggle that has worth and purpose. Let it find me while I fight a battle of hope for the safety of those who look to me for protection. I will not wait. I will go, and I will escort death to those who stand against our people. Death to the Dragon!"

Calum realized that he had been yelling only as the sound of a hundred returning shouts washed over him. Mimicking the Sword Bearer's stance, they stood with weapons raised overhead, the ancient silver steel moving like a wave over the swordsmen.

Calum let them yell for a few moments and then sheathed his sword with a snap of his arm. The warriors stopped shouting as they followed their leader's example and stood waiting for whatever he had to say next. Bending slowly, Calum picked his helmet up from the ground and held it in front of him.

"Meet me here in two days at daybreak. Bring provisions, weapons, and as many members of your teams as will come. Most importantly bring your courage, your desire, and your love for this people. For what we do, we do for them. Death to the Dragon."

Calum turned on his heel and walked back down the street as the sound of a hundred returning war cries shook the earth. Thirty seconds later the city center was empty except for the hushed scurrying of citizens, talking about what had happened.

...Flecks of blood from the wound on its head decorated the dragon's great neck and shoulders, the red spots standing out against the black armored scales. It tried desperately to push its way into the house with repeated shoves against the front wall.

Pieces of plaster from the walls and ceiling fell to the ground with each determined thrust from the reptile. The body of its mate lay like a great boulder at its side. The remaining dragon had paused only momentarily to sniff the remains of its companion before attacking.

When he first saw the creature come around the corner of the house, Calum had bitten his tongue to keep from crying out. The huge, foreign animal, with its lopsided face and blood flowing down its neck was a horrible sight.

58

Judging from the monster's actions, he guessed that Artair must still be alive and hiding inside the house. It wouldn't be long before the determined animal shoved its way inside. Then it would be all over. The boy's hands were getting sweaty from holding the unfamiliar sword handle and he carefully wiped them on his pants one at a time.

His mother had threatened him with a whipping if he ever dared to even touch Grandfather's sword after he had teased his little sister with it a few months earlier. The threat held no weight now, for there was no one to administer the promised punishment.

His mother had been working in the fields with some of the other women when these two dragons had found her, and his father had died in the street, torn nearly in two by one of the armored creatures. Now Calum stood watching helplessly as the demonic reptile tried to find a way to get to his best friend.

He jumped as his sister's scream ripped from the window behind him. He had told her to lie down and remain still, but she was now standing and staring as the dragon pummeled Artair's house.

Her brother hissed to her to be quiet, terror coursing through him. It was no use. The girl's body was quivering with fear and her screams only grew louder as the massive reptile paused and drew its head from the window of the other house.

Calum stopped breathing as the monster's wrecked head swung around and looked straight at them. Standing right in front of his sister, the boy couldn't tell whether the animal was looking at him or at her, but he knew that in the end it would not matter. If the beast attacked them they would both die.

The dragon's head swiveled from them back to the window it had been trying to enter, then returned to stare at them. He again tried to quiet his sister, his mind racing. He had seen what had happened to his father in the street. He knew that he would have only one chance, maybe not even that, to stop or slow the animal before it killed him and his sister.

The dragon turned its head further to the left to use its good right eye to look at them. Then it snarled, bloody foam dripping from its sagging jaw. Calum's eyes narrowed, a strange calm settling into his chest. Then the predator leapt at him.

He watched the creature's great feet hit the ground in the middle of the street. Small clouds of dust rose up between its clawed toes, and then it was airborne again with a jump long enough to take it to its intended quarry.

Calum darted to his left and swung the sword as hard as he could. He watched as the dragon's large eye twitched to follow his movement. He realized in that moment that it hadn't been looking at him at all. It had been entirely focused on his sister. He would later claim that the dragon had looked surprised to see him, as if he had come out of nowhere.

The battered head began to turn in mid-air to face this new threat when Calum's sword found its mark. The dragon's forward rush carried him right by the youth and its back right leg knocked Calum rolling. He somehow managed to keep his grip on his sword.

When he righted himself and looked back, the monster was roaring and rubbing its head in the dirt along the side of the road. A bloody furrow cut right across the forehead of the mighty beast, as if picking up where the first wound left off. It extended far enough over the head to ruin the right eye, completing its blindness.

The youth stood slowly, bringing his sword up in two hands, his eyes locked on this nightmare made flesh. His sister had thankfully stopped screaming. Later he would find out that she had fainted. The only sound he could hear was the roaring of the monstrous dragon.

A lone figure raced across Calum's vision and seemed to fuse itself to the dragon's side. It was Artair. The youth had left his house, and was now holding onto the handle of a sword that he had plunged between the reptile's ribs.

The monster threw itself skyward and twisted towards the pain in its side. The bloody head slammed into Artair, throwing him into the wall of Calum's house. He crumpled to the ground without a sound.

The dragon roared and tore at the sword deep within him. Frustrated and mortally wounded, the animal stopped thrashing and lowered its head to the earth, its great nostrils opening wide as it searched for a scent.

"He's looking for Artair," Calum whispered to himself.

The dragon no longer had the luxury of sight, but it knew the general location and scent of at least one of its enemies. Reaching down to the ground the youth picked up three small stones. Taking aim, he threw the first one, striking the animal at the base of the tail.

Calum was startled at the dragon's reflexes as the huge reptile whipped around at the area where it thought the attack had come from, tearing at the ground with its claws.

Just as suddenly, the animal turned itself around again and resumed its search for its unconscious foe. The boy had also acted quickly and was now two steps closer to Artair's unconscious form.

The second stone clattered against the wall to the dragon's left. The entire house shook with the force of the monster's attack, its terrible claws leaving deep gouges in the walls. By the time it turned around again Calum had taken three steps and was now almost to his friend.

Struggling to keep his breathing steady, he readied his last rock. This time the stone, thrown from only five feet away, struck the dragon in the wound on its head, the very one Calum had inflicted only a minute ago.

The creature rose up on his hind feet and roared. Calum ducked as the beast's tail sliced through the air above him. The boy was now in the position he had wanted to be in as the dragon resumed its dogged search for Artair.

The young Helvetian had placed himself in front and a little to the side of his friend's body. He could only hope the dragon, in its search for the unconscious boy, would not recognize his own scent mingled with his friend's.

He held his breath as the dragon came closer to him, its nostrils flared open in the dust. The newly orphaned youth waited silently with his sword raised over his head.

It took an eternity of heavy heartbeats before the dragon had inched its way forward and stood directly in front of the young man. Beads of sweat stood out on Calum's forehead, and his arms ached from supporting the unfamiliar weight of the sword.

The dragon paused and lifted its head slightly from the dust. With the sixth sense animals often had, it sensed a danger its other senses could not. A slurred growl rumbled from its throat. By the conclusion of that growl Calum's sword was slicing through the air, aimed at the creature's neck.

The blade separated the beast's head from its neck and buried itself in the ground below. The monster's body, in obedience to its last reflex, threw itself up and back, landing against the wall of the house. The boy watched, trembling, as the reptile quivered for a few seconds longer and finally lay still.

Calum awoke with a start and sat up as the sound of his spoken question faded away in the darkness. Lying back down, he wondered if Artair or he would ever be free of the nightmares that haunted them.

They seemed doomed to replay their first encounter with the dragons over and over as if it were some kind of price they had to pay for killing them. After that first fight Artair had moved into Calum's house and soon after they had confessed that they shared the same dreams.

In the fifteen years that had followed that awful day the two of them had become legends, heroes, and leaders, but it would all come to naught if their fight against the dragons were not won in the next couple of months. It felt good to know that one way or another there would finally be an end to it all.

He wished that he knew the answer to the question that he had asked of the darkness. The Sword Bearer closed his eyes and tried to relax. A few minutes later he was asleep again.

Chapter 9

When Calum approached the City Center at daybreak he was greeted by a once-in-a-lifetime spectacle. The entire square was packed with men. Before him stood more than had been represented two days previous, and with them stood the finest archers and lancers of the Sword Bearer order. The news of the coming expedition had spread like wild fire.

The first thing he did was to order a count taken. The number that returned to him was staggering. He had hoped to get at least three hundred men. Instead he was dealing with over five hundred. To be precise, five hundred and thirty four men had showed up, all of them either Sword Bearers or seasoned members of their teams.

The army quieted slowly after Calum drew his sword from its sheath and held it above his head to call for their attention. As soon as there was silence, he lowered the weapon to his side and addressed the crowd.

"Comrades, I welcome you to the beginning of the dragons' end. I thank you all for coming. As quickly as possible, for time is short, I want fifteen teams assembled. I want a leader and a second-in-command chosen out of each group. I will lead one of them, and I have already spoken to those individuals who will be working with me.

"The leaders are to meet me in my home in half an hour. We will depart as soon as our meeting is over. Let it be done." Calum turned and started walking back toward his house as the square behind him burst into activity.

Calum stopped, his eyes fixed on one man standing in the shadows at one side of the square. This was the man he had not dared to hope would join him.

It was Ragnal, the Hammer that Lives. Not a Sword Bearer, as he was both married and had children, he was still the best dragon slayer in Hellveti. He was the best without question, a legend whose stories were usually disregarded as impossible fantasies. Ragnal would join him on his team, he was sure, though the famed warrior could easily lead his own team. He had no interest in power or leadership, he only wanted to kill dragons.

It did not take them the full half-hour to assemble in the one-room house, so the meeting began early. The head Sword Bearer was pleased with those who had been selected to lead the teams. He knew all but two personally, and he had heard of the others. Overall, they were reasonable, experienced, and courageous. Excluding himself, there were nine swordsmen, three archers, and two lancers.

"Are the teams assembled to your liking?"

Calum's question was answered with a scattering of nods and a few voiced replies to the affirmative. "All right then, let's get started. Our mission is two-fold; we are going to slaughter the dragons, and find the men who are taking our people."

"We will refer to the individuals who have been kidnapping our people as men from now on. Any discussion as to them being half-beasts, changeling demons, or death in human form will not be permitted.

"I know that those rumors have gone around in our villages, but I have seen their tracks and they are men, nothing more. Is that understood?" Calum scanned the faces in the room for confirmation before unrolling a map that lay on the table in front of him. The team leaders crowded around to get a closer look.

"I have made copies of this map for each of you. Our fifteen teams will spread out along our eastern border. I have marked locations on this map, and you may all pick where you would like to begin according to how well you know the area.

"From each designated position, your teams will head east toward the Spine, with the intent of killing all dragons you find. You will also be searching for clues that will lead us to the kidnappers. In this fashion we hope to take out all dragons that are headed into our country before they get here.

"Tell everyone you meet up with to move into the larger villages or cities for protection. There will be no one left behind to protect them if there are dragons behind our line.

"Use every opportunity to live off the land and preserve your provisions. Head straight east for as long as possible, then work your way toward this point." Calum pointed to an "X" on the map.

"We will meet there and proceed to the Bleeding Tooth. According to scout reports from fifteen years ago, this is one of the only ways to get past the cliffs.

"Once there, we should be able to prevent more dragons from getting through. If, for some reason, you find cause to take a different path, or if you require assistance, contact the group closest to you. The teams will be identified by the number assigned to the position they start from.

"Take no unnecessary risks, and do not allow your men to take any. If one unit fails that will leave an avenue open for dragons to attack our people. The men we are leaving behind will not be sufficient to stop a large attack. We all know that our militias are all but worthless when it comes to dragon fighting.

"Bury casualties where they fall. There will be time to bring them home later if we are successful. If we fail there will be no home to bring them back to." Calum paused for a moment and looked into the men's eyes.

"You will decide, in the end, whether we win or lose. The men are excited and enthusiastic now, but their spirits will not remain high without your help. Make sure that they remember who and what they are fighting for.

"Make no mistake; this is our chance to win this war, but failure is more likely than success. This could well mean the end of our people. Are there any questions?"

When there were none, he let them pick where their teams would begin and dismissed them to see to their men, instructing them to be ready as soon as possible.

When they had gone, Calum sunk heavily into his favorite chair and let his eyes rest on the blade of his sword, which lay unsheathed on the table.

"Where is Artair," he wondered aloud. This would all have been much easier with him here. At the same time, maybe his being kidnapped was the push the people had needed to get them to this point.

Calum rubbed his right temple with his thumb. Runners had been sent from most of the village leaders already. Some supported his action and some tolerated it. The leader of Greenock had given his support, though he had also expressed his concerns. Without the swords and the Sword Bearer teams, the village's militia would break itself on the first few dragons that came along, leaving the town to the mercy of the beasts' appetites.

Calum shook his head to clear his thoughts and stood, sheathing his sword. They had no other option than to succeed, and success was not found in thoughts of failure.

Picking up his helmet, he walked out the door and closed it behind him without looking back.

Chapter 10

Artair stirred from a deep sleep as his cage was dropped to the ground with a thump. Fighting his way through a white fog inside his head, he struggled to open his eyes. The attempt sent shooting pains through his temples. After a few seconds, he tried again to open his eyes and this time succeeded. The light hurt him abominably and he shut them quickly.

"Good morning, Artimus," he mumbled as his hands massaged his aching skull.

"It's evening, actually, but thank you. How's your head?" the kidnapper replied.

"It feels like I have a storm cloud inside it, thank you. Did you drug me again? Wait a minute..." Artair's hand had found the wound on his chin. It had been neatly stitched closed, but what surprised him was that it was partially healed. He checked his throat to find a similar wound there, made by the other man's sword. This one was also healing nicely. The prisoner opened one bloodshot eye to look at his captor.

"How long has it been since we fought?" he asked, his throat was raw and his voice sounded rough and forced to his own ears.

"About a week." Artimus answered, a grin spread on his face.

Artair's other eye opened wide in surprise. He snapped them both shut again as the painful light flooded in.

"Do you mean that I've been unconscious for nearly a week now?" He groaned.

"Actually, you've been semi-conscious a few times when we decided to feed you, but other than that, yes." The kidnapper's tone was patronizing, as if he were speaking to a young boy.

Artair grunted. "No wonder my head hurts!" he said and subsided into silence as he rubbed his temples.

Artimus seated himself in front of the cage. "In case you'd like to know, I was the only one in the squad here that voted against killing you immediately. I figured we should kill you later." That remark earned him a grunt from his prisoner.

"The only way that I could convince them was to promise to have you drugged up so hard that you wouldn't be able to even twitch out of turn. Even then I was nearly outvoted.

"We stayed at that camp for four days after your little escapade, tending the wounded. Luckily for you no one died, or else you would have been killed anyway, even if I commanded them not to. You'd best watch your step around here since you've wounded almost everyone at one time or another. They don't like you much," Artimus concluded.

Artair growled deep in his throat, an unintended sound of frustration and anger. "You know what? That just breaks my heart that I might have made this trip uncomfortable for them. Maybe you all should have thought about the risks before you took up this profession." Artair said and glared at Artimus out of one eye.

The other man glared back, his customary smile gone. "We're not the only ones that should have thought more before we acted. That other prisoner saw your little escape attempt and decided that he'd try it for himself a couple of days later. I killed him before he could touch even one of my men. He was not as lucky as you were, nor as fast."

Both of Artair's eyes were open now and he fought his way to a sitting position to face Artimus.

The prisoner finally broke the silence. "Then why didn't you kill me? You told me, on that day, that my worth to you would not save me again. You said that, and I believed you, but I'm still sitting here while my friend, that 'other prisoner' as you call him, is dead. Why?" Artair asked.

Artimus was silent for several seconds, opened his mouth as if he were about to speak, then closed it again and shrugged his shoulders.

"I didn't want to. Let's leave it at that. Be grateful that I didn't, it was a hard decision."

Artair's hand subconsciously moved to the wound at his throat, as if checking for himself how close that decision had been.

"Anyway," Artimus continued, "I didn't wake you up for the cheery conversation. The boys want me to keep you drugged for the duration of our trip. I'm against that due to the adverse effects that these drugs have sometimes. Not to mention it's a pain spoon feeding you morning and night."

Artair's eyes narrowed at the comment and Artimus laughed.

"So, I'll give you a choice. You can either remain asleep for another couple of weeks, or you can give me your word not to try to escape, and we will leave you awake. It's up to you." the kidnapper said.

"You would accept my word, as simple as that?" Artair questioned, watching the other man carefully.

"Yes."

"Why?"

"That has to be your favorite word." Artimus sighed. "I trust your word because none of my men are dead. You are deadly enough to have killed them instead of wounding them, in fact it would have been easier in some instances, and yet you didn't."

"So because I don't want to kill, you will accept my word?"

"No, because you have shown yourself to be a man of honor, even when you had a lot of reason not to be. I would accept your word as binding."

Artair looked at Artimus quizzically for a few seconds and then asked, "Before I decide, would you tell me what those adverse effects are?"

Artimus laughed and shook his head. "I don't think so; you'll have to find out for yourself."

"Then I will only promise not to try to escape as long as we are travelling. When we reach our destination, all deals are off. This is only if you will answer a couple of questions for me." His words brought a small smile to his kidnapper's face.

"Let's hear your questions and I'll decide whether it's worth it or not," the other man responded.

"All right, one: where are we going? Two: what am I going to be doing when we get there? Three: why is it that you come to kidnap my people?" The prisoner looked at the other man expectantly.

The swordsman shook his head slowly. "Now, now, you said a couple of questions, and you have three. So, I'll either answer the first two, or the last one. You choose. Do we have a deal?"

Artair paused for a moment and then nodded. "Sounds good enough to me," he said, "would you shake on it?" He extended his hand through the bars toward the other man, who clasped it firmly.

"Okay," the Helvetian said, leaning back against the bars in his cage, "let's hear the answers to the first two, where and what."

Artimus lay back on his elbows and stretched before responding. "We are heading to a city called Cyrene, the capitol of our nation. Without wounded men we usually make the trip in about two weeks. Thanks to you we will be a little late. Another week or so would be my best estimate.

"Once we get there you will be sold to a man by the name of Tullius who is in charge of entertainment for the nobles and the rich of our society. He will set up a time and an occasion for you to fight in the arena." Artimus spoke the word as if he were afraid of it and the grave tone of his voice was not lost on his prisoner.

"What if I refuse to fight in this arena? I do not fight for sport or for other people's entertainment," Artair asserted.

His captor waved a hand to dismiss the question. "It wouldn't matter in the least, but I'm willing to bet that you'll fight."

"So, that's what I have to look forward to, is it? I spend the rest of my life fighting duels to make rich people cheer?" he asked, sarcastically.

The other man shook his head. "Yes and no. You will end up fighting a duel, and it will be for the rest of your life, but not in the way you're thinking. You will fight for your life, and then you will lose it. It doesn't end until you die, and it does not take long."

Artimus stood up with his last comment and walked away without a backward glance, leaving Artair alone to contemplate what he had been told.

*

The landscape began to change slowly as they travelled. The rolling hills and sudden ravines gave way to flatlands. Here the grass was more sparse, and the men had to search longer every night to scavenge firewood from the few trees.

Artair spent his time watching for landmarks and memorizing the route they were taking. Artimus noticed that he was looking around a little more than usual, but he made no attempt to discourage him from doing it.

The Helvetian took some satisfaction in the fact that the majority of his captors were recovering from some wound that he had inflicted. He wanted them to remember him, and to remember how unpleasant kidnapping him had been.

When he made eye contact with the man with the scars, he feared that he might have overdone it a little. He guessed that only the head man's presence kept the large man at bay even now. When their eyes met there was unmistakable hatred in the other man's eyes.

He would not be worried about it if he were free, but as long as he was in a cage he was vulnerable.

More than all of this, however, he was disturbed by the foreign nature of his kidnappers. This was no band of marauders or tribal raiders. Their clothes and weapons marked them as soldiers of a civilized nation. Where had they come from?

Chapter 11

Are your people worth your life?

Iain's eyes opened slowly, carefully. He had heard the Cyrenians leave with Artair fully an hour before. Still, he had lain there quietly, barely breathing, for another hour.

He had to move, he could not wait any longer. He tried to sit up, failed, and rolled onto his stomach instead. He pushed himself up with his arms, his face stony as the pain hit him afresh. Once he made it to a standing position he looked down, parting his undershirt to inspect his wound.

The pain had been severe, but it wasn't what stuck most in his mind. The feel of steel passing through his body was stuck in the front of his mind, and the sensation still echoed down to his fingertips.

It was an intensely unnatural feeling. All people know that they will die, but none truly believe it. Feeling his body run through with the cold blade, he had felt the reality of his mortality.

After he fell in battle, he had remained still for the rest of the night. His training helped him in that. It was with these men as it was with dragons: to move was to die.

He recognized the weakness that came with loss of blood, but that did not concern him. He was stronger than most men and the loss of blood itself would not stop him.

What he had to worry about was the rot. He had seen it many times in other men, especially with wounds like his, when the skin around the wound grew red, then green, then black. Some survived, most didn't.

He would not. He knew from where the wound was, and from experience, that he would not. The only question was how long.

He looked the way the Cyrenians had gone. For a moment he wondered what would become of Artair. He quickly cleared his mind of such thoughts, and his eyes turned to the ground. It took only a few seconds for him to find his sword, discarded in the dust and weeds.

He frowned as he picked it up, then wiped it clean with the clean parts of his shirt. Even foreigners and bandits should know better than to neglect a good blade. Even an archer knew that. His blade was not one of the Olden Times, but it was the sword of his father, and that was enough for him.

Once the blade was cleaned to his satisfaction, he carefully returned the sword to its sheath. It hurt more than he expected as the movement pulled at his torn stomach.

He saw a fresh trail of blood leaking from his shirt. He pressed his hand against the wound, applying what pressure he could. He took off at an easy lope, the fastest he could do without doing more damage.

If he had been at full strength, he could have reached Greenock easily in two days. As it was, he'd be lucky to make it in three. And that was only if the rot didn't set in too fast.

Are your people worth your life?

He had misjudged his own capabilities, or underestimated his wound, for two days of the fastest travel he could handle had him only half of the way to Greenock. His wound had long since stopped bleeding, but he knew that the damage was far from over. He could feel something wrong in his center, and the weakness he felt from loss of blood had not diminished with time.

His sword, ever a part of him, was now a heavy weight on his back. That above all scared him. He had worn the sword since childhood, and had years ago stopped feeling it where it hung. The lack of it he could feel even in his sleep.

He was climbing his third hill in an hour when he heard it. A clear bugling note hung in the air for several seconds before evaporating into silence.

Iain did not spare the energy to turn toward the sound; he didn't need to. He had heard it many times before. Every other time he had been with his team. Even with his brothers in arms around him there had been ample reason to fear. Alone and wounded, the sound made his mouth go even drier.

Somewhere behind him a dragon had sounded its hunting cry. Worse, the only reason it would give away its position like that is if it knew that its quarry could not run. It was hunting him, and it knew he was injured.

He had run another mile after hearing the dragon's cry, but he had no illusions about outrunning the beast. Once a dragon was on a trail it would not stop until it found its prey. The only reason he was still alive was that the dragon was playing with him, enjoying the slow kill.

He found what he was looking for in a steep gully. The overhang was crumbling, and after he had himself situated it took only a few pokes with his sword to cause a minor landslide that covered him in a solid foot of dirt and rocks. The impact drove the breath from his lungs and his wound flared with pain. He kept poking at the overhang above him until he was completely covered. He left a space in front of his mouth so he could breathe, but other than that even his sword was covered.

His only hope was that the dirt would mask his scent. Otherwise the dragon was sure to find him. He had seen how dragons ate. Once, he had watched a dragon that was hunting deer. It had caught a young doe by one of its back legs, and with a dreadful twist of its neck it tore the entire leg off. The dragon dropped the limb and kept attacking, silencing the animal when it tore the spine in half.

He had watched until the deer was consumed, bones and all. The dragons used their weight and leverage more than they did their jaws, tearing their meat instead of chewing it.

Dirt and rocks slid ahead of the dragon as it entered the gully, piling even more debris onto Iain. He froze, holding his breath in exchange for total immobility. He heard the animal sniffing, and then the crunch of gravel as the monster came closer. For a long few seconds everything was perfectly quiet, and Iain knew the dragon was trying to puzzle out where his prey had gone.

Are your people worth your life?

A horrible weight crushed down on his calf and Iain lunged to drag his sword out from under the dirt.

The dragon was faster. The horned muzzle knifed through the rocks and gravel. Massive jaws clamped shut on Iain's leg. He screamed as the dragon hopped backwards, yanking him from the debris. With a flip of its head, the giant reptile flipped him up into the air.

He felt the bones in his lower leg shatter as his body was twisted around the leg still held in the monster's jaws. When he finally hit the ground again he nearly lost consciousness.

By some miracle, his sword was drawn and in his hand. He hewed at the giant head with it. Injured and using normal steel, it wasn't enough to fully penetrate the dragon's armor. Still, his pain gave him rage and he managed to open a furrow on the beast's forehead.

The reptile flinched, more from surprise than pain, and spat out the leg. It wasn't in a battle rage or mortal struggle, there was no reason for there to be all this trouble.

The dragon stepped back, still watching Iain, and reached up to touch the wound with its forepaw in a terrifyingly human gesture. It knew what damage it had done, and it was in no hurry. Above all, it cared for itself, and prey that could defend itself was worth studying.

The dragon circled, watching its wounded quarry. It charged, jaws gaping wide, aimed for the head of its human prey. It would be quick now, an ending without further injury. The quarry moved only slightly, a twitch to the dragon's eyes. The jaws snapped down, blurring with speed, and swallowed an arm's length of steel.

The blade stopped a hand's length out the back of the dragon's skull, and the dragon's teeth were locked on Iain's shoulder. For a moment they were eye to eye, the armored great eye of the dragon before the fierce gaze of the Helvetian. Then the dragon slumped, dragging its dagger-like teeth along the warrior's arm as it fell.

Iain's laugh turned to a cough, that turned into a grimace. He had killed a dragon! By himself! Only a small handful of men in all of Helvetia could claim such a thing. And those had special weapons. He had slain the mighty beast with only his father's sword. The only red on it was the dragon's blood. What songs would be sung in his honor in Greenock if ever they knew.

If ever they knew…they would never know.

His leg was destroyed, broken and shredded. It didn't matter much now if he was found, the bite of a dragon was deadly. While not venomous, their diet of rotting meat made infection a sure thing with every bite. Even the cuts on his sword arm would be enough cause for concern. All his wounds combined to promise him a swift death.

He made his way to a seated position, the pain in his stomach was now the least of his concerns. He tied shreds of his shirt just below his knee. He was able to stop the bleeding, but he knew it was only temporary. He was dying, and he would die without making it back to his countrymen.

With only a glance at the cuts on his arm, he started to crawl. He was leaving his sword behind, and that pained him, but he knew that it would be no more use to him now. It would stay where it was, lodged in the dragon as a testament of his greatest feat when it was found...

...even if he never was.

Chapter 12

On the second day after Artair woke up, Artimus surprised him by approaching his cage and unlocking the chains holding it closed. Usually several men with swords accompanied the opening of his small prison every night, but this time the head man alone was going to let him out.

Asael noticed what was happening as the second chain rattled to the ground. Ripping his sword from its sheath with a word that could only have been a curse, he stomped toward them. Several other men stood to follow him.

Artimus did not bother to turn when he heard the men coming, but spoke several words of his own language in a light, conversational tone. At his words all of the men except Asael stopped in their tracks. Artair watched as the scarred man drew closer, his jaw set and his eyes shouting defiance and hate.

The head kidnapper repeated whatever he had said, but this time the tone different. His words were slow, but each one pierced the air like a knife. Several of the others took a step back, but the large man kept coming. The warrior's eyes flicked to Artimus's belt. He was not wearing his sword.

The big kidnapper was only three feet from them when the swordsman finally spun around, knocking Asael's blade from his hand with his left and punching the man in the jaw with his right. The scarred head snapped around and he fell to the ground, a dust cloud rising from the impact.

He immediately started to rise, and then stopped when he looked up at Artimus. The cut on Asael's face had started seeping blood again, mingling with the dirt. The team's leader snapped out several more words that Artair did not understand, and then looked up at the rest of the men gathered nearby. They stumbled over each other to return to what they had been doing before the excitement started.

The head man waited until Asael had picked himself up from the dust and returned, grumbling, to the group before he resumed unlocking the cage.

When he had freed all the locks he opened the top and swung it open. Artair raised an eyebrow at him from inside. Artimus motioned toward a stand of trees in the distance.

"Come on, let's take a walk," he said, speaking again in Helvetian.

The prisoner stood slowly, his muscles stiff from their prolonged inactivity. He looked around before stepping over the side of the cage to the ground. Artimus did not speak, but began walking in the direction of the small forest. Artair followed, doing his best to keep the limp from his step as his muscles worked the knots out of themselves.

When they were a safe distance from camp, he turned to Artimus and asked, "So, are you always so... *persuasive* with your friends?"

The other man glanced sideways at him and shook his head. "I don't think there's a man or woman alive that would call that man their friend. He's mean as a snake with a double toothache, and he doesn't like people telling him what to do." The head kidnapper kicked a rock in his path; it rolled into a patch of grass and disappeared.

"If he doesn't like people ordering him around, I'll bet he loves what you just did." Artair bent down and picked up a couple pebbles and rolled them in his right hand as he walked.

"Yeah, well, I don't like people trying to stab me in the back, so I guess neither of us were having a good time," Artimus answered.

"Now wait a minute," the Sword Bearer demanded. "He did have his sword out; but how did you know that he was planning to do more than stand guard over me when you let me out?"

"How did you know that you could break your cage open on that first day? The answer is that you just knew. I know my men like you know your strength and your armor.

"I've been working with Asael for a couple of years now. Usually he does well enough, but in case you haven't noticed, you've made him more than a little mad lately. He especially doesn't like that I didn't let him kill you before. He was the one most in favor of having you never wake up. The fact that I stopped him does not endear me to him, as you might expect." They walked in silence a few more steps before Artimus changed the subject.

"So, how much of your story about the swords was a lie? There's more to them than you told me before. What didn't you tell me?" With the conclusion of his question Artimus stopped walking and looked expectantly at Artair, who turned to face him.

The Helvetian scratched his head and made a show of thinking it over before he responded with a mischievous grin. "I did forget to mention that they're a lot better than any of yours, didn't I?"

Artimus rolled his eyes at the comment and Artair laughed.

"There are a few things that I left out of my story," the warrior admitted, "But let's keep walking while we talk. My legs are killing me from sitting in that cage all day."

The other man nodded his assent and the two resumed walking.

"When our ancestors found the steel that those swords are made out of, they were in the middle of a civil war. They used all they could find to make weapons. As you've seen, they're stronger and sharper than a sword made out of regular steel.

"In fact, it's pretty good against almost any material. I don't know if they ran out of metal first or the war ended, but they stopped making weapons like that.

"In our day, we've been able to find some of the raw material, but we no longer know how they processed it. Usual methods don't work. So, the weapons that have survived are highly prized in our society."

"That makes the picture a little clearer, but what do you use them for? You and I both know that there hasn't been a serious war among your people for a long time," Artimus interjected.

Artair looked at the other man for a moment, wondering how this foreigner could know that. He shook his head. "For once you're wrong, Artimus. We've been at war for close to fifteen years now. A war more desperate than any fight we've ever been in."

The Helvetian lapsed into silence and his captor stared at him.

"Are you lying to me again? From what I've been told, the last thing that could be called a war among your people was decades ago, so don't fool with me about this." When his prisoner didn't respond, he continued.

"So tell me, if you've been at war for fifteen years, who is it that you've been fighting?" Artimus insisted.

Artair stopped abruptly and looked into the other man's face, his eyes blazing with anger and frustration. Artimus knew a lot about his people. Too much. It was impossible that he didn't knnow about the dragons. Why would he feign ignorance like this?

When finally spoke his voice was low and deliberate.

"When I was thirteen years old I watched my father die when a pair of dragons found our town. I killed one of them before it could kill me. My best friend finished off the other as I lay unconscious."

"You've killed a dragon?" Artimus interrupted, incredulous. He found himself unable to look away from the other man's eyes as they reflected the bitterness and frustration that boiled inside him.

"The dragons destroyed whole villages and slaughtered thousands before we found a way to beat them." Artair continued as if he had not heard the other man. "Since then we've been fighting them with the same weapons that our ancestors created to kill each other."

The Sword Bearer's eyes bored into the other man. He finally turned away and began walking again, cursing himself under his breath. He had said too much, but perhaps it would be for the best.

The blades' true potential was no longer a secret. Now at least they might let him out if they were attacked by a dragon, giving him a chance to bargain for his freedom. His captor followed after a couple of steps.

They walked in silence for more than a minute before Artimus spoke. "So, you've killed a dragon with those swords back there, by yourself?" he asked.

"Yes, I killed that first one alone, but after that I was always part of a team. To go up against a dragon alone would be foolhardy," Artair said after a brief hesitation. He had already given away the information, so it would do him no good to deny it now.

Besides, he still wasn't telling him everything. He saw no reason to tell him about the one man who did exactly that, over and over again. No need to tell him about the Hammer.

"Okay, but you're saying that those swords back in our camp will actually penetrate a dragon's armor? I had heard that nothing could do that, at least not consistently," he protested.

The prisoner shook his head. "The swords were made long ago. They have some unique qualities that make them better for dragon fighting. Regular steel immediately blunts itself when it hits a dragon's armor.

84

"While they might cut or scratch a bit, they are as blunt as a staff before they can penetrate. These swords can't be dulled by anything we've tried. You can cleave stone with them and not even scratch the finish. These swords will do the job, but it's far from easy.

"A dragon's armor is actually two layers thick. The outside layer is extremely hard but also fairly brittle. That layer can be shattered by a hammer blow. The second layer is thicker and heavier and almost as strong. These are the only swords capable of shattering through the first layer and still stay sharp enough to cut through to that lower layer."

Artair looked at Artimus as the other man turned and looked toward the horizon, a small smile growing on his face. The smile grew into a grin that remained on his face for several seconds.

"What are you laughing about?" The Sword Bearer demanded.

The kidnapper only shook his head and chuckled. "Nothing, Artair, it's nothing. However, I feel a little better about what you've done to my team now that I know that you're not some farmer hauling his daddy's sword around.

"Fighting against men must be pretty easy after fighting dragons for fifteen years, am I right?" His voice was cheery, and the grin was still stuck on his face.

His prisoner looked at him, judging his sanity, and then nodded. The easy smile on Artimus's face had warmed his own mood and he smile a bit as he responded. "It is a lot easier. Most of your men seem like they move in slow motion when they're fighting. In fact, Calum would laugh me to shame if he knew that you and Asael had beaten me."

"Who's Calum?" Artimus asked.

"I told you that it was a pair of dragons that attacked my town when I was younger. He killed the other one. He's my friend." The smile had disappeared from the warrior's face now.

Artimus kept silent as he watched the other man sort through his memories. "Most people we kidnap would have started talking in the past tense by now. You still expect to be able to escape, don't you?"

Artair ignored the question and, after a minute of silence, turned to his captor and asked, "Artimus, why are you here?"

His voice was serious now. "You aren't like Asael, you don't enjoy seeing people suffer. I could even go so far as to say that you seem to be a decent person. So why are you here to kidnap my people?

"You're taking me to what you believe will be certain death. Doesn't that bother you? None of the rest of the men on your team even think of me as a human being. I can tell by the way that they look at me. But you do. You're not the same kind of person as they are, so why are you doing this?"

The kidnapper refused to meet the other man's gaze for several seconds as he considered how to answer the question. In the end he answered with one of his own.

"Are you married?" he asked finally.

"I'm serious, Artimus, I want to know," the Helvetian insisted, not letting his captor redirect the flow of conversation.

"Answer my question." he commanded softly.

The Sword Bearer shook his head in frustration and then shrugged his shoulders.

"Fine. No, I'm not married." he responded. "I will eventually, when my sword goes to another, but I am not worthy of that honor yet."

"Have you ever been in love?" the head man asked.

The Helvetian glared at him. "I've spent my entire adult life fighting dragons and expecting not to see the end of the next fight. So no, I haven't," Artair answered, openly frustrated now at this domestic line of questioning.

"Then you cannot understand why I am here, or why I do this," Artimus said and turned to look back at camp. Before the other man could ask anything else, he motioned toward it with one hand.

"We'd better get back, they should have dinner ready by now," he said casually.

His prisoner stared at him incredulously and then began walking back toward the campsite. As they drew close to the light of the fire, Artair looked back at him and asked, "Hey, what did you say to Asael after you knocked him down?"

Artimus chuckled at the memory. "I'm afraid there's no direct translation," the swordsman answered, and both men laughed.

Chapter 13

Artair watched the mountains inch closer as the days passed. Every night Artimus let him out of his cage to walk around, something that displeased Asael greatly.

The Helvetian only grew more confused with every conversation he had with the head kidnapper. Had they been back in Greenock he suspected that they would have been good friends, but under their current circumstances that was impossible.

Artimus had warned him one night to never mention his history with dragons, and especially to never mention what his swords were used for. The warning was unnecessary, but appreciated.

Artair could not decide if that meant that Artimus himself did not plan to tell anyone, or if he simply did not want to have the information divulged to his men before he could tell them himself. Regardless, Artair had no reason to tell anyone anything more.

The journey toward the mountains concluded one evening as the party camped at the base of a solitary peak that curved as it reached into the sky. Artair's eyes widened when he caught sight of it, studying it with a mixture of disgust and curiosity. When Artimus came to unlock his cage, he stopped him with a gesture.

"I'd rather stay in here tonight, if you don't mind," he said, to his captor's surprise.

"I knew that if we kept you in there long enough that you'd get to like it. Am I right, or is there some other reason that you'd rather stay behind bars than stretch your legs?" Artimus asked, with a touch of sarcasm in his voice.

Artair rolled his eyes. "The only thing that could ever be comfortable in this box would be a rock, and you know it. I just don't want to take a walk right now," the caged man responded.

His captor snorted. "I know that we don't cook very well, but you must have a real low opinion of my taste buds if you think I'm going to stomach that nonsense.

"Come on, what's so different about this place that spooks you? You don't seem like you'd be afraid of the dark, so what's the matter?" He waited expectantly for a reply.

"Fine then. Let me out of here and give me back one of my swords and then we can take a walk," Artair responded with sarcasm of his own.

"I'm afraid that one's impossible. Why would you need a sword, though? You think we'll meet up with a dragon around here or something?" Artimus asked lightly.

His prisoner looked at him. Then he pointed up at the peak that loomed above them. "Unless your drugs have gone to my head that is the peak my parents' generation named the Bleeding Tooth. The name of 'Tooth' is self-explanatory, but they named it 'Bleeding' because this is where they first met up with the dragons.

"Only one of the men in that party survived long enough to get back home. Somewhere at the base of this peak there is a cave and we suspect that the monsters originally came through it into our lands.

"No party sent to find this place has ever been heard from again. I'd suggest we either find a new place to camp or let me have one of my swords. One dragon would kill everyone here, including me. Have you ever fought a dragon before, Artimus?" He challenged.

The other man grinned and shook his head while beginning to take the chains off of the cage.

"As a matter of fact, I haven't ever had the pleasure, but don't worry. We've never been attacked here and we always use this camp. Let's go," he said as the last chain fell to the ground and he swung the lid open.

The Helvetian shook his head.

"Get out of the cage. In case you're wondering, you do not have a choice about this," Artimus insisted.

The Sword Bearer considered a moment, then stood up. The other man took his arm to help him over the side of the cage. He nodded toward the looming monolith.

"This way, let's go," he said and waited for his prisoner to start walking before falling into step on his left.

Artair walked catlike, his hands held slightly away from his body, his eyes searching the deepening shadows around every tree. His captor was as relaxed as ever and by the second grew more amused with the antics of the other man.

Artimus led him up to the base of the peak, and then headed along the side of it. The solid rock gleamed white in the failing light. They were halfway around a large boulder when Artair jumped sideways, throwing the other man against the back of the boulder while clamping one hand over his mouth.

"You daft fool!" Artair hissed through clenched teeth. "We're there. That's the cave on the other side of this rock. It fits the description perfectly.

"You've led us right to the dragon's lair and you didn't even bring a sword. We're dead if they catch wind of us, you idiot." The Sword Bearer's head twitched back and forth, furiously scanning their surroundings, noting possible cover or routes for escape.

Artimus had been trying to remove the hand from his mouth, but without success. Artair was infuriated and terrified. Suddenly the kidnapper's knee crashed up into the other man's groin and his right fist buried itself in his prisoner's stomach.

The steel-like grip loosened as all air was driven from the warrior's lungs and pain lanced through his groin and up into his belly. Artimus grabbed Artair's left hand, the one covering his mouth, with his own and twisted it while driving his free hand up into his elbow.

The fierce attack caught the other man off guard and his captor slid behind him smoothly, shifting his right hand to the Helvetian's shoulder while pulling the other arm up behind his back.

Artimus's elbow dug into his prisoner's back as he half carried, half pushed the gasping swordsman around the boulder and shoved him into the mouth of the cave.

The dragon fighter's training and instincts kicked in as he hit the ground and he rolled to his right, coming up hard against a rock wall. His mouth filled with dirt as he struggled to gain his breath, shaking in terror. He couldn't help the noise he was making as his body struggled for air. His eyes darted among the deep shadows of the cave, searching with desperation for the dragons he knew that he would see.

To make matters worse, the cave floor immediately around him was clear of anything that he could use as a weapon. There were no rocks, no sticks, nothing. Then his leg brushed against something smooth and hard that moved as he touched it.

Reaching back, Artair pulled it up in his right hand, his eyes still scanning the dark recesses. It felt like a rock, except that the weight was wrong, it was too light for the size.

He glanced down at what he had in his hand and his body stiffened in horror. He was holding a human skull, the empty eye sockets staring at him as if in accusation.

His lungs finally cleared and he screamed in pure fury. Jumping to his feet, he threw the skull at the blackest area of shadow.

He heard the sound of it hitting the wall and then landing in the dirt. Then there was only silence.

"Artair."

He jumped at Artimus's voice and spun around to face the speaker, his entire body quivering with rage.

"Look down." The other man's voice was calm, and he stood leaning against the wall at the entrance to the cave.

The Sword Bearer stood stock-still as his eyes slowly lowered from Artimus to the dirt floor. The rage slowly melted away from the warrior's body to be replaced with wonder and confusion. Sinking to his knees, he stared at the ground.

The floor of the cave was covered with the footprints of both men and dragons. The prints were all crowded together, those of dragons covering those of the men, and the tracks of men covering the dragons'. For several minutes Artair stared, his mind racing. When he looked up at Artimus, his bewilderment shone in his eyes.

"This is the cave they spoke of." It was more statement than question, but the other man nodded affirmation anyway.

"What does this mean?" Artair asked, his voice hoarse from shock and strain.

The kidnapper did not answer, but instead pulled a sword from a sheath hanging on the wall inside the mouth of the cave. Stepping away from the wall, he motioned to his prisoner with it.

"Stand up, Artair. We need to get back to camp." Artimus's voice was quiet, a rare touch of sympathy in his tone.

The Helvetian stood and faced the other man. "Why did you show me this? What is this place? Curse you Artimus! What is going on?" he shouted. His words echoed back into the cave and repeated his final question.

His captor shook his head. "I can't tell you anything yet, but I promise that you will have your answers eventually. Let's head back, now," he answered. His voice left no room for argument.

Artair looked around once more and then stalked out of the cave. The other man followed him, sword in hand, all the way back to camp where the prisoner immediately lay down in his cage and did not move for the rest of the night. The food they brought to him was ignored, and his eyes were still open as the rest of the group fell asleep.

The morning dawned on the party as they were finishing breakfast. The men kept their distance from the prisoner's cage as they made preparations to leave. A blind man could have felt the rage emanating from the warrior.

When they finally left camp, they headed straight along the base of the Bleeding Tooth until they made it to the site of the previous night's activity. There Artimus returned the borrowed sword to its sheath and led the way into the forbidding shadows.

Three of the men had torches lit in their hands as they entered the dark opening. In their flickering light, Artair could see his own tracks from the night before. This time he was only slightly apprehensive about entering the legendary cave. The men around him were at ease, more than they had been the whole trip. This was nothing new or dangerous in their eyes.

Ahead of them the path led deep into the mountain and slanted downward. Artimus paused momentarily to pick up the skull that now lay in the middle of the tunnel. When he stood up his eyes met Artair's.

He held his gaze for a moment and then looked away to toss the skull past the cage and toward the mouth of the cave. None of the other men turned their heads to watch it hit the ground, but the Helvetian watched as it rolled up against the wall where he had stood the night before. He kept looking back, fixated on the gruesome sight, until it disappeared from view.

Artair noted with some interest that the men carrying his cage were moving faster now than they had on previous days. If they knew that dragons lived in this cave, they wouldn't have come near it.

Where even Artimus had admitted that he had never fought a dragon and that their swords were no better that those if the village militias; it was clear to him that a single dragon would have no trouble shredding its way through the entire group.

The only thing he could think of that would allow the tracks he had seen to exist, and for them to use this tunnel, would be if the dragons had certain patterns of movement inside the caves that allowed for windows of time for safe passage. That would explain why they were hurrying, since they would have to make it out of the dark interior in time to avoid an encounter.

Artimus's actions of the night before were unexplainable in and of themselves. His captor did not seem like one who would need to nurture fear. Yet it appeared as if that was exactly what he had been trying to do; startle him, shake him up for no reason. Either that or he had been trying to show him something that the Sword Bearer couldn't yet understand.

His train of thought was broken when the group neared a fork in the passageway. The only light they had was from the torches the men had brought with them, and Artair wondered what was going to happen when they burned out.

The men carrying his cage didn't pause, but took the right side of the fork which headed further downhill. The pace quickened even more with the change of direction, and the Sword Bearer wondered how much longer they could keep it up. He glanced over his shoulder as the torch behind him burned out and the darkness grew. Another fork appeared, and they took it left, the path leveling out this time.

The second torch burned out, and the only one left burning was starting to flicker. The Helvetian only caught occasional glimpses of the leader's back as the swordsman trotted ahead of the group beyond the reach of the torches. The third torch burned low and then went out.

The caged warrior was surprised when the cave didn't go completely dark as he had expected. Looking around, he noticed that there was a dim light coming from up ahead. Soon Artair could see the head man clearly as the light grew brighter the closer they came.

After another few steps he could make out a dim doorway with torchlight spilling out of it. A few seconds later the leader stepped through it and the captive could hear voices coming from inside.

Artair watched, fascinated, as the group stepped through the opening and into the light. The dark cave had opened up into a huge underground cavern. Lamps hung at intervals along the walls. The prisoner could see several crude shelters built up in the back of the room.

To the left, another tunnel continued to lead downhill into the bowels of the mountain. He guessed that by now they had passed underneath the Bleeding Tooth and were somewhere in the mountains behind it. Beyond that, he could not guess.

Artair's searching eyes finally found Artimus. The black-garbed leader was talking with a weasel-like fellow who was dressed the same as his captors. The two soon approached the cage, talking in their own language, and the new man looked the prisoner over appraisingly.

When the newcomer made some comment and began to point towards Artair's healing wounds, Artimus stopped his hand before it got within arm's reach. Anger flared in the man's eyes at the unwanted restraint, but after another few words from the kidnapper, his eyes widened. He subconsciously stuck his hand into his pocket.

The Sword Bearer was grinning at him the next time he looked up, though he didn't understand what was said, he was amused at the stranger's actions.

A couple minutes later, their conversation finished, Artimus bade farewell to his companion and they continued on down the tunnel that led left.

They passed three more checkpoints that day, each time stopping for a few minutes. As usual there was no break for lunch. The group exited the caves in time to see the sun set over the mountains.

Artair was glad to breathe fresh air again, and found that his appetite had returned when dinner was finally brought to him. The caged warrior could feel that a certain tension had been lifted from the men around him.

They were more relaxed, more jovial. When they turned in for the night, no guard was posted. The Helvetian knew the reason for the change, and it made him uncomfortable. These men were home now, and he was trapped in the secure confines of their country.

Chapter 14

Artair was awake and had been impatiently waiting for more than an hour before anyone else stirred in the camp. Not surprisingly, Artimus was the first of them to wake up. He went about making a fire and starting breakfast with a nonchalance that the Sword Bearer would have expected to see if the man were in his own home.

The head kidnapper artfully avoided looking in his prisoner's direction for several minutes until one of the other men woke up and took over cooking at the fire. Then he came walking over toward him.

"Good morning, Artimus, nice to see you up and around." Artair quipped with his usual sarcasm.

"There is a time for all things, my friend," the other man replied with a sleepy grin. "The day after we get through those dreadful caves is used for much-needed rest. You don't know how stressful it is being in the kidnapping business, or how hard it is for my poor, wounded men to carry your big carcass all over the map."

The swordsman sank to the ground by Artair's cage and sat plucking blades of grass as he absentmindedly looked into the sky.

"What did you tell that first guy back there in the cave? He looked like he was scared he was going to lose his hand if he didn't hide it from me." Artair asked. Artimus chuckled.

"Oh, I told him that we found you running around on all fours chasing rabbits. I said that you had nearly bitten the fingers off of the last man who had put his hand too close.

"He wouldn't have believed me if there hadn't been so many bandaged hands around to prove my point. You showing your teeth at him like you did helped too," the kidnapper replied. This time both men laughed, causing some more men to stir from their night's sleep. The two could hear muffled curses coming from the general direction of Asael's bed, signifying that he was now awake.

"Artair, just to let you know, in a few days we'll be at Cyrene. After that we probably won't see each other again. Along the way there will be a lot of people wanting to take a look at you. You've already figured out that my countrymen don't think of you as an equal.

"That's not their fault, but it's the way things are right now. I'm hoping that someday that will change. You know, it's interesting to me that although they think of you as animals, most of the people have found ways to learn pieces of your language. If you spoke simply, most people would understand you.

"Anyway, if I don't get another chance to tell you, good luck in the arena." Artimus rolled over to lie on his back and his eyes began to trace the solitary cloud that hung in the sky.

"You said that no one has ever survived a fight in the 'arena', as you call it. Is that true?" Artair asked. The other man nodded his head in response to the question, but kept his attention on the cloud.

"Do all people you take from my country end up in the arena, or am I an exception?" the Sword Bearer probed. This time Artimus glanced at him for a moment and then returned to looking into the sky.

"All of them go there eventually," he answered finally.

"Then my next question is do you ever apologize to the women and children you kidnap before you send them off to be butchered?" Artair's voice had gone cold. He could see his captor's body stiffen at the question.

"You say that your people do not see me as an equal. You even have the gall to act sorry about that. How do you rationalize sending innocent people to die? How do you see us, Artimus?

"You're a real good talker, but when it comes right down to it you're as barbaric as that animal Asael you keep under your heel. I won't die in the arena. I'll live and I'll escape and I'll come back with an army of my countrymen.

"When I do, I'm going to find you, and before I kill you, you'll apologize to the brothers, husbands, and fathers of all the people you've sent to die, because all the people you really should apologize to are already dead."

Artimus roared in anger as he left the ground, throwing himself against the cage, rolling it over on its side.

The dragon fighter hastily righted himself and glared back at his captor, who stood looking in at him from out of arm's reach.

"Artair, you do just that. You bring on your armies if you can raise any. I'll see them die like cattle in a slaughtering pen. If you bring them back through those caves you will be bringing them to their deaths.

"You're a bitter man with a mouthful of fear, so don't you try to lecture me when all you're trying to do is save your own skin." Artimus kicked the bars of the cage and stormed off.

The rest of the day was spent in leisure. Most of the men spent their time sleeping, lounging around the fire or, curiously, washing their clothes. Their prisoner wondered why they didn't consider bathing in the creek they drew water from, but they appeared to be more interested in appearances than hygiene.

Artair was surprised to see that even Asael took time to clean his clothes and went so far as to shine his sword. Artimus didn't return to talk to him that day. When he was let out of his cage to walk around, it was with an armed guard.

The next morning the group set off again, this time walking in formation, Artimus in the front, with Artair's bearers and his cage following right behind. The rest of the men walked two by two following the prisoner.

Every effort had been made to conceal the men's wounds, but it had not been very successful. The Sword Bearer guessed that their entrance into Cyrene was going to be some type of ceremony or procession.

He wondered why the preparations had been made so far in advance. According to the head man's estimations, they were still a couple of days' journey from the home city.

The reason became clear later that same day as they passed a small scattering of farms. As soon as the houses came into view, Artimus pulled a horn out of his pack and blew three long blasts.

The Helvetian watched as the inhabitants came running from their homes and stood along the side of the road. As the cage passed them, the people looked at him with uncloaked curiosity, and no small amount of fear.

He saw the same fear in the eyes of most of the people the party passed for the next couple of days, whether the group was large or small. At one point, while they were passing through a small town, a random person threw a melon at him. It broke against the bars of the cage, spraying pieces of the ripe fruit into his face and onto his clothes.

The Sword Bearer was surprised when, in response to the attack, his kidnappers quickly formed a protective ring around his cage.. The men on the outside drew their swords. There had not been a second attempt to attack him, and they passed through the rest of the town without incident. Twice the group passed what looked to be abandoned farms. In both cases the house had been crushed almost flat, and there were no people around the area.

Thus far Artair had been surprised at the similarities he saw between these people and his own. They looked the same, dressed similarly, worked land that appeared comparably fertile, and the produce he saw growing was as it was in his own country.

The only differences he could identify were that these people were poorer than his own, and there was fear in their faces. Most did not even look up at the soldiers who marched behind the Helvetian's cage. Rather they stood with their heads down as if afraid they were going to be punished for merely existing.

On the evening of the third day a party of five men approached their camp soon after they had stopped for the night. Three of the men looked like fighting men, possibly bodyguards, while the other two were definitely not. The one was extraordinarily fat, his overly fancy clothes not quite able to conceal the rolls of excess that hung around his waist. The other was skinny and slightly bent over, with pale skin and hands that looked better suited to holding a quill than a weapon of any kind. Artair could tell that the walk had been a terrible strain on the fat man, for as soon as he got closer the Sword Bearer could see the sweat rolling off his red face.

When the party finally arrived at the fire, Artimus greeted them, and a place was prepared for the round visitor to sit. The caged warrior strained to hear the conversation that went on, but what he could hear was not in his language, and so he contented himself with watching.

*

Artimus had never understood why a man so overweight and so unaccustomed to physical activity always insisted on seeing the prisoners before they had made their way into the city. He had asked him about it once, but he had received only an annoyed look as an answer.

"Master Tullius, how are things in Cyrene these days? You are looking well, and I suppose that I can only wish that all were so well taken care of." Artimus commented after allowing an acceptable amount of time for the other man to catch his breath. His comment brought a small smile to his visitor's flushed face.

"Thank you, General Artimus, I am well and so is Cyrene. The city is clamoring for some good entertainment, as always, and I suspect that you have brought me the balm I will need to soothe that particular itch?" The man's voice was one that had been overly refined over years of culturing his words before kings and nobles. That he was able to express himself with so few words was an exception made as a personal favor to his host.

Artimus nodded. "You can be sure, my old friend, that what we have brought you will keep the city buzzing for weeks. In fact, I judge our prisoner to be the most dangerous creature alive, with the exceptions of the dragons and myself of course." The General smiled slightly as he spoke and Tullius rolled his eyes.

"Now Artimus, you should know by now that your job is to bring them, not to present them to an audience. That's my job. I'm sure that this poor fellow is as pathetic as all the rest of the vermin you've brought me over the years, you just want more than your usual price for his hide," Tullius responded.

The other man didn't answer, but clapped his hands together once, bringing his cohorts around him in a half circle facing the newcomers.

"Master Tullius, please take a close look at my men. I can promise you that it is all real and that I caused none of it," the General said.

Tullius glanced quickly around at the men, and then studied each of them individually, his attention lingering on the bandages and healing wounds the soldiers displayed. His gaze stayed on Asael's face for the longest period, and his left eyebrow rose once before he moved on. When he had looked them all over his eyes returned to Artimus.

"Okay, let your men go sit down and rest themselves. I'm convinced," he finally declared.

Their leader waved the men away and they returned to their places around the fire. The large man leaned over to the head kidnapper and lowered his voice.

"If your prisoner did those things to your men, then he is truly a warrior, but what about you, General Artimus? Did this creature find his way past your defenses as well?" he queried. His host nodded his head slightly and responded in the same low voice.

"I carry a wound on my leg and in my side, but I would ask you to take my word for it since I would like to keep the fact a secret from my men, you understand." Tullius's eyes were wide as he sat back in his seat. A second later he let his breath out in a heavy sigh.

"Well then, you may be right. This man may have potential in the arena. What are you asking for this special animal?" The fat man asked the question and then sat back, assuming a pose that Artimus recognized. The negotiations were now open.

"I'll make this simple for you Tullius…double the usual," the General said.

The statement made the other man's mouth drop open in mock astonishment. "Double?" he gasped, looking slightly like a large fish out of water. "I wouldn't pay that much if you dipped him in gold and stuffed diamonds in his ears. You've been traveling in the sun for much too long General Artimus. I'll give you the usual upon delivery, as well as an extra bonus based on his performance." Tullius finished speaking and looked coolly at the other man, who sat with a smile on his face.

Artimus reached behind him and then tossed Artair's sword into the dirt in front of the other man's feet.

"What is this? Some trinket you think will sway my…" Tullius stopped, staring at the name engraved in the hilt of the sword. The blood drained from his face, leaving his usually ruddy face pale and slightly gray.

"A trick, General?"

Artimus shook his head, slowly.

"An heir? It can't be. Dromeda's heir?" Tullius asked, as if a nod would not suffice as an answer.

"There is no way to be sure, of course, but I'm sure you recognize the steel. They have been handed down by families, and there can be no explanation other than that. He is either an heir or as close as you will find."

"What will the King say?"

"He won't miss the festival, I can assure you of that."

Tullius suddenly shook his head, visibly trying to regain his composure and purpose. "Well, with no proof I see no reason to pay you any more for the savage."

Artimus chuckled. "Oh, no, my old friend, you won't get away with paying a corpse's price for a prize such as this. It will cost you double and I can guarantee you that you will gladly hand me the price after you've seen him in action. That's the deal, Tullius, you can either take it or leave it. Let me remind you that I can make my money with him in other ways, and you wouldn't like that at all." Artimus's grin widened as he finished speaking and the other's round face turned bright red with anger. "In fact," he continued, "Drake himself would probably pay more than that for the privilege of killing him, don't you think?"

The fat man was silent for several seconds as he composed himself and then he spoke. "I knew the first time I laid eyes on you that you would turn into a lying, cheating scoundrel, and now I see the fulfillment of my prophecy. You have that mongrel at my door by noon tomorrow or I'll have you whipped for theft."

Artimus laughed as Tullius stood up and marched out of the camp followed by his bodyguards and his scribe, who had written down the final figures of the deal.

Artair spent the night in silence. He hadn't understood anything that was said but he guessed that the night's meeting had determined his future. The thought was not a pleasant one. Neither was the fact that his captors celebrated as if some great victory had been won. Not since he was thirteen had anyone determined his destiny for him, and having someone do so now was extremely displeasing.

He did have to admit that he was curious about the reaction he had seen to the name carved in the hilt of his sword. He had asked about the name, from as many people as he thought might know more about his people's history than the one he had asked before. Not a single person even knew of the last time the name had been used, much less who the original owner might have been. Thanks to his captors, he might find out finally about Dromeda, but his life was a little bit much to trade for that bit of information.

Chapter 15

The next morning Artair watched from his cage as the men around him once again looked over their clothes and weapons, making sure that each was as clean and presentable as possible. Their preening delayed their departure and he was glad when they finally broke camp and resumed their journey. He was apprehensive about what was going to happen next, but anything was better than simply waiting. Artimus led them on the same path they had been following for the last couple of days. It led across a small valley and then up and over a hill at the far end.

When the party came over the crest of the hill Artair caught his first glimpse of their final destination. The landscape before them dropped down and opened up into a huge valley. Nearly covering the valley floor was the city Artimus had called Cyrene.

The entire group stopped to look down on the city as it came into view. The Cyrenians were grateful to be home, and Artair couldn't help but stare at the sight before him. He had never seen a city so large or so beautiful in his life. He calculated that it had to be at least ten times the size of his home, and Greenock was certainly one of the largest cities in the empire. A high wall surrounded the bulk of the area with only a few massive gates providing access to the inside.

Even from their distant vantage point Artair could easily see that the architecture also surpassed that of his home city. Two buildings in particular stood out from all of the rest. One was obviously a palace of some kind with tall spires and white walls that shone in the morning sun. The other one was also large, but with less beauty. This second structure was simply massive, and it sat directly in the middle, as if the city had been built around it. There was something about the impressive edifice that made chills run down the Sword Bearer's spine, yet he could not take his eyes off it.

The Helvetian's ponderings were interrupted as the group began moving again, heading down the hill into the city. Crowds of people met them at the bottom. Artair had thought that he was used to the stares and the strange antics of these people, but he was mistaken. His captors could hardly restrain the people, who, encouraged by their numbers, tried to press closer to his cage.

The group was met at the entrance by a band of fifty soldiers, dressed in black uniforms with silver trappings. Artair could only guess, but he assumed that these were not their typical dress. The uniforms were too fancy, too new. These fifty men formed a protective ring around the cage and Artimus's team before the gates were opened to admit them into the city.

The caged warrior was astonished at the sight that opened up before him as the giant doors creaked open. Thousands of people stood in the street, sat on housetops, and hung out of windows. Several hundred soldiers held open a path through the throng. The people making up the crowd alternated between cheering for Artimus and his men, and screaming at Artair while he sat in his cage. He could not understand their words, but he understood the meaning of what they were saying. They hated him, hated him a lot, and they were not afraid to let him know it.

The black-garbed parade slowly made its way through the crowded streets, sometimes pausing to wait for the soldiers to clear a path as the Cyrenians pushed and shoved to get closer to the spectacle and the caged prisoner. Artair figured that they were headed toward the palace-like structure he had seen from the top of the hill. When they finally reached the building, he looked up at it in wonder from inside his cage. Up close it was even more spectacular. The wall surrounding the edifice was made up primarily of white rock, with red stones scattered along the outside as accents. The building itself was made out of similar materials. Artair could only wonder at the time and expense that had to have gone into constructing a palace like this one.

The crowd thinned out and then disappeared as they neared their destination. When they finally reached the outer gates Artimus stepped up to the wall and pulled on a cord that hung there. A chorus of bells, not unlike chimes, sounded in response. The general then stepped back and stood facing the entrance. Looking around, Artair noticed that all of the men around him stood at attention facing the massive gates in front of them. None of them moved as a minute passed, then two, and then three. Artair guessed that they had been waiting for fully ten minutes before the gates finally swung inward to admit the group.

The inner courtyard of the palace was dotted with statues and flowerbeds, but the thing that caught the Helvetian's eye was the crowd standing on the steps of the palace itself. Twenty men stood in a line across the steps, all of them dressed in white with two swords slung across their backs. In the center of the line were three men with a white dragon symbol engraved on the front of their armor. Although a part of the line, the three seemed to stand alone.

Several steps above them stood another man, dressed in a red robe with white accents. He appeared to be middle aged, and stood with an air of authority. A golden crown sat on the man's head. When still twenty yards from the white line of soldiers, the entire procession stopped, and all the men bowed down on the ground, pressing their foreheads against the stone of the courtyard. They held that pose for several seconds before Artimus stood and walked up to the middle man of the trio Artair had noticed earlier. Once there he bowed at the waist and then straightened.

"I, General Artimus, request to be allowed to speak with King Drake of Cyrene." He spoke with a tone laced with formality, and perhaps a little boredom. He did not move as several seconds passed.

At long last, the guard in front of him reached forward and laid a hand on his shoulder. "The king does not often speak with those he has not invited, but on this occasion he will permit it. Leave your weapons and proceed."

The general stepped up and handed the man the short sword that hung around his waist, as well as a dagger he produced from between his shoulder blades. The guard took the weapons and then moved aside to allow the visitor to pass.

"All hail and praises be yours, great king." Artimus stated as he once again bowed to the steps in front of the man.

"Artimus, my good friend, welcome back. Cyrene has missed you." Despite the tone of his words, the king's posture did not soften. Drake had been king for over twenty years now, since Artimus was a child. He had assumed the throne when he was barely nineteen years old.

"The journey went well, and we have brought back a man who exhibits their finest swordsmanship. He is to be sold to Tullius at noon today, and the festival will be held within a few days." Artimus reported. For the sake of those around him, he could not allow himself to speak informally.

"Does he know anything?" King Drake inquired in a low voice.

"No, Your Majesty, he knows nothing. They fight the dragons now with all the resources they can muster," he answered.

"How effective are they in this?"

"We have seen evidence of them killing a dragon, but they clearly lost men of their own in the attack. They were hauling a body when we found this one.

"This man bears many scars from battles. From what we can see they are holding them back but are not able to push them back. It is good that this man will die in the Arena. He would be a dangerous enemy to Cyrene," Artimus said.

The King's sudden stillness silenced him. He had not been animated before, but he had turned to a block of stone at the end of the last statement.

"You have been away a long time, but that is no excuse for your forgetfulness." The King's voice was calm and too quiet to be heard farther than a few feet away, but there was an edge of steel in the words that made the words painful to hear.

"Forgive me, Your Highness, for my speech. I truly have been away for a long time, and have forgotten myself. With your permission, I have one more bit of news for you, after which I will withdraw so as to cause no more aggravation to His Majesty."

Drake waited a moment, then nodded, his head moving no more than an inch.

"The savage carries a sword bearing the name of Dromeda, and claims that the weapon has been handed down from his ancestors. Sire, I believe that we now have Dromeda's heir in our possession, or at least one of them."

For a moment no one spoke, and Artimus was careful not to drop his gaze from the King's.

"He is to be sold to Tullius?" Drake asked finally.

"Yes, sire."

"Then he is of no consequence or use except to draw a crowd. You are dismissed, General."

Artimus bowed, took his weapons back from the men holding them, and walked back down the steps.

Without looking back, he ordered his men to stand up, and led them out of the palace grounds, his feet crunching slightly on the crushed white gravel of the courtyard.

Once, when he turned to look back, he caught Artair's gaze. The other man's eyes were filled with curiosity mixed with another emotion that angered the general: pity. It was a strange type of pity he had seen in the other man's eyes. It was the same type of pity that Artimus would have for a man who got himself killed by his own foolishness, where he was more sorry that the man had been stupid than that he had died in the act.

The group soon arrived at their destination, and the prisoner was not at all surprised to find himself looking up at the building he had stared at from the top of the hill. It was indeed massive, and the ornamentation was a futile effort to mask the building's true identity.

Artair was startled when Asael spoke from behind him, even though the big fellow kept his voice low so as not to be heard by the leader of the party. "Welcome to your grave, savage. Welcome to the arena."

The Sword Bearer's head turned slowly from the low voice to look once again at the building. His foreboding was justified if this was indeed the place where his people had been taken to be killed. This was the location Artimus had said no one ever escaped from, a statistic he had vowed to prove inaccurate.

Artair shook his head, trying to clear the thought from his mind, and then began tracing the designs on the outside of the structure as he waited for the next turn his fate decided to take. Like a red rose placed on a decaying corpse, the ornate decorations did little to change the effect of the whole.

Chapter 16

Tullius met Artimus at the door and the two clasped hands. The arena manager waved his visitor inside to sit in one of two chairs on opposite sides of a small table. Between them was a small silver teapot and two cups. The General declined the tea, as he always did, and then waited as the other man poured himself a cup and sampled it.

"I assume that you've already made your visit to the King's palace," Tullius remarked.

Artimus let the statement go without comment and sat in silence.

At length, Tullius finished his tea and then pulled two bags from the floor beside his chair and set them on the table. For all his excess fat, he lifted the heavy bags without any appearance of effort. Those in the past who had underestimated him because of his vast size had been sorely disappointed. "Double, as promised, you cheating dog." the fat man said without malice. The swordsman nodded, but made no move to pick up the money.

"Is this man really as good as you say he is, Artimus, or was all of that just a ploy?" Tullius asked, then smiled a wide, genuine smile. "You can tell me now, the deal's already made."

The General smiled painfully, and then nodded. "Unlike you, I have no need to improve upon my facts for the sake of presentation. To be frank, he's so good that he almost got away from us, if you can imagine that. In my life I have only fought one man who was better at the sword than he is, and that's the truth. It's a shame to have him go to the arena like this, because we could use him in the army as an instructor. That's how good he is," Artimus said.

"His lineage would make that a problem, would it not?"

"His supposed lineage, Tullius." Artimus corrected him.

The fat man waved his free hand in dismissal as he took another drink from his cup.

"In my business close is good enough. The people will know him as Dromeda's heir, and I will thank you not to try to change their minds. The sword and his skill with it will do the rest." Tullius shook his head in wonder and sat back in an attempt to ease his bulk in the under-padded chair.

"But, unfortunately his skill will only affect one thing now," Tullius said with the beginnings of a sly smile.

The other man raised an eyebrow. "Oh, really, and what is that?" Artimus asked, playing along.

The other's broad grin grew even wider. "The admission rates into the festival, of course." Tullius said and roared with laughter at his own joke, his hanging jowls bouncing.

Artimus rolled his eyes and stood up, lifting the bags from the table. The manager of the arena stood to follow him as he opened the door and stepped outside.

Artair eyed the fat man coolly as he approached his cage. He was used to people looking at him as if he were some animal on display, but this fellow was especially obvious about the fact.

Tullius, in accordance with Artimus's instructions, kept a safe distance from the cage as he coolly appraised its contents. When he had made two complete circles around the prisoner he cast a glance at his old friend that was more doubtful than anything else. Then, as if consigning himself to his fate, he shrugged, then clapped his hands loudly and barked several commands to his men.

The arena guards had been congregating ever since Artair had been brought to the building. The men hurried to take the cage from Artimus's companions and carried it quickly through a large door to the left of the one the two had just come out of. Artimus raised a hand as they disappeared into the building, but the procession disappeared before he could see if Artair had returned the gesture.

"The festival will start in a couple of days. Will you be there?" Tullius asked Artimus. The general turned to face him.

"That all depends on how high you raise the admission prices." he replied with a smile. The other man laughed and then waddled his way into the building in pursuit of his newly acquired attraction.

Artimus paid his men, bade them a temporary farewell, and headed for home. The other soldiers would be partying for the next week, or until he decided to gather them up to head back to Helveti, but he had never had a taste for the same types of celebration they did. The invitation was always there, of course, but he suspected that the other men were glad to be rid of their leader after being ordered around by him for so long. Also, he was sure that most of the jokes told over the next week would be about him, and he would hate to take all their fun away. The weary swordsman smiled slightly at the thought as he walked home.

*

Artair's cage was carried through a dark passage with only occasional lamps hung on the walls, which seemed to give birth to more shadows than light. They continued along the tunnel for a couple hundred feet before coming to a formidable iron-strapped door with a large lock. One of the men produced a key from inside his vest and took a moment of clattering to unlock the door, swinging it inward.

The Sword Bearer's eyes strained in the darkness to see what might lie ahead, but his nose told him, first of all, that the room in front

114

of him was used to hold large numbers of people. He could smell sweat, blood, and human waste so strongly that it turned his stomach. At the same time he could hear the murmur of voices and a couple muffled screams coming from inside.

"Don't wait for me, I'm coming," came a voice from behind them. Artair turned to see the fat man hurrying along the tunnel towards them. Obediently, his men stepped forward, carrying the cage through the door and into the room.

Once inside, the Helvetian could begin to see what his other senses had been telling him. Iron-barred cells lined the walls, taking up most of the free space, and a larger circular pen had been constructed in the very center of the chamber. Artair could see the figures of people in some of the enclosures, and a large body of them in the pen in the middle of the room. The cellblock was dark and the air was close and humid, filled with the smell of human waste and unwashed bodies.

Artair was carried until they came to an empty cell where his cage was set down. At this point Tullius handed the keys he had received from Artimus to the same man who had opened the outer door. The guard immediately began removing the chains that held the lid of the cage closed. While he was doing that, the rest of his companions drew their swords and formed a half circle around the prisoner with the only opening being the entrance to the cell.

When the lid was finally opened, Artair stood slowly, stretching his cramped muscles. His eyes glanced around the circle at those who stood guarding him, and then his gaze returned to the individual who had unlocked his cage. The fellow motioned for him to step out and then gestured toward the open door with a flourish as if inviting a distinguished visitor to enter a dining hall. He paused only momentarily and then stepped out of the cage and into the enclosure, turning as he did to face the man who had welcomed him in. The guard took a torch from one of the other men, who were visibly unsure about whether they should put their swords away or not, and stepped into the cell with the Sword Bearer. Stepping back to allow the man in, Artair waited expectantly.

"My name is Marius, and I'm the captain of the guard here," the man said with a certain bored tone in his voice suggesting that he had made this speech many times before. His Helvetian was sloppy, with an accent that made it obvious that he did not care whether he improved upon it or not.

"As you will soon discover for yourself, there is no way to escape from this cell. There are iron bars on all sides, even under the floor and on the ceiling. You cannot break or cut them and you cannot squeeze through them so make yourself comfortable. Meals will be delivered twice a day, morning and night. If you make any attempt to attack the person who brings your food you will no longer receive any. If you cause no trouble, I will have no reason to make your life any more miserable than it has to be. Do we understand one another?" The guard asked the question without expecting an answer, but he got one anyway.

"No, we do not understand one another." Artair replied coldly. "I live my life trying to keep people safe and protected while you live yours to put them in submission until they can be conveniently disposed of. So no, I don't think we will ever understand one another."

The statement caught Marius off guard, and it took several moments for his words to sink in. When they did, Marius's eyes narrowed and Artair's right hand moved up to scratch casually at his chin. The guard said nothing more but cautiously stepped back out of the cell and swung the door closed.

Tullius had watched the vocal confrontation with more than a little amusement. If this man had been able to stand toe-to-toe with Artimus and survive, not to mention actually wounding him, then he might be the greatest candidate for the arena in the history of the event.

116

The manager pulled himself from his musings as he realized that his men were all looking at him, waiting for his next order. He dismissed them to go about their regular duties, then stood for several minutes more, looking at Artair in his cell.

The prisoner might have been a statue as he returned the other man's gaze. The light coming from torches on the wall was not enough to allow the two men to see each other's faces, but were bright enough for them to know that they were both still there, and watching each other.

"What is your name?" the Helvetian asked suddenly.

"My name is Tullius. Why do you ask?" the other man responded. He was surprised at the question; prisoners didn't often have the state of mind or the courage to be curious about anything when they were first brought to him.

"Do you do this because you have to, or because you want to?" Artair asked, ignoring the other man's query.

"I suppose it's a combination of the two, to be honest," the fat man answered, only slightly disturbed by the question.

"If you didn't have to lead this operation, would you still do it?" the prisoner inquired.

Tullius squinted in the darkness to try to see the other man's face, but he could not. These questions were getting a little too probing for him to be comfortable with the conversation, but he could think of no reason not to answer, so he replied simply. "No, I don't suppose I would. Why do you have so many questions?" he asked in response.

This time the Sword Bearer answered the other man's question. "I'm trying to decide whether I have to kill you or not." Artair said simply, then turned away and stretched out on the cot at the back of the cell.

Tullius stood in the darkness, his mouth gaping in amazement. Although every logical sense told him the answer was irrelevant, he still wanted to ask the question the other man's statement had brought to his mind.

"So, will you?" he asked finally, trying to keep his voice casual and impartial.

"That is up to you. You may leave now." The voice that came from the darkness made shivers run down the fat man's spine, and Tullius had taken several shuffling steps toward his office before he realized that he had just taken an order from one of his prisoners. The realization made him pause, but the call of duty kept him from returning to the cell. The work of promoting a festival had just begun, and he had hopes that this one would be the greatest of all time. Never again would he have a contestant with such a name.

Chapter 17

Calum didn't even wince as the needle slid through his skin, making the final stitch to close up a long gash in his upper arm. Looking around, he mourned silently the loss of yet another man from his team.

Today they had killed three dragons. The first they found had been alone, while the second two had been mates. It was in that fight that a lancer, a man named Rork, had been cut nearly in half by the tail blade of the male, and it was then that he himself had also been wounded. Of the thirty-two men that had begun the trip with him, twenty-seven remained, while two of them were badly hurt. Those who died had died well, and thirty-three dragons had fallen so far to accompany them in death. The other teams reported comparable success, and similar casualties.

Calum thanked the man who had stitched up his arm, then walked over to check on the two that had been wounded in an encounter the previous day. One had been clawed down the chest, and the other had lost his right hand in a dragon's jaws. They were good men, and most expected that they would live, but such things were never certain. Often the wounds received when fighting dragons simply refused to heal, as if some type of venom was at work.

Calum was glad for the fact that his wound had been caused by the broken shaft of an arrow sticking from the reptile's side instead of by the animal itself. He assumed that the reason the wounds from dragons sometimes never healed had a lot to do with how dirty the animals were, instead of venom. From what they had been able to inspect from the dead dragons they could not find venom sacks like in a snake, but a dragon's mouth and claws were always coated with bits of decaying flesh and dried blood.

After checking on the two, the team leader sat by the fire and stared into the flames. He had not expected to find the sheer numbers of dragons that they had found. The teams traveled slowly, and not a day went by that they didn't encounter at least one of the beasts. They infested the land, and resisted the intrusion. As of yet spirits were high, even after the long period of fighting. The Sword Bearer teams seemed grateful to finally be doing something that had potential value, and these men were truly good at what they did. As they went, the team had combined into a real fighting unit, and it was surprising how much easier it was to kill dragons with the larger numbers of people. Of course, there was also a larger chance of human casualties, but so far they had been lucky.

Calum guessed that it would be another couple of hard weeks before they reached the rendezvous point he had described, and after that he could only guess how long it might take them to find the cave. The disappointing thing was that none of the teams had reported finding anything that would lead them to where the phantom kidnappers had gone. They had found a couple of used campsites, but none of them looked new enough to have been used in the last couple of months. They still did not have any idea as to where or who these individuals might be.

When it had started, many had believed that it was the work of their old enemies, the people who occasionally raided their western borders. The facts did not support the theory, however, since all the kidnappings took place on their eastern borders, and there was no evidence of anyone being taken on the north or south. How the kidnappings were connected to the onslaught of the dragons, no one knew, but that thought haunted the leaders of their nation.

A whistle from one of the sentries brought Calum to his feet, the bright steel of his drawn sword glistening in the firelight. There was a murmur of voices at the perimeter of the camp and then a lone figure stumbled into sight. The Helvetian general recognized him as a young man named Màrtainn from Greenock. He was an applicant to become a Sword Bearer due to his speed and extraordinary reflexes, but now the youth looked exhausted and dust covered his clothes. Approaching the fire, the young man looked uncertain whether to speak or remain silent.

"Well, speak up boy, you've got no reason to wait for my permission. Why are you here?" Calum demanded.

Màrtainn looked relieved at the question and seemed to relax. "I've been sent to find you, sir. You need to come back to Greenock immediately." Màrtainn paused to breathe and the older man interrupted him.

"What is the matter? Have dragons attacked the city?" He asked urgently.

Màrtainn shook his head. "No, sir, there is no such problem. We found Iain. He must have escaped but he was hurt in the process and met a dragon on the way back. He left a message for you. I'm supposed to bring you back as soon as possible." Màrtainn stopped talking and looked at Calum expectantly.

The Sword Bearer stood staring into the woods as if he was not paying attention and then suddenly he grabbed the youth by the shoulders so hard he winced. "Yes, I will leave immediately; you stay here until tomorrow morning and then follow me. You're in no shape to travel right now." He turned his head and sought out his second in command. "Ragnal, keep pressing forward, I will return as soon as possible. We need to know what Iain had to say."

The Hammer that Lives simply nodded from his place next to the fire. Just as well-known as the two original Sword Bearers, the warrior was one of few men alive that had fought dragons one-on-one.

Calum turned back to the messenger, who had become distinctly uncomfortable due to the bigger man's grip on his arms, and released the boy. "Thank you, Màrtainn; I will see you on the trail." With that he collected his things, swung his pack over his shoulder and dove into the darkness of the trees.

"Doesn't he need someone to be with him? What if he meets a dragon along the way?" Màrtainn inquired of the warrior Calum had left in charge.

The older man just smiled. "Boy, if I were you I'd spend my time feeling sorry for any fool creature that may get in his way tonight." Ragnal chuckled at his own joke and then resumed looking into the fire.

Ragnal was not as worried at the thought of a man alone against a dragon as the rest of the Hellvetians were. One-on-one was the way he usually fought dragons, and how he preferred it. When the dragons had first arrived, he was a young blacksmith, barely out of apprenticeship. The reptiles killed half the people in his village while they were still out in the fields. He could still remember the terrified screams that had reached him at his forge. He had run toward the carnage, then had turned back for a weapon as soon as he had seen the dragons.

Once back inside his shop, he had reached for the biggest hammer he owned, a ridiculously large war hammer that he had come with the shop. He had not even bothered to try to move it yet, it was so large. He had been so intent on getting back out to the dragons that he had not realized much of what happened next until later. As his hands touched the hammer's handle, the metal warmed to his touch, and a

122

high keening whine filled the small building. Ragnal had run from his shop with the massive hammer, and a legend had been born.

When the rest of Hellveti had recovered from the dragon attacks, they had sent parties to check on the outlying villages. Most had been destroyed completely. The party that had found Ragnal's village had discovered the young blacksmith in the newly plowed fields, surrounded by the bodies of a dozen dragons. Their heads had been smashed almost flat.

From that day until the present, the Hammer that Lives had gone out every night in a circular sweep of the surrounding countryside, killing dragons in the darkness as he found them. A man had once claimed that Ragnal made up the number of dragons he killed every night, so he had invited him along on the next patrol.

The naysayer was delivered home over the shoulder of the dragon slayer, exhausted and twitching in terror from what he had seen.

*

Two days later Calum trotted into Greenock. It was dusk, the sun barely setting on the horizon.

Màrtainn was at least half an hour behind him; he had left him on the trail earlier that day. The boy had only taken a couple hours of rest at the camp before following him into the darkness. Màrtainn's youth and lack of battle armor had allowed him to catch up to the Sword Bearer in the beginning, but Calum's drive to see what awaited him soon allowed him to out-distance the boy.

The warrior's eyes were bloodshot and he looked exhausted as he grabbed the first person he found and asked where the men who had found Iain were. The first individual didn't know, but a friend of his walked by just then and directed him to the home of Seumas.

People turned their heads to watch as Calum jogged by. They all knew him and most knew why he had returned. When he reached the front door of the house he sought he opened it as he knocked. Seumas was sitting at his table, but stood as the dusty traveler stepped inside.

"Where is he?" the weary traveler demanded.

The older man seemed slightly taken aback by the abrupt question, but he was calm as ever when he stepped closer to Calum and put his hand on the younger man's shoulder. "Young man, you are worn out. Come, have some dinner and rest yourself, we will speak after you are better." Seumas's tone of voice was that of a father looking after a wayward child.

Calum shook his head. "No, sir, there is no time. Where is he? I must know," he pleaded.

Seumas shook his head and let his hand fall to his side. "We buried him yesterday."

Chapter 18

The old man's words struck the Sword Bearer like blows from a hammer. All of the air rushed out of him and his knees nearly buckled. His head swam as he reached out and grabbed the doorway to steady his buckling knees. Seumas helped the younger man to a chair where the Sword Bearer collapsed and let his head sink onto his folded arms on the table. After a few seconds he composed himself and looked up at the city leader.

"Who spoke to him before he died?" Calum asked.

"A number of people spoke to him, but he spoke to my wife at length right before he lost consciousness for the last time. He also left something for you, something he says he was instructed to give to you," Seumas answered.

"Where is your wife now and where is what he left for me? Please sir, time is precious," Calum said, seeing the other man's hesitation.

"My wife will be home shortly, and she knows where the object is. Until then, I implore you, sit still and have something to eat. You look famished."

When Calum did not object, Seumas stepped to the fire and ladled some stew into a bowl. The weary warrior hadn't thought much about food in the last couple of days, but as soon as the savory stew entered his mouth he realized how hungry he was.

The old man refilled his bowl three times before the door opened and an elderly lady with long white hair walked in. Her dirty houseguest immediately stood to welcome her and she returned his customary greeting. This time he was patient enough to wait for her to sit down in her chair before he began with his questions.

"Juliana, I need to know everything that Iain said to you, or anything that you have overheard him say. Was he really taken along with Artair? And if so, how did he escape? What did he have to tell me? Please, ma'am, I am in a terrible hurry and I need to know all I can." Calum spoke with all the urgency he could put into his voice.

The white-haired lady looked at him coolly and then nodded. "I can see that you are in a great hurry, Calum," she began, "so I will tell you all I know as quickly as possible, but please keep enough control over your manners to not interrupt me." He felt vaguely the way he had when being scolded as a child, but simply nodded his agreement and tried to assume a relaxed posture.

"He was taken the same time as Artair, that you already knew. He said they were placed in cages and taken toward the Spine. He escaped after he was wounded by the group's leader. He says that Artair was alive when he last saw him, but that he had failed in an escape attempt. He said that Artair was beaten by the group's leader."

"Wait a minute." Calum interrupted. "Iain said that Artair was beaten by one man?"

"Well, he did mention that another one of them jumped in at the end, but he was beaten by them, yes." Juliana replied.

The Sword Bearer shook his head in disbelief. "I've never met anyone who could have beaten Artair, even with two men I would not bet on their success." Calum said with suspicion in his voice.

The woman looked at him with kind eyes. "You are too modest, young man, the rest of the Sword Bearers argue about who is the better with a sword, you or he. However, if that part of his tale is hard to believe, the rest of it will be even more difficult for you. He said that the same man who had beaten him was forced to guard Artair for the next

126

couple of days because of how angry the rest of the kidnappers were. They kept him unconscious with some type of drug after the fight, and Iain never got a chance to speak with him."

"The day after the fight they stayed in camp to allow some of the men to heal a little bit, and the same individual who played the biggest part in beating Artair came and talked to Iain. He told him that if he wanted to, he could stage his death, but that he would have to play along and then do what he asked of him. He agreed and the stage was set for his mock-death. This man gave him a roll of leather and made him promise to deliver it to you. Iain wouldn't admit it, but I think he knew what he was getting into. The wound he received in the fight would likely have eventually killed him. He was stabbed in the stomach, and you know how those wounds can be."

"He lay in the bushes without moving the entire night and the next morning until the kidnappers left, and then he headed for home."

"We don't know the details about what happened after that, but we know that a dragon caught up to him." Her eyes shone with pride for a moment. "He killed the dragon single-handedly, Calum. Alone, wounded, and with only his father's sword, and he killed an adult dragon all by himself. We pulled his sword from the carcass a full five miles from where we found him. You should have seen him, Calum, any normal man would have simply stopped and died. He crawled five miles dragging one leg that had been nearly torn off his body."

"He was a warrior, Juliana."

She nodded slowly, as if that explained her own story.

Juliana pulled a small roll of leather from her pocket and handed it to Calum, who took it from her fingers gently. The material was tied together with two strings, and judging by appearances neither Iain nor anyone else had opened it. Roughly seven inches wide, he guessed that, when unrolled, it would be roughly two feet long.

127

Pulling a dagger from his waistband, the Sword Bearer carefully cut the strings and spread it out on the table. The three of them stared at it for nearly a minute without speaking before he re-rolled the leather and stuck it into a pouch hung on his belt. The elderly couple remained seated as Calum stood up from the table.

"Thank you both for your help, I know you understand how important it is that I leave quickly. Tell no one what you have seen until I contact you again."

With that he opened the door and left quickly, jogging down the streets and out of town the way he had come. On the way out he passed Màrtainn, who was barely making it to the first buildings of the town. As he jogged past he clapped the young man on the shoulder, causing the lad to stop and turn to watch the seasoned warrior's retreating back in the failing light. The young messenger shook his head in wonder and wearily headed for home.

Chapter 19

"On your feet, slave, it's time to go." Marius's voice was not a welcome one as he swung open the door to Artair's cage. With him were several men, all with swords drawn. The Sword Bearer noticed, with some puzzlement, that all of the men were dressed up as if for some important occasion. Instead of the weathered iron breastplates he was used to, they were wearing armor that glowed golden in the torchlight. Plumes of feathers rose from their helmets and even the swords they held were shiny and decorated with jewels.

Artair stood and looked at Marius for a moment before obeying. He could not be certain what was about to take place, but he knew that, whatever happened, his chances would be better outside of the barred enclosure. The guard stepped back to give the prisoner room as he stepped out the door and into the hallway. With the encouragement of the swords behind him, the Helvetian followed Marius as they walked between the cells and into a dimly lit hallway that turned abruptly to the right.

It was in this hallway that Artair began to hear a booming sound coming from above them. It sounded like a distant thunder, or the muffled roar of a continual rockslide. The hallway ended at a door, which his captor unlocked, and the small procession entered a room with large double doors at one end. In the middle of the room, stacked on a table, was Artair's armor. The Sword Bearer looked questioningly at the head guard as he motioned for him to step to the table.

"Come on, man, don't you recognize the stuff? Suit up; it's time for the festival to begin. Just don't get any ideas once you get it all on. We're not beginners at this, you know." As if to prove the point, three more men entered the room as he finished speaking. They were carrying crossbows, loaded and drawn.

With every weapon in the room pointed at his back, Artair stepped forward and ran his hand down his breastplate as it lay on the table. He could feel the adrenaline pumping inside of him as the familiar feelings of anticipated battle seeped through him. The men watched in silence as he strapped on his armor. He worked slowly, savoring the experience. He had spent too long in the dark in his cell and he was in the mood to see the sun again. Though he had been promised death, he did not plan to go easily and he expected at the least to have his passing talked about for years to come. The Helvetian could hardly suppress a smile as he looked up at Marius. The other man looked at him quizzically and then motioned toward the double doors.

"Well, now that you're all dressed up, let's go to the festival. You walk ahead of us, and stop when I say so. Understand?"

Artair just nodded his head and smiled, then turned and strode to the double doors. Jerking the latch, the swordsman threw them open, and was knocked back by the sound that assaulted him. The thunderous boom he had been hearing was the roar of people yelling. He did not dare guess how many people would be needed to cause that much noise, but certainly thousands—if not tens of thousands.

The exit opened up to an outdoor passageway with no ceiling and a dirt floor. On both sides the walls rose up fifty feet at its highest. Artair stepped forward and then down a step onto the hard-packed dirt. The blades of the men following him prodded at his back and he continued forward. When he reached the end of the passageway he stopped to stare at the sight that lay before his eyes.

130

He was standing at the entrance of a large dirt area, circular in shape, about a hundred yards in diameter, and surrounded by high structures filled with people. Thousands were packed into the stands, using every scrap of available space. Artair could not begin to guess the number of spectators who were yelling, no, roaring down at him. Above them the sky was blue and the sun shone brightly. To one side he could see a large tower with an open window set to overlook the floor.

It was toward this tower that Marius directed him, and as they drew closer he recognized the man he had seen a couple of days previous, the king of Cyrene. Today he wore a black dressing robe decorated with white dragon emblems.

Marius hissed for Artair to stop when they were directly in front of the tower. The man in the black cloak stood and the roaring ceased as if it had been simply turned off.

After a couple of quiet seconds the ruler raised his right hand in a fist and the crowd roared again. The tyrant sat down as Tullius stood up. The round man began to speak in a voice that filled the huge arena. He could not understand what was being said, but he guessed that what was being said was about him. He heard the name "Dromeda" spoken twice, and both times the crowd gasped in unison.

Artair scanned the other occupants of the tower and was only mildly surprised to see Artimus standing to the left of the king. He stood in a full suit of armor as if guarding the older man. He also wore a helmet topped with plumes.

The Helvetian tore his eyes from him as he realized that Tullius was nearing the end of his oration. At the conclusion of his speech the crowd began roaring again, and Marius guided the prisoner back toward the middle of the floor. Artair felt something crunch under his boot and he glanced down. A small bone, obviously human, bleached white from the sun. While his eyes were down he saw the pool of blood. Someone had kicked dirt onto it, but the edges were still wet. Further on he could see some damp earth where he guessed more blood had been recently spilled.

As they walked, Artair saw a sword, partially buried in the dust. A little farther on he saw a spiked club, wet with blood, lying in plain sight. He looked around him, at the screaming crowd, and tried to imagine what had happened before he was brought out. He obviously was not the first person to fight in the arena, had anyone else lived? Once in the middle of the arena, the men left him alone and hurried back to the door they had come out of. Before following the others, Marius turned back toward the Helvetian.

"Goodbye, savage." He said just loud enough for him to hear, and then ran, dust rising up from each foot fall.

As they disappeared another set of doors opened and the cheering intensified once again. Artair watched the man that walked out, and watched as the doors were closed behind him. Dirty and unkempt, the man's beard made it almost to his chest, and blood soaked what he could see of his long hair. The newcomer raised his arms and yelled to the crowd. He wore dirty armor, the breastplate looked like it had been made for someone larger than he, and he carried no weapon. The stranger lowered his arms and looked at Artair. His smile was wide, but had no cheer or friendliness. Walking forward, he scooped a wide battle ax out of the dirt and stood looking at the Helvetian—and then he charged, screaming fiendishly.

Artair ran toward him, then slipped to the side, ducked under the ax, scooped a dagger out of the dirt, and stabbed it into the back of his attacker's knee.

The gladiator screamed in pain, the blade jamming his knee joint. Turning, he swung the ax again, desperately hoping to make contact with his enemy. Instead, the ax stopped halfway as the Helvetian stepped in close and shoved the heavy weapon back into his face. The side of the blade flattened his nose and threw his head back as if on a hinge.

Artair turned from the unconscious, falling man as the door opened behind him.

The next gladiator came out of the gate running. He blinked as the sunlight hit his eyes, and he opened it just in time to see the butt end of the ax handle coming toward his face. He ducked, which meant that the blow landed between his eyes instead of in his mouth. His limp body fell against the door he had come out of—which was now closed again.

Artair swung the ax and sunk it two inches deep into wood where the door and the wall met. It would not stop them for long, but it might give him a minute's respite. He ran away from the door, searching the arena floor for a sword. He found one, half-buried, and scooped it out of the dirt as a door across the arena slammed open. He glanced up as another armed man ran from it. He watched him come for a moment, and then kept looking for another weapon.

A new gladiator stepped through the shattered remains of the first door. He held a sledgehammer with a three-foot handle. The wood near the head was stained dark from the blood of past enemies, and there were flecks of blood on the big man's chest and shoulders. This was obviously someone who had contributed to the blood pools.

Artair glanced at him, his eyes lingering on the weapon and then he ran for a shield lying a dozen paces from him. He could sense the movement as both gladiators closed on him, but he needed the shield if he was going to beat both men. He scooped the circular shield out of the dirt and turned toward the man with the sledge hammer. He ducked under the first hammer blow and thrust forward at the big man's legs with his sword. The attempt missed as the gladiator dodged, and Artair threw himself backwards, away from the next hammer blow that buried the head in the ground where he had been.

The second gladiator swung a sword at the downed Helvetian, but the blade bounced off the round shield with a sound like the ringing of a bell and Artair's sword buried itself halfway into the man's thigh before he ripped it back again and rolled to his left.

The hammer left a small crater where Artair had been a moment before, and Artair lunged to his feet, backing away from the hammer as the man he had wounded fell to the ground, clutching the massive hole in his leg.

Artair heard another door open and lunged forward, deflected a swing of the hammer with his shield, and nearly separated the gladiator's arm from his shoulder with a hammer-like blow of his own.

The sledgehammer thudded on the ground and Artair shoved its owner onto his back and turned toward the sound of the last door opening and something hit him in the chest. His feet left the ground and he landed on his back. The thrown spear landed next to him and he stared at the dent in his breastplate that restricted his breathing. Gasping, he looked up at the two men who had come through the door. The one who had obviously thrown the spear now held a short sword ready in his hands. His eyes were locked on the spear next to him, however, and Artair knew that was his weapon of choice. The other man held two swords, each roughly three feet long and over four inches wide. They were the swords of a true swordsman, and this man was obviously that.

Artair, gasping, struggled to free his breastplate while backing toward where the first man he downed had dropped his sword. The straps holding his breastplate in place finally gave way and the heavy plate fell to the ground. The Helvetian gulped air and moved faster. The gladiator swordsman saw what he was doing, and ran toward him, the two swords pumping like extensions of his arms.

The Helvetian stumbled over the fallen sledgehammer, judged the distance to the fallen sword, and then threw his shield at the advancing gladiator. One of the twin swords slapped the flying shield from the air without a break in pace, and Artair dove for the sword. His hand closed on the bloody handle and he rolled forward, coming to his feet facing away from the swordsman. He pivoted, swinging one sword high while bringing the other in front of him in a blocking motion. Both swords connected with the other man's weapons, and the two men both struck again, and then one more time, without effect. Artair was backing up, blocking attacks while trying to mount his own offense. The enemy swordsman flowed smoothly from one attack into another, never breaking stride, never slowing down. Each time Artair blocked a thrust it was if the opposition had been expected, a backup plan already in motion.

Artair saw the walls of the arena coming in his peripheral vision and threw himself sideways, rolling to his feet as he had done thousands of times against dragons. The move surprised the gladiator, and he broke stride, turning to chase his target. The Helvetian took his chance and ran forward, back toward where the spearman had just retrieved his weapon. The gladiator saw him coming and suddenly the spear was flying at his now unprotected chest.

The dragon slayer twisted out of the way of the projectile and made a desperate grab for it as is cut a thin slit in his shirt along his side. His hand closed on the haft right at the end, and he let the spear continue on its flight, into the upper arm of the swordsman who had been running behind him. The spearhead tore out the back of his tricep and Artair jerked hard, tearing the blade free.

He pivoted, spinning the bladed end of the spear to block the short sword of its owner, and then rammed the butt end into the gushing wound of the swordsman. He spun, hitting first one, and then the other of his opponents with the ends of the spear. The swordsman was down, blood from his arm soaking the ground, and then the spearman fell with Artair striking him twice more before he could land.

The Helvetian stood quivering; his chest bruised and cut, and looked for the next gladiator to come out of the door.

None came. The fighting had taken no more than five minutes.

Slowly he started to recognize where he was again, heard the crowd, and finally looked toward the tower. Artimus was staring at him, his expression unreadable. In front of him, the king sat with a bored look on his face, hardly paying attention.

Artair pointed with the bloody spear at the tower.

"I win, Artimus." He yelled over the roar of the crowd.

The doors opened on all sides of the arena and a flood of black-garbed soldiers poured into the arena. Artair watched them come, dropped the spear, and walked toward the door where he had entered. The soldiers closed the space behind him as he went, but none touched him until he was safely back inside the room where he had put his armor on. The crowd had already stopped cheering.

Marius was waiting for him, a pair of shackles in his hand. "Take off the armor, Artair. Do it quickly."

Artair shrugged, stepped to the table, and started unbuckling his gauntlets. He didn't see the blow coming, or who gave it, but something hit the back of his head and he slumped forward onto the table. He fought in vain to push back the darkness that invaded his mind, and then slumped to the floor.

Chapter 20

Artair groaned as he woke. He opened his eyes, but for a moment it didn't make a difference. The darkness of his cell was almost complete. He was dangling from his wrists from the top bars of his cell. A thin chain cut into his skin and he could feel the wetness from his own blood. He did not know how long he had been unconscious, but he could not feel his hands and his shoulders ached from the strain of holding his weight. He kicked his feet, and found that by stretching his legs he could just touch the end of his toes to the bare floor, but he could not ease any of the pressure on his shoulders.

"Sounds like someone is awake." A series of torches and lamps was coming down the corridor toward Artair's cell. The noise of the key in the lock was not a welcome one.

"You know, it's been months since someone survived the first round. I'm sure you would like me to say that I'm impressed, but really I'm just grateful." As he spoke he was unrolling something from a bundle. In the flickering torchlight it was not possible to see what it was, but there was a quiet tinkering of metal.

"Officially round two will come tomorrow, but I like to think that the real second round is just between you and me." He let his arm fall to his side and metal-wrapped tips of the whip brushed the ground. The handle was over a foot long and built to serve as both whip and club.

"As I said, it's been a long time." Marius's smile beamed in the darkness and a couple of the guards chuckled from their positions outside the cell.

Artair watched the jailer in silence. He knew that nothing he would say would stop what was about to happen, so he did not try. The only consolation he took was from the thought that Marius could not go too far if they expected him to fight the next day. Correction, he thought, they only expect me to die.

"Nothing? You care that little about your own skin?" The first blow slashed across Artair's chest, leaving a dozen bloody streaks. Artair stiffened, but made no sound.

Marius smiled again. "Strong, I like that."

The second blow turned Artair all the way around, twisting him on the biting chain. The whip tore his shirt to tatters and blood immediately pooled in the cuts and started to drip down his stomach.

Before he could twist back to face it, the whip struck again, gouging his back like a dozen claws. He tasted blood in his mouth and realized he had bitten through his lip.

The end of the handle prodded his shoulder, turning him back toward the light.

"Still nothing?" Marius was still smiling. "That's okay with me." The handle pushed up against Artair's chin, forcing it up roughly. "We've got time."

The next blow was the hardest yet, and Artair's body spun on the chain. He could feel blood running down his arms to join the wounds in his chest. He kept spinning as the whip continued its work. It struck across his thighs, then against his arms. A savage blow across the back of his shoulders tore away the rest of his shirt, leaving only the collar and shreds of the sleeves. The punishing metal tips even found their way to his hands, and the numbness there was replaced with pain.

There was a pause, and then a solid blow across his stomach drove all air from his lungs. Marius was now holding the whip by the blood-soaked tips, and was wielding the handle as a club. The second strike smashed Artair's lips, spilling blood down his chin.

The beating slowed as Marius began to tire. His breathing was getting heavy and the smile had finally disappeared.

Artair had yet to make a sound. He hung from the chain, eyes closed, his breathing shallow.

Marius paused for a moment, then stepped forward and gripped Artair's bloody chin in one hand, wiped sweat from his face, and smiled at his unconscious victim.

Artair's eyes snapped open.

The Helvetian's legs locked around Marius's waist, pulling him forward as his body jackknifed, crushing the top of his head into his jailer's face. Marius's nose and lips flattened, and his head snapped back. The jailer's body sagged, and Artair let him fall, guiding him with his legs to keep him within striking distance. The men who had been watching the beating now stumbled over themselves trying to get inside.

Marius's head landed on cold stone and Artair brought both knees up toward his chest and then drove both heels down. One missed, but the other found its target and Artair felt something give.

The first guard through the cell door threw his shoulder into Artair's midriff, swinging him up and away from Marius. He wasn't able to do any more damage before the guards cleared the cell.

Artair hung, dripping blood until he finally lost consciousness. His last thought before his eyes closed was that he would be in no condition to fight anymore.

*

"Marius's work?"

There was a quiet word of confirmation from someone else in the room.

Artair's eyes opened, then closed against the light of the room. He was hanging from his wrists again, but this time his feet were on the ground. He stood, his knees almost buckling, and noticed there were chains on his feet as well.

"I don't usually have to chain my patients, but you'd have to admit that you're a little different than my usual." The words came with a brief stab of pain from his back and he arched away from it.

"Easy Artair. He's actually trying to help."

Artair glanced to the side, opening his eyes only long enough to confirm what he already knew.

"I find that hard to believe." The words hardly made it past his shredded lips, and it alarmed him how he sounded.

"That's fairly cynical of you, just because the rest of us are trying to get you killed doesn't mean he is."

Artair knew Artimus was smiling even without looking, but he couldn't possibly smile back even if he wanted to. At that moment the doctor was cleaning a long cut that went from just below his shoulder blade all the way down to his hip, and, good intentions or no, the Cyrenian's touch was none too gentle.

"Why bother, Artimus? I'm dead soon anyway."

Artair glanced down at his chest, then decided looking was a bad idea. His chest was a maze of cuts, all connected by dried blood. He could tell where the doctor had been cleaning before he had regained consciousness. Strangely, it didn't look any better.

For a while, the only sound was the dull scrape of the doctor's tools on skin as he chipped away dried blood from Artair's wounds. He made his way back around to his chest after a while, and eventually he was pronounced clean. The doctor then turned back to his table and came back with a jar full of white powder.

140

"I know that what I have done so far has not been pleasant, and for that I apologize," he said, pulling the top off the jar. "This is also necessary but will be far worse."

"It will keep your wounds from getting infected, Artair, but he's right about the pain." Artimus said from the wall.

"What's the point if…" Artair hissed in pain and then couldn't catch his breath again as the doctor started dusting his chest with the powder. Everywhere the white substance touched torn skin it burned like hot coals. Soon he was dusty from his neck down to his knees and he was trembling with pain.

The doctor stepped back, inspecting his work. He nodded, put the top back on the jar, and placed it back on the table.

"It will stop burning in a couple of minutes, and then you're as healthy as I can make you. Better than I can say for your friend by the way." The doctor smiled and opened his mouth to say more but shut it abruptly after a look from Artimus.

Artair glared at the doctor as he made his exit from the room, taking his medicines and tools with him.

Chapter 21

Sometime around the time that the jailers came to deliver the first meal of the day, Tullius came to supervise Artair's release from the shackles. This time the Helvetian did not struggle as the shackles were removed and he was allowed to collapse onto the bed, his body screaming with pain. Even so, he was asleep before the men had left the room.

At the first sound of Marius's voice, Artair's eyes popped open and he tried to sit up. The movement aggravated his many cuts and bruises, and he had to grit his teeth to keep from yelling out loud.

"Time to go, Artair." Marius's voice was different today, as he tried to speak around a broken nose and bruised mouth. "I heard who you're going up against today, and you won't last long enough to run out of breath. Too bad, I was looking forward to seeing you again." He smiled cruelly, and then opened the cell door gingerly, favoring his ribs on the right side.

Artair struggled to his feet, his body stiff and sore. The walk to the armor room loosened him up a little bit, but he knew he was in no shape for a fight. Putting on his armor was made harder by the fact that he was trying not to show Marius the pain he was in. Just before he was done, a man walked in carrying his two swords. Artair's eyes locked on the weapons and then glanced at Marius.

"Wasn't my decision. Put them on." Marius grunted.

Artair felt a thrill of excitement when he took the swords into his hands. If it weren't for the men with crossbows he would have been tempted to try an escape, but he knew that it would be expected, and he was no fool.

The walk out into the arena was terrifyingly familiar, and Artair caught himself looking forward to the challenge. He just hoped that his skill would allow him to last this time even though his condition didn't suggest that he was capable of it.

After the speeches, different this time, but almost the same length, Artair was once again left alone in the middle of the arena. Drawing his swords, he began doing drills, quickly, like he had done a thousand times. The movement loosened up his body even more, and the swords felt good in his hands. He knew he had only a few seconds, so he moved faster. He knew how silly he must look, doing drills in the middle of an arena with thousands of people watching him, but he had no other choice, and he did not have to worry about impressing anyone anyway.

He heard the door open, and then close. He finished the drill he was doing, sheathed his swords, and then turned toward the newcomer.

For a moment he thought that his eyes were deceiving him, but as the man started walking forward he knew they were not.

Draklin, as he was called, his real name had been forgotten long ago, was the largest man most people had ever seen, unless they had known his father. Easily topping seven feet, he was nearly as wide as he was tall. Convicted of killing his own father while he slept—most claimed there was no other way for the deed to be done—he had been given the chance to live as a gladiator for as long as he could win the battles they set for him. His father had been a weapons master and a teacher of arms for Drake's army. Draklin grew up learning every conceivable weapon and the arts of war. Right after he turned twenty he had used his father's own ax against him while he slept, cleaving the giant's skull in two. Drake's love of the arena turned the murderer's crime into a profession, a job that Draklin obviously relished.

So far he had lasted ten years, and those who tended him told all who would listen that he was less human than animal at this point.

Artair watched the giant approach, still almost not believing the man's sheer size. The giant was carrying a sword that complemented his size, and a forked dagger that in any other man's hand would have been called a full-fledged sword.

Draklin stopped at the middle of the arena, faced the tower, and roared a sentence. The crowd cheered, Draklin clashed his weapons together and charged.

Artair's quickness saved him. He had underestimated the giant's speed, and he didn't have time to pull a sword free before he had to throw himself sideways, rolling to his feet with both swords in his hands. He blocked the dagger, ducked under the scythe-like swing of the sword, and then flew back as the giant's wide foot struck him in the chest. The kick landed on the exact spot of the bruise made by the spear the day before and the pain took his breath away. He rolled back to his feet as Draklin closed on him, ready to end the fight. This time the forked dagger caught Moray's sword and the giant twisted it, tearing the weapon from Artair's hand.

Draklin paused, scooped the fallen sword from the dirt and grinned at Artair revealing broken, blackened teeth. The behemoth barked a short laugh and charged again, grunting like an animal.

Artair watched him come, his sword held in his right hand. He had forgotten the roar of the crowd, and even his distaste of fighting for them. He was in a fight for his life, and it was a feeling he was used to. Draklin came at him again, surprisingly fast, and the Sword Bearer gave ground quickly, defending himself with every trick he could think of. The fight had hardly begun, and yet Artair was already tiring, his

144

defenses slowing. Draklin sensed his weakness and pressed forward harder, the broken grin displayed on his scarred face.

The giant stopped advancing and turned to wave at the crowd with both arms, roaring something unintelligible. The crowd thundered a response as Artair tried desperately to catch his breath. Finally, Draklin turned back toward him and leapt with his customary speed. The Sword Bearer was waiting for him, and at the last moment he threw his weapon from his right hand to his left and slid to his left, ducking under the massive sword's swing while sidestepping the dagger. His sword, meanwhile, sliced past the giant's swinging right hand. The ancient steel sliced through skin, tendon, and bone as one.

The giant roared in pain, desperately trying to make his right hand obey his commands. His sword lying in the bloody dust, he clenched his bleeding wrist and cursed in a language foreign to his opponent but heard by every person in the now-silent arena. They had seen Draklin wounded before, but never crippled, never like this.

The people in the crowd murmured with surprise as Artair's blade slowly filled in with blood red. In the tower, King Drake sat up straight in his chair.

Artair knew the extent of the injury, knew the man would likely never wield a sword again, and suddenly felt sick. Though his life had always participated in death, there was no cruelty in him. Slowly, his sword held ready, he walked forward toward the bleeding giant. As he neared, the bloodshot eyes locked with his, screaming hate and pain while his mouth continued with its cursing.

"I have had enough." Artair said slowly. "I never wanted to fight you in the first place. Have someone take care of your arm." With that he glanced up at the tower and turned to walk away from the giant.

Several thousand people gasped at once, and Artair heaved his sword over his own shoulder. Leaping forward, he scooped Moray's sword from the dirt and swung the sword as he turned.

Draklin had picked up his sword with his left hand and charged one last time, his right hand dangling useless at his side. Artair's thrown sword pierced his armor at the right side of his midsection and the gladiator felt the sickening feeling of the steel's invasion into his organs. His pace did not slow, however, as it was death he sought, and hoped to give. Without the use of his hand he would no longer be of use to the king and therefore was already slated for death. In his last moments, he wanted to win this last battle.

The two swords crashed together and Artair was driven back with the force of the giant's charge. He parried the next blow, and the next, and then leapt to the side, avoiding a strong thrust he would not have been able to stop. Another sequence of blows and Draklin was visibly slowing. An overextension by the giant, and Artair kicked forward, catching the protruding sword hilt and driving it another foot into his opponent's belly. Artair felt the sword stop as it hit bone and he leapt back away from the giant.

This time Draklin said nothing, didn't even bother with a curse, simply slid to his knees and toppled backward. His spine severed, he was still alive and would be until he bled to death, but he would not move again.

Artair stood with his hands on his knees, breathing heavily. Finally he stood and walked forward. The arena was quiet enough for him to hear his own footsteps as he approached the dying man. He pushed the huge sword away from the giant's hand with his foot. The giant was looking at him, hardly blinking.

Artair heard the doors open behind him and dropped his sword to the dust only seconds before he felt the poke of a sword at his back, not too gently. In his peripheral vision he could see over a dozen more men with swords, all of them in the same fancy armor.

"I'm sorry." Artair said as he was led away from the dying man.

Chapter 22

This time Marius took no chances. With plenty of help, he chained Artair's hands as before, and then chained his legs also. Then, to increase the apprehension, he showed the Helvetian the whip he was planning to use, a heavy black creation with bits of metal hanging from each tip.

"You know what I'm going to do with this, Artair? I'm going to cut you up in little pieces, and maybe, if I miss, I'll take out an eye."

"No, you won't."

Marius froze, and slowly lowered the whip down to the end of his arm. Artimus had stepped into the circle of light provided by the torch. He was holding his plumed helmet in his hand, and suddenly everyone acted uneasy.

"Take the chains off, Marius, and then go. All of you." Artimus never raised his voice over a conversational tone, but there was no doubt that he would be obeyed.

Marius tossed the whip out of the cell and quickly unlocked the chains. One of the other jailers gathered them up and carried them out. Artimus stood still until they had all disappeared into the darkness at the end of the hall, and then he stepped closer to the cell. Inside it, Artair had already relaxed onto the bed and turned his head away from his visitor.

"I feel like I should reintroduce myself." Artimus began, smiling slightly. "My name is Artimus, son of Arkane. I am the head general of King Drake, and have been for many years."

"For some reason I'm guessing that I'm supposed to care about something you just said?" Artair asked without moving and without looking at the Cyrenian general.

Artimus cocked his head to the side, peering at the prisoner. "You really don't know who you are, do you? You don't know who Dromeda was, or Drakus?"

"I already told you that I didn't, and I don't have the energy to convince you of it now. Who was Dromeda? You people definitely make a lot of fuss over that name." Artair truly did not care to hear what Artimus had to say, he really just wanted to get some sleep, but he sensed that he would not get rid of the other man so easily.

Artimus laughed. "We'll see how interested you are, Artair, because it has just as much to do with your history as it does mine. Dromeda and Drakus were both leaders of tribes in what you call Helveti, although that name came after both of them. Drakus was a king, while Dromeda was a general for a different tribe. Are you interested now?"

Artair groaned as he sat up, swinging his legs off the side of the bed. "Not really, but if you insist on keeping me awake, I might as well listen to the story. So, go ahead."

"It is not just a story, Artair." Artimus snapped. "It is the history of both our peoples. Obviously your people have forgotten it, but mine never will."

"How long ago was this?" The prisoner asked.

"About two hundred years."

"Sounds like your people need to let the past go." Artair said and started to lie back down.

"Stop baiting me, Artair."

"Or what?" The Helvetian was suddenly standing. "Let me guess, you'll have me beaten? Or maybe you'll send me into an arena to watch me die, or take me away from my people? What am I supposed to be scared of, Artimus son of Arkane?"

"Don't you want to know why?" The general answered.

"Why what?"

"Why all this has happened to you? You've noticed how much my people hate you, it's obvious. Don't you want to know why?"

Artair stepped back toward the bed and sat down. "Yes, I would." He said quietly.

"Okay then. I don't have a lot of time and I have too much to explain as it is. As I said before, Drakus was a king in Helveti. At the time there were seven tribes, all battling against each other for power and territory. It was a continual war that went on for several decades. Most of what you are most proud of with your country can be dated back to this time period. The warrior code, the endurance and training, all went into sustaining this war. They went to such extremes that for years they would battle over a border change of only a few feet. Thousands died, so many that they lost count of the casualties. Finally, Drakus and Cyrenius, two of the kings, decided to meet.

"They took a month, an entire month, Artair, to decide how they would sit to negotiate. In the end they set up a table, exactly straddling the border, and each sat on his own side. Had either man crossed the border there would have been a battle. From their negotiations, which took another three months, they came up with an alliance. With their two armies combined they would be stronger than any of the others, and they bet on the fact that none of the other tribes would join together to defend themselves. They figured that there was too much animosity between the tribes to allow them to work together."

"I know about our tribes, but there are only five." Artair stated tiredly.

"I know, Artair, keep listening." Artimus snapped. He looked around to make sure they were still alone and then continued. "The combined army rolled over two entire tribes before the rest knew what was happening. It worked just as they expected it to. Those who tried to retreat from the behemoth army were slaughtered by the other tribes as soon as they crossed their borders. A third tribe fell while the rest scrambled to mount a defense. Drakus' army continued to grow from conscripts and from people who flooded to them to be a part of what they saw as being the next ruling group. Now, for some reason, after the third tribe fell to them, they stopped their advance for a little over a week. I'm sure they figured that it would cause them no harm due to the fact that it had taken them months to create an alliance, and their army was larger than any they thought could be built. If it hadn't been for Dromeda, it wouldn't have been a problem either. Without him, Drakus and Cyrenius would have accomplished their design almost without opposition."

"So, what did he do?" Artair asked, fatigue obvious in his voice.

Artimus frowned at the interruption. "The remaining kings and the thousands of warriors who had retreated from the combined army now had a real problem. They realized that they had to combine their power to have any chance at all, but they could not decide who should lead them. Obviously none of the kings would allow another king to take such power on himself. Finally, Dromeda, a young but obviously talented general, volunteered. He would lead the combined army but would have no political power once it was over. It was a situation that everyone could agree to. He organized the men into separate units according to their kingdoms, allowing their own men to lead them under him. In this way he was able to retain their loyalty and teamwork while harnessing their combined strength."

"The two armies met at the same border Dromeda had always defended. He stood in front of his country's army only, and the combined army facing him looked large enough to trample them under their feet. The battle began, and Dromeda started giving ground, retreating into his own country. Drakus followed, never thinking that this was what his enemies wanted. The rest of the newly allied armies lay waiting for them, and attacked the larger army's flanks and rear. Over the next ten days, over half of the men who came to that battle died. Cyrenius was killed, and the attacking army was routed. Dromeda's army chased them all the way across Helveti until he trapped them against the mountains. It could have ended there, should have ended there, but it didn't. Dromeda kept attacking, and the battle continued. They continued until Drakus and his men were starving to death as they fought for their lives. Sometime during this fight, they found the tunnel we brought you through. Drakus, knowing that he would receive no mercy from his enemies, chose the unknown over death. He, and as many of his men as could, retreated through that cave into this country."

"And let me guess," Artair said from the darkness, "your king Drake, who I assume is a descendent of your buddy Drakus, has been telling this same story to everyone for as long as he has been in power."

"Good guess, and now you come in with a sword passed down through the generations with Dromeda's name on it. The chances are good that you are his heir—at least that's what everyone here already believes."

Artair stood up, stretching carefully as he walked to the front bars. "So, what happens now, Artimus? I'm assuming that monster I killed today was the best of your gladiators, and if not I will gladly surrender to the man who could have beaten him before this. Who will I be facing tomorrow?"

Artimus opened his mouth as if to speak, but right then one of the jailers came walking down the corridor, holding a dinner pot. The general stepped back from the bars and glanced toward the coming man. He nodded to him as he passed by and then looked back at the prisoner.

152

"Goodbye, Artair." He said simply, turned on his heel and soon exited the door at the end of the corridor.

The Helvetian stood at the bars for a minute longer, trying to decide what he thought about the Cyrenian general, but finally his fatigue got the best of him and he retreated to his bed.

*

Artair wouldn't have believed that Marius could look any more unpleasant than he already did, but the next morning his expression was absolutely sour. They took him out of his cell and down the hall to the armor room. Putting his armor on hurt more than he wanted to admit, and this time he wasn't able to conceal the fact from his captors. He knew without doubt that he wouldn't be able to continue fighting every day like this for long. He would wear out soon, very soon, and then Artimus' prediction of his death would come true.

"You thought Draklin was bad, didn't you Artair?" Marius asked as Artair strapped his swords across his back. "He almost beat you didn't he?"

He didn't answer.

"Well, Draklin wouldn't have lasted five minutes with what you're going to go up against today."

Chapter 23

"Draklin was our greatest gladiator, and he was undefeated, but no one ever survives the last day of the festival. Everyone dies, savage." Marius enjoyed saying it far too much, and Artair didn't bother looking at him, but simply turned toward the door, unhooked the latch, and threw it open.

The Helvetian walked to the middle of the arena without prompting from his captors. He was used to the speeches, used to the crowd, and he was tired now of the wait. He wanted to know what his next challenge was, and he was slightly heartened by what Marius had said. If this was truly the last day of the festival, he might have a chance of surviving if he could just last one more fight.

One more time, the speech ended, and the jailers left their prisoner standing in the middle of the arena.

As they disappeared, four other doors opened up and dozens of people began streaming out into the arena. Artair's hand had already grasped the handle of one of his swords before he realized that these people were, like him, prisoners. They did not have the same look as the gladiators he had faced, nor did they enter the arena with the confidence he had seen in his former opponents. They were armed with an assortment of weapons and a few of them had armor, but they all looked as confused as he felt about this situation.

Out of some instinct of human nature the other prisoners ran toward him, congregating in the middle. He counted twenty seven of them, mostly men with a few women and a couple of children.

The roar from the crowd rose to a fevered pitch as a massive door at the side of the arena began to rumble open. The gate was about half open when a stray breeze carried a familiar scent to the Sword Bearer's nose.

Dragons.

His eyes darted to the left and right, evaluating his fellow prisoners, and then he jumped at the person nearest him, a small man with a rusty dagger, and shoved him down into the dirt.

"Everybody get down. Get down and dig into the ground." The people around him stood as if paralyzed, staring at the foreigner as he scooped dirt over his chosen victim.

"You. Get down on the ground and cover yourself with dirt. Move it." This time Artair directed his statement to one of the men closest to him, who finally dropped to his knees and began to dig. Several people followed suit.

"That's it, cover yourselves up. Whatever you do, don't move. If you move, or if it smells you, you're dead."

The majority of the people were now following his commands. Those who did not understand him soon got the picture as the prisoners around them began to throw dust over themselves.

Artair picked out three men working in a group and ran toward them. The door was mostly open now, but he still could not see the creature.

"You three, do you understand what I am saying?" Two of the three nodded their heads in response.

"Okay, you huddle down here, and when I yell the word "go" three times, I need you to get up and run in different directions as fast as you can. Run hard and don't look back. As soon as you get close to the walls jump to the side, roll once and then lie still. Whatever you do, don't move after that unless I tell you to. You got it?"

The two nodded their heads and then turned to the third and seemed to be explaining it to him. Artair looked up at the door in time to see it click completely open. Behind it he saw another gate swing wide and light suddenly flood the passageway.

"Down, down, everybody down. Don't move, don't breathe, and don't make a sound."

The Helvetian warrior stood out in the open, his cloak moving slightly in the wind, eyes locked on the open door. He could see a massive figure moving in the passage thanks to the light coming from behind it. These people were as safe as he could make them, but now it was his job to stop the creature before it could scare them into confusion. He knew from experience that as soon as they ran the dragon would have its victory.

The beast's head appeared first, quickly followed by the rest of its body. It was huge, with a massive head and long claws on its feet. The dragon moved lightly, as if walking on its toes, its armored skin changing colors as it moved and the sunlight played off its scales.

Artair's mind raced. To attack a dragon alone was unheard-of except as an accident, and his hastily made plan had more possibilities for failure than success. He was pitting his knowledge of dragons and his own skill against an animal nearly thirty times his size and just as fast.

The monster's eyes scanned the floor of the arena, looked and then looked again. Due to the lack of movement, the dragon could not pick out a suitable target. Then the breeze whispered through the arena again and Artair's cloak shifted slightly. Instantly the reptile's gaze snapped to the lone figure and it leapt forward. In the same moment the Helvetian sprinted toward the animal, pulling a sword from its sheath as he went.

Up in the tower Artimus murmured a farewell that he knew would not be heard.

The distance between Artair and the dragon closed surprisingly fast as both ran at full speed. Then the Sword Bearer drew back his arm and threw his sword toward the dragon while drawing the other blade with his free hand. As soon as his weapon came loose he stopped dead in his tracks. The dragon's attention was drawn to the flying sword that landed fifteen yards ahead of his opponent, the point sunk into the dirt. It was still swinging from the impetus of the throw when the dragon was upon it, snatching it up in his jaws while clawing at it with his front feet. The dragon spat the steel object out in disgust just as the other blade left the warrior's hand.

Struck without warning, the dragon screamed as the lethal weapon buried itself in its multi-colored flank. Jack-knifing violently, the beast tore at the offending object with its jaws. Artair darted in as the dragon's throes carried it away from him and picked up his other sword. Checking his position he took a deep breath and yelled.

"GO! GO! GO! Move you motherless dogs!" He did not turn to see if the three strangers had followed his instructions, but kept his eyes on the dragon. At the sound of his voice the animal seemed to forget the pain in its side as its head snapped around to find the speaker. Bloody froth dripped from the reptile's massive jaws as it locked eyes with Artair. The Sword Bearer held still, silently cursing the men behind him.

They had not moved; they had failed him.

The beast opened its mouth to roar when suddenly its gaze shifted to something behind the Sword Bearer.

The three prisoners were up and running.

The dragon, confused by the movements of its enemies, reared up on its hind legs and roared. The intent of it was to frighten its adversaries into flight, and it had the desired effect. Artair could hear movement as the rest of the captives began to stand up and run, ignorantly following the example of the trio.

The swordsman stood stock still, waiting for the creature to move. He would have only one more chance, and then people would begin to die. The dragon would attack the running prisoners, hopefully leaving him exactly one chance to make one more strike with the sword he held in his hand. If he missed, or if the beast did not give him that one chance, they would likely all die.

It attacked, leaping straight at the Helvetian, but with its eyes locked on the crowd behind him. Artair stood with his sword in his right hand. As the dragon's back feet lifted off the ground, he swung the weapon up and forward, hurling it at his adversary with all the strength he possessed. The wounds in his back ripped open with the effort, blood soaking the inside of his armor.

Again the monster realized too late where the real danger lay, and could do nothing as the second sword buried itself in its chest.

Artair tried to jump out of the way, but the dragon's right front foot slammed into his legs as it crashed to the ground. The blow from the monster threw him twenty feet, where he landed face-first in the dirt. The dragon tore and clawed at the blade that had pierced its heart, but to no avail. As the animal's death throes slowly weakened, the warrior staggered to his feet. Blood ran down his face and dripped into the dust from a gash above his eye. He watched the dying reptile intently for a few seconds and then walked up to the animal's body. Reaching up, he ripped the sword from the beast's flank, releasing a fountain of hot blood in the act. Walking to the animal's head, he swung the heavy blade, severing it from the rest of its body.

Artair leaned on his weapon and tried to catch his breath as he looked down at the dead animal in amazement. It had worked. He had killed a dragon single-handedly, and none of the other prisoners had died in the process. Had it gotten away from him, his only course of action would have been to get close to it while it was distracted with the other people, but that would have cost many lives.

158

Out of simple habit, he moved to retrieve his other sword from the chest of the dead animal, but then something on the ground caught his eye. Reaching down, he pulled the object out of the dirt by the dragon's severed skull and looked at it intently. Shaking his head in disgust and disbelief, he dropped it back to the dust and stood up. Even through the rush of adrenalin he could hardly keep from groaning in pain.

The swordsman suddenly realized that the only sound was his own labored breathing. The arena was silent; the crowd stood quietly, staring at the spectacle before them. Artair stared up at the spectators as they looked down at him. He had not been angry as he fought the dragon, but as he faced the people who had come to see him die he could feel fury rising inside of him. Reaching down, he picked up the dragon head from the dirt with both hands. Taking two running steps, he threw it into the stands in front of him.

"People of Cyrene," Artair shouted, holding his sword above his head, the handle hot in his hand.

The multitude quieted at the sound of his voice, and he continued. "You all came here to see us die. You came here to see blood, and I gave you the show you came for. You came here to watch me die in the dirt, but instead I've slain your executioner and given you his head as a prize."

"You are a bloodthirsty people; but there will come a time when you will beg your leaders to stop the shedding of blood. You have seen what I can do, but I am not the champion of my nation. One day, that man will come, and on that day your king will fall. That day will come, and I will bring it. People of Cyrene, you have seen the beginning of your end this day." With that Artair stepped up to the dragon and, with a powerful jerk, wrenched his second sword from the beast's carcass.

The Helvetian returned both swords to their sheaths and then turned to look up at the box where Artimus was seated. The man he had assumed to be the ruler was on his feet, looking down at him. Artair returned his gaze without flinching, and held it until one of the men standing next to the king asked him a question, interrupting the brief contest of wills.

The king snapped an answer and the man scurried off. A couple minutes later soldiers flooded the arena, disarming the stunned prisoners and surrounding Artair, who stood defiantly with both arms folded across his chest. The soldiers gave way to allow Artimus through to stand in front of Artair. There was no smile on the general's face now.

"Give us your swords, Artair," Artimus commanded. "Give us your swords, or we will kill you right here and now. You're smart enough to know that we can, so hand them over." Artimus's command was clear and cold, leaving no room for another request.

"You said no one ever survives, Artimus. I did, just like I said I was going to. Now, you remember what else I said I was going to do, and you just get ready." Artair's hands flashed up and jerked his swords free, flicking them forward to land in the dirt at the general's feet. The handle of his sword flashed cold as he let it go, obviously disapproving of the surrender. The movement made the men around him jump, but their leader stood as if hewn out of stone.

He did not struggle as they made him remove his armor, nor as he was led back to his cell in the bowels of the building. Marius was uncharacteristically silent and did not bother to attempt another torture session. It seemed that Artimus's order the day before was still in effect.

In the darkness, Artair replayed in his mind every scene, every detail of the day's events. A lot had happened in only a couple of minutes, and he sensed that what had just occurred would change more than his own future. He had beaten Cyrene's unbeatable, and he had done it in front of thousands of its citizens.

The warrior smiled as he wondered what the king was saying about him right then.

Chapter 24

After overseeing Artair's recapture, Artimus walked home, accompanied by the five men who made up his own personal guard. He would rather have walked alone, but the king had ordered the soldiers to accompany him at all times when he was at Cyrene. Artimus sometimes wondered if they were truly bodyguards or simply men ordered to watch his every move. As he opened his front door he could hear the five spreading out to watch all entrances to his house.

A fine protection they would be, he thought wryly. I could kill them all without working up a sweat. How good would they be against someone who could endanger me?

Artimus sat at his table in the near darkness of his dining chamber. He kept the windows covered to keep the men outside from watching him, and he was in no mood to go around and light candles. As he relaxed, his mind returned to the spectacle in the arena and he smiled. Then the smile turned into a grin, and the grin into laughter until he was laughing uncontrollably, pounding his fist on the table.

As his laughter abated, he reached out and pulled a portrait toward him that was sitting on the table.

"He killed the dragon, honey, killed it and tossed its head into the crowd. I wish you could have been there to see the look on old Drake's face. It was all I could do to keep from laughing out loud."

His merriment faded, and he touched the face in the portrait tenderly. "We won't have to wait too much longer. It has begun. I can feel it. It won't be long now."

The general stilled suddenly as a knock came at the door. Returning the portrait to its former spot Artimus stood, composed himself, and walked to the front entrance. As expected, it was a messenger from the king, summoning him to the throne room.

∗

Tullius was busy having a private celebration in his office when Artimus burst in to tell him of Drake's orders. The fat man immediately called in one of his guards and sent him to round up his messengers and anyone else he could find to help. When he finally left, his boss closed the door behind him.

"Our friend really caused an uproar today, didn't he?" the manager of the arena asked Artimus, who simply nodded.

"No one else has ever done more than scratch one of those animals, much less kill one. What manner of man is he, General? He not only knows how to handle himself, but he's fought dragons before, too, if I don't miss my guess. Will the beast truly be able to kill him tomorrow?" Tullius asked.

The other man shrugged his shoulders. "Before today I wouldn't have given him one chance in a hundred to survive alone against a dragon. Now I'm not so sure. Maybe he'd be more willing to talk now that he's been shaken up a bit. Can I speak with him?" Artimus inquired.

"Well, of course, you can speak with him, and I wish you the best of luck. I spoke to him when he was first brought in, or rather he talked to me, and it was about as fun as sitting on needles. Just don't let any of your people get too close to his cell; I don't want to have to figure out how to get a sword back from that man if he were to get his hands on one. Go ahead; I've got work to do." Tullius waved a hand dismissively and worked his way over to his desk where he began to write quickly.

Artimus let himself out and then headed toward the darkness where the prisoners were held. His bodyguards followed him with some reservation. No one enjoyed going down to see the condemned people held in the depths of the arena. The smell of the place seemed to attach itself to a person, following you home. Marius met them at the first door and, after hearing the request, led them to Artair. The warrior lay unmoving on the cot at the back of the cell, and did not seem to notice the men approaching.

"Up, prisoner, you have visitors," the guard ordered as he approached. The command had no effect on the cell's occupant.

"I said get up, slave." Marius ordered, his voice rising. Again there was no response and he glanced quickly at Artimus, who was silently amused and not at all surprised by the situation.

"Artimus, you get rid of that yapping dog and his fleas and I'll talk to you alone. I'm in no mood to listen to his barking."

Marius stiffened at the insult, jerked his keys out of his pocket and stuck one of them into the lock. "By the Gods, I'll…" he began.

"…get yourself killed." Artimus finished the other man's sentence as he reached over and jerked the keys from his hands.

"Leave us," the general snapped and turned to look at his bodyguards. "All of you wait for me at the door." One of them began to protest but stopped when he saw the look in his superior's eyes.

Marius had a sick look on his face. "General Artimus, may I…" he began, reaching for the keys Artimus still held in his hands.

"No, you may not. Wait for me with the others and hope that I do not see fit to report to Tullius your utter lack of self-control that I have just seen exhibited."

The guard shrank from him and hurriedly headed for the outer door. Artimus's bodyguards followed after only a moment's hesitation.

When they were gone, the General looked back at Artair, who was now sitting on the cot. Blood from the cut on his face had dried and in the dark it appeared as if he were wearing a dark mask on one side.

Artimus grasped the bars and shook his head at him, smiling. "Well, you sure stirred up a hornet's nest today, Artair. You're the first person to beat a dragon in the arena in the entire time it's been running. Congratulations." the general said jokingly.

The prisoner did not return the smile. Standing slowly, he crossed the room to face the Cyrenian. "What was its name, Artimus?" he asked.

The other man just looked at him, his face showing nothing in the dim light of nearby torches.

"That dragon I killed today, did you know its name?" the Sword Bearer asked again after he received no answer.

The General looked at him for several seconds more and then shook his head. "Artair, you must have hit pretty hard when that reptile threw you, because that animal didn't have a name. It was just a dragon, caught in the wild and released into the arena," he responded.

The Helvetian glared at him. "You're a liar, Artimus. That animal I killed today had a collar around its neck. I picked it up after I cut its head free. It was a collar, Artimus, but not some big restraining device you would have used to harness a wild creature. It was a simple leather band with a metal ring on it that would not have survived one toss of that dragon's head had you tried to tether him by it. That monster was somebody's pet, trained and conditioned to kill people. Now make up some other story because your last one doesn't cut it." Artair's voice rose in volume until he was shouting and his eyes flashed fire.

The Cyrenian returned his gaze coolly. "Okay, you're right. It was domesticated. I'm not too sure but I believe that its trainer called it

Bartimaeous. So what? You killed it, and tomorrow a dragon is going to kill you. This time, though, you won't have anyone there to help you. You'll be alone, and you'll die in front of all the people you tried to scare today."

"Then, in a week or so, I'll be headed back to your homeland to get another couple of your countrymen to come and take your place. Is there anyone special back there you'd like me to meet?"

The swordsman jumped back from the bars as Artair's hands darted toward his throat. "Open this cage, Artimus, or are you afraid to face me again?" the Sword Bearer hissed.

"I should have killed you last time Artair. I won't make that same mistake again. Give my regards to the dragon."

Artimus turned on his heel and walked to where his men were waiting. Tossing the ring of keys to Marius, he pushed the door open and walked out, his bodyguards trotting to keep up.

*

Several years previous to the day's events, a number of men and women had been brought from the barbarian lands and had been forced to teach a select few of the Cyrenians their language. For a time it became a common hobby to learn and speak this new dialect. After a short time period, however, the allure had faded and there were few now that actually used Helvetian on a regular basis. However, the majority of the upper and middle classes could understand it, and there were several who were still nearly fluent.

Those who understood Artair's speech in the arena quickly translated it to those who did not, and within an hour of the end of the fight everyone in the city had heard what he had said, in one form or another. The people's responses were varied. Some were only offended by his words, while others actually believed that what he had predicted would come to pass.

The festival, as it was called, had been introduced by King Drake a couple of years after he came into power. Originally, it had been only criminals or traitors that had been fed to the dragons, but later some of the barbarians had been caught and brought to fight in the festivals. At the beginning, people had only come to them in obedience to orders given by the king himself, but over the years the people had become desensitized to the practice and now came of their own volition.

Artair's victory and words, however, had pricked the people's public conscience. They also had to deal with the fact that a man, a barbarian nonetheless, had beaten one of the monsters in fair combat. Although the dragons had always been a part of life for the Cyrenians, King Drake had made them a symbol of his power and military might. That a man had beaten one of them could easily be seen as an ill omen against the king's power.

The king now fought against this suspicion, and it was a battle he did not intend to lose.

Chapter 25

Artimus stopped in to talk to Tullius one more time before heading for home. The arrangements for the festival were coming along according to plan, and he had once again raised the price of admission. Artimus guessed that no one would complain this time. Artair had become quite a hit in his first appearances. The only difference was that now some of the people would be coming to see him live, not just die.

After speaking of a few more things with his large friend, the general left him to his work and turned toward home.

The general's last command to his bodyguards was to send one of them with a message to the king to inform him that his wishes were going to be met. On the next day, the barbarian would again face a dragon.

*

The door to the cell next to Artair's was thrown open and a man was tossed inside, banging his head against the frame of the cot. After locking the door, Marius ran his keys across the bars of the Helvetian's enclosure and then disappeared down the hallway.

The newcomer groaned in the space next to him and the Sword Bearer turned his head to look at him. There was something vaguely familiar about the man, although he could not identify what it was.

"Is that guy always so friendly, or did I just catch him on a good day?" he asked sarcastically, testing to see if the other man understood him.

The newcomer groaned in response. "He's just mad that his parents traded him for a three-legged dog when he was six months old, that's all." The other man responded in Helvetian.

Artair sat up and looked through the bars at him. "Have we met before? I know it's dark in here, but I'd swear I've seen you somewhere."

The other man slowly picked himself off the ground and sat down on the cot before answering. "Well, if I remember right, the last thing you called me was a 'motherless dog,' so we have met. Although I wouldn't call our association very friendly." he responded, with a smile that Artair could see even in the near-darkness.

The Helvetian laughed at the comment. "So you were one of my runners today? That's unbelievable." Artair exclaimed.

His fellow prisoner shook his head. "No, my friend, that isn't unbelievable. What's unbelievable is what you did to that dragon. I've never seen anything like it. We were sure we were dead. How did you know what to do?" the other man asked.

Artair cocked an eyebrow at the question and then shrugged his shoulders. "When you've been around those animals your whole life you have a lot of opportunities to learn their instincts."

"Take the one today for example. After I wounded him and all of you ran, he could see that he had several enemies, and he was feeling pretty vulnerable with one of my swords stuck in his ribs. So, he rears up and roars to let everyone know that they are messing with a dragon and that they'd better look out. He would expect then for all of us to run, and he was going to head for the closest enemy that appeared active. That's where the gamble was."

"If he had headed to either side of me the best I could have done would have been another side shot, which would have killed him eventually but not fast enough to stop him from tearing apart anything that he got his hands on for at least another five minutes. Luckily, though, the entire mass of people got up and followed you and your two friends in running for the walls. The dragon leapt for them and forgot about me, since I hadn't moved for a while. Now, had I missed he would have killed most of the people there before I could get to him again, but we don't have to worry about that anymore."

"What's your name, anyway?" Artair asked.

"My name is Conaf, and don't ask for a second name because I can't remember the last one I used. How about you?"

"I'm Artair. Why are you in here Conaf?"

"They caught me trying to stir up a rebellion against our beloved king, and the sentence for that is death in the arena. I can only imagine how mad ol' Drake was when you screwed up my execution." The rebel chuckled to himself at the mental image.

"Yeah, I'll just bet. Hey, I've got a question for you, Conaf. The dragons, they're domesticated aren't they? The ones they use for the arena I mean."

His fellow prisoner responded in the affirmative so he continued.

"How do they catch them?" he asked.

"What do you mean, how do they catch them?" Conaf responded with a confused look on his face.

"I mean, how do they get close enough to take them alive?" Artair said with some exasperation in his voice.

"I still don't understand what you're getting at, friend. Why would that be a problem?" the rebel asked, to Artair's bewilderment.

"Okay," the Sword Bearer began slowly, "there are dragons out there, living in the wild…"

"No, they don't, Artair. Who told you that?" Conaf interrupted.

The other man just stared at him. "Dragons don't live in the wild, they haven't for over a century. At least, so far as I'm told."

"Did you see those weird-looking buildings by the arena when you came over the hill? That's where the dragons are. They're just animals, Artair. They used to be used as draft animals until King Drake rounded them all up and made them into his own personal pets. A lot he killed off, talking about keeping the bloodlines pure or some nonsense. They stay in those buildings unless they're headed into the arena or when General Artimus and the Chosen take them out to go repulse some of your people who have attacked our villages." Conaf looked like he wanted to say more but stopped when he saw Artair's face.

For a couple of minutes the two sat in silence. The Cyrenian opened his mouth several times as if to speak, but then decided against it in favor of waiting.

"So now they use dragons as war animals?" the Helvetian finally asked, his voice strained.

"Yes, of course. Artimus and a hundred of his men ride them against you people when you attack us. How is it that you've never heard about this?" Conaf asked incredulously.

"The answer to that is very simple; my people have never come across those mountains except in cages. Your king has been lying to you. If your armies march out to attack someone, it wasn't my people. Let me guess: entire settlements are wiped out every time there is a so-called attack, and the king makes you all pay more taxes to aid in the defense of your lands. Am I correct?" Artair concluded grimly.

Conaf only nodded, thinking.

"What kind of man is General Artimus?" the Sword Bearer asked, changing the subject.

"He's the king's top general, that's all I need to know," the other man snarled.

"Is he married?" Artair questioned.

"He was. His wife disappeared a couple of years ago and no one really knows where she went. Some people think he killed her himself. There are those who think he's been twisted enough by the king over the years to do something like that. Why do you ask?" he responded.

Artair just shook his head. "No reason, just wondering. I'm tired; we'll talk about this later, okay?" Artair suggested.

Conaf grunted his consent and silence closed in around both men.

Artair's mind raced, trying to process the information he had received in the past few hours. Artimus had inadvertently informed him that the next time he went into the arena he would be alone against a dragon. In a way, that was comforting in that he would have no one other than himself to worry about, but at the same time he would have no one to help distract the creature.

The main philosophy of dragon fighting had always been that of multiple attackers. The only thing that kept the reptiles from being a perfect enemy was their short attention span. Used to things running from them, they did not care about objects that were holding still. In fact, it almost seemed as if they didn't see them at all. Also, if you stopped moving while at the same time something else began moving, a dragon would most often forget about you and go after whatever moved. That one concept was what allowed them to fight the dragons effectively, and it was something that Artair would not be able to use if he was going to be alone in the arena.

He had to find some way to get in an early hit, something to slow the dragon down or disable it in the first pass. Concerned, he reached up and gently examined the cut on his head with his fingers. It was not a bad one, but he wished that he had a way to clean the blood off before the next fight. The only water they gave him was barely enough to quench his thirst, and nothing more. The smell of blood on him would be virtually impossible to hide from the dragon.

Although he would rather have planned his next fight, he couldn't keep his mind off what Conaf had just told him. It was hard for him to accept what he had been told, although if he was truly a rebel against King Drake then the other man would have no reason to lie. Dragons had been his enemies since his teenage years, and to find out that they were little more than pets or draft animals here made his head swim. He wondered what the difference was between the dragons here and the dragons he was used to. From his experience in the arena he knew that they were definitely the same animals, but how were they connected?

Artair suddenly sat up in his bed. "Conaf, have you ever owned a dragon?" he asked.

The sounds coming from the other man's cell told Artair that he had been at least partially asleep. "What? No, I've never had one; I told you they took them all away a long time ago. My dad had one once, though," he said sleepily.

"What are they like usually? I mean, I've fought them in the wild and I've fought one in the arena, but how are they in normal life?" Artair pressed.

Conaf yawned. "Well, they're nothing like what you saw in the arena. They're just big, docile, strong animals. Like a huge ox, that's all. They cut off those big horns at birth, when they're not much bigger than your fingers. Not much to them after that."

"Well, then how do they end up trained killers like that one I faced today? Of all the words I'd use to describe them, docile is not one of them." Artair said incredulously.

"From what I've heard, and I've heard from some pretty trustworthy people, dragons are very easily trained—if you know how, of course. Also, once you train them in something they don't forget it. My dad had a dragon so well trained that all he had to do was hook it up to a plow and it would plow our fields all by itself."

"Since I've been around here, I've seen several people get taken out of their cages who were definitely not headed for the arena, but never came back either. My guess is that they train those dragons to kill, using prisoners as practice targets. Kind of morbid, but that's what I think." Conaf looked quizzically at the other man. "Why are you so interested in all this anyway? You think it will help you win your next fight in the arena if you know the dragon's history or something?"

Artair shook his head. "No, I know all I need to know to win the next time I go into the arena. What I'm learning from you might help me win a war."

With that the Helvetian lay back down and said no more. After a few minutes both men were asleep.

Chapter 26

The following day, in the early afternoon, Marius and his men arrived at Artair's cell, again dressed in their better armor and the plumed helmets. This time there were twice as many men with crossbows standing guard.

Artair had awakened much calmer than he had been when he had fallen asleep. He knew that he would have to concentrate on the issue at hand, or else what he had learned and what he had figured out would do no one any good.

Marius opened the door and swung it wide, motioning for him to come out. Artair sat still on his bed for a full minute, enjoying the angry look on the guard's face, before he stood and walked slowly to the door. As the procession moved down the hall, Conaf called out to him and wished him luck. He raised a hand in response.

The group moved quickly, taking the same route as before. This time the Sword Bearer took even longer to put on his armor, to his captors' obvious displeasure. As before, he could hear the roar of the crowd as they approached the arena, but it was not as loud this time as it had been the day before.

The Helvetian finally swung his swords into place and nodded to Marius. Stepping forward, the guard pushed the double doors open and then waited for Artair to step through before following.

As it had the day before, the procession headed across the floor of the arena and stopped in front of the tower at the opposite end. This time the crowd stopped cheering long before King Drake stood up.

Looking around at the densely packed stands, the city's ruler began to speak in his own language. As he did, Artair scanned the occupants of the tower. Of the ten or so people present, there were a couple men and one woman who might help him, he decided. He hoped he was right, because his life would depend on it.

As the king finished his speech he looked down and locked eyes with Artair. "To you I wish a terrifying and pain-filled death. Say hello to your countrymen for me." King Drake said in Helvetian, and then sat down.

Tullius stood and motioned to Marius and his men to leave the arena. It had been decided that another speech would be a waste of time. Artair turned to watch them go and then shifted his gaze to watch the gate where he expected to see the dragon emerge.

There was a collective intake of breath from the audience as the gate began to move, sliding open slowly. The Sword Bearer watched the door until it was halfway open and then he turned his back to it and walked toward the tower. Craning his neck, he looked up at the king, and next to him, at Artimus.

"King Drake, I've already told your people and your general what their fates will be. Your people will beg for peace, and your general will beg forgiveness." Artair heard the massive gate click open behind him as he continued. "You make my countrymen and me out to be barbarians and killers, while at the same time you send your soldiers out to kidnap my people and to destroy your own villages."

The king sat with a face like stone. One of the men Artair had noted earlier shifted in his seat with his eyes glued on something behind him. At the same time the warrior heard slight murmurings from the crowd. Sweat broke out on his forehead as he kept himself from turning to look.

The dragon had entered the arena. Even without turning around he was sure of it. Reaching up with his right hand, the Sword

Bearer drew one of his swords, the one that had belonged to Moray. Pointing at the king with it, he yelled.

"You have ruled too long and with too much power, and your rule will soon come to an end. Yes, King Drake, I know exactly how it will end."

One of the men and the woman up in the tower stiffened suddenly, the woman reaching up to cover her eyes, and Artair flattened himself to the ground. His right hand drove the hilt of the sword into the dirt as he fell, and a split second later it was torn from his grip as the monster's front feet shook the ground on either side of his body. The feet left again as the animal screamed and fell, rolling to its right. The Sword Bearer rolled to his left, coming to his feet with his own sword in his hands. The handle was warm in his hand, and he felt a slight tremor, like excitement, run through the weapon.

The dragon had been sneaking up behind him as he talked, zeroing in on his voice and his movements. Like any large predator, dragons would kill from ambush when possible to prevent injuries. The two people in the tower had reacted just as the beast had pounced at him, aiming for his shoulders with its front feet. Had it made contact, its jaws would have snapped down and separated his spine between his shoulders.

Moray's sword was now jammed up through the beast's right front shoulder, disabling it. The dragon, a male that was mostly crimson in color, was now glaring at Artair through its red eyes.

In the next moment it pounced. It was slowed by its injury, and its right leg hung virtually useless. The swordsman rolled to his left and slashed backward at the beast's right foreleg as it passed. The attack only bounced off the monster's armor and did no damage.

Turning toward the dragon, Artair threw his sword as the reptile spun toward him. The red-eyed beast caught the blade with its tale as it flew, knocking it down into the dust.

The Sword Bearer stood unarmed, waiting for the dragon's next move. In his mind rang his own words said to Calum on the night he was captured: "You'll get nothing but a good chance to practice your rolling after you lose your sword." There would be no rolling here, for there was no one to distract the dragon.

The monster's eyes burned into Artair's as it jumped for him. The Sword Bearer waited for a heartbeat after the dragon left the ground and then threw himself backwards. Massive jaws snapped shut above him, missing by mere inches. As the dragon's jump carried it over the top of him the Helvetian caught the handle of Moray's sword. The blade came free with a terrible wrench, sending him rolling.

Artair shook to clear his head as he stood, dragon blood covering his hand and the sword.

The monster came again, this time running flat out at him. Even with one leg nearly useless, the beast was dangerously fast. Artair jumped straight in the air, the dragon's head passing right below him, and then placed a foot on the reptile's down-turned neck and leapt again.

Twisting in the air, he slashed downward as he hit the ground. His haphazard attempt cut deep into the end of the monster's tail, next to the blade. The dragon roared as it curled its hurt appendage up to its face to look at the new wound. Artair turned and ran for his other sword that lay in the dust a few feet behind him.

As he reached the weapon he could hear the dragon coming again, and he threw himself onto his back and shoved both swords upward at the oncoming monster. One of the blades missed altogether, but the other went into the reptile's mouth as it swung down toward him. The red steel cut through the right side of the massive jaw and stuck out the back of its head.

At the same time, the beast's one useable foreleg ripped away Artair's breastplate, tearing a gash across his chest. Only the animal's forward momentum kept it from falling on its face as its wounded foreleg attempted to support its weight. The beast screamed in frustration as it stopped to tear at the pain in its mouth with its one good front limb.

Artair stood up, gasped for breath, and charged his enemy. With a roar of desperation he stabbed his blade through the dragon's side and into its heart. The beast's head whipped around as it roared and Artair grabbed the handle of the sword stuck in its mouth, jerking its head past him. The reptile reacted violently, whipping its head around and bucking away from its attacker. The Sword Bearer jumped free as the monster's movement helped pull out the blade that had been in its mouth. He stood shakily and watched as the dragon helplessly tried to pull the killing steel out of its side with jaws that no longer worked.

The monstrous beast turned to look at Artair, its blood-red eyes filled with pain and anger. The creature bunched itself as if to jump, but Artair did not bother to move. The reptile's last attempt at victory turned into a final pronouncement of defeat as its back legs buckled and it fell to its side in the bloodstained dirt.

Artair walked up to his beaten foe slowly, trying to catch his breath, and then finished the fight with a final swing of his sword. It took him nearly a minute to gather enough strength to pull his other blade from the dragon's side.

The spectators watched as the Sword Bearer's legs buckled and he fell to his knees in the blood-splashed dust. The Helvetian warrior did not move for several seconds and then he looked up at the tower's occupants. The women seated there looked down at him in horror. Dried blood on his face, a long wound seeping blood that ran across his chest, and two bloodstained blades complemented the look on Artair's face.

"You lose, Drake." Artair shouted, pointing at him with one sword. "You lose and I win. Now stop sending these animals to do your dirty work. Come down here and fight me like a man, and I'll lay you down right here next to your pet."

"Be it today or another day, I will see you dead at my feet. I will see you dead as punishment for the hundreds of innocents you've killed. What do you say, King Drake? Do you fight with men, or do you restrict yourself to butchering women and children?" Artair's voice rang throughout the deathly silent arena.

Indeed the congregation was holding its collective breath. After a long pause, Drake turned to Tullius and said in a quiet but direct voice. "Bring in the Titans."

The fat man's eyes widened and his mouth dropped open.

"Sire, no." Artimus exclaimed, stepping up to the king's chair. Drake backhanded the general in the mouth viciously, throwing him into the wall. Turning back to the arena manager, he placed a hand on his sword.

"Release the Titans, Tullius, or your successor will do so over what remains of your fat carcass."

His quivering servant bowed and nodded feverishly as he struggled to find his way from the room. When he had gone, Drake turned on the man he had struck.

"Do not question me again Artimus, not one more time."

The other man nodded dumbly, blood covering his chin.

The king looked down at Artair in disgust as the swordsman struggled to his feet.

Chapter 27

Marius could not believe his ears when he heard Tullius's stuttered order. The fat man repeated the demand and then staggered back up the stairs. Marius gathered his men together and sent them en masse to fulfill the king's wishes. He went no further than the bottom of the stairs. He wanted nothing to do with what was about to happen.

*

Artair stood by the carcass of the dragon and waited. He did not know what was going on, but he had seen the altercation between the king and Artimus and he knew that something unexpected was happening.

The crowd was getting restless. From the appearance of things, not many of them had heard what went on in the tower, but they knew that something was going on.

The warrior tried to refasten his breastplate, but was unsuccessful. He would need an entirely new set of straps to fix it. The wound on his chest worried him. It was not terribly deep, and he would have thought that it would heal quickly if it weren't for the reputation that dragon-inflicted wounds had earned over the years. As it was, the long tear burned as if salt had been poured into the gash.

Looking up at the tower, he noticed that Tullius had returned to his seat, his round face red and covered with drops of perspiration. It was obvious that it wasn't just from exertion.

Then Artair heard human screams. These weren't cheers, they were terrified, bone-chilling screams. Looking around, he noticed that the gate through which the dragon had come had remained open. It was through that tunnel that the shrieks were coming. The sound got louder every second and soon Artair could hear shouts and the sounds of conflict coming from the passage. Instinctively, he began walking toward the middle of the arena. His feeling was that he would need maneuvering room for whatever was to happen next. His knees were shaking as he walked, and his arms felt almost too weak to hold them up.

He stopped in his tracks as a huge dragon exploded from the opening. Carried in its mouth was the body of a man. Artair held stock-still as the massive creature dropped its victim and rose to its hind legs, roaring at the crowd. This was the biggest dragon the Helvetian had ever seen. Not only that, but the animal had more muscle packed onto its massive frame than he had ever imagined possible.

The beast finally stopped roaring and dropped to set its front feet on the ground. The Sword Bearer watched in horror as it turned its head to watch a second dragon of equal size step into daylight.

"Goodbye, Artair," King Drake said, just loudly enough for the man in the arena to hear. The swordsman didn't bother to acknowledge the remark, but kept his eyes on the two creatures in front of him.

The warrior's mind raced furiously. There was no way to fight two dragons at a time without distracters, people to keep one occupied while you attacked the other. Seldom had a team ever attacked two dragons at once, and never when they had a choice.

Artair waited until the male stood up and roared before he reached up and slowly untied his cloak from his neck. The dragons had not yet noticed him. They stood looking at the crowd, as if they could not figure them out--apparently these two were not used to the

182

multitudes of people. The Sword Bearer moved slowly as he wrapped his cloak around his chest and tied it, re-securing his breastplate and covering the wounds on his abdomen. His hands were steady now but his heart was racing. One of the dragons had to die quickly or there would be no chance for him. He didn't think he really hadn't any chance anyway, but it wasn't in him to give up.

Artair swallowed hard and reached up to pull Moray's sword from its sheath. Without turning, he tossed it behind him and to one side. The sound of the weapon hitting the ground and his movement caught the attention of the female. Opening her mouth, she roared at him and attacked, bounding across the arena with cat-like agility. The male followed her, just a jump behind.

The Helvetian pulled his sword from its sheath and glanced down at the red blade. In another few seconds it would either save his life or witness the end of it.

A roar began in the Sword Bearer's throat and echoed in the arena as he burst into a run, heading straight for the attacking monsters. To the Helvetian, everything moved in slow motion as he watched the female dragon close the distance between them, her bloody jaws snapping.

His sword swung back in his right hand as the beast's hindquarters bunched and then propelled the huge animal into the air, a jump that would bring her to him. Artair's left foot hit the ground, stirring up a small puff of dust. His left hand moved back to join his right grasping the handle of the sword. His right foot hit the ground. The reptile was fully in the air now, its clawed paws extended and ready to meet him. His left foot hit the ground again, and he swung the sword forward, propelled by all the strength in his battle-weary body.

With the sound of a hammer striking steel, dragon and man joined into one in the eyes of those who watched. The bulk of the animal hitting the ground threw so much dust into the air that for several seconds no one could tell what had happened, or which of the combatants had lived.

As the dust cleared, a cheer went up from the crowd. King Drake was on his feet, the echoes of his shouted "NO" ringing in the tower.

On the floor of the arena the male prodded the body of its mate with its snout. The red-bladed sword could be seen where it had ended the female's life. The Sword Bearer's stroke had split the dragon's head in two, from the end of its snout to the middle of its head, killing the behemoth instantly.

Artair was nowhere to be seen.

The male ceased his futile efforts to wake his mate and began searching around her body, sniffing in the dirt like a large dog. Deep growls emanated from the big animal's throat as it looked for its prey.

Up in the tower, King Drake sank slowly back into his chair with a sigh. "Well, isn't that an undeserved end to the man? He died killing one of the greatest creatures that has ever existed," the king said to no one in particular, then stood and leaned out over the edge of the tower.

"Kronos, come." he shouted to the remaining dragon, that still circled the body of its mate. At the sound of its master's voice the animal raised its head from the dirt and ran to the base of the tower. Once there it looked up into the face of the king as a dog looks at his beloved master.

"It's okay, Kronos, you did just fine. Good boy, Kronos."

Artimus was always disgusted to watch the king when he talked to his pets. This man had no compassion or mercy toward his fellow men, but was as loving as a good mother to these beasts.

Down at the bottom of the tower, Kronos rose up on his hind legs and set his front claws on the rock of the building, trying to get closer to his master. The king looked down on his beloved pet as a

184

cheer erupted from the crowd. Confused, he looked toward the stands. The people there were not looking at him or the dragon, but at something on the arena floor. Drake's muscles began to tighten as his eyes scanned across the arena to a sight he was desperate not to see.

The king's eyes locked on Artair at the same time that he heard Kronos scream. Glancing down, he was horrified to see a sword protruding from the back leg of the massive animal. The blade had cut through the dragon's hamstring, and the king watched as the limb buckled underneath the dragon's immense weight and Kronos fell to his side, scrambling desperately to his feet to stand facing his attacker.

"Kill him, Kronos, kill." King Drake shouted in a frenzy. Unconsciously he had drawn his sword and was pointing with it at the battered man.

Once his eyes again locked on the Helvetian, he found that he could not look away. The man stood bare-chested, his upper body armor now completely torn away in his fight to get out from underneath the dragon's carcass. Blood covered him from head to foot, a combination of his own and the female dragon's. What truly caught the King's attention, though, were his eyes. He had never seen such raw fury in the look of a man. The king took an involuntary step backwards from the edge of the tower and watched what happened with a mixture of horror and fascination.

Artair had retrieved his own sword from the body of the female after throwing the sword he had dropped at the beginning of the fight at Kronos. The male, his one leg now useless, roared at his tormentor and backed up against the stone wall of the tower. His injured limb now protected, he roared again at his human enemy, daring him to come within reach. Artair stood looking at his opponent, fire raging in his eyes, and nodded as if to accept the challenge. A half second later he charged at the dragon, his sword clutched in his bloody right hand.

Kronos waited until his small foe was within reach and then struck viciously with one clawed paw, slicing at the human's head. Artair ducked under the blow and then dove into a roll to escape a sweeping attack from the dragon's tail. Coming to his feet, the Sword Bearer slashed the beast's left paw as it swung at him, and then ducked under it as it passed him. Exploding from a crouch, the swordsman ran in close to the dragon. Instinctively swinging his weapon upward as he ran, the Helvetian felt the point of his blade stab into the creature's jaws as they swept down to grab him.

To the watching crowd all that was visible was the furious actions of the dragon—blurred by the speed in which it moved. The monster's size, and the dust kicked up by the fight, mostly hid the Helvetian from the watching eyes. The furious monstrosity looked to be battling itself, like a large man swatting at gnats.

The dragon's head reared back, and Artair stepped up next to the beast's great chest. After ducking once and sidestepping to avoid the two sweeping paws, the warrior crouched and jumped backwards, propelling himself under the dragon and landing slightly to the side of the huge beast. Gathering his feet under him, he thrust his sword up into the dragon's belly, the red blade sinking in to the hilt. He followed his sword and ducked under the reptile to the other side as the creature screamed and pivoted to grab at the intruding implement.

The dragon had yet to move its back legs in the fight due to the injury it had sustained, and that was what was saving the weary Helvetian. Nonetheless, the beast managed to jump straight forward as Artair laid hold on the handle of the sword that was stuck in the dragon's back leg. The monstrous animal's jump only helped him pull out the blade, and Artair stood ready again to face the monster, Moray's sword held in both hands. The Sword Bearer's fingers struggled to keep hold of the bloody handle as fatigue and blood loss

186

threatened to overcome him. He knew that this fight would need to end soon, or he would not survive it.

Kronos humped his back against the pain of the wound in his stomach and sat waiting. Artair gasped for air for a moment and then attacked, running straight at the dragon. This time the armored creature struck with both his paws and his jaws as his enemy drew near.

The warrior twisted away from the strike and took two steps closer to the dragon before slashing at the beast's shoulder with his sword. The blow did nothing but incite another attack, but that was what the Sword Bearer had planned. As the dragon slashed at its own right side, Artair dropped and rolled forward underneath the reptile's neck. The great head had just begun to curve to attack him when the Helvetian stabbed his sword up into the dragon's throat. Again he dove under and to the side of the beast as it reared up and tore at its throat in agony. The warrior jumped out of the way as the monster fell to one side, thrashing. The great claws extracted the sword from its neck, releasing a great gush of blood in the process. The animal clawed at the fatal wound, tearing away its armored scales as it thrashed in pain.

The most terrifying part for the crowd was the animal's silence. Only muted gasps escaped from the dragon's ruined throat as it desperately tried to live.

Artair got to his feet wearily, watching the huge animal until the death throes ceased and the arena was again still. Then he walked up and pulled the sword from the dragon's belly and then slowly made his way to where his other sword lay in a puddle of the dragon's blood. He made a weak attempt to wipe it off, then gave up and stuck both swords into the ground and stood leaning on them facing the people in the tower. After a moment, a small smile made its way to his mouth.

The king sat looking down on him, pure hatred in his eyes. Artimus looked disbelieving, as if he simply could not accept what had just happened. The rest of the occupants looked like they were going to be sick.

"King Drake, your dragons have failed. They cannot kill me. If you want me dead you'll have to come down here and try it yourself. I challenge you. I am wounded and tired, but I challenge you to come down here and face me like a man. Do so, and I will lay your body alongside of these beasts you trained to kill my people and yours. What do you say, Drake? Are you coming, or has a simple barbarian taken away your courage?"

The crowd murmured at Artair's challenge, but their leader's composure did not falter as he stood to give his answer.

"The King of Cyrene does not dirty his hands to kill an animal like yourself. I will see you die, barbarian, you can be sure of that. I look forward to it." With that the King returned to his seat and turned to look at Tullius.

"Take this wretch to his cell. I will visit him as soon as I am ready."

His servant nodded and bowed slightly to his king as Drake left the room. Artimus followed after a few seconds and sent word for his men to be assembled.

Five minutes later a hundred soldiers flooded into the arena, weapons in hand. The king's head general led the way with his sword still in its sheath. As ordered, his men stayed a few yards behind him as he approached Artair

Up close the Helvetian looked a lot worse than he had from up in the tower. He had cuts and bruises all over his body, the slashes on his chest still oozed blood, and there were several other large gashes under his arms and on his stomach from when his armor was torn from him under the weight of the female dragon. The man's entire body seemed to cry out for rest, but in his eyes a fire burned.

"Come on, Artair. It's time to go back to your cell. You're done fighting today," the Cyrenian said brusquely.

The Sword Bearer's eyes bored into his head. "I don't need to beat all of you, Artimus. Look at the people in the stands. I became a hero today, and for the simple reason that I defied your king and I'm still living. Look at them." Artair insisted.

The general glanced up at the people in the stands. Now on their feet, the entire crowd was offering their unspoken support for this bedraggled warrior. When his gaze returned to Artair the Helvetian had a small, bitter smile on his face.

"They support me, and I'm a barbarian. How fast would they support you if you tossed that madman out of the palace and decided to lead them? What's keeping you? Is it fear, or is it the simple fact that you enjoy doing his dirty work for him?"

"Is he the only maniac that sits in that tower, Artimus? You give the order and do your worst, because if the men of this city don't have the guts to stand up for their freedom you haven't brought enough to stand against me." Artair stepped back and swung his swords up into ready position.

Artimus just stood looking at him, admiring the fact that he was able to hold up the two swords even though it must have taken much of his remaining energy. "You speak well, and you fight better, but it doesn't matter anymore. Either you die now or you die later, and the king will crush anyone who even speaks of you after that. Heroes die just as easily as normal people do, so prepare yourself. You people must be born stupid if you haven't realized yet that no one man can change the way the world works. Didn't your father teach you that before he died?" Artimus asked tauntingly.

The general's sword leapt from its sheath as the bloody warrior attacked him, but he never had to use it. As soon as Artair began moving forward nets smothered him from both sides, tangling his swords in the ropes.

While the Sword Bearer's attention had been drawn to Artimus, the men had followed his orders and waited for the prisoner to attack him.

Without the restraints it was sure that the Helvetian would not have been taken alive. However, even with their help, two men were wounded in the process of taking his swords away from him. Finally, Artair was carried unconscious to his cell. When he woke up, he was once again hanging from his shackled hands. His ankles were also chained to opposite walls—keeping him standing but unable to move. After almost an hour, he could see a torch coming down the halls and he could tell that three men, maybe four, were approaching his cell.

Chapter 28

Calum found his men just as they broke camp in the morning. The fire was almost out, a thin trail of smoke rising from the ashes. Stumbling down a hill, covered with dust and grime, he was quite a sight. As he came closer the warriors could see that not only dust, but also blood covered their friend. Ragnal was the first man to reach him and half caught him as he tripped. The rest of the group crowded around as their leader leaned on his second in command, breathing heavily.

"What happened, Calum?" Ragnal asked urgently, concern creasing his face. The dust-covered Sword Bearer took a few deep breaths and then looked around at the men surrounding him. The worry on their faces turned to confusion as a wide grin split his face. When he looked up at Ragnal the other man was almost sure that he had gone insane.

"I found a dragon, a dragon we missed." Calum started to laugh and ended in a fit of coughing.

His boyhood friend motioned for someone to throw him a water canister and the head Sword Bearer drank deeply. Afterwards he threw it back to its owner and stood up straight, the grin still plastered across his face.

"All right, let's get going. Do you know where any more dragons are?" Calum asked with all the enthusiasm of a small child. His comrade shook his head in exasperation.

"Old friend, you are in no condition to go anywhere. You need to stay here in camp and rest today. We will find some dragons tomorrow," Ragnal said as soothingly as he could. Calum was usually the coolest head amongst them, and to see him in this condition was very alarming.

Calum shook his head and the grin disappeared. "No, we will go now. There is something you all need to see, something I've learned. Trust me, and I guarantee we will all celebrate together at the end of the day. I ask again, do you know where any dragons are?" He insisted.

Ragnal looked around at the rest of the team in desperation. A couple shrugged their shoulders, but the majority looked as confused as he was.

"Fine," he sighed. "We sighted a dragon last night just as darkness was falling. We were heading out to find it right now, but I sincerely doubt that you're up for a fight in your current condition. I mean, look at yourself, man." he insisted.

The Sword Bearer just shook his head and grinned at his friend. "Ragnal, you have no idea what I am still capable of. I am fine, let's get going. Which way?" Calum asked and looked expectantly at his second in command, who sighed in defeat and pointed in an easterly direction.

The lead man headed off immediately, stepping through the crowd who had been standing around him. A couple seconds later the rest followed, all of them more than a little worried about their leader.

After they had been walking for a few minutes, Ragnal stopped the original Sword Bearer and told him in a low voice that the dragon they had sighted had disappeared over the top of the hill that lay in front of them before they had broken off the hunt and made camp. Calum motioned for his men to come in together and when they were gathered around him he grinned at them.

"All right, this is how we're going to do it. You archers, spread out and follow me at about twenty yards. The rest of you walk behind the archers. Nobody attacks or does anything unless I order it, is that clear? Ragnal, I don't want to hear it," Calum said as he raised a hand in protest. "This will be a day none of you will ever forget, but you have to do what I say right now. No matter what I do, and no matter what happens, stay in your positions unless I give an order. Now, is everyone ready?"

The determined warrior waited until he had received an answer to the affirmative from every member of his team before he nodded and turned to walk up the hill, the fighting men assembling behind him.

As he reached the top of the hill, he caught sight of the dragon halfway up the side of another rise about a hundred yards away. It had no idea that it was being hunted, and was climbing slowly. Dragons always looked clumsy when they were moving slowly, as if their bodies only worked well at high speeds. The Sword Bearer cupped his hands around his mouth and shouted.

"Dragon!" Calum's voice must have just barely reached the beast, because it paused for only a second before continuing its ascent. The Helvetian warrior started jogging down the hill, trying to close the distance between him and the huge animal. "Dragon! Get back here!" he yelled again, and then laughed.

Ragnal walked with his hammer hanging from one hand as he walked behind the archers. He alone in this team might be able to kill the dragon in time if it attacked, but he had to trust his friend. This time the dragon heard Calum's shout and turned around to see what was making the noise. It acted only mildly interested.

Spreading his arms wide, the blood-spattered man kept walking in its direction, a big grin on his face. "Come on, come to your old buddy Calum, come on boy." the Sword Bearer yelled. Behind him

Ragnal exchanged glances with the rest of the men. They had never seen their leader act like this, and only a mad man would act this way with a dragon.

The monster roared in response and leapt forward, running at its human target with jaws snapping.

"That's it, come on buddy, time to die," the warrior growled, all joviality lost now in his tone. Instead there was rage and simple certainty. Calum's posture and step showed total confidence, while the men behind him gripped their weapons in apprehension and waited for some order that would allow them to return to their usual battle strategy.

"All right, you big lizard, come and get it." the head Sword Bearer roared as the dragon closed the distance to less than thirty yards. He stood with his sword sheathed, his arms spread wide as if asking for a hug from the monster.

The men behind him stirred, their trust in their leader battling with the instincts a hundred dragon fights had instilled in them.

"Keralti tock na." Calum shouted suddenly.

Confused at the unfamiliar words, the other men stared at him, and then looked past him as the dragon abruptly slowed, stopped and then lay docilely down on its stomach. The beast set its massive head on the ground and closed its eyes, the enormous body relaxed and still.

Finally pulling his sword from its sheath, the lead man walked up to the enormous reptile. The creature seemed to be oblivious to the presence of his enemy as the swordsman approached and set the blade of his sword on the top of its neck.

Calum looked back at his men, who now stood open-mouthed, staring at a scene they had never dreamed possible. Then he turned back and, with a powerful swing of his sword, cut the beast's head off its body. Calum jumped out of the way as the dragon thrashed a few times and then lay still.

For several seconds none of the men could decide whether to look at the body of the animal or at their leader, who had started laughing again as soon as the reptile had stopped moving.

"I wish you could see the looks on your faces." Calum roared and kept laughing. Finally his laughter diminished and the Sword Bearer stood looking at his friends.

"You know what? I'm hungry," he said suddenly. "Let's go get something to eat, what do you say? I've just done the work you all planned to do today, so let's go back to camp."

The statement got no response so he simply started back the way they had come and then waited at the campsite of the previous night until the rest of the men came wandering in, looks of disbelief and raging curiosity on their faces. It wasn't until a fire was going and food was cooking that Calum decided to answer the unvoiced question showing so plainly in all of their eyes.

"Màrtainn's story was the truth. They found Iain. The sad thing is that he died before I could get there," Calum began as his men gathered around him. "He left something for me, though, let me show you."

The head Sword Bearer pulled the roll of leather out of the pouch at his waist and displayed it to his comrades. "For some reason, the leader of the kidnappers made a deal with Iain and they faked his death. Part of the bargain was that he was to make his way back and give this message to me."

As he spoke, Calum unrolled the piece of leather and then turned it around to show to his men. "This is a map leading to a cave in the Bleeding Tooth. It shows the way to navigate the tunnels that apparently branch off from that cave, passages that lead all the way through the mountains and come out on the other side. At different points on the map, as you can see, there are notes telling of guards and fortified positions inside the passages."

"Also, there is a simple piece of instruction at the bottom that says: For when you meet up with the dragons: Keralti tock na," Calum read and then returned the roll to his pouch.

"At first I didn't know what that meant or how I was supposed to use it. I thought that maybe it was simply a joke or that they were wishing us luck in their own language or something. Then I met a dragon along the way. I was stupid and making too much noise and it was on top of me almost without warning. I went a couple of passes with it before it occurred to me to try saying those words, like a command or a spell or something. Well, I didn't say it right the first couple of times, and I nearly got myself killed, but when I finally did say it correctly that dragon did the same thing the one I just barely killed did. I couldn't believe it." Calum laughed, "That big dragon just sat there, still as a stone for a couple of minutes while I just stared at it. Finally it opened one eye and looked at me, as if expecting me to do something. I did, although I guarantee what I did wasn't what it expected."

"Calum, do you realize what this means?" Ragnal asked, his voice quiet.

Oddly, the other man's face became serious again and he nodded. "Yes, I do, but I don't think that you do." he responded.

Ragnal looked at him questioningly and Calum continued.

"Those words are not some spell over the dragons, they are a command. It is a command that all of these animals know and obey."

"You're saying…" Someone in the crowd began.

"They've been trained. Someone trained these dragons at some point. No, more than that, a person or a group of persons trained all these monsters."

"This map," Calum said as he jerked it out of his pouch again, "shows us how to get through the mountains using a network of tunnels protected by people we've never seen. The kidnappers come from there. There is a civilization on the other side of those mountains that trained these animals, and that has been sending people to kidnap us for the last fifteen years."

"With these three words we will defeat the dragons, but I fear that our real enemy might be the one we've never seen. The war may have only just begun." Calum looked around at his men as what he had said sunk in.

"Bring me two pieces of parchment. Choose amongst yourselves who wants to run tonight."

When the writing utensils were brought to him Calum spent a couple of minutes alone while his men talked amongst themselves. When Calum returned to them he held the two pieces of material rolled up in his hands.

"All right, who's going?" he asked, and two men raised their hands. Calum handed each of them a roll of parchment. "Take these to each of the teams closest to us. One of you heads north, the other south. I've written those three words on each message and also new instructions for everyone as a whole."

Turning to the rest of his men, Calum continued. "We will stay here for the rest of the day and leave tomorrow morning. The other teams will proceed as we planned previously, except that they will each take on a little wider area to cover for our absence. We will follow this map to the cave and press on through the tunnels. I want to see what is on the other side and I want to know what we need to expect from these people."

"Anyone who does not want to come with me is free to go with these two and join one of the other teams." Calum looked around at his men, and then continued when he saw that no one wanted to leave.

"Included in those orders are instructions for them to proceed and meet up at the Bleeding Tooth. If we are not back from inside the tunnels by that point they are to leave sufficient forces there to watch for people coming through and to stop any kidnapping parties. The rest are to head for home and help the empire to prepare. Although we cannot be sure of the extent of their plans, we do know that these people are not all friendly, and we will plan for the worst possible scenario. If they sent dragons against us they might not hesitate to send soldiers."

Turning back to the two runners, the lead Sword Bearer asked if they had any questions. When they did not he sent them on their way.

The rest of the day was spent preparing for the mission ahead, both physically and mentally. Calum slept for several hours and ate as if he had never tasted food before. By nightfall he looked like his old self again as he sat next to the fire, staring into the flames.

"Calum?" Ragnal asked, and the big man raised his head to look at his friend. "Why do you think that kidnapper sent that roll back to us? I just can't figure out why he'd want to. I mean, if he wanted to lure us into a trap then he didn't have to include the command for the dragons. In fact, why lead us anywhere if they are the ones who let those beasts loose on us? Those blasted reptiles have been doing a good job of keeping us busy for the last fifteen years."

"As far as that goes, why send dragons into our country? They have to know they're dangerous. I guess what I'm trying to say is that I'm as confused as I've ever been in my life. I'm wondering if you've figured any of this out."

Calum was silent for several seconds before answering. "You know, Ragnal, I always like to give people the benefit of the doubt, and there could easily be a good explanation for all of this. The dragons could have simply gotten away from their country and escaped over here. If they were domesticated once, but then spent some time in the wild, they'd get hungry and return to their survival instincts."

"The kidnappers could simply be a bad element from their society that comes over here to take people for their own reasons. What I'm saying is that it's possible that the people on the other side of those mountains are the same as we are, just with a bad set of circumstances making them look like they wish us harm."

"The man who sent us the message, for example, could be in favor of opening up communications between our two peoples, and included the command to the dragons as a gesture of good will. With those cursed reptiles gone and the kidnappers' identity revealed, we could be witnessing the end of our society's major problems," Calum said with an insincere smile.

Ragnal raised an eyebrow at him and then looked into the fire. When he spoke again he had lowered his voice. "Calum, what do you really think?" Ragnal looked up at the end of his question and met the other man's gaze.

The firelight reflected in the Sword Bearer's eyes as he responded. "I think we're already at war."

Chapter 29

"Artair, wake up."

The Sword Bearer's eyes opened slowly and tried to focus in the near darkness.

"Someone's coming, Artair, and I don't think it's good news." Conaf hissed in the darkness.

The Helvetian groaned involuntarily at the pain in his shoulders at being hung from his hands as he slept. In truth, it was more that he had simply passed out after a time. He had no idea how long he had been asleep, but his wounds told him that he was still in the same nightmare he had been in when he last checked. He flexed his legs, putting his weight back on them and groaned again. He had never been so weak or battered, and it scared him. His fight was not over, and yet he felt as if he would not last another fight.

The door at the end of the hallway stood open, light spilling through it. They could hear voices coming from the outside corridor. One was obviously Marius, but the others were not as familiar to the prisoners.

"What happened out there Artair? No offense, but you're supposed to be dead."

"Sorry to disappoint, does close count?" Artair could hear the weariness in his own voice and he struggled to shake himself awake, blinking in the darkness to try and clear his vision.

A small knot of men passed through the doorway, following the one in front, who walked without hurrying—seemingly unfazed by the smell and the raw human suffering on every side.

Artair watched as the group stopped in front of his cell, as he knew they would. He heard the jingle of keys as his door was unlocked and then swung open.

"Come on in, boys, make yourselves at home." Artair croaked, his voice cracking. He was able to smile, a sneer that hurt more than he expected it to.

King Drake ignored the comment, stepping through the cell door as if crossing a throne room threshold. He was silent as he approached the prisoner. Circling around the cell, he studied the Helvetian in the almost complete darkness. He moved smoothly, so that even his footsteps could not be heard on the rough floor. Finally he made his way back to face the prisoner and for a moment the two were eye to eye. Turning, he gestured toward the door and one of the men there stepped forward, placing a gold-plated stool behind the king. He sat, sweeping his robe around him. He sat upright, his back as straight as if it had been a sword blade.

"When I took power, it was with the simple philosophy that if I were to enter into any battle, I would win not only that conflict, but every fight thereafter in one meeting. The first rebellion against me therefore became the last." He spoke as if this were a social call, a conversation between friends. He spoke Helvetian as if he had been born to it, without a hint of an accent. He stood slowly, deliberately, and walked forward until he was only inches from Artair.

"It means that any would-be enemy has a memory of the thousands who died that day to keep their thinking loyal." The king's eyes blazed with the fire of barely suppressed rage. "It means that any time someone rises up against me, anytime someone is so insanely foolish," Drake's voice shook with anger as he glared into Artair's eyes, "there is only one thing that can be done."

Artair stared back into the king's eyes, and slowly smiled. "Your philosophy works well when dealing with frightened sheep or men in chains. I would ask you to let me out of these chains so we could settle this like men, but I've already given up hope of that. You may have been something once, *Drake*, but now you are a coward who sends others to do his fighting for him."

Drake stood slowly, his hand on his sword. "If I didn't already have plans for you I would kill you for those words. Words spoken in desperation by the heir of a man so despicable as to hardly be worth speaking of."

"It is obvious you have grown bored if you have to dredge up enemies from the past." Artair snarled.

The king smiled, a brief flash of teeth in the darkness. "I do not kidnap your people in order to find enemies; I do it to even the score. Don't worry, I know where my enemies are, and I will deal with them soon enough."

"Bold words for someone who had me chained before you dared enter my cell. What type of king are you if you have to have your unarmed enemy bound before you dare invade?"

Drake stiffened visibly, and a snarl curled his lips. "A king does not brawl with savages."

"Words of a coward." Artair spat. "Unlock these chains and I will show you how a king should handle an enemy." The Sword Bearer strained forward in his chains, forcing his face closer to the king's. "I would feed you your own heart." He snarled.

For a few terse seconds the two men were silent, looking at each other.

"We'll have to see about that." Drake said, and then snorted a laugh that had no cheer in it. The king turned, then, and left the cell.

He walked down the hall without a single glance backwards. His servants pulled the stool from the cell and scurried after him. Artimus, who had stood silently watching the exchange, stood still while Marius and his colleagues unhooked the chains and then locked the cell door after them.

Artair stood still after being unchained, watching the Cyrenian general. For nearly two minutes the two stared at each other without speaking, until the prisoner's legs threatened to buckle under him. Finally, Artimus simply turned and walked away, leaving the cell block in silence.

"Hey, are you all right?" Conaf asked as Artair collapsed onto his bed. He had waited for as long as he could before daring to talk to the other man, but his curiosity had finally gotten the better of him.

The wounded warrior just groaned and hoped that Conaf could take the hint that he did not want to be bothered.

"Come on, man, tell me what happened out there."

Artair rolled his eyes and sat up. The action reminded him of the wounds on his sides and he sank back down onto the cot, gasping.

"Excuse me for saying so, but you look terrible," Conaf said.

The Helvetian just glared at him. "You'd look a lot worse if you'd been out there with me, believe it." Artair retorted.

"What happened out there, Artair? You've got to tell me," Conaf pleaded. "I've never seen anyone speak to the king that way, and I don't think anyone ever has."

"I fought a dragon, killed it, then they set two more on me. I killed them and they nearly killed me. Then the guards threw a net over me, knocked me on the head, and tossed me back in here. The rest, you saw. If you want more of a story than that you'll have to ask someone else to tell you about it," Artair said.

Conaf just gaped at him. "Do you mean to tell me that you killed three dragons today, and that the last two came both at once?" the other prisoner asked incredulously.

"The king called one of them 'Kronos' I think."

Conaf gasped, his mouth opening and closing without sound. "The Titans. You killed the Titans?"

"I believe so. They're dead and I'm alive, so as long as they were the 'Titans' you are talking about I guess that I did."

"I'm sorry, Artair, but I don't envy you one bit. Those two are the king's personal property. They are the only dragons allowed to breed in Cyrene. Drake valued them over any ten thousand people in this world!"

"The king has a torture chamber. Only his worst enemies end up there, and I'm guessing that's where you'll be headed next."

The Helvetian nodded. "For better or for worse, I think I am done with the arena."

The sound of the outer door opening turned Artair's head, and then he whipped back around to face his fellow prisoner.

The two men exchanged a glance and then Artair leapt toward the front of his cell.

Chapter 30

Five men came through the outer door. Four of them were dressed in the common uniform of the Cyrenian soldiers, a short sword at the waist and a dagger at the upper arm. One of the four carried a crossbow. The fifth one was Marius, who came along to show the others where they could find their target. He carried a short sword only, the blade dirty from not having been cleaned in ages.

The darkness of the prison prevented the intruders from seeing clearly into the back of Artair's cell as they approached. The jailer stayed back as the door was thrown open and the trio with short swords rushed in, followed closely by the man holding the crossbow. A small smile started on Marius's face. The Helvetian had survived the arena, but he would wish that he hadn't after a while in the king's torture chamber. No one had ever given a reliable report of what was in that fearsome room, but the king always returned the bodies of the dead to their friends or family for burial, and the sight of the mangled corpses was enough to start every horrifying rumor imaginable.

The three front men spread out as soon as they got inside the cell and moved forward toward the bed. They did not expect the barbarian to be awake, as they had heard that he had collapsed as soon as the king had left. Wounded and beaten, they did not think he would be any trouble. The fourth stood two steps inside the door, his crossbow ready in case of any tricks.

Time stood still for a moment as the soldiers stared at the bed.

It was empty. An unspoken question hung in the air, and yet suddenly none of them wanted to know the answer.

A soft sound came from behind the man with the crossbow as Artair dropped down from the bars on the ceiling, and the three soldiers in front turned as one. The Sword Bearer wrapped both arms around the owner of the crossbow and held him tightly while reaching forward to jerk the release on the weapon. The bolt buried itself in the chest of the middle swordsman, who screamed and clutched at the deadly shaft. The man to his left jumped back, away from his fallen comrade, and Artair saw Conaf's arms grab the soldier and pull him up against the bars.

The enraged Helvetian jerked the dagger from his captive's arm sheath and stabbed the blade into its owner's right arm. Pulling the blade free, he yanked the crossbow out of the leader's weakened hands and slammed it up into his captive's face, and then flicked the dagger across the cell where it slid into the fourth soldier's throat right above the collarbone.

Conaf's shouted warning was unnecessary as the warrior twisted and jerked the intruder he was holding backwards, impaling him on Marius's sword. The jailer recoiled in shock and Artair was on him. Driving his knuckles into his captor's throat with his right hand, the escaping prisoner swung the crossbow with his left, the heavy weapon crashing into the other man's jaw. Artair caught him before he could fall and threw him back into the cell, where he landed on the body of the soldier he had accidentally killed. Artair jumped after him and pulled the crossbowman's sword from its sheath.

The fellow Conaf had pulled against the bars was dead; the rebel had used the man's dagger against him. The Sword Bearer did not bother to check the intruders he had struck. The only one who was alive was Marius, and he would be unconscious for quite a while unless someone woke him.

Acting quickly, Artair pulled the uniform off the soldier who had been killed with the dagger and put it on over what remained of his own. All of the dead men's clothes were soaked with blood, but the black material would not show it as soon as they dried. A minute after the fight ended the Helvetian was standing fully dressed in his attackers' attire. Even the act of putting the clothes on nearly made him gasp from pain, but he was in a fight now, and his wounds would need to wait. He searched the men quickly and then turned to look at his fellow prisoner as he slid a dagger into the sheath on his left arm.

"You know, now I can believe your stories about killing dragons. You, my friend, are a demon on two legs," Conaf laughed, and shook his head in disbelief.

Artair stepped toward him and extended his left hand toward the rebel. "You're pretty good yourself. Thanks for the help," he said.

The Cyrenian reached through the bars with his own left hand and gripped the Sword Bearer's.

"Hey, anytime I can h…" Conaf's statement was interrupted as Artair jerked the man toward him, pulling his arm through the bars until his shoulder crashed into them. The swordsman's other hand slid the dagger from the sheath on his arm and held the edge against the inside of the rebel's wrist.

"Hey, what are you doing?" Conaf demanded angrily.

Artair pulled a little harder on the captive arm until the other man winced in pain. "You know what I'm doing. Why were you moved over here? It would not be too smart to put a rebel prisoner who speaks my language into the cell next to mine, now would it? What were you supposed to get out of me? What were you supposed to find out? Talk, man, or I'll cut you so bad you'll bleed dry before you can make your peace with your Maker," Artair hissed.

Conaf shook his head. "You've got it all wrong, I'm not a spy; I hate King Drake. That's why I'm in here, remember?"

Artair glared at him. "You're lying to me; stop lying or start bleeding; I'm all out of time," the Sword Bearer said, and began to press with the knife blade.

"All right, all right. I was put in here for a reason, but I don't know what. After they got done beating me for helping you out in the arena General Artimus ordered them to put me over here. When our beloved jailer protested, Artimus told him that if he didn't put me where he told him to, he would be put in instead. So Marius brought me over and that's it. I swear that's the whole story. I don't know why Artimus wanted me next to you. You've got to believe me, Artair," he pleaded.

The Helvetian paused for a moment before returning the dagger to its sheath and then let go of Conaf's hand. Reaching down, he picked up the ring of keys from off the ground where they had fallen and tossed them into the other man's cell.

"As soon as I'm gone let yourself out and come and get into one of these uniforms. After that, release the rest of the prisoners. Head straight out of those doors you came in through. I'm going to go ahead of you and eliminate the rest of the guards."

"If I fail, you'll have to do it, so give some of these weapons to the more able prisoners. If you encounter no resistance and you can get those people free, meet me at the southwest corner of the nearest of those dragon stables as soon as it is dark. I'll wait for you there. If you betray me I will escape again and then I will find you. Is that clear?"

Conaf did not speak but nodded his head.

Artair turned and walked out of the cell. "Leave our friend Marius locked in here, he'll appreciate the experience," he said over his shoulder as he left.

Conaf smiled as he picked the keys up off the ground.

*

Artair stepped out of the cell and walked down the hallway separating the rows of prisoners. As he walked he reloaded the heavy crossbow. The Sword Bearer took a deep breath and then broke into a run just before he came into view of the iron-strapped outer door, waving his arms over his head.

There were four men standing at the exit awaiting the return of their comrades. Already nervous because of the amount of time that had gone by, his frantic approach was a confirmation of all their fears. Drawing their swords, the soldiers ran to the escaped prisoner, who dropped to his knees and gasped for breath, waving the men back the way he had come. Three of the four ran on without hesitating, while the last followed after only a moment of hesitation.

Artair swung himself around as the last man went past him and fired the crossbow, catching the straggler in the back of the leg, right above the knee. The wounded Cyrenian cried out in pain as he fell, his sword sliding across the stone floor as he reached back to grab the offending projectile.

At the sound of his cry his comrades stopped and looked back. Artair scrambled forward and hunched over his victim, seemingly trying to help him. Still ignorant of what had caused the injury, the three who had run on followed suit and returned to try and assist their friend. The man in front of the trio slowed as he neared his wounded comrade and his eyes squinted in the dim light. It looked almost like the first man had his hand over the mouth of the one who had been wounded.

The front soldier's eyes widened an instant before a crossbow bolt sank into his shoulder. Artair jumped up, swinging the crossbow as the first man stopped and his two comrades rushed around him. The swinging weapon downed the first to come around and then the Sword Bearer dropped it and drew his sword. The last Cyrenian brought his own weapon up in a confused effort to defend himself from what he thought was his fellow soldier. The Helvetian knocked the weapon out of his hands and then kicked him backward into an empty cell. Swinging the door shut he turned and held the tip of his sword at the throat of the soldier with the wounded shoulder.

Prodding with the sword, Artair guided the man into an empty cell next to where his comrade was. The remaining two soldiers were similarly put away, although he had to drag the one he had hit with the crossbow, as he was still unconscious. Putting the men in cells not only kept them out of the way, but it would also save their lives. Their own prisoners would gladly kill them if given the chance.

Picking the projectile weapon up from the ground Artair checked it over for damage and then loaded it with the last bolt he had taken from its previous owner. As he walked past he also picked up one of the swords that lay on the ground.

The door that led to the hallway was still open when he reached it, since the soldiers had seen no reason to lock it behind them. Going through the opening, he closed it behind him. Conaf had the keys, so it would not stop the prisoners' escape, but it could slow down the guards outside if any got away from him. He had never seen anyone with keys except Marius, and those were with the prisoners now. No doubt Tullius also had keys, but the fat man didn't seem like the type to personally tend to suppressing a rebellion.

Artair moved carefully along the hallway, the crossbow held ready. He met no one as he walked up to the doorway he remembered seeing when he had been brought in. He had glanced inside as he had been rushed through and recognized it as the guards' barracks. As before, the entrance was open and he could hear voices coming from inside.

Consciously keeping his breathing even, Artair slid along the wall until he was right next to the doorframe. In the time he had been a captive at the arena he had watched the guards and kept a count on how many were around at any given time. With Marius beaten, he expected that another four or five of them were still inside. What he could not guess was whether or not there were more soldiers with them.

Holding the crossbow in one hand and a sword in the other Artair took a deep breath and prepared himself to step into the open.

Chapter 31

A short, solidly built guard stepped out of the door, turning into him and nearly colliding with the warrior before stopping, his eyes wide in surprise. The man's mouth opened to yell and Artair slammed the haft of the sword into his throat, cutting off the coming warning.

The Sword Bearer grabbed the man as he bent over, gagging and gripping his throat, and pushed him back into the room he had come from, shoving him across the floor and then stepping back, the crossbow covering the five men who either sat or stood in the small enclosure. Most of them wore looks of utter incomprehension as their eyes lay fixed on the weapon in Artair's hands. One of them, the fat man he remembered as Tullius, looked like he was going to be sick.

"All right, everybody just settle down," Artair said. "Your men ran into some trouble trying to pull me out of my cell and they died. I don't want to kill anyone else today and I'm sure none of you want to die, so let's make everyone happy, shall we? Everyone put down your weapons and lie down on the floor. Come on, no one else has to die today." he ordered.

The fat man dropped to the ground immediately as if struck on the head and lay down on his face. The rest of the men just stood watching, making no move to comply.

"Come on, guys, you can understand what I'm saying, so do what I tell you. Put your weapons down and…"

Two of the guards' eyes switched to something beyond him and Artair pivoted on his left foot, swinging the short sword up along his body and stabbing it through the chest of the man who had come up behind him. He continued to pivot and fired the crossbow as it came to bear. The four Cyrenians with Tullius had jumped for him as soon as he had taken his eyes from them, and the crossbow bolt smashed into the man closest to him, throwing the attacker backward into one of his comrades. Artair threw the crossbow at the next individual who came at him but he ducked under it and thrust at him as he came up. The Helvetian parried the blow, stepped in close, and punched the man in the throat. He felt the guard's windpipe collapse under the blow. The second borrowed sword slid out of its sheath as another Cyrenian jumped over the downed body of his comrade.

Artair slapped the other man's blade down with one sword and stabbed him in the chest with the other. Releasing the weapon, he let the man fall as the last guard rushed him from the side. He blocked his blow and then counter-attacked, forcing his opponent to back away from the sweeping blade until he tripped over the guard who had stepped out into the hallway. As the man began to fall, he knocked the sword out of his hand and kicked him in the stomach.

Artair spun around, scanning the room. The fat man was trembling on the floor and the last guard he had hit stayed down and just looked at him when he turned toward him.

"You stupid fools, I tell you all to settle down and no one believes me except the scared fat one. Did you all wake up hoping to die today?"

Artair gestured with his sword to the guard who lay on the floor. "You just behave yourself over there while I talk to your large friend, and you just might live to see tomorrow."

The Helvetian sheathed his sword and walked over to the man lying on the stone. Sitting down on the chair the fat man had been sitting in before the battle began, he sighed.

"All right, now, get up big man," Artair said.

"Please don't hurt me," Tullius whimpered without lifting up off the floor.

The escaped prisoner smiled wearily. "I won't hurt you, Tullius, just so long as you do as I say and get up. I don't like talking to people's backs."

Tullius rose stiffly and sat himself down in a chair next to Artair's. Sweat beaded on his brow as he turned to look at the Sword Bearer. "What do you want from me?" Tullius asked with a slight tremor in his voice.

Artair leaned forward suddenly, making the arena manager sit back in his chair. "I want answers. First, how many more guards are there in this building? Second, why was Conaf put in the cell next to me? Third, where are my swords?"

Tullius took a deep breath and glanced around. "There might be one or two guards running around in the building somewhere, but only if they're on their way out. The shift just changed, that's why they were all in here when you came. Conaf was put into the cell next to yours because General Artimus wanted him put there, and your swords are in a case in my study," the arena manager answered, his voice slowly returning to normal.

Artair pulled the dagger out of the sheath on his arm and held it lightly in one hand. "Now, Tullius, I think that you could have guessed that I didn't want to hear lies out of you, so I'll ask for the last time: Where are my swords, and, since you mentioned it, who would be there waiting for me if I went to your study?" Artair asked, the dagger gleaming in his right hand.

Tullius stared at the blade and swallowed. "Okay, your swords are right over there on Marius's bed. He claimed them after we knew that you weren't headed into the arena again," he said, and looked down at the floor. "He wouldn't have kept them, of course, but I didn't bother telling him that. Is he dead too?"

214

"Not the last time I saw him."

"Pity. The other men were decent enough, but he would not be much missed."

Artair didn't bother to look to his swords, but kept his eyes on the fat man. "You didn't answer my second question Tullius, but that's all right. You just answer yes or no to the next couple and I might forgive your past infractions. Is Artimus in your office?"

Tullius nodded his head slowly.

"Is he alone?"

Again the other man nodded.

Artair stood and walked to the other side of the room where his swords were laying in their sheaths on a cot. The warrior swung them up into place but kept the short sword at his waist. Returning to the two men he grabbed Tullius by the arm and pulled him to his feet.

"Come on, you're coming with me. As for you," Artair pointed to the man on the floor, "I'd stay in here and stay really quiet. The prisoners you've abused, beaten, and starved are going to be coming through here in a minute, and I doubt they'll be as merciful as I was." Pushing Tullius in front of him, Artair left the room and shut the door behind him.

"Lead the way, big man," the Helvetian said as soon as they were in the hallway. "Just don't get any ideas about leading me anywhere but to your office. If we are ambushed the only thing you can be sure of is that they will find your body on the ground after the fight."

Tullius moved as quickly as his bulk would allow, walking down the hall to a small door Artair had not noticed when they had brought him through. The Sword Bearer stopped him when his hand touched the handle.

"You go first, but go slowly. If anything happens, drop down on the ground and hold still. I can't promise you won't get hurt but I

215

can promise that I won't touch you just so long as you don't move around."

Tullius took a deep breath and then jerked the handle and the door swung inward to expose a small, well-decorated study with another door on the opposite side. In the middle of the room Artimus sat in a chair, a thin-bladed sword lying across his lap. As the two came into the room the general smiled at them.

"It took you long enough, Artair. How many of them did you leave alive?" Artimus asked casually.

The Sword Bearer shoved Tullius to one side and stood facing his old enemy. "How were you so sure that I was going to get away from them, Artimus?" Artair demanded.

The general shrugged his shoulders. "That's very simple. I know my own men and I know you. My bodyguards didn't have a chance. You did me a favor if you killed them," he said.

"I didn't kill all of them, Artimus, though I could have. You should have whoever trains those guys whipped for incompetence. Why are you here?"

The king's head man took a drink from a glass sitting on a small table to his left before answering. "I came to supervise the transport of a prisoner, you, to the king's private torture chamber. Luckily for you, the king forbade me from going in after you, but rather had me send my bodyguards, a useless lot, along with a couple other men I picked out of the ranks."

"By the way, you look like you're already dead and decomposing. If you go outside looking like that you'll be caught in five minutes," Artimus informed him, gesturing at Artair's head.

Lifting one of his hands, the Sword Bearer touched his head. Blood caked his hair and covered half his face; no wonder the arena manager had been scared!

216

Artair glanced up at Tullius as the big man brought him a pitcher of water, a small basin, and a dark towel. The warrior kept the hand holding the sword free of the liquid as he quickly splashed water on his face and ran it through his hair. Then he rubbed his skin gingerly with the towel.

Artimus watched him coolly. "You can't escape, Artair. There are walls surrounding this city and my men watch all the gates. Fifteen minutes after it is found out that you are gone my men will be alerted and then everyone in the city will be watching for a big, lone soldier with cuts on his face and a scar running down the middle of his chin. It will only be a matter of time before you're brought back in, and the king will have his fun with you. You can save us all a lot of time and effort if you give yourself up now, or you can give me a chance to test my men and my systems and try to get away. That's your choice," the Cyrenian said, and then took another slow drink.

Artair shook his head slowly. "Artimus, you should know already that I won't give myself up, so why give me the chance? What do you gain by letting me escape?" he asked, his sword still raised in ready position.

"I don't think I'll answer that question for the time being, Artair; you will forgive me, won't you?" Artimus answered almost flippantly.

"Then answer a different one for me and I'll be on my way." the escaped prisoner said.

"Oh, and what question would that be?" Artimus asked absently, his fingers tracing the handle of his sword.

"The same one I asked you back when we were on the other side of the mountains. Why do you kidnap my people just to send them into the arena? You didn't answer this one before, but now I want to know," he said, his eyes locked on Artimus's.

The other man smiled at him and shook his head. "Ah, come now, Artair. That's not the whole question you want answered is it?" the general asked mockingly. "What you'd really like to know is why we released the dragons on your people fifteen years ago, as well as kidnapping some of you. Am I right? Isn't that what you'd really like to ask?" he asked sarcastically.

The Helvetian stared at him, confusion on his face.

Artimus shook his head in exasperation. "Oh, Artair, you mean you haven't figured that out yet? Goodness, but you're slow. Didn't you ever wonder why you never found a pair of dragons with little hatchlings running around, that you never found nests? Wasn't it conspicuous to you that the same place your ancestors first met the dragons is the only way to get from your country to mine? My drugs must have slowed your brain if you haven't figured this out yet."

"We trained them, Artair. We trained them, and then set them loose on all of you. There, is that clear enough for you to understand?" Artimus questioned.

The Sword Bearer stood staring at his former captor. "Why? Why would you…?" Artair began.

The other man interrupted. "See, I knew that that would be your real question. It's very simple. A civilization weakened by fifteen years of dragon attacks and kidnappings will be easy prey when we decide to invade them. Good plan isn't it? By the way, what I said about heading out soon for another kidnapping trip was all a lie. Thanks to you, King Drake has ordered me to move up the schedule and get our armies ready. The next time I see your country I will be riding on a dragon in front of the full might of Cyrene. Do you think your people will even put up a fight, or will they just give up?" Artimus asked, his tone now serious.

Artair dropped the short sword he had in his hands and had pulled his own weapons from their sheaths before the borrowed blade hit the ground. Artimus moved at the same time and stood up, his sword held lightly in his right hand.

At that moment the sound of footsteps and hushed voices were heard in the hallway and they all froze.

"Those are the prisoners you helped set free, Artair. As soon as anyone catches sight of them the alarm will sound and hundreds of men will flood this place. As much as I would enjoy fighting you again, I don't think you want to be caught in this building when my soldiers arrive. Run now, and be caught again later, or stay and try your luck. Either way it will all end up the same."

Artair hesitated for only a second, torn between anger and logic, and then ducked out of the door to the hall. Artimus and Tullius waited until they heard the outer door swing shut and then the fat man sighed heavily and wiped his brow, shaking his head at his friend.

"Don't you think that was a little close, General?" Tullius asked.

Artimus nodded. "Yes, it was, but it was perfect. Go sound the alarm. According to the rest of the city he killed your guards and escaped while you were in here with me. The king will believe that and not punish you but only if you sound the alarm now. Go, quickly," Artimus commanded and the fat man hurried out the door opposite the one through which Artair had left.

A couple of minutes later bells pealed throughout the city and the manhunt began.

Chapter 32

Darkness settled on the city of Cyrene like a heavy, black blanket. The entire population had been put on house arrest as the whole of the military took to the streets in search of the escaped prisoners. Several of the Cyrenians had already been found when they returned to their homes in search of refuge. In obedience to orders, all those who were recaptured were executed immediately.

The order had a negative effect on the situation.

As soon as they heard about the executions they began fighting without surrender when discovered. Most shared the feeling that they would rather die fighting than decapitated on their knees. Nothing had yet been found of the escaped Helvetian savage, the man who had beaten the dragons and defied their king, but he was the focus of the search.

The people had spoken of little else since the fights earlier in the day. Some admired him, others hated or feared him, but no one could help but respect the warrior. Anticipating this, the king issued an order that anyone found helping the escaped barbarian would be executed, along with his or her entire family.

With thousands of soldiers combing the city, and the people adequately threatened against assisting the barbarian, King Drake nearly howled with impatience as the hours dragged on without news of his capture.

Drake paced the floor in the throne room as, outside, his soldiers continued the search.

Conaf walked like the soldier who had once owned the uniform he was wearing as he approached the corner of the stable. He held a sword in his hand. His nerves were on edge, his senses heightened. He had called in too many favors that day just to stay alive, and there were still several close calls. Although he believed in Artair's abilities as a fighter, he doubted that he would be able to meet him as he had planned.

When he finally reached the southwest corner he stopped and looked around. His doubts seemed to be validated by the silence of the area.

"If I were you I'd stand real still, Conaf, and drop that sword into the dirt." The soft voice came from behind him, and there was a whisper of a touch at his throat that he recognized as the edge of razor-like blade.

The rebel held perfectly still and held on to the weapon.

"Maybe you don't hear so well, Conaf. I said drop that sword," the warrior repeated.

"I don't think so, Artair, not until you tell me your intentions. If you want to cut my throat I think I'll hold on to the only chance I'll have at taking you with me." Conaf responded, doing his best not to allow himself to move as he spoke.

After a few terse seconds the knife blade left his throat and he turned around to face Artair, who had a sword in one hand and a dagger in the other.

"I have to give it to you, Conaf, you've got guts. I hope you have enough of them to be of some use. Did everyone get away?" he asked.

The rebel's hand checked his throat for a wound before answering. "Yes, everyone got away, at least for a couple of hours.

They've already caught a few of them, and they kill them immediately when they do. How did you hide this long? Those soldiers have been combing this entire city and you don't even know anybody here," Conaf asked incredulously.

Artair shrugged his shoulders as he returned the dagger to the sheath on his arm. "I learned a long time ago that the best place to hide something is right out in plain sight. I hid my swords as soon as I left the arena and then hid myself until all the soldiers showed up. After that they were all running around so much and making so much fuss that they didn't notice they'd picked up an extra man. Fairly simple really," Artair said lightly.

Conaf just stared at him. "Do you mean that you've been running around for the last couple of hours with the same people who are looking for you? How did they not notice you?" he asked, disbelieving.

"When people are looking for something, all you have to do is be different than what they think they're looking for, and they'll pass you by. They expected to find me hiding somewhere or running away from them. I did neither. Several times a soldier would look me right in the face and never think twice. It was quite funny, actually. In truth, one man did make the connection, but he had the misfortune of figuring it out while we were alone in an empty house. I'm sure some nice person will let him out of there as soon as he regains consciousness and starts moving around. He will have a frightful headache, though." Artair responded as if telling a campfire story.

Conaf just shook his head in disbelief. "All right, so what happens now? What are we going to do?" the rebel asked.

The Helvetian raised an eyebrow at him. "Well, we are going to find a way to get me out of this cursed city, and then there will be no more we. How does that sound?" the Sword Bearer said, much to his companion's dissatisfaction.

"Oh, I don't think so, Artair. You're not just going to run off and hide in your country now after all you've done. You've got to help us get rid of Drake," he said in exasperation.

The swordsman's eyes bored into the other man. "Okay, Conaf, tell me the truth. Even with me, how big of an army could you raise to go against your king?"

When the Cyrenian didn't answer he continued. "Do you think you could raise a hundred men, maybe as many as five hundred, that aren't afraid of their own shadows? I'm sorry to break it to you, Conaf, but rebellion isn't going to work. If your people had the heart to fight against that monster, they wouldn't have let you get sent to the arena.

"The people are all too scared of Drake to actually be able to fight him. He's going to send an army to take over my nation too and then we'll all be in the same situation unless I can get out of here and warn them that he's coming. The only chance you'll have at taking your king out of power is if somebody else takes away some of his military support. Otherwise you'll just end up back in the arena again."

"Now, unless you have a better plan, let's figure out how to get me out of here and let me do some good on my side, all right?"

Conaf hesitated for a few seconds and then sighed. "You're right, of course. I just hope your people can do the job. One piece of advice: take out the dragons first. If you can figure out a way to destroy them you'll be halfway to victory. I don't envy you the task, though. Come on," Conaf said, and motioned for Artair to follow him.

"I know how to get you over the wall. One of the gatekeepers is a sympathizer of our cause."

"Wait, we need to get my swords," Artair said, and headed back toward the arena.

Conaf followed him after only a moment of hesitation.

*

Asael bowed to his king in the courtyard of the palace by the light of torches. Drake stood over him, looking down at the man with a gaze that served to pin him to the ground.

"Remember, I want him alive, but no more escapes and no more mess ups. You bring that barbarian to me or you bring the one responsible for letting him get away. If I think that that person is you, you will beg for death in my torture chamber. Is that perfectly clear?" Drake's voice left no room to doubt the seriousness of his words.

Asael nodded without looking up. "Yes, sire. I will not fail you," the soldier replied.

King Drake looked down at the man before him and nodded to himself before turning around to return to the palace. When he had gone, Asael jumped to his feet and trotted out of the courtyard, a lopsided grin creasing his scarred face.

*

After the two retrieved Artair's swords, Conaf led the way through back streets and alleyways in the general direction of the outside walls. Lamps, hung at intervals along the streets, provided a scant amount of light, but Conaf's feet seemed to know the way by heart, and he moved with confidence. Several times the pair had to stop and hide as patrols of soldiers marched by. After a little more than half an hour, the rebel opened the door to a small building and stepped inside, beckoning for Artair to follow. The Helvetian stepped inside and then crouched down, mimicking the other man's movements.

"All right," Conaf whispered, his breathing heavy from excitement, "we're about fifty yards from the west gate. Stay here and stay out of sight. Close the door when I'm gone and don't go near the windows. I'm going to go ahead and find the guy I told you about. When I know it's safe, I'll come back for you."

The Sword Bearer nodded his agreement but Conaf wasn't finished yet.

"Artair, will you really come back and try to take King Drake off the throne? Seems to me that it would be easier to just cave in the tunnels and stay on your side. Why would you come back? I mean, you don't owe any of us any favors. Much the contrary." Conaf said and waited in silence for an answer.

"I've been fighting their dragons for fifteen years, Conaf. Then they kidnapped me and made me fight for their entertainment. Even if I weren't trying to defend my country, do you think I would let those offenses go unpunished?" Artair replied.

Conaf hesitated for only a second before standing up and moving back into the street, the matter settled.

Artair remained in his crouching position and surveyed the room around him. He was in some kind of blacksmith shop. The shutters were closed on both windows, blocking out any light that could have come from the lamps outside.

He stood slowly and worked his way to the window at the back of the room. The shutters were set on the inside of the frame. Reaching out with his left hand he grasped the shutter handle and pulled on it lightly. When it didn't budge he pulled harder. Artair felt adrenaline begin to course through his body as he gave up pulling on it and felt along its edges. His fingers had only moved three inches before they found the head of the first nail. A few inches further he found another one. The shutter had been nailed shut from the inside.

He was in a trap!

Turning from the window Artair's eyes searched the racks and table in front of him while his arms began pulling the soldier's shirt off over his head.

Chapter 33

Conaf slipped through the darkness to stand next to a large-framed man with a beard who had just stopped walking in front of the gate. The big guard looked around at him in surprise.

"Conaf, what are you doing here? I didn't expect you for a while yet. Is everything ready?" he asked.

The rebel nodded, grinning. "Yeah, everything's ready. I'm telling you though, you should see this man fight. He's as fast as a dragon and twice as mean. He killed three soldiers and incapacitated another one right in front of me in the time it takes a regular man to take a breath." Conaf said.

The other man just shook his head in wonder. "I believe it. I don't think the people in this city will ever forget him killing the Titans. I'll bet old Drake busted an artery when Kronos died. I sure don't envy the man when the king gets a hold of him, you know what I mean?"

Conaf shrugged his shoulders noncommittally.

"Well, I'd better go get him; you keep your eyes open, okay?" the rebel said in parting and then slipped back into the maze of buildings.

A group of shadows broke off from the darkness and followed him.

*

Conaf paused at the door of the blacksmith shop. Looking around, he tried to put his finger on what had stopped him. Something was different from when he had left the small building. Finally, he shook his head and eased the door open, stepped inside, and crouched down as he had before.

"Artair," Conaf hissed into the dark interior of the small shop. There was no answer.

"Come on, buddy, it's time to go," he said, his voice a little louder this time. Still there was no answer. Conaf stood slowly, his eyes straining at the darkness.

Suddenly, the door was thrown open behind him and a rush of bodies burst through it into the room, their feet making small splashing sounds. Asael was the first one in, and shoved Conaf out of the way, his back crashing against the wall. The ten men with the scarred soldier crowded their way into the blacksmith shop and spread out, swords up, searching.

"You idiots, you were supposed to wait for my signal." Conaf protested.

The leader of the party didn't bother to turn around as he replied. "It doesn't matter now, he's hiding somewhere in here and there's no way out."

Asael jumped forward as the clang of metal on metal echoed in the room. Following it was a grunt of surprise and pain. In the darkness one of the soldiers had attacked Artair's shirt, which had been stretched out on an anvil at the back of the room. Without sufficient light it looked like a man crouching. The brute tore the shirt off the anvil and looked at it curiously.

The entire group swung around as light flooded the room. Standing in the doorway was Artair, a lamp taken from the street in his right hand. His left rested on a spike that had been driven into the front of the door.

"Asael, does it hurt to be wrong all of the time?" The Helvetian's taunted as he stepped out and pulled the door shut behind him.

The men inside rushed for him but Artair was a step faster, looping a chain over the spike in the door and then hooking it over another spike he had hammered into the doorframe, securing the entrance shut. The hunters had been caught in their own trap.

Conaf pounded on the door from the inside. "Artair, come on, at least let me out. If you leave me here they'll execute me. We're on the same side!"

On the other side of the door the Sword Bearer shook his head. He could hear the men pulling on the shutters that covered the windows. In no time they would cut their way through.

"Wrong, Conaf. You're on nobody's side but your own. By the way, you might want to tell those men to get away from the windows; it's going to get pretty hot in a second," Artair said, and began unscrewing the top off the lamp in his hands.

Inside the shop, Conaf suddenly realized what had seemed different to him when he had approached the door. It was too dark outside. The lamps on the street were missing. Behind him, Asael shifted his feet, producing the same wet sound that they had been hearing all along. The turncoat looked down and then jumped back, pushing the scarred soldier out of the way.

A half-second later Artair lowered the flame in the lamp to the puddle of oil outside the entrance. Fire shot up both sides of the door and raced into the room on the oil Artair had poured on the floor. Moments later the two windows burst into flame in similar fashion as the Helvetian circled the building. Finally, he re-secured the top on the lamp and threw it onto the roof. The lamp broke on impact, sending out a blanket of flames on the top of the building.

Artair turned and disappeared into the shadows as the flickering light of the fire reflected off the neighboring buildings.

*

At the gate, the large man who had spoken to Conaf noticed the fire lighting up the sky at the same time he heard the alarm bells start to ring. Torn between his duty to watch over the gate and his desire to see if the fire endangered his friend, the guard took several hesitant steps toward the glow in the sky and then turned to look at the gate.

Heaving a heavy sigh he relaxed his body and walked back to his post. After a couple of steps, he turned his head back to look again toward the fire.

As his head turned, his eyes crossed to look at a sword point placed between them. The man holding the sword could have been no other than the barbarian. Bare-chested, with cuts all over his body, the big man with the double blades was unmistakable. The gatekeeper held stock-still and tried to breathe evenly, the sword at his waist forgotten.

"Now listen very carefully, and everything will be fine. Can you understand what I am saying to you?" Artair spoke slowly and deliberately and moved the sword slightly away from the man's face to allow him a little bit of movement.

The gatekeeper shook his head, panic showing in his eyes. Artair sighed and then reached forward to unhook the Cyrenian's sword belt from his waist. The weapon fell into the dirt as Artair lowered his blade. Gesturing, the Helvetian indicated that he wanted him to open the gate. The man glanced only momentarily at the blade before moving toward the middle of the exit, and heaved for a few seconds at the great beam that held the huge doors closed. As it fell to the ground he pushed the gate open a few feet and then turned around.

As he turned, he was shocked to see that Artair was no longer there. General Artimus stood where he had been, a severe look on his face and the infamous thin-bladed sword in his hand. The guard stood paralyzed in panic as he looked at the swordsman. Suddenly a group of soldiers appeared, running from the direction of the fire.

Artimus turned as they came and waved them toward the gate. "The barbarian has escaped, find him or do not dare return."

The large man jumped out of the way as the soldiers rushed past him. His eyes were still locked on the general. After a few seconds Artimus walked up to the terrified man. No longer able to meet his eyes, the man dropped his gaze to the ground.

"Speak to no one of this event and I will be silent about who it was that let the barbarian escape. Is that clear?"

The gatekeeper's head snapped up at the comment.

"But, sir, the barbarian hasn't escaped, I had only barely opened the gate when…" The gatekeeper's stammering was interrupted as Artimus grabbed him by the front of his shirt and shook him violently.

"I will have no more of your insubordination! You will speak of this to no one. If you do I will personally inform the king of your incompetence. Is that clear?" Artimus spoke each word separately with a force that made the gatekeeper wince at each pronouncement.

The man stuttered his agreement and the general released him.

"Go back to your watch, and do not allow yourself into my sight again. Leave this gate unlocked for when those soldiers return with the savage."

The big guard nodded and hurried off, his eyes on the ground. Artimus stood for a few seconds and then turned and disappeared into the shadows.

A full minute later a bare-chested figure slid from the shadows and slipped through the gate into the night. Behind him the sky was still glowing as flames rose from the remains of a blacksmith shop.

*

Luckily for the men inside the burning building, an entire detachment of the king's troops had been sent as backup for Artair's capture. Asael's haste cost him his eyebrows and some of his hair, but the door was broken down fast enough to save the men from a fiery death.

As the soldiers lay choking and coughing in the light of the burning structure behind them, a lone man appeared from the darkness and stopped in front of Conaf's charred figure. The turn-coat soon noticed the general standing near him and looked up into Artimus's face.

"What happened here, Asael?" he asked without taking his eyes from the escaped prisoner at his feet.

"This scoundrel told us he knew where Artair was, but then he…" Asael was half way to his feet when his words were cut off as Artimus buried the toe of his boot in the bigger man's midsection. Collapsing with a dull grunt, he stayed down.

Artimus turned back to look at Conaf, who had finally stopped coughing. "Now that you know my attitude toward lies, how about if you try and tell me what happened here?" the General said, his voice icy.

Conaf swallowed hard. "I was captured earlier today. The king said he would grant me my freedom if I led these men to the barbarian. It would have worked except that these fools rushed in before I could find out if he had remained where I left him. Asael gave the order, sir," the turncoat said, and then lapsed into a barely hopeful silence.

"So, you led the barbarian into a trap, he escaped, and some of the king's soldiers were injured. Does that sound about right?" Artimus asked.

Conaf thought for a moment before answering in the affirmative.

"Asael, do you agree with this traitor?" he asked, turning to the soldier as he stood.

Still gasping for breath, the scarred man simply nodded.

Selecting a soldier from the men who stood watching the fire, Artimus shoved him toward Conaf. "Take this rebel to the king. Tell him he was responsible for the barbarian's escape." he commanded.

In the end, it took three men to haul the struggling traitor toward the palace. The king's treatment of those who failed him was worse, by far, than death.

Turning back to Asael, he said, "You. Take some men and go after that barbarian. I don't care if you have to follow him all the way across the mountains. Find him, and bring him back, or the king will have your head. Is that clear?"

Asael nodded meekly at the order and then, after gathering some men together, headed toward the nearby gate.

For a few minutes, the general stood and watched the building burn, and then he disappeared again into the darkness.

Chapter 34

The Bleeding Tooth rose into the twilight sky like a dagger, piercing the black expanse. Calum stood at the base and looked up at the solid-rock pinnacle. They had arrived an hour before twilight fell and made camp. His men sat quietly around the fire, sharpening weapons and staring into the flames.

Much had changed with Calum's discovery. The last they heard the dragons were dying in droves as the larger groups split into smaller killing squads. Since that day only one man had died in battle, and his death was due to an ambush.

The war against the dragons was all but won, and yet there was no rejoicing in Calum's camp. On their minds weighed the possibility that they had been victorious over the dragons only to find a greater foe coming for them; one they were not at all prepared to meet.

Deciding to plan for the worst, Calum had sent another of his men back to Greenock with instructions that were to be delivered to Seumas, and then to be passed on to every village leader. He was suggesting that all militia units be activated and that each should begin drilling for a possible battle.

Calum's thoughts were interrupted by a footfall behind him and he turned to face Ragnal, who had come out from the campfire.

"It sure is a pretty evening, isn't it?" he asked lightly.

Calum simply nodded and turned to look back up at the peak.

"You know, we've all heard about this place since we were kids," the team leader mused. "As well as stories of those first explorers who awakened the dragons."

"I've fought these animals since I was thirteen. Most of my memories revolve around them. My only dream for the last fifteen years has been to see them fall, and now that dream is being realized. They're doomed. The war is over." Calum paused a moment.

"But another one could be starting; a far worse one. Do you think the men are up to it?" he asked and turned to look at his second-in-command.

"Oh, you know them," Ragnal answered, shrugging his shoulders, "the younger men are excited for the adventure. The older ones are more apprehensive. What's your plan for tomorrow?" he asked back.

Calum turned to look at the mountain. "We'll head into the caves early and follow the map until we hit the first place where there are guards. Then we'll see what they have to say. With any luck, they'll be just as nervous about meeting us as we are about meeting them. If we're unlucky, they'll attack us and we'll have to kill them before they can alert the other guard stations further on."

His matter-of-fact statement caught Ragnal off-guard. "You've thought this out pretty well, haven't you?" he asked.

Calum didn't move or respond for several seconds. When he finally spoke his voice was low.

"If those people sent the dragons against us, and have been coming into our lands to kidnap our people, then they will know exactly how strong we are, and where our weaknesses lie. If they plan to invade us, we need to know. If they were thinking about attacking us, I plan to make them think twice about it. If they want war we will have no choice but to give it to them."

234

Calum turned to look Ragnal in the eye. "I don't want to have to kill anyone, either, but neither did I want to raise my little sister since I was thirteen, while fighting dragons. I didn't want to lose my best friend right when we needed him the most. I don't want a lot of things, but I know that I'm going to have to do my best with what life hands me."

"Right now, we have the choice of either doing nothing with the vain hope that these people will just leave us alone, or we can find out what they have in mind. Then, if needed, we will have to fight the battles that need to be fought to keep our nation safe." Calum turned back and resumed his study of the peak in front of him.

"Tell the others that we'll leave an hour before sun-up." The lead Sword Bearer said.

Ragnal nodded and walked back to the fire in silence.

Only the sentries were still awake when Calum returned to camp and fell asleep, praying that the dreams would stay away for the night.

*

The team arrived at the cave in the predawn light. Footprints of men and dragons were plainly seen on the dirt floor of the opening. Calum paused only momentarily to look back at the men who followed him. All held their weapons in hand, swords were bare and arrows placed at bowstrings. Beside himself, every fifth man held a torch, lit from the morning fire, and spares had been prepared.

The Sword Bearer nodded to his friends and then smiled and headed into the darkness of the cave. He moved cautiously but quickly through the dark bowels of the mountain. In the days of traveling he had memorized the map Iain had left him, and so it remained in the pouch at his waist.

He paused momentarily when he saw the approaching light that marked the first guard station. All of his men knew the plan, and there was no need to go over it again. To do so would only give away the fact that he was nervous about what might happen.

Calum slowed his walk as he approached the doorway and then stepped through and took several quick steps straight into the middle of the cavern that opened up in front of him. The rest of his men waited out of sight on each side of the doorway, archers first, then Sword Bearers and lancers. Calum held his torch in his left hand although it was no longer needed. His right hand hung at his side, itching to draw the sword he had left in its scabbard.

He was amazed at the size of the cavern in which he stood. His eyes flicked over the crude structures and stopped on a thin, narrow-faced man who stood staring at him from twenty yards away. The man seemed undecided about whether or not to yell for help or pinch himself to make sure he was awake, when the Helvetian spoke.

"Hello, my name is Calum. What is yours?" His voice was steady, but he had to force it to be so.

The words seemed to strike the smaller man and he jumped.

"Don't be scared, I'm not here to fight. I am a messenger from Helveti. Who are you?" he asked again as adrenaline pumped through his veins.

The small man was silent for another half second and then turned his head toward the structures up against the wall and began to yell in a language Calum didn't understand. At the same time he pulled a short sword from a sheath at his hip and pointed it at the intruder. The Sword Bearer heard movement inside the dwellings as men jumped to their feet and grabbed for weapons.

"No, no, no, settle down, I'm not here to cause trouble. I'm from the nation on the other side of the mountains. I come in peace. Look, I'm alone and I haven't even drawn my sword. Come on, man, don't be

236

a fool." Calum yelled as men poured out of the rough structures and ran toward him.

"Don't do this, don't make us do this." he yelled again as he backed away from the charging soldiers.

His words unheeded, Calum threw the torch at the men running at him and drew his sword. Arrows sliced through the front of the attacking group as his archers fired from the doorway. Three men fell screaming, and the rest turned to see the second volley of arrows fly through the air, accompanied by a stream of warriors that poured out of the door and crashed into their surprised ranks. Steel flashed in the dim light and screams accentuated the bitter struggle.

The last five Helvetians to leave the doorway ran straight for the mouth of the tunnel that led deeper into the mountain. Calum charged forward and barreled into the stranger closest to him, slapping the soldier's sword down as he came, and shoved him into the middle of his comrades, knocking several of them off their feet.

Calum crossed blades with another man, knocking his sword down and then dropping to the floor as he swung again. He thrust from the floor, shoving his sword up into his opponent's stomach and chest. Tearing the blade free, he parried a lance thrust and kicked another attacker in the stomach. The kick drove all breath from the man and he stepped back from Calum only to be struck in the side by an arrow. Another shaft hit him in the back as he fell and the Sword Bearer leapt over his body to stab a guard who was about to finish off a disarmed member of the Helvetian team. His blade stopped the attack and the wounded man screamed as he fell.

Only seven of the soldiers were still standing when Calum looked around, and as he looked another fell. The remaining six broke and ran almost in unison, heading for the mouth of the tunnel and the five men who waited there. His eyes slid to the archers who had moved out of the doorway and now stood in a line.

In unison, the five men loosed their arrows and the Sword Bearer glimpsed the darting shafts as they left the strings. Before he could turn his head to see, Calum heard the arrows strike. Five of the six men were down, and the last was still running, the rest of the Helvetian men following him. One of the warriors standing in the soldier's way yelled for him to surrender, but the stranger would have none of it. Calum looked away and returned his sword to its sheath as steel clashed and the last enemy died.

The Sword Bearer counted the bodies on the ground. Of the nineteen men who had attacked him, only one was still alive, and he would be dead soon. Calum shook his head. They were used to fighting armored dragons. These men had no armor and died far too easily.

His men grouped around him and the team leader looked them over. Amazingly, they had lost no one. Only a couple had visible wounds. The element of surprise and the men's Helvetian armor had saved them from serious damage.

"Ragnal, take two men and search those houses. I only count nineteen bodies, and I wouldn't be surprised if number twenty is still around somewhere. Bring back any rations, weapons, or anything else that might be of interest.

"The rest of you help me check these men. If they're alive, we want them to stay that way. If not, I want their pockets emptied, their weapons taken, and everything piled right over there." Calum indicated an area by the entrance to the cavern.

Turning, he could see the five men who were positioned at the mouth of the tunnel. They had stayed in place, as per orders, and were now facing into the darkness that descended deeper into the mountain.

*

The searching and the stockpiling of the dead men's possessions took only a few minutes. It soon became apparent that

Calum had been wrong about the twentieth man; they were alone in the cavern.

His previous evaluation had been correct concerning the surviving soldier, however, the man died only a few minutes after the fight ended. Calum tried to stop, or even slow, the bleeding from a wound in the man's chest, but in the end he was unsuccessful.

As soon as everything useful had been taken from them, the dead bodies were taken into a small cave that branched off of the cavern. Ragnal and his associates had found it as they looked around, and decided that since the soldiers had used it as a trash dump, it would be a suitable resting place for the soldiers themselves.

As soon as that uncomfortable chore was completed, all useful materials were cached in one of the crude structures. Once done, Calum gathered his companions around him at the mouth of the tunnel where the five men had been keeping watch.

"All right," Calum said as he looked around at them, "there's no stopping now. We have to assume that the people ahead of us know that we are here. So we do it again, the same way, at the next stop; except this time give the archers time to fire three volleys before the rest of you attack. Let's lessen our casualties as much as possible. If you're wounded, keep toward the back and watch our flank. If they want to talk, we'll talk, but plan on them not wanting to."

"Remember the people who are counting on us. Let's go." The head Sword Bearer punctuated his statement by heading down the tunnel at a quick walk, a torch in his left hand.

As they went, two men placed captured weapons in places where they could be used in case of a retreat.

The flickering light of the torches played in the faces of the warriors, now hardened with resolve.

Chapter 35

Artair winced as he pulled the poultice away from his chest. Luckily, the cuts made from the dragon's claws were beginning to heal. He would wear scars for the rest of his life to remind him of the arena, but at least he would survive it in the end. The Sword Bearer held his breath as he tied the last poultice in place with a strip of cloth and eased his shirt back down over his wounds.

He had stolen some clothes from a small farm a few miles from Cyrene, and he was glad to have found them.

The land he was in was amazingly similar to where he had grown up. Were it not so, he would not have been able to find the plants he needed to make the healing concoction that was now attached to his chest.

The swordsman looked around as he stood and swung his twin blades into place. The Cyrenians were still looking for him, and he had to hide from columns of soldiers every few hours, but he figured he was only half a day's journey from the tunnels now, and if he could only slip past them he could find his way home. Artair smiled at the thought. He couldn't wait to see Calum's face when he walked up. The smile stayed for a couple more minutes as he moved through the woods, headed west parallel to the path they had taken as they had come to Cyrene.

The sun had climbed to its peak when Artair saw the soldiers coming. He dropped to his stomach in the tall grass and cursed silently at his bad luck. The trees had been thinning out for several miles, and he had decided to head across the path to the other side where there was more cover. When he saw the soldiers coming he was only a few yards from the trail they were using. Now he had no other recourse than to hold still and hope they didn't see him.

Artair kept his eyes on the ground at the soldiers' feet as they passed. There were twenty of them, and Asael was leading them. He'd recognize that man's walk wherever he saw it. The column had almost passed by, and the hidden warrior felt a rush of relief, when the last man in line stopped suddenly and turned toward him.

He held still and watched the man's feet for a split second before his eyes moved to the soldier's face. The man was taking a drink from a water canister, his eyes closed as he enjoyed the rush of cold liquid down his dry throat. When his eyes opened he was looking right into Artair's face. Barely ten feet separated them, while more than twenty feet separated the careless soldier from his comrades.

Neither man moved as they stared at each other. The Sword Bearer locked the other man's gaze and waited for his chance. It came as the soldier turned his head to look in desperation toward his comrades who had marched on, now fifteen yards away. When he looked back the barbarian was gone.

The man immediately yelled and ran toward the rest of the column. Artair crawled frantically through the grass as the soldiers charged his last position. Soon he could hear them coming behind him as he jumped and ran for the cover of the forest. As he neared the trees he could feel them coming on as a crossbow bolt slammed into a tree trunk ahead of him.

When he entered the trees he cut left, heading deeper into the forest and away from his pursuers. He had no more than a fifteen-yard lead on the soldiers behind him, but that was enough to give him an advantage.

Suddenly, Artair broke out of the trees and entered another clearing. On the other side he could see the mountains, and the entrance to the tunnels.

He tossed a glance over his shoulder as he ran, and then threw himself to the ground as the man closest behind him fired his crossbow. As the bolt sailed over him the Sword Bearer exploded from the ground, his sword coming free of its scabbard. The crossbowman put another bolt into his weapon just as the Helvetian's blade sliced it in half. The soldier looked up in surprise and shock as the escaped prisoner took off again, his legs pumping as he sprinted for the entrance to the tunnels.

His mind raced as he ran. He knew there were guards inside the cave. If he were caught between them and the soldiers behind him it would be all over, but his mind couldn't conceive of any other option.

Artair glanced over his shoulder when he had closed the distance between himself and the tunnels to a mere fifty yards. The soldiers were gaining on him, with Asael in the lead. Looking forward he could see men standing inside the mouth of the cave.

Reaching up, he pulled his other sword out of its sheath and slowed to a stop. Turning around, he held his weapons at ready as Asael and the rest of the soldiers stopped as well, the tall grass hugging their legs.

"It's all over, Artair. I'm supposed to take you back to the king alive, but I don't think he'll be too disappointed if I just bring him your body. That's up to you, but you can't take all of us," Asael growled between heavy breaths. The big man was missing his eyebrows and most of his hair had been burned off.

Artair looked at the soldiers who stood facing him, swords in hand, and weighed his options. He didn't have many. Wounded and weary, he knew that he could not expect his body to give him the speed he would need to take on multiple enemies. Neither did he have the strength to run any farther.

"Remember the last time we fought, Asael? Artimus isn't here now to save all of you this time." Artair watched the other man's eyes narrow at the statement, and then flick to something beyond him.

The original Sword Bearer grinned as a familiar voice filled the clearing. "No, Artair, I think he's right, it is over," Calum said with a hard smile.

The scarred Cyrenian stared at the new arrival. Confusion was obvious on his face.

"Asael, get out of here," Artair warned. "If you try to take me now you'll all die here today. Go back and tell Drake that you never saw me. I'm sure none of your men will dispute it, since that would get them killed. Go home. Give it up, you can't win this fight," he insisted.

He could see Asael's breathing elevate as the big man took several quick breaths, and then open his mouth to yell a command to his men. On his order all twenty of them rushed forward and Calum pulled Artair backwards. Arrows appeared at the chests of several of the attackers as archers rose from the tall grass.

Helvetians slid out of the brush between Artair and the Cyrenians and engaged the charging soldiers, pulling them down to the ground. Calum let go of his friend and the two joined their countrymen as they attacked the remaining Cyrenians.

Artair used Moray's sword to slice through the first man to come at him and then he closed with Asael. The scarred man pulled a dagger from his waist and held it in the hand opposite his sword. Artair slapped away the first thrust and then darted in and slid to the ground beside Asael's feet, evading a sweeping slash and knocking the dagger away with his sword blade. The Sword Bearer kicked up with his right leg, connecting with the big man's hip and lifting him half off the ground. Artair's blade followed his kick, stabbing up into Asael's body.

Jerking the weapon free, Artair rolled away from him as he fell. Standing slowly, he looked down at the Cyrenian as he clutched the wound in his side. The rest of the soldiers were already down and Calum was standing nearby, his bloody sword held at his side.

"Asael, I tried to warn you. You see, I am crazy enough to try and take on all of you at once, but Calum would never come over here unless he had brought some men with him."

As the Helvetian watched, the man's eyes close slowly and then his entire body relaxed.

Artair turned to look at his friend.

"Wow, Artair, you look terrible."

The weary dragon fighter just grinned wearily. "It's good to see you too. Just when I thought the situation couldn't get any worse you had to show up and prove that anything is possible. Do you get uglier every day or is it just me?" the battered Sword Bearer asked in mock seriousness.

Calum laughed and the two clasped hands. The team leader glanced around at the group of men surrounding them.

"Is everybody all right?" he asked.

Each of the men nodded in turn.

"Those boys were so surprised I think most of them died from heart failure." Ragnal quipped with a smile.

Artair looked around at the men with undisguised curiosity on his face. "Who's guarding Greenock right now if you are here, Calum?" Artair asked with concern. "How did you guys find your way through the tunnels? Not that I'm not glad to see all of you, but this is kind of confusing."

Calum just nodded understandingly and placed one hand on his friend's shoulder. "Wait until we take care of these soldiers and get back to the caves, and then we'll sit down and have a good long talk. From the look of you I'll bet you'll have plenty to tell us also," he said.

Artair nodded in agreement and then helped his countrymen search their fallen enemies and hide the bodies.

*

Half an hour later, Artair sat back and whistled through his teeth in wonder as Calum finished telling him about Iain, the command phrase, and their journey through the tunnels.

"So, the dragons are out of the picture? That is unbelievable," Artair said, and then laughed with sheer relief and wonder.

The rest of the men laughed with him.

"So, how long did it take you to get through the tunnels?" he asked.

"Oh, it took us about a day," Calum answered. "We caught the last group of guards sleeping last night as we came out. Since then we've been waiting for one of those patrols to come close enough for us to try and talk to them. When one finally came, though, we had to kill them to save your sorry carcass." Calum said sarcastically.

"Well, Artair, it's your turn, tell us how you got yourself drug all the way over here and then ended up beat up, uglier than ever, and running from the local army."

The escaped prisoner thought for a moment and cleared his throat before speaking.

For several minutes the Helvetians listened with rapt attention as Artair told them of his capture, his experiences in the arena, and his escape. When he was done, he leaned back against the cold stone of the tunnel and smiled wearily at his friends. "Pretty much a normal type of time for a Sword Bearer, you know, fight dragons, get out of tight pinches, struggle to survive, all the things we do every day, right guys?" Artair asked and then chuckled at the incredulous looks the men gave him.

"Sure, Artair, just standard stuff," Calum agreed with a smile. "Hey, in all your running around in there, did you ever find out what their plans are with us? I mean, none of the groups we met up with in the tunnels really wanted to talk, so we are all still wondering about these people's true intentions. Now that you're here, though, I suspect you can enlighten us on that matter," Calum said hopefully.

Artair nodded at the same time the smile slipped off his face. "Fortunately, I do know what they are planning. Unfortunately, it's not anything good. They're planning an invasion, the plans are already being carried out."

Artair's statement did not incite much of a response. Most of the men there had already guessed that much.

"When?" Ragnal asked.

Artair shrugged his shoulders. "As soon as a couple of weeks, as late as a few months. I don't know exactly," he answered.

"How many?" Calum asked. He had been drawing in the dirt with one hand, but raised his head as he asked the question.

"All I know is thousands, and they'll be led by the man who put this scar on my chin," Artair said, touching the mark on his skin.

His friend nodded and dropped his eyes again to the dirt.

"There's more. At the head of that army a hundred men will be riding dragons trained as war animals."

A couple of the men in the group gasped, and Calum looked up at Artair sharply. He nodded to signify that he was not joking, and then stood up.

"All right, listen up. A lot has happened in the past month, in fact, our entire world has changed. But there's a lot more we need to do. Tomorrow, at daybreak, I'm headed back to their city. I know where they keep the dragons and I'm going to get rid of them. You all know as well as I that no army of ours could stand up to the charge of a hundred of those armored reptiles."

246

"After that I'm going to do everything I can to hurt them, slow them down, and generally dampen their enthusiasm for this invasion. We have to give Calum enough time to gather an army."

The Sword Bearer looked up at the other man as his name was mentioned but then lowered his gaze again to the cave floor. It went unsaid that, of all the men there, Calum was the one best suited to begin the preparations in Helveti.

"As soon as we've done all we can in Cyrene we'll head back through these tunnels and head for home. If no one meets us as we come out of the tunnels to tell us that an army is ready, we'll do all we can to slow their army as it comes through."

"I say 'we' because I know that some of you will be willing to come with me, but know that not too many of us will be coming back. These guys are good, and their general is as sharp as they come. Some of us will not come back, but we'll do our part and we'll win in the end." Artair said with conviction.

"Those who don't want to continue on will go back and help Calum." he concluded.

"All right, who's coming with me?" he said and looked around expectantly.

Nobody moved for a second and then Ragnal raised his hand. One after another the rest of the men followed his example until twenty-five men had volunteered. The first Sword Bearer nodded as he looked around at them.

"Thank you. We leave at daybreak tomorrow." Artair paused. "Calum, let's take a walk, I need to talk to you."

The team leader stood and followed Artair as he walked out of the cave and into the sunlight. As they left, the men behind them all started talking at once.

Chapter 36

The two friends walked in silence for a few moments before Artair cleared his throat to speak.

"There's more about this whole situation than what I told in there, but a lot of it shouldn't be known by too many people," Artair said, glancing at his friend out of the corner of his eye.

Calum grunted. "Yeah, I figured as much. How did you get that scar on your chin?" he asked, gesturing toward it with his hand.

"When I fought them the second time I almost got away. Artimus, the general I spoke of, stopped me and we fought it out one-on-one. We were pretty even for a long time, but then another one of his men jumped in and the two of them beat me."

"He's a strange one, and I have to admit that I can't figure him out. He's the top general for the king of their nation, and that man is as evil as the devil himself. Yet the general had to be the one who gave that map to that fellow Iain. What's more, Artimus told me that he had killed him. He didn't even want me to know that he was helping us. He does things like that a lot."

"Sometimes I feel like he's a friend, but I find that I always feel like that right before he does something to prove that he is an enemy. Whatever he is, he's dangerous, and we'll have to be careful."

"These people do not think of us as equals; they think we're barbarians. Let's use that to its full advantage," Artair said.

Calum nodded in agreement. "Artair, I'd never ask you this in front of the men, and if I did I wouldn't expect a complete answer, but how much chance do we have here? I mean, they've been preparing for this for a long time and we're going to be scrambling to get it together before they're on top of us, so how much chance do we have?" he asked.

Artair walked in silence for a few seconds before answering. "If they come through those tunnels riding dragons we will have no chance at all. The monsters would break through our lines and wreak havoc while their army wiped us out. Without them, and if we succeed in dampening their spirits before they get to our army, we have a chance."

"I think that in the end it will come down to how much we want to win. Our people will be fighting for their families and homes, but they're going to have to believe they can actually save them. We'll see," Artair concluded.

"You know, I knew that I was going to be headed back to Greenock, and that I wasn't going to stay here with you. Don't think that I don't want to stay, but we both know I can be of more use back in Helveti. Still, I'd stay and fight with you if the situation were different. Good luck over here," Calum said.

His friend thanked him and the two walked on for a moment in silence.

"Have you had the dreams lately?" Artair asked finally.

The other man shook his head. "No, I haven't had any since we started using those words on the dragons," Calum answered.

The weary Sword Bearer smiled suddenly at a thought. "You know, if the dragons are no longer a problem, and if we win this war somehow, we might even get to relax and be regular people for once." he said with a chuckle.

Calum tossed a glance at him and then snorted.

"Yeah, right, Artair, no one in their right mind will ever be justified in calling you a regular person, not even if you were to finally put those swords away. If it's not this challenge, it will be another one, but you'll keep yourself busy," Calum said with a chuckle.

*

The following morning Artair bade farewell to Calum and those who went with him. It was with an uneasy feeling that he watched his friend disappear into the darkness of the tunnels. Their entire lives they had fought the battles life had thrown at them together, but now the battles that had to be fought required their separation. Calum was the better leader, and Artair had a knowledge of the enemy city, but they shared a common love for the people who looked to them for protection.

Both unmarried, many back in Greenock wondered how long it would be before they tired of fighting and settled down. What they didn't understand was that they would never be able to leave the war un-won--they were simply incapable of it. Both had lost their childhoods, their families, and many of their friends to the dragons, and it seemed as if they fought to recover all they had lost.

Now the war had taken on a larger scope and a greater urgency. It would take all they had to survive it.

Artair's thoughts were interrupted as Ragnal cleared his throat. He turned his head to look at the warrior and realized that the rest of the men were also watching him, an expectant look on their faces. Artair looked back coolly for a moment before speaking.

"Ragnal, thank you for volunteering. Take one man and go pull a uniform that will fit me off one of those soldiers we killed yesterday. The rest of you gather up any money those soldiers had on them and put it all in a bag, we need to get some new clothes."

The men looked at him strangely, but headed off to complete his instructions. Artair followed them after only a moment's hesitation.

If they hurried, they could be to Cyrene in a day and a half, and then he could begin to fulfill the promises he had made in the arena.

Chapter 37

The Sword Bearer camp at the base of the Bleeding Tooth boiled with activity as the warriors prepared for the evening meal and then to retire for the night. The earliest of the parties had begun arriving the previous morning, while other groups had been trickling in since then.

As soon as they realized how easy the dragons were to destroy with the code Calum had passed on, the groups had broken up, until sometimes a single man would comprise the entire killing squad. They had stopped counting the number of the armored reptiles that had been killed since Calum's message had arrived, but it must have been hundreds.

If it hadn't been for the news of a passage through the mountains that had come along with the command phrase, there would undoubtedly have been a great celebration under way. As it was, the camp was tense with apprehension and uncertainty. The dragons were no longer a problem, a concept still unreal to many, but the fear of yet another previously unknown enemy kept the exultation to a minimum.

Twenty men stood at watch, most of them facing the Bleeding Tooth. They had already found the cave at the base a few hundred yards away, and everyone in the camp glanced in its direction on a regular basis.

If Calum and his team did return, they would come through that cave. However, if they failed, the only things that would be coming through those tunnels would be dragons and kidnappers. The thought of a possible attack was enough to keep every man on edge.

It was to this audience that Calum shouted greetings from the approaching twilight.

"Comrades, what's for dinner?" he yelled. Immediately there were weapons in the hands of all that heard his voice, and in a half-second's time the rest of the men followed suit. It was not until several moments after that they recognized Calum and his men that the weapons were laid aside.

The head Sword Bearer insisted on eating before he would speak of what they had learned inside the cave, and so the entire camp crowded around him and the warriors who had come back with him.

They ate quickly, and then Calum stood to address the crowd, wiping his hands on the front of his pant legs.

"Well, I'll start with the good news. We found Artair on the other side of these tunnels." Calum kept talking over the murmurs of surprise that rose from the men around him.

"He had escaped from the kidnappers and had nearly made his way back to the caves when we met up with him. Twenty-five of the men who were with us went with him. He is well, though a little worse for wear, and he was able to find out a lot about what those people have planned."

"That brings me to the bad news. For over twenty years we have lived without fear of battle with other men, but the time for war is here again. Artair and those with him have gone to try to delay and weaken their forces, but we have to deal with the possibility that they might not be able to," Calum said as murmurs rippled through the crowd.

"So we should expect that, in as little as a month, there will be a trained army coming out of that cave that will number in the thousands. That is the situation we are in, and now it is time to talk about what we are going to do about it. Any man here who wants to attempt surrender will please see me later tonight and I will give him directions on how to get through the tunnels. Once on the other side he can try and negotiate with the people he will meet over there!" There was a round of snorted laughter at the ridiculous thought.

"The bitter fact is that, of the several groups we met up with in the tunnels and on the other side, not one of them even attempted to communicate with us. They attacked without a word and we can expect nothing different from the people who will be leading their army."

"We will break camp immediately. Thirty men will return to the caves and wait in one of their way-stations with the sole purpose of keeping the tunnels clear for when Artair and those with him come back through. If you are overpowered, retreat and fight them as well as you can if they follow you out of this side of the cave. Five more men will remain here to redirect the rest of the Sword Bearer teams that will continue to meet here."

"As we break camp I will select one man from each village or city to act as an ambassador. Those men will return immediately to their homes to deliver the messages I will give them."

"We are now at war, my friends, and our people will be counting on us once again. Do not fail them and do not fail me." He concluded.

There was feverish intensity in the air as tents were taken down and packed away, weapons were checked, and black-garbed men began to disappear into the night like shadows in the light of dawn. Half an hour after their leader had finished his speech all that was left of the camp were a few fires tended by the five warriors selected to remain at the site.

Calum ran alone in the night. He was the ambassador to Greenock and the thought of an army crashing into his unprotected home spurred his legs into action.

Chapter 38

Artair and his men crouched in the bushes outside the walls of Cyrene. Fifty yards to their right was the main gate of the city, the one by which Artair had entered when he had first reached the enemy city. Everything had already been discussed, so the only thing left to do was wait for the right time.

Luckily, all five archers had opted to come with the group headed to Cyrene, and they waited with arrows ready at their bowstrings.

All of the men wore plain peasant clothing on the outside, with black garments underneath. Artair wore the uniform taken from the dead soldier, with a plain cloak thrown over it. They had taken the civilian clothes from little settlements along the way, but they had left money taken from the dead soldiers to compensate the owners. The last thing they wanted to do was to give the people proof that they were savages. Part of their mission was to breed confusion and doubt in these people, and showing themselves to be fair, instead of brutal was one of the ways they planned to do so.

Finally, Artair nodded to himself and leaned over to the archers. The light was quickly failing, and the men on top of the walls could only barely be seen.

"Fire as soon as you decide on targets, but remember that we want noise and confusion more than casualties."

Turning to the rest of the men, he tapped a finger on his temple to show that it was beginning. A couple seconds later the archers' bows twanged and arrows flew.

*

Fifty yards away, on top of the wall, a guard stopped his pacing to peer into the darkness. He was sure he had seen movement out there, but he could not determine if it had been an animal or a man. No one had attacked Cyrene since King Drake came into power, but with the barbarian still at large, the soldiers were on edge.

The man grunted as something slammed into his side. Looking down, he saw the feathered shaft of an arrow protruding from the solid part of his hip. He had a moment to be amazed at how precise the bowman had had to be before the pain struck him. His mouth dropping open, he screamed in agony and collapsed to the stone, clutching the shaft where it protruded from his body.

Another guard farther down on the wall was already yelling for assistance and pulling at an arrow lodged in his shoulder. Immediately soldiers came running from other sections of the outer wall. As they came, four of them were swept from the parapets as if slapped by some invisible hand. Their bodies fell to the earth below, arrows sticking from their chests.

The sound of the guards hitting the ground struck the people standing nearby like a slap to the face. Women began to scream, and people near the walls broke and ran from the scene.

As one of the guards looked out over the barricade to try to find the hidden assailants, he was surprised to see what appeared to be torches in the bushes a short distance from the walls. A second later, Artair's archers released the flaming arrows. The burning projectiles flew over the surprised Cyrenian and smacked into the houses and shops directly inside the enclosure.

Alarm bells pealed from the bell tower and soon the sound could be heard throughout the city. At the signal, every soldier in the city jumped for his weapons. The alarm gave the guards on the tower confidence, and several stood to fire their crossbows into the night. The hastily fired bolts had no effect, but another two Cyrenians screamed in the twilight as arrows found them.

At that point Artimus ran from the cover of buildings and neared the outer wall.

"Stay down, you fools. If you stand up you skyline yourselves," Artimus yelled as another volley of fire arrows found their way into the wooden planks of a large building. The general grabbed the first bunch of soldiers to arrive and sent them to fight the fires that had begun to spread.

Yet another volley of flaming arrows sailed over the walls as Artimus looked over the soldiers that had assembled in the space between the walls and the houses, then yelled for the gates to be opened.

The huge doors creaked open and over a hundred soldiers roared out into the night in search of their enemies. As soon as they left the safety of their city arrows whistled through the night and sliced through their ranks. At the same time, a group of ten Helvetians jumped up and ran from the advancing force. The soldiers ran after them, swords bared and yelling into the night, away from the massive gates that had begun to close.

Before the opening could be shut off, another force of ten men materialized from the brush on the left and rushed in quickly, killing the gatekeeper and forcing their way into the city. Once there, they attacked the soldiers who had remained inside the walls with a ferocity that terrified the Cyrenians. Another volley of flaming arrows flew over the walls and lit several more roofs on fire, sending eerie shadows dancing amongst the fighting men.

258

The walls of Cyrene had been breached.

Breaking away after only a few seconds of fighting, the invaders, as if by command, retreated out the opening and into the now-complete darkness. A group of soldiers followed them, blinded by rage and driven by instinct. Artimus only succeeded in stopping some of them and ordering them to close the gate.

The great doors had almost swung closed when a wounded soldier returned, hobbling, through the opening. Blood seeped through his hands as he gripped the shaft of an arrow embedded in his thigh. The gates were swung shut and secured before anyone noticed that the archers outside had ceased their attack.

Inside the walls there was utter confusion as the cries of frightened women and children mingled with the screams of the wounded and the cursing of the men fighting the fires caused by the arrows. Soldiers poured into the area, adding to the chaos with the addition of more bodies. Over it all, Artimus's voice could be heard plainly, yelling orders to soldiers and civilians alike.

In a few minutes, order was restored and the wounded were cleared from the area. Several more patrols were sent to search the outside of the city and to watch for the return of the soldiers who had run after the attackers.

In all the confusion, no one noticed as a single soldier with a bloodstain on the leg of his pants ran back into the crush of buildings and disappeared.

Chapter 39

Artair ran amongst the buildings while trying to travel parallel to the walls. The crowded interior of the city made him worry that he would lose his way if he lost his bearings. When he passed the second gate he slowed down and began working his way closer to the barricade. At length he found and climbed a ladder that lead to the top of the parapets.

Once on the top, he walked up to the nearest guard, smiling. The unfortunate soldier didn't realize he was in danger until it was too late. Artair knocked him unconscious with the flat of his borrowed short sword and then tied and gagged him with a length of rope brought for the purpose. Two more guards fell the same way before the Sword Bearer whistled into the darkness. A similar whistle returned to him and he smiled.

Pulling his shirt up, Artair began unraveling a long length of rope from around his waist. The rope, like the civilian clothing, had been stolen from the Cyrenians along the way. After tying one end to the wall, he tossed the rope down to the ground. It only took a few more seconds before Ragnal gained the top of the wall. He tied off another length of rope and tossed it down to the men below. Before long, fifteen men crouched on the top of the wall and the ropes they had used were safely stashed away.

Artair swung his swords into place on his back and nodded his thanks to Ragnal. Whispering, he directed the men as they carried the unconscious guards to a nearby house. After assuring themselves that it was empty, the soldiers were dumped onto the floor and the door was jammed from the outside.

Without another word, Artair started off toward the middle of the city, his men following him in silence. As they went, each of the warriors pulled lamps down from the tops of the light poles and blew out the flame. The party had to hide several times, and twice they had to circle around an area that was too open or too lighted. Even so, it took less than half an hour until the men got their first look at the arena. For Artair it was an unwelcome memory, and he hardly glanced at the gargantuan structure as he passed it in the dark. The men with him couldn't hold back their gasps of surprise in the darkness at the gigantic structure and the realization of what it was.

In a short time the band had reached their destination. The original Sword Bearer pressed himself against the wall of the first of the dragon stables and gestured to Ragnal. When he had come near, Artair put his mouth close to the other's ear.

"Go on with the plan as we discussed. It must be fast. If someone cannot be knocked out and gagged they will have to be killed. We won't have another chance at this, so let's do it right," he whispered urgently.

The shorter man simply nodded and moved past him. Half of the warriors followed the stocky individual.

Artair waited for a moment to allow them to get out of the way before moving to the entrance of the stable he was hiding next to. The door creaked slightly as it opened, and then he was inside, moving with the fluidity of a large cat. His men followed, the smell of dragons filling their noses and adrenaline pumping through their veins.

The inside of the stable was filled with spacious stalls. The monstrous animals stirred at the intrusion and several of them roared.

Artair was amazed at the workmanship of the interior and the care taken to ensure the comfort of the dragons. The insides of the stalls were padded, and there was a nameplate placed on every door. It still revolted him to see how they treated the monsters, but he could understand to a certain extent if they truly were domesticated at one point. Despite this, the stalls were of solid construction, and the walls looked strong enough to hold the animals they contained. That would be important for their plan to succeed.

The small team swept through the stable like a dark wind. In the end, three keepers were carried out of the building unconscious. Only one knew that he was being attacked before it happened.

Artair left three of his men at the first location and moved to the last of the four buildings. Expecting to see something similar to the first stable, he was surprised when he opened the door. Instead of multiple stalls, there were only two. There were no dragons or people in sight and he almost left before he noticed a small structure in the corner of the building that looked like it might be a small guardhouse.

Signaling to his men to begin the preparations, Artair moved toward the small structure.

*

At the same time the Sword Bearer was nearing the small structure, a guard on the opposite side of the city grunted in surprise as an arrow sliced through his shoulder, and flaming projectiles lanced through the darkness. In a few moments bells again pealed through the night.

*

When Artair got to the guardhouse, he was surprised to see a lock on the outside of the door. He had half turned away when he heard the sound of movement inside. After a moment of indecision, he sliced the lock off with his sword and kicked the door in. He paused for half a second and then stepped into the structure.

In the next instant he had to duck as something flew at him from the darkness. The warrior swung as he stood, his sword sweeping the darkness as his free hand pulled his second weapon free. The blade met something metallic and was deflected as an object bounced off the swordsman's stomach. Confused and startled, Artair backed out of the door and waited for his attacker to step out of the enclosed space of the guardhouse.

His mouth dropped open as a feminine figure exploded from the dark interior, slapped his sword blade down, and planted an iron pot along the side of his head. He grunted and dropped one of his swords as pain mixed with shock at the unexpected attack. The woman threw the pot at him and then swept his fallen sword from the ground with a deftness that belied familiarity. The Helvetian was driven back as she attacked, the ancient blade dancing in her hands. Steel rang on steel for several seconds before Artair parried a particularly wide slash, stepped inside, and grabbed the woman's sword. Letting his other weapon drop, he threw his shoulder into the female stranger and tore the blade from her hand.

Artair's shove threw her back onto the ground, and she immediately began to get up, but stopped as her opponent placed the point of his sword against her chest. For a moment, the two simply stared at each other as both tried to slow their breathing. Blood dripped from a cut on the Sword Bearer's temple and he looked at the woman in amazement.

Although of above-average height, she was slim and attractive. There was fire in her green eyes, and though her dark hair was in disarray, there was no denying the fact that she was beautiful.

The entire encounter had taken less than thirty seconds, but Artair could almost feel precious seconds passing by.

"Can you understand me?" he asked, his voice low.

The fire in the woman's eyes was replaced with curiosity and she nodded.

"Okay, then understand this. In another minute we are going to burn this stable down. So, you can either let me gag you, and you can come quietly, or you can be knocked unconscious and left outside on your face. What will it be? If you don't decide quickly I will decide for you," he warned.

The woman looked at him for a second with defiance in her eyes and then stood slowly, allowing Artair time to move the sword point as she stood.

"If you're against King Drake you don't have to worry about me doing anything to get in the way. But if you must, you can gag me," she said. The woman's voice was cool and clear, showing no sign of emotional strain from the fight or the fact that the sword still threatened her chest.

The men at the door whistled to Artair and he stepped back from his female prisoner.

"All right, you can do whatever you want now, but I'd suggest you leave quickly," he said and then ran toward the door, picking his other sword up as he went.

The woman followed close on his heels.

As soon as they were outside, the three men each struck sparks into stacks of straw covered in lamp oil. Flames erupted as the trio ran for the door. Pulling it closed, they barred it shut and then struck sparks against the wall, sending fire shooting up the oil-soaked exterior.

As he looked around, he could see flames already licking through the roofs of the stables next to him. From where he was standing, he could hear the screams of dragons. The black-garbed forms of his men ran toward him as the doors of the other stables erupted in flames.

Artair turned and ran into the darkness, his comrades following him. After they had gone a short distance, Artair stopped and counted his countrymen. They were all there, and there did not appear to be any serious wounds among them.

As he turned to continue a hand grabbed his arm. Turning, he saw with irritation that it was the woman who had grabbed him.

"Take me with you," she said simply. She spoke Helvetian as well as he had heard from a Cyrenian except for the king himself.

The Sword Bearer gaped at her and then pulled his arm free from her grasp and headed into the darkness. His legs buckled and he fell to his knees as something rammed into him from behind. The Helvetian rose angrily and faced the woman who had kicked him, now surrounded by his men. Ragnal had a massive grin on his face, and the rest of the men were obviously holding back smiles of their own.

"If you think that I'm going to be a burden in a fight, you better check your head again, because it's still bleeding." The woman was taunting him.

Artair glared at her.

"Listen," she continued. "I've been a prisoner in that stable for a long time, so any love or loyalty I ever had for King Drake died long ago. Take me with you and let me help. I'm as good as any one of you, and better than some," she said, looking around at the men who surrounded her.

Artair shook his head in exasperation. This woman had the confidence of a queen. "It's your life, girl. If you want to lose it, that's your problem. I warn you, though, get in our way and you won't be conscious long enough to realize it. Let's go," Artair said to his men, and they ran on into the darkness of the unlit streets.

Behind them, the flames broke through the roof of the first stable and roared into the heavens.

Chapter 40

"Is everyone mad? Are you all insane?" King Drake screamed at the group of men assembled in his throne room.

They wisely remained silent. As soon as things had cooled down at the wall they had been summoned to report to their ruler.

"The barbarian escaped and then returned with an army in less than a week? It's inconceivable. An attack has been made on Cyrene, our soldiers have been wounded and killed, and yet you say that we didn't even find one of the attackers? Is that about right, General Artimus?" Drake demanded and glared at his head man.

"Sire, no army attacked Cyrene tonight. Only a handful of men came against us. Other than that, however, you are right. We did not kill any of them, neither could we catch them." Artimus replied coolly.

King Drake walked down the steps from his throne to stand in front of the speaker. "You say that there were only a handful of men attacking us tonight, while I have been getting reports for the last hour that it was a full army of barbarians. How do you explain that, General Artimus?" Drake questioned.

"The explanation is very simple, sire. You have been receiving reports from incompetents who have not seen enough battle to teach them to keep a cool head. At no time were more than five arrows fired over our walls. If they had had more archers than that they would have had no reason not to use them."

"Between ten and fifteen men came in at the gate, and no more than that could have run from our men who first went outside or else they would not have been able to disappear so easily. My estimation is that we were attacked by between twenty and forty individuals. I also dare to say that a fair number of them are probably inside the city itself at this moment." Artimus spoke matter-of-factly, but even the king seemed visibly shocked by the statement.

"Why do you believe that, General Artimus, and how could that have happened?" Drake questioned, his voice severe.

The rest of the men in the room waited anxiously for his answer.

"I do not know how it might have happened, but I know that an attack such as the one that just occurred would have no other purpose. In their second volley, their archers killed four guards from off the top of the wall in semi-darkness with nearly identical placement of arrows, and yet their first volley did nothing but wound our men. They did not have to settle for wounding the men like they did. They easily could have killed them, but instead they chose to wound them in ways that would allow them to scream, make noise, and call for help. It was all a diversion."

"Also, the fact that they have not attacked again in force would also suggest that they are occupied with something other than our walls." Artimus was interrupted as another set of alarm bells rang in the distance.

The men in the throne room waited the few seconds it required for a messenger to arrive at the door.

"Another attack, sire. This time on the north wall," the messenger said, with a slight note of fear in his voice.

Artimus turned back to look at King Drake and his eyes noted the bare sword in the ruler's hand.

"Stop them, General. I don't care how, but stop this immediately. Go." the king roared.

The rest of the men caught up to him as they reached the outer door. The general opened it and stepped out into the cool night air but then stopped suddenly.

A couple seconds earlier the flames had eaten through the roof of one of the dragon stables and now the light of the fire illuminated the sky above it. With all the attention being paid to the outer defenses, and the fact that the arena area had no houses in it, the fires had yet to be reported. Exclamations of disbelief came from all around him as the rest of the men crowded around him and stared. They all knew where the fire had to be coming from, and yet none of them wanted to believe it.

"He's killed the dragons. He did it." Artimus said to himself in wonder.

He felt the people around him shift and move away as King Drake himself stepped through the door to stand next to his head man. The general did not dare look at his sovereign, but he could feel the raw anger that seeped from the man. When the ruler finally spoke it was with a tone that sent chills up Artimus's spine.

"How long until our army will be ready to invade, General Artimus?" the tyrant asked.

The other man paused for a moment before answering. "We had planned to begin the invasion in two months, but we could do it in one. Any earlier and we will not have sufficient provisions to sustain us if there is resistance," he answered carefully.

"We will invade in three weeks' time, General Artimus, and if need be we will steal the food we need from the peasants. I want his people to scream in fear of our army, and I want his city burned for this offense. Fix this, General, and prepare the men. In three weeks we will repay the debt we owe him."

King Drake turned on his heel and disappeared back into the palace as Artimus dashed off into the darkness, followed by his men. It was going to be a long night.

Chapter 41

The town was quiet as Calum stumbled through the main street toward Seumas's house. It was evening, and no one saw him as he passed by their homes and knocked on the door. Fully a minute later, the old man answered the summons, dressed in his nightclothes. It was apparent the older man had been asleep, but when he saw the warrior all sleep dropped from his eyes. Stepping inside, the Sword Bearer turned to face the village leader as he closed the door behind him.

"It is as we feared; they are going to attack us. We don't know how much time we will have, but we know that it will not be enough. I need to speak to the people immediately; there is no time to waste. Will you help me call them together outside of town in an hour? Also please send someone to fetch me as soon as they are assembled. Believe me when I say that my urgency is warranted." Calum finished and looked at James expectantly.

The older man simply nodded and the Sword Bearer stepped to the door, opened it, and walked through the streets to his home. Once there he fell on his bed and for the first time in weeks his body relaxed.

Calum slept soundly as the town bells rang and people stirred from sleep to stumble to the town center. Once there, they were redirected to an open area outside of town that was quickly being illuminated by a forest of torches. Seumas had a makeshift stand made that would allow the Sword Bearer to stand a few feet above the crowd.

When Calum was finally roused and directed to the site, more than thirty thousand people waited to hear him. Needless to say, not all of them were very happy to be awakened at that hour, but they all knew that what he had to say was important, so the murmuring was minimal.

The Sword Bearer looked over the population and his heart stirred inside him. These were his people, and he'd been fighting since childhood to keep them safe. He hoped that this would be the last struggle in that fight. As he stepped onto the stand prepared for him, he smiled at the crowd assembled in front of him.

"People of Greenock, Helvetians, the dragons have been defeated. We have killed them by the hundreds and they are no more." He raised a hand to quiet the throng as it erupted in surprise. When they were quiet again, he continued.

"However, in the process of eliminating that threat we have discovered another. For fifteen years we have supposed that our scouting parties woke up the dragons in the cave at the Bleeding Tooth, and that it was from there that they originated. We know now that this is only partly true. The monsters did come from that cave, but they came first from a land on the other side of the Spine. They were trained and released by the people of that area to weaken us over these many years." He had to pause then, and it took nearly a minute for the crowd to quiet itself.

"People from that civilization have come into our lands to steal away our children. They are the kidnappers, the Dragon Masters, and our enemies."

"These people, they call themselves Cyrenians, are right now planning and preparing for an invasion into our lands. We do not…" Calum raised a hand for silence as the people reacted to his words.

"We do not know exactly when they will be coming, but we know that we do not have much time. If these people conquer us we can expect nothing but slavery and oppression, but I am here to promise you that that can be avoided. They cannot be sure that we know they are coming, and if so they will underestimate us. In that lies our advantage."

"Forces from Greenock will join those from every city in Helveti, and with that army and all of your help, we will be victorious and end the reign of fear they imposed upon us fifteen years ago."

"For those of you who are in the militia, this is the call to arms you have been preparing for. Furthermore, any man who can wield a sword is invited to join us in the defense of our land, our city, and our lives."

"From the rest of you I would ask for your labor. All blacksmiths, those who know how to make weapons, any man who is not able or willing to fight, and all capable women and children are invited to gather tomorrow morning in the town center. You will receive direction there as to how you can assist in this cause. For all those who are able to fight, meet me back here in the morning. Bring your weapons and your resolve. We can win, but it will take all of us working together."

"You may have noticed that I have ordered no one to assist us in this matter. I will be honored to fight for the cause of freedom alongside those who fight for that reason, and no other."

"I bid you a good night, and I will see you in the morning," Calum said, and then stepped down from the stand and headed for home.

Behind him the talking turned quickly to a dull roar as thousands tried to digest what had just been explained to them.

Of all the occupants of Greenock, Calum was one of the only people who slept soundly that night.

*

The following morning dawned bright and clear, and Calum stood looking over those who had decided to fight. The militia was there, standing in their ranks at full force with three thousand men. Above that, another thousand stood ready. The Sword Bearer was pleased as he looked out over them. He had grown up with most of the men who stood ready to defend their country.

From the time the dragons first attacked fifteen years earlier Greenock had grown dramatically. In response to the danger, people from smaller settlements moved to the relative safety of the larger city and the protection of the original Sword Bearers. Now, Greenock was the second largest city in the empire, and had the third largest militia. Calum knew that it was in the militias that they would find their greatest strength. It took longer than a few weeks or even a month to train a man to be a soldier. So many of the people who had just barely volunteered would still be unprepared when the battle began, but they would still be a great benefit. All Helvetians knew how to fight, but it was the militias that knew how to work together as a fighting unit. The most important thing they would have to learn was obedience, and that they could learn in the time they had.

The leader of the militia was a man named Bhaltair, a former Sword Bearer who had given his blade to another after a dragon wounded his leg, making him walk with a limp for the rest of his life. Against a human he was deadly, but against one of the armored reptiles he would have little chance. Calum motioned to him and he came walking over, as always doing his best to hide his infirmity.

"How are you feeling today, Bhaltair?" Calum asked with a friendly smile.

The other man chuckled ruefully. "I figure I'd feel better if I were still sleeping in my bed instead of talking to you, if I must be honest." he said and the younger man laughed.

"All right, I'll try not to waste your valuable time," the Sword Bearer said with a smile. "I want you to take control of our force. The men from the other villages will be arriving in the next few days, and I need to be here." Calum paused as he pulled a piece of parchment out of the pouch at his waist. "So, take these men and follow this map to the site I've indicated. That will be your training area."

"You know that I cannot tell you how much time you have, so waste none. Work all of the men together, but try to keep your militia functioning as a unit. We'll be using them separately, but use those who already have training as much as you can to help in the instruction of the other men. Is that understood, Captain?" Calum asked with a small smile.

Bhaltair nodded. "Perfectly, sir, join us as soon as you can."

The two shook hands and then the Sword Bearer headed back into town. Behind him he could hear the boom of the militia leader's voice as he addressed his troops. He smiled. Those who were inexperienced with such things would hate their lives for the first week, but the captain would get results.

When Calum arrived at the town center there were several hundred women and a hundred or so adolescents and older men waiting for him. The group fell silent as he approached.

"I thank you all in advance for your service. You will be as crucial as the soldiers in this war. You can believe that, because if it were not true I would not have said it. This is no time for any type of deception. Your tasks will be varied, but for today I want you to divide yourselves into four groups. One group will go into the woods and cut branches to be used for making weapons. The next will clean the branches and prepare them for use. Another team will consist of all those with know-how on making bows. The last one, all the blacksmiths, will make arrowheads and fasten them to the shafts. Work together, and work quickly. We will need many thousands of arrows and several hundred bows for our soldiers. Go to it, friends."

Calum watched for a few seconds as the natural leaders in the group took charge and pretty soon the units were assembled and one of them was headed toward the forest.

Around noon, the first detachment from a small neighboring city arrived. Their militia contained only one hundred warriors, but along with them were four hundred men who had also answered the call to arms. Accompanying them were two hundred civilians who had come to assist in other ways. Calum instructed the leader of the militia to head for the same place he had sent Bhaltair.

The Sword Bearer that had gone as an ambassador came with them and Calum asked him to stay in Greenock for the rest of the day. The man's name was Cassus, and he had been a part of Calum's team when they had begun the campaign against the dragons. All that day the two talked extensively, and several times the head Sword Bearer knelt down and drew in the dirt to clarify what he was explaining.

The day passed quickly as groups of soldiers and helpers arrived periodically from different villages and cities. By the end of the day, over ten thousand prospective fighting men had been sent to the training area, of which roughly seven thousand were militiamen, and over five thousand civilians were involved in the production of weapons.

Calum was quietly pleased with the accomplishments of the day when he turned in for the night, but he still could not sleep for worry. He was busy preparing for a war in which he did not know how strong his enemies would be, or even how long it would take for them to arrive. Would there be enough time to prepare the men? When would the battle begin? Did they have any chance at all of winning?

Chapter 42

On the night after the stables burned down, the arena caught fire. The blaze was put out quickly, and the main structure of the massive building was undamaged, but the tower the king used to view the spectacles burned to the ground. Assaults continued on the city despite regular patrols along the outside of the walls. The people were now afraid to leave their homes after dark and the guards kept low on the parapets.

Those of Artair's men who had remained outside the walls, primarily the archers, had the simple task to torment and sting the Cyrenian forces. While Artimus still claimed that the attacks came from only a small group of well-organized men, others believed that an army of barbarians had finally made their way to the capitol city. The fact that no one had seen an army only made the people more fearful of the phantom barbarians.

On the third night there were more fires set on different sides of the city. Artimus ordered all lamps taken down after he found out that the attackers were using the oil to set fires. The lack of a ready source of lamp oil certainly hindered Artair's party, but the increased darkness allowed them even more freedom inside the city.

It was on this third night that the invaders lost two men. The pair was leaving an arson site when they ran into a column of soldiers. It was not in them to be taken alive, and they died only after several enemies had fallen to their dancing blades. That evening the rest of the team met in an abandoned house to rest and report to each other the events of the day.

Artair took the news of the two men's deaths stoically when Ragnal informed him. They all knew that the war they were fighting inside Cyrene would lead to their demise if they stayed long enough. They were fighting as guerilla fighters, and that kind of strategy was never without casualties.

They were succeeding, though. The citizens of the city were afraid, an emotion Artair wanted to permeate the society. He wanted the soldiers who would be headed toward his country to have fresh in their minds what even a small number of Helvetians could do. There was no better way to dampen a nation's thirst for war than to take the fight into its own home. He was sure that the people of the city had no desire for war, although they had no love for his countrymen. No, the thirst for blood came from the king himself, and it had sifted down into his subordinates. Artair could see that he was right when he saw that the civilians were reacting with fear instead of anger at his invasion.

The people were driven by fear, not by loyalty or a sense that what they did was right. What he hoped was that that fear would give Helveti an edge in the coming battle.

Turning, Artair caught sight of the woman who had joined them at the dragon stables. She had told them that her name was Caelia, but other than that they knew little about her. He suspected that she might be a spy of some kind, but the girl had proven herself during the night's activities. She had quickly procured a short sword, and the one time they had encountered resistance she proved to be as willing as any of them to fight against the king's forces. The rest of the men were intrigued by her, as was Artair, but she flatly refused to talk about herself, or to speak at all unless absolutely necessary.

The original Sword Bearer idly traced the blade of a dagger with his finger and stared into the darkness. He only hoped that all was going well for Calum, because he knew that they would not be able to delay them for long. As they traveled inside the city he could see signs of preparation as the soldiers not only sought to root out the invaders, but also visibly prepared for a future conflict. The invasion was coming soon. Very soon.

*

Artimus struggled to keep his expression neutral as King Drake raved. The ruler was dressed in full armor, a sign that he was pushing the outside boundary of his fleeting sanity. He wanted to fight, to kill, to war with his enemies. The fact that he could not find them was what angered the man. Artimus had never known man or beast with a blood lust like his king. He enjoyed the death and pain of his fellow men like most people enjoyed a cool breeze on a hot day.

King Drake finished yelling at the walls and turned to Artimus. The two were the only ones in the throne room. The rest of the generals and officers were out searching for Artair. The swordsman did not move as the king walked up and stood nearly nose to nose with him. His breath was foul and his eyes were bloodshot.

"Are you a traitor, General Artimus?" King Drake asked.

The swordsman was careful not to blink or do anything that would show surprise at the question. "You know, sire, that I am not," he answered coolly.

Drake glared at him and then turned away, walking toward a small door at the side of the throne room.

"Come with me, Artimus, and we will see," the king commanded.

His general followed him, a sick feeling swelling in the pit of his stomach. He always hated going to the king's torture chamber, and he could tell that he would like it even less this time.

As they passed through the door the putrid smell of human waste assaulted their nostrils. Artimus followed Drake into the middle of the dimly lit room. It was cool, dark, and filled with different machines of torture.

Conaf, the man the king had used to try and catch Artair, had died on the rack the day before. It had taken him several days to succumb, and the tyrant had taken it as a personal challenge to keep the rebel alive as long as possible. He finally stopped walking and, turning to face his subordinate, gestured with his arms at the implements that filled the room.

"Take a look around, Artimus. Take a good look," Drake said, his voice cold.

The swordsman looked around obediently even though he knew the room by heart. When his gaze returned to the king the older man was glaring at him.

"I make you a promise, General. If you betray me, or if I even suspect that you might have it in mind, the last thing you will say before I rip out your tongue will be to choose how your wife will die. Am I being quite clear?"

Artimus stood his ground as the king once again walked up to him.

"Now let me be just as clear about something else. If this little disturbance, these barbarians tormenting my city, is not cleared up in two days' time, I will take it as a sign of your weakness and betrayal. You have the resources of this entire city at your disposal, and I expect you to flush these men out of Cyrene. If you fail I will fulfill my promises. Do you understand, General Artimus?"

The other man simply nodded, not trusting his voice. The king looked at him for another second and then walked out of the room without another word.

Artimus was left in the near-darkness, surrounded by the instruments of the madman he served, trembling with rage.

*

Flames engulfed the roof of a large storehouse on the fringes of the city and Artair jumped down to the ground next to the building. To his left and right, several more structures added their burning light to the night sky. This time they had split up, each picking their own target, and then started their fires exactly as the sun slipped completely below the horizon.

As soon as he was sure that the blaze he had set would continue to burn, the warrior began to run, ducking into alleys and running along the darkened streets. The rendezvous point was a fair distance away, and he had only five minutes to rejoin the group before they headed for cover. Security on large targets had been stepped up, and they had changed tactics to include multiple targets at once. He slowed as he approached the small, abandoned hut that was to be the meeting place. There was no one there.

Artair stopped and circled the small shack, taking cover alongside the buildings. His head snapped up as a new blaze erupted from the direction of the other fires. This one was closer to the rendezvous point. In a half instant his swords were in his hands as he began to hear the sounds of battle, swords crashing on steel and men yelling. The Sword Bearer was at full speed in three steps as he headed toward where he was sure his men were fighting.

Artair slowed and then stopped as a familiar figure appeared, running toward him with a short sword in her hand. Caelia was running hard, a wild look in her eyes and blood on the edge of her sword. She hadn't seen him yet, so he stepped deeper into the shadows. As she passed him, he caught her sword between the two of his and flipped it out of her hands. She took several steps before she could stop and then turned around. When Caelia saw Artair she gasped and took a step toward him. The Helvetian's upheld blade stopped her.

"Why are you here? Are you running from a fight or are you trying to capture the one who got away? What is happening? Tell me." he demanded.

Caelia shook her head and struggled to catch her breath.

"No, Artair, Ragnal sent me to warn you. They found us, the soldiers did, hundreds of them. They are going to try to hold them off long enough for us to get out. It's over, Artair. If we stay here for another minute we'll end up as dead as the rest of them are going to be." Caelia pleaded.

The Sword Bearer shook his head in disbelief and she continued.

"Artair, Ragnal told me that you needed to go help Calum back at Greenock. He said that without you there would be no hope. That's why they are trying to hold them off, so you can get away. Think about it, please. You've made sure that no one mentioned any names around me for the last couple of days, so how would I know about Calum or Greenock if he hadn't told me? Come on, let's go." Caelia yelled and, grabbing him by the front of his shirt, began pulling the warrior away from the sound of fighting.

Artair looked back dumbly toward the sounds of struggle and then turned and ran with the girl into the maze of buildings.

Chapter 43

A sudden calm dropped onto the battlefield as the Cyrenians took a step back away from the last remaining invader. The Helvetian paused as well, turning to scan the bodies of his countrymen. It took him only one look to see that he now stood alone. The massive hammer had been thrown in an attempt to save the last of his men. The hammer had done its work in killing the Cyrenian soldier he had targeted, but it had connected a full half second too late, and now the Helvetian leader stood unarmed.

Artimus watched, transfixed, from a clear vantage point on a roof as the lone warrior reached up to lift the visor of his helmet. The heavy gauntlets the man wore were flecked with blood but moved without trembling. His face was made up of rock-hard planes that showed nothing but calm appraisal, and nothing of the fear one would expect from someone in such a precarious situation. His head turned, taking in the entire army surrounding him, one man at a time. Artimus realized, with more than a little shock, that the Helvetian was cataloging each man, his position, and his weapon. He was not just looking, he was planning at an unthinkable level.

"You men with blood on your blades," Ragnal's voice swelled across the courtyard, ignoring the sheer mass of humanity that should have muffled it, "your lives are forfeit. Drop your weapons, and kneel. I will make your deaths honorable." He spoke it as both promise, and as comfort, Artimus realized. He was proclaiming judgment, but also offering some rationale for his command.

Artimus was part amused, part horrified to see how many of his men looked startled at the demand. Several looked toward their leaders as if to ask if they were going to be ordered to comply. A couple looked like they might simply obey.

A short bark of laughter from one of his captains was a welcome sound in the terse silence. "Your life is in our hands, savage." The captain stood stiffly, proudly, as if he had not just lost over half of his command in a single skirmish with the barbarians. "Our king has requested a survivor be brought to him for questioning. That is the only reason you are still alive. You will come with us, or you will join your men." At this, the captain pointed to the fallen Helvetians for emphasis.

Ragnal barely glanced at the speaker, then ignored him, as if he had not understood. His eyes were following a Cyrenian soldier who had stooped over the thrown hammer. He peered at it, and then bent further to pick it up off the stones. He dropped it back to the ground with a grunt of surprise. He tried it again, lifting with his legs this time, and managed to half-carry, half-drag it back to where he had been standing in the crowd. It was obvious he intended to take it home after the battle as a grisly souvenir.

Artimus planned to make sure that he didn't. He could tell, even from a distance, that the hammer was no ordinary weapon. It was forged of the same steel as the Sword Bearers' swords, the steel of the ancient kings. To the wrong man, it would be far too heavy to be used. To one meant to wield it, it would be light as a willow switch but with deadly effect.

"Those of you who have helped to kill my men must die." His voice boomed again as his eyes starting to move, with the whip-crack of authority. "You may do so honorably, and kneel, or you may fight for your lives. I am comfortable with either choice. Both paths end with your deaths." Even unarmed, surrounded by an enemy army and his dead countrymen, he stood as if in command of legions.

Artimus was tempted to laugh out loud at the ludicrous scene. A single unarmed man, surrounded by the bodies of all he had brought with him, telling an army that they should kneel to be executed for the crime of killing his men. And yet, no one was moving to try to apprehend him. Even unarmed, the Helvetian commanded a lot of respect, or fear, sometimes it was hard to tell.

"You will come with us or we will simply kill you and leave your body with these swine you brought with you." The captain was speaking again. He was getting angrier now. Flecks of spittle flew from his lips as he spoke. Artimus could tell that this young captain believed himself the equal of the Helvetian, believed he deserved to be obeyed. The fact that he was not being obeyed was infuriating to him.

Ragnal smiled, though the emotion did not make it up the solid planes of his face to his eyes. "Neither of those things are going to happen."

The captain was obviously confused for a brief moment, trying to remember what he had said that could be rejected in this manner.

"I will not come with you because the men around me must be avenged. They have no sons, so that duty must fall to me." Ragnal talked as if lecturing a small child, one who was barely learning to speak. "Also, I have two sons." There was a pause in his speech at this pronouncement, and Artimus could almost see the Helvetian allow himself to think of his family exclusively for a moment, a mere heartbeat that would likely be the last time. Then it was over. "I have two sons who will likely be my superiors in every way. They would follow their responsibility to come to avenge my death. I would not have them spend their lives trying to find the men who eventually kill me. Instead, I must die in such a way as to leave no doubt that I need no vengeance." He paused at this, glancing pointedly at the soldiers who stood with bloody blades.

284

"I also have a wife, whose name even you are not worthy to hear, who believes herself married to a man, not a cowering dog. I could not return to her knowing that I am no longer worthy to be called her husband."

"We will not kneel to be executed by a savage." The captain shouted, as if to reclaim control by sheer volume. "You will kneel here before the might of Cyrene!"

Ragnal raised an eyebrow at the comment, and then turned slowly, conspicuously inspecting the army around him for a second time. His eyes missed nothing, even if the look was meant to be contemptuous. "If this is the might of Cyrene," he mused, "our war might end here tonight."

The captain laughed deliberately, the sound loud and brassy. "Do you really believe yourself the equal of my entire army?"

"No," Ragnal answered, his voice quieter, but still heard by all in the square, "I believe you all unworthy to stand on the same battlefield with the very least of my men." He paused and appraised the look on the young captain's face. "The thought that you all might be my equal had not even occurred to me." This last statement was delivered with such pure venom as to be nearly damaging to one's ears.

"You," the captain hissed, "will kneel before me or I will remove your ability to do so!"

Artimus knew, though the young captain did not yet, that he was quickly losing control of the situation. He was making greater demands without his getting obedience to his lesser. It was the work of an amateur, one who would not likely live long enough to learn any better.

"A Helvetian bends his knees only to God." Ragnal thundered. The army surrounding him twitched back from him at the sudden outburst. Several men clenched and re-clenched their hands around the handles of their swords. "You in this city bend your knees to a king not worthy of my hammer, or the pursuit of my sons. You blame your history on my people, instead of on yourselves for being the descendant spawn of cowards and murderers. You play the sheep to a deranged shepherd and yet have the gall to raise your voice to me?"

"I am a leader of men and a slayer of dragons. I am the Hammer That Lives!" Ragnal roared.

"Yet you do not have a hammer!" The young captain shouted back, grinning triumphantly, "you are unarmed and can choose to either die or come with us!"

Ragnal nodded slowly, as if conceding the point, and looked down at the men lying around him. Reaching down, he scooped up a staff that had been lying next to his foot. The staff was as tall as he was, and had a blade coming from one end and a hook at the other. He set the hooked end on the ground and leaned on it like a walking stick. "You ask me to kneel before you? A boy barely a man who believes that arrogance is somehow a replacement for experience, and ambition a substitute for honor? Kneel before me, insolent youth, and I will make your death more honorable than your life has been."

"You will kneel now, or you will die by my own hand!" The captain yelled, raising his sword as if to remind Ragnal that he had it.

Ragnal surprised everyone, including Artimus, by laughing. Not a mere chuckle, but a full-throated roar of laughter that made the army around him shift nervously. He threw his head back and howled with laughter. Then the laughter changed to something else, something primal and angry. The army of Cyrenians shifted fearfully as this last invader roared his rage to the heavens. Artimus could not be sure, but he believed heard a name come out of the Helvetian's lips as the roar ended—and then the visor snapped into place as if by obedience to an unspoken command.

The next movement came far too quickly for even Artimus's trained eye to follow. From the sheer size of the Helvetian, Artimus had

286

expected a powerful, yet ponderous, attack. He had expected sweeping blows with the staff, as if it were the missing hammer, and men pushed back by the Helvetian's superior strength. Artimus realized, in the first half moment of battle, how wrong he had been.

The young captain died in that first instant, so quickly that surprise was not even able to register on his face before his death was assured. The Helvetian struck him three times in the first instant. A jab that crushed the windpipe, then two blows that broke the Cyrenian's arms. All he had left to do was fall.

In the next instant, another man fell, and then another. The Helvetian fought with a style better suited to a man half his size, but from someone with his strength it was terrifying. He was in their midst with his first movement and with obvious intention. It defied any strategy Artimus had ever heard or taught about fighting against a group. Instead of finding a place where his back may be protected, the Helvetian pushed forward at all times, deeper into the mass of soldiers. It meant that he would be continually surrounded by enemies, so that none of them could fully engage him without endangering their own comrades. At the same time, it was apparent that being surrounded was exactly what he wanted. The staff moved too fast for Artimus to see anything beyond the Helvetian's hands, and both ends found their targets as if living, vengeful things.

The hook at one end of the staff would be pulling a soldier from his feet while at the same time the blade killed another man behind the Helvetian. Then the blade would swing over to dispatch the man on the ground while the hook tore the breastplate from another soldier in preparation for the coming blade.

A part of Artimus's brain was horrified to see the vicious, efficient brutality that was suddenly tearing through his men, while the largest part was absolutely mesmerized by the spectacle in front of him.

Only once had Artimus seen such a thing, and that had been back when he was only a boy. He had begun training with the sword and his instructor had challenged the entire training group to attack him en masse. It had ended quickly and with laughable ease, with all the children lying on the ground at the instructor's feet.

Though, in this case, the people falling to the ground were not laughing, or getting back up. Indeed, the massive Helvetian moved as if dancing, but to a dance unfamiliar to the Cyrenian soldiers. They could not stop his weapon as it came at them, and could only slash and stab at the place where he had been a half moment earlier. They swung and lunged, but they were as children before a master.

Ragnal pushed forward, seeking out the tightest knots of men, ever deeper into the throng. Men started to scream as he approached, pushing now to run away from the Hammer That Lives.

A tight fist of men came pushing through the crowd at that exact moment, slicing through as if cutting through butter to reach the center. These, Artimus knew, were the king's personal guard. Drake himself had to have sent them into the fight as soon as he heard that there was one. Taught the sword from childhood, they were rarely allowed to leave the palace grounds without the king. They were killers without scruple and without restraint when without their master.

Artimus watched with a detached sense of curiosity as the small band made their way to the Helvetian. Against one of them, he was sure the savage would have triumphed. Against the full squad of five that had come, even he would have no chance.

He watched in mute horror as the first man of the five reached the Helvetian. Reached him, and then fell as if deboned. The warrior leapt over his still-falling body and bore another of the white-cloaked guards to the ground with his blade, killing him as he struck the paving stones of the courtyard. The other three attacked where he had just been, but he was already gone, sliding away from the blades as if

288

he had asked them to attack him in precisely that way on the practice field. The final three died in quick succession. He struck them thigh, midsection, and neck with a contemptuous ease.

Then the Helvetian glanced to his left. It was a quick look, a simple dart of the eyes, but Artimus saw it. He didn't have to look to know what he was looking for. He had glanced toward the soldier still holding his hammer.

Artimus wanted to yell a warning, wanted to point and tell his men where the warrior was headed next, but he was out of position, and the Helvetian was too fast. He was already moving back along the army toward the desired weapon, killing as he went. The Cyrenian soldiers were being pushed forward by their leaders and reinforcements from behind, while those on the front lines tried in vain to escape the Helvetian's notice.

The soldier holding the hammer tried foolishly to raise the heavy weapon, but was not a tenth the man he would have needed to be to make the strategy work. The blade of the staff pierced him before he could get the hammer as high as his waist, and he dropped it, clattering, to the ground.

The Helvetian took one more swing with the staff, clearing the space around him, and then he reached down for the hammer.

Artimus would swear for the rest of his days that the hammer rose from the ground to meet its master's hand, a faint glow coming from the massive head.

The Helvetian let loose a sound that could only be compared to a dragon's victory cry, filled with rage, triumph, and ecstasy. The men around him, those who weren't already trying to flee, threw themselves back against their comrades in a desperate attempt to escape.

Then he struck.

Artimus saw the blow coming not because the hammer started moving, but because of the set of the man's feet, the bunching of muscles in his legs that signified a tremendous effort. Then the hammer struck the men closest to the Helvetian with a sound like an anvil shattering. Artimus covered his ears with his hands and cried out in surprise. The sheer impact was indescribable. The damage, if so small a word could describe the effect, was unthinkable.

To the Helvetian's hammer, armor was insignificant. Bone was an amusing suggestion, and flesh an afterthought. His first blow killed one man outright, and two more were struck and would die on the ground. The hammer did not pause in its travel from one point to another, no matter how many men stood in the way.

The warrior charged forward into the crowd again, swinging the hammer as if scything wheat. Then he slipped one hand through the strap at the end of the handle and started to spin. Artimus would have told anyone that such an act would never have enough power to be effective on the battlefield, but he had never witnessed a man like this. The hammer swung at the end of the Helvetian's right arm as he spun, the hammer going from low to high on every rotation. The low blows shattered legs, knees, and ankles. The high blows caved in helmets and broke necks. At the same time, the length of the hammer's handle, and the length of the warrior's arm, meant that no one could get close enough to counterattack. His speed meant that no one could come up behind him to get in close either.

It was a lopsided massacre. By this point the Helvetian had left behind the dead members of his team, but had left a wide swath of broken, dead, and dying Cyrenians across the battlefield. The Cyrenian army had been reduced by losses, but had been reduced more by the soldiers who had fled a battlefield controlled by just one man. For a moment, Artimus had to ponder the fact that this one man might actually be able to win this battle, all by himself.

Then the first archer found a position on a rooftop surrounding the courtyard. The Helvetian was waiting for him, and threw a stolen sword into the man's chest from thirty yards away. As that archer fell, another gained a roof on the other side of the courtyard. A third came into view on another roof.

The Helvetian stopped his disastrous spin, and gripped the hammer's handle with both hands. Working in close, he almost disappeared from view in the crush of Cyrenian soldiers…almost.

The archers apparently had very specific orders that included nothing about caution or care.

The first dozen arrows fired found only Cyrenian targets. The Helvetian was moving too fast and was far too good at keeping himself surrounded by his enemies. The first arrow that connected with the invader sunk deep into his left shoulder. His armor had kept it from going all the way in, but it hadn't saved him entirely.

Without stopping, Ragnal reached up and broke the shaft off a couple of inches away from his skin.

The second bounced off his armor plates, but the third sunk a full foot into his broad back. After seeing this arrow hit home, Artimus slipped down off his rooftop perch.

It took him more than two minutes to reach the Helvetian, but he could tell from the men around him that the warrior was slowing down. Soldiers had stopped running, and now stood in a shocked daze, staring at the dead and dying around them. Over their heads, the sound of the hammer blows was slowly diminishing.

Artimus stepped into a clearing carved out of his own men, and stared at the hulking Helvetian. He now had six different arrows poking from different parts of him, but he was still standing. The archers had stopped firing, likely against orders, out of awe that he was still standing. The only sign of weakness, other than the fact that he had stopped attacking, was that the head of the hammer now rested on the ground, and he was leaning on the handle.

The Helvetian monster was dead, even if he hadn't fallen yet.

"Artair told us about you." Artimus spoke with simple certainty. The Helvetian did not move, did not speak.

"He told us that he wasn't the champion of Helveti, that there was another man who would be coming." He paused, waiting for any reaction. "At first I thought he was just trying to mislead us with some bizarre kind of false modesty. May I say that you are certainly everything he said you would be."

The Helvetian answered by slowly lowering himself to one knee, still leaning on the hammer. His weakness was now obvious, his life blood staining the stones beneath him. With his free hand, he reached up and tugged at his helmet until it came free. The face underneath was wet with sweat, but no emotions registered.

"Your abilities will be talked about for longer than anyone here will live, of that you can be sure." Artimus said, searching for something to say that would incite some kind of reaction.

"I am not…" Ragnal began, then had to stop as a new wave of pain took his breath away. "I am not the champion of Helveti." He finished, his breathe coming in rasping gasps. "I am a father." He choked, gagged, and then continued. "And I am a husband."

With a surge, Ragnal regained his feet, swayed slightly, and then steadied himself. A discarded sword he had knelt to pick up was in his free hand, partially hidden behind his leg. "That is all the champion I need to be." This last was too quiet for anyone but Artimus to hear. Then Ragnal suddenly smiled, looking right into Artimus's eyes. "You won't like meeting the real champion."

Then, with a smooth motion, lacking any hesitation, Ragnal shoved the sword under his breastplate and through his own heart. For a moment, nothing happened. Everyone stared at the hilt of the sword that had suddenly appeared. Then the Helvetian toppled slowly backwards, landing flat on his back with a solid thump.

292

The hammer fell after him, more slowly as if by afterthought. Artimus stood watching the dead man, waiting for him to stir again.

Out of curiosity, Artimus stepped forward, crouched, and grasped the handle of the hammer. He started to stand, but was jolted to a stop in the motion when the hammer refused to move.

He tried again, using both hands this time.

It didn't budge. The hammer had decided that it was not going to move anymore.

Chapter 44

Artair followed Caelia as the two of them raced toward the outer walls. He sensed that she knew where she was going and so he simply followed, a sword in his hand. At one point they had to huddle in the shadows of a building and wait as a large group of soldiers went by, apparently on patrol. Artair took the opportunity to ask his female companion where they were headed. She responded simply that she knew how to get them out of the city, and to follow her lead. He nodded his compliance and they continued on.

The two stopped in sight of one of the main gates. In front of it there were several dozen armed guards. Artair glanced at his female companion with a question in his eyes. She looked back and just shook her head slightly.

Handing him her short sword, she rubbed her hands through her hair to make it look even more messed up, and then stood and ran screaming toward the group of soldiers. Her movement startled Artair, and he almost leapt after her before retreating into the darkness again.

Her screams had quite an effect on the guards, and in an instant they had all drawn their weapons. She slowed as she approached the men, and then began crying and pointing off into the darkness. The Sword Bearer watched in fascination as the entire company dashed off in the direction that she had indicated, leaving only the two official gatekeepers to protect the exit.

As soon as the men left, Caelia collapsed to the ground in a sobbing heap, her entire body quivering. The remaining guards huddled around her, not at all certain what to do but determined to help console the hysterical woman. They did not even notice Artair's approach until he was too close for them to escape. Their unconscious bodies hit the ground and the woman's sobs ceased. The Helvetian shook his head in grudging admiration for his female companion and the two of them dashed for the gate.

As Artair slipped through the opening after her, he could see the returning soldiers running hard toward them. The girl was already ten yards ahead of him as he came through the gate, and he ran after her.

Suddenly, she fell to the ground with a crash. Artair didn't have a chance to slow down before something grabbed his legs and he also fell to the earth. Strong hands covered his mouth and the stars disappeared from his vision as some type of covering was thrown over him. He began to struggle but stopped as his captor whispered into his ear.

"Artair, you hold still now, and the worst that will happen to you will be to get stepped on once or twice."

The voice belonged to one of the men on his team, and he stopped struggling. After a few minutes, the sound of footsteps subsided and the hands that held the dragon fighter released their grip. Standing, he could see Caelia with one of the archers. The unfortunate fellow had a bloody lip, which he had obviously obtained very recently.

Wasting no time, they ran away from the walls of Cyrene and did not stop until they had come to one of their old campsites over a mile from the city. There they reported on the varied successes and failures of the past few days. None of the archers had been killed, although one of them had been wounded. Artair and Caelia told them of their experiences inside the city and the certain death of Ragnal and his men. The group managed only brief snatches of sleep that night.

When Caelia awoke the next morning Artair was sitting next to her. Startled by his appearance, she jumped and looked at him with a question in her eyes.

"Who are you?" he asked.

Caelia waited for a moment until she realized that there would be no more to the question, and then she sat up and looked at him quizzically.

"My name is Caelia, I already told…" she began with an impatient tone.

"Don't give me that." he snapped, interrupting her. "You were a captive in the stable where the king kept the two dragons he prized the most, and you fight your countrymen with the same passion that we do. So, I ask again, who are you?"

She returned his angry gaze for a moment and then shrugged. "Okay, you want to know my story? My husband and I rebelled against that bloodthirsty tyrant. Or rather we started to rebel against him. As it turned out, he knew all about it. We were betrayed, the king killed him, and he put me in that horrid little hut to rot," Caelia said bitterly.

"Why didn't he kill you?" Artair asked, unconvinced.

She rolled her eyes at him. "You, being a man, should know that without asking. He wanted me, but he said that before I would make a 'suitable' wife he would have to break my will. That's why he put me in a box instead of in a grave. Now you've given me a chance to fight back, and I'm taking it." She paused to take a long look at Artair and then continued.

"The people of my nation don't have what it takes to defeat King Drake, he has too much power over them. You might actually be able to change that. That's the reason I am helping you. Now, are you convinced that I'm not a spy?" Caelia asked.

The Sword Bearer stood up slowly. "No, I'm not, but we need to leave anyway. The rest have already gone, and there are several hundred soldiers on their way here right now." he said casually.

Caelia stared at him, her eyes wide as she jumped catlike to her feet.

"You mean that you've been sitting here talking while there's an army on their way to kill us? Are you completely mad?" she demanded.

"You know, I've never been able to figure that one out." Artair responded after visibly thinking for a few moments.

She rolled her eyes and ran after him as he left camp.

*

A half-mile behind them Artimus marched at the head of five hundred men. The tracks of the group's late-night flight were easily followed, and the soldiers he had with him were eager to be known as the ones who would destroy the remaining invaders.

Chapter 45

The grass had long since been chopped into dust along the entire length of the training field. Fires burned at the different camps and shouts could be heard from the instructors as thousands of men drilled and prepared for the coming battle. Calum held still and tried to take in the entire spectacle as he arrived at the training area.

It was late afternoon and the day was already beginning to cool. He had come from Greenock with the bulk of the non-combatants and left them with Clarke to work at a different site a few miles closer to the Bleeding Tooth. All those who had not come with him remained at Greenock and were still producing weapons.

Calum could identify the men from different villages and cities from the banners each unit had posted where they trained. He calculated there were a little over twenty thousand warriors who had been sent to prepare themselves in this valley. Although he expected that there would be more that would trickle in, these fighters were to be the army that would either win or lose against the coming attackers.

The men around him stirred with impatience and Calum glanced at them. Many of those with him were barely more than boys, but if he ever tried to argue that any of them were too young, the fact that he had become a Sword Bearer at age thirteen always came up, and the youths were permitted to train as warriors.

The original Sword Bearer finally had his fill of the sight and led those with him down the hill to join the rest. They did not have much time, and there was much to do.

*

After a day's march, Artair and the rest of his men had widened the gap to a little over a mile, and then both parties had stopped as darkness fell. The Helvetians ate a cold supper and scattered into the brush to sleep.

Two hours before dawn five hundred Cyrenian troops broke the morning's silence with war cries as they descended on the camp, quickly seeking out the cloaked forms that lay in the woods and tall grass. They found only empty blankets and spare clothing.

At that same moment, Artair and those with him were running west, more than five miles ahead of their pursuers.

Artimus cursed under his breath as he saw his men's swords rip apart the abandoned clothing before he ordered them on. The race was futile, he knew. The Helvetians would reach the tunnels before the end of the day, but he still had to make sure that they were gone before he could return home to face the king.

At noonday Artimus halted his company to allow them to rest and eat lightly before forcing them back onto the trail, this time with scouts flanking them to ensure that the barbarians did not double back to Cyrene. They reached the head of the tunnels at twilight, a full half an hour after Artair and the Helvetians had disappeared into the dark passage.

Something lay in the mouth of the cave and as Artimus walked in he saw that it was a short sword. There was a piece of parchment wrapped around the blade. His men stared at him as he examined the message. After squinting at it for a moment in the dim light he ordered a torch to be brought to him. The leader read the writing and then had camp set up in the mouth of the tunnel.

Although they all wanted to know what the message said, none of the soldiers dared ask.

＊

When he was alone, Artimus couldn't help but shake his head and smile in admiration for Artair. The message left on the blade of the sword had to have been made in haste as they escaped through the tunnels, but the warning it gave showed that the escaping men were in no way beaten.

Turning the weapon toward the light, he read the inscription once more: "Your dragons are dead and your people are terrified; visit us in our own lands and we will sadden your women with the news of your deaths." Artimus chuckled again as he read it and set the sword down beside him.

On the following day he would start back to Cyrene, and he would prepare his armies for the coming invasion.

Only once had he ever lost a fight, either as an individual or as a general, and with him at the head of the armies of Cyrene, nothing would be able to stand against them.

Chapter 46

Two days after entering the tunnels, Artair and Caelia walked out at the base of the Bleeding Tooth into the twilight. The Sword Bearer breathed deeply of the cool night air as he stepped from the cave. He was glad to be home. They had rested for a day with the men Calum had sent to wait inside the tunnels, but Artair was too anxious about the preparations that had to be made to stay any longer. Caelia didn't want to stay either, and the two of them left the others and continued on alone. After a day's rest neither of them had any need for sleep and they decided to press on for a few more hours.

They met up with the camp of Clarke and the non-combatants in a large valley along the path that led to Greenock. Caelia chose to stay there for the night, but Artair followed Clarke's directions to the training area.

When the returning warrior found the camp he sought Calum out and the two spent several hours talking before falling asleep. Artair was impressed with what had been done, but the amount that still had to be accomplished was staggering.

At least now they would be able to fight together, as they had always done. The children who had fought dragons were now men, and they would either win or lose this conflict together.

*

As ordered, the armies of Cyrene left their beautiful city three weeks after the dragons died in the fires. The civilians watched in awe from their houses as the massive army marched out of the gates. With the black and white dragon banners of the king waving in the slight breeze, it was a sight not soon to be forgotten.

Thirty thousand strong, each soldier was well trained and loyal to his superiors. More importantly, not a single one was concerned that they would not be victorious. The barbarian invasion had convinced them that their opponents were dangerous, but they still had no doubts in the ability of their leader.

General Artimus marched at the head of the men, his white battle armor setting him apart from his black-clad soldiers.

King Drake rode in a litter carried by eight bearers dressed in pure white. Up until three weeks earlier, the tyrant had not planned to come along with the first army, but his plans had changed as his hatred for Artair and his people grew.

The fact that the ruler would be accompanying them bothered Artimus. As a rule the general tried not to underestimate his opponents, whereas the king seemed unable to keep himself from underestimating everyone around him. There was one thing for certain, though, Artimus thought. With the king accompanying the army, there would be no quarter given, no mercy, and no chance for their enemies to surrender. The madman would not be satisfied with anything less than the complete decimation of any army that came against them.

As they traveled to the tunnels, the ruler's disposition became more and more ugly, anxious for the coming battle. He ordered one of his bearers executed because the fellow stumbled as they entered the caves, jarring the royal litter. Even his personal guards had never seen him in such a state. It took almost three days for the prodigious army to squeeze its way through the tunnel network, and when they were all finally through the passage Artimus ordered a halt for the night. The king approved the rest break when it was reported to him, but his general could almost feel the man's impatience at the delay.

Artimus was always amazed when he looked back on his experiences with Drake. When he first assumed power, it was as a young, strong man with a certain cruelty that frightened his enemies into submission. In the years since, that cruelty had grown into a maniacal craze. Kings had been extreme in the past, but Drake had reminded the nation what it meant to be ruled. The King of Cyrene, Artimus had long since admitted, was a madman. Drunk with power and blood lust, there was nothing left of the tyrant to be admired.

As the swordsman left the king's tent that night, the bitter thought came to his mind that in the next few days, unless everything worked out perfectly, both peoples would be under this man's rule. For that, he was sure, he would never be forgiven. Not by his nation, nor by Artair's. He would be known as the general who began the oppression of an entire people instead of freeing his own.

When he returned to his tent, his scouts met him with the news that an army was positioned a few miles from their location. Artimus simply nodded at the news and sent the scouts on their way. When he entered his tent and secured the flap, however, the general sank to his knees and gripped his head in his hands. Doubts and questions pounded against the inside of his temples, and he struggled to push them away.

Finally, he stood and walked over to his makeshift bed and pulled the portrait, wrapped in velvet, from his pack. Uncovering it slowly, he peered into the woman's face until his eyes burned.

"It will end tomorrow. One way or another, I promise that it will end tomorrow." He spoke softly but with an intensity that made him tremble.

After studying the portrait for another few moments, Cyrene's head general rewrapped it in the velvet cloth. Then, taking the bundle in his right hand, he walked out of his tent and to the closest fire.

Soldiers surrounded the small bonfire as they relaxed after dinner, but the crowd dissipated as if under orders as Artimus stood silently holding the misshapen package in his hands. When he was alone, he threw the cloth and its contents into the flames. Some of the soldiers who had left their spots stood watching their general as the flames licked into the night sky. However, only a couple of them were close enough to see the tears coursing down his cheeks as he stared at the burning bundle.

As soon as the portrait was completely consumed, Artimus returned to his tent and collapsed on his bed, but sleep eluded him, chased away by the image of a weeping woman in a blue dress.

*

The morning dawned beautifully, with the cool air and gentle breeze welcoming soldiers from two nations to a new day. Artimus awoke early and reported to Drake what the scouts had told him the night before. Pure excitement lit up the King's face as he heard of the proximity of his enemies.

"How many of them are there?" the tyrant asked eagerly.

"Our scouts estimated nine to ten thousand," Artimus responded.

A look of disappointment crossed Drake's features. "Well, that is hardly a challenge, but beating them will show the rest that resisting is useless. Is the barbarian Artair among them?" the ruler asked.

"He has not been seen, but I suspect he is there," the swordsman answered.

The King stood and clasped his shoulder. "You will lead our armies to victory today, General Artimus. Then, as promised, you will rule this land as my appointed leader. Take pride in your work, this is a glorious day." the tyrant exclaimed.

The ruler gripped his shoulder a little harder and then released him. Artimus backed his way out of the tent and then sent for his captains.

Within an hour, his subordinates had their orders, and the men were set in ranks. At the king's bidding, the massive army moved toward the battlefield, each soldier either eager or nervous, but all with the knowledge that this day would be an incredible victory.

Chapter 47

The site Calum had chosen for the battle was a large, open valley fringed by woods. It was at one end of this location that the armies under the original Sword Bearers stood ready.

Five thousand militiamen stood at the front, their matching armor and weapons impressive in the early morning light. Behind them, in loose ranks, stood another five thousand warriors armed with swords, axes, and bows. Behind them, hidden in the trees, were all of the older men and boys who had insisted on remaining to help if needed. These too carried weapons, but Artair and Calum shared the hope that they would have no need of them.

Such was the sight that greeted Artimus and his men as they entered the valley. As ordered, his troops were deployed and set at readiness by ranks. In divisions of five hundred, each troop was a composition of crossbowmen, footmen, and lancers. Each group was under the direct leadership of a man Artimus had personally chosen and entrusted with the responsibility. At the front, there were several units of only foot soldiers. It was these individuals that would take the brunt of the initial attack. The footmen were to absorb the damage of the enemy's attack, while the units behind them were to gain strategic advantage over them.

Soldiers were sent out to check for flanking parties and, when they found none, returned to report to Artimus. Their leader was speaking to the king. After waiting to be granted permission to address their superiors, the scouts reported that there were no other forces in the area other than the ones who had assembled on the far side of the valley. Artimus nodded quietly at the news and waited for the king's next statement. The king said what he expected him to say, and he was moving before he finished talking.

"What are you waiting for, General? Destroy that pitiful army." the madman demanded impatiently.

As he walked away from the tent, Artimus could feel the adrenaline pumping through his veins, and he breathed deeply of the cool morning air. It was days like this that let you know you were alive, and sometimes made you wish you were not.

By the time he had made his way to the front of the army, everyone knew that there would be no more waiting. The time had come.

When he reached the front of the ranks, Artimus turned and held one hand up for silence.

"You men of Cyrene, in front of you stand the enemies of your homeland. Today is the day they will fall, never again to invade our borders or kill our people. The wrongs they committed against our forefathers will today be avenged. We have been preparing for this battle for…" Artimus stopped speaking as murmurs broke out amongst the men.

Following the soldiers' gaze, he turned to look toward the opposing army. It was moving. The ragged-looking force was advancing toward them slowly, at a walking pace.

Artimus held up a hand to quiet his men as shouts and cheers called for the order to attack. The Cyrenians waited impatiently as their enemies slowly closed the distance between them.

Artimus watched them with curiosity as they came. It was not until the other army stopped about two hundred yards from their adversaries that he turned and motioned to his nearest captains to come to him.

The murmurs began again as a lone figure detached himself from the rest of the opposing army and continued walking forward. Anyone who had not seen him in the arena could still recognize the warrior from his reputation and by description.

His two swords still in their scabbards, Artair walked toward the Cyrenian army with his head high and an arrogant jaunt to his step. At about seventy-five yards, he stopped and stood waiting.

The meaning was obvious. The champion of the Cyrenian army was being challenged to a duel in front of his men. The challenge was obvious, and there was no other person that it could be intended for.

From his position in the rear, King Drake jerked as if stuck with a pin and stood up on his litter.

Artimus nodded to himself and turned from Artair's waiting form to his assembled officers.

"He's challenging me, and I must answer it. Until I return, keep these soldiers in line. Do not, under any circumstances, send these men across this valley. Make that army come to you. Is that clear?" Artimus asked.

The officers each responded in the affirmative.

Turning toward the battlefield, the Cyrenian swordsman pulled his two thin-bladed weapons from their scabbards and checked them over quickly. Returning the blades to their sheaths, he began to walk forward when one of his captains raised a hand to stop him.

"General Artimus, pardon the question, but if you fall on the field, who should lead the army?"

The swordsman turned toward the man and smiled. "I will not fall," he said, and continued walking toward Artair's solitary figure.

Over forty thousand pairs of eyes watched as the distance between the two decreased. The chill of morning was gone, and the heat of the day warned them of its advance. The only sound Artimus could hear was that of his own footsteps as he walked toward his adversary. Artair stood silently watching him, his face showing no expression.

Since the other man had not drawn his swords, Artimus left his in his scabbards. He stopped when he was within ten feet of the Helvetian.

"You can't win, Artair, you know that. I've beaten you every time we've fought, and now you can only lose again. After you fail, so shall your army," Artimus said, baiting him.

The other man seemed to think for a moment and then nodded slightly. "Let's see if you're right, shall we?" Artair asked, and leapt toward Artimus, both swords coming free of their scabbards and sweeping in toward the general's body.

Steel rang on steel as the Cyrenian's swords flew from their sheaths and met with Artair's. Artimus's counterattack failed as the Sword Bearer slapped his blades away, crouched, and swung both weapons at his legs. The general jumped up and back, evading the deadly attack and putting some distance between the two. Surprisingly, Artair did not advance immediately, but rather stood holding his swords and looking at his opponent.

"Tell me truly, Artimus," he began, his breathing even. "Why didn't you kill me the last time we fought?"

The Cyrenian looked at him quizzically and began circling the other warrior, his swords always at the ready. "I answered that already, Artair. I didn't feel like it at the time," Artimus said simply. "That decision was important to you, but not to me. You were a simple slave, to be killed or allowed to live at my pleasure. Kind of like right now!"

The statement incited another attack as the Helvetian dashed across the distance that separated them and again the clashing of steel rang in the valley. After a few seconds of intense, yet fruitless, contest, Artair jumped back and roared his frustration.

"Don't lie to me, Artimus, there's more to it than that," he yelled. "Why did you fake the death of the other prisoner, tell me that. Why did you let me escape from Cyrene? Why did you keep giving me information if you thought I would only die in the arena?"

Instead of answering, the Cyrenian launched an attack of his own, and for a few minutes the two fought back and forth, neither gaining an advantage. Finally the general stepped away and began circling once again.

"Tell me, Artimus, are you as mad as that king you serve, or are you just too scared to face him? He's a maniac, and you're his puppet. You might be our friend or our enemy, no one can tell. No one behind me can say whether I should kill you or let you live, because no one can understand why someone would do the things you've done." Artair parried a searching thrust from his opponent and continued.

"Are you insane, Artimus, or do you have reason for what you do? If you are not mad, then what does that lunatic have on you to keep you doing what he commands?"

The Cyrenian attacked again, and Artair was forced back by the ferocity of the other man's advance. Then suddenly the general stepped back from the Sword Bearer and lowered his blades. With a sigh he gave the answer he had been wanting to give.

"He has my wife, Artair. He took her from me when I first planned a rebellion against him. I can't find where she's hidden, and no one knows where she is. I can't let that monster hurt her."

The two crossed swords again and then backed away from each other. The continued struggle held both armies captive as all eyes were glued on the two champions.

"My people will never be able to overthrow Drake without help. He's too powerful, and he is feared too much. The only way he will ever fall will be if some other force beats him first. You asked why I didn't kill you, why I let you escape? It was for this. You were supposed to win this fight." Artimus said and threw his arms wide toward the two opposing armies.

"And now, after all is said and done, you've failed me. There is no way that your pitiful little army can beat us. Even if you kill me, my army will overrun your men as if they were children. There is no way out Artair, it's over. I will find another way," Artimus said and attacked again, this time with deadly intent.

The ancient blades of the Sword Bearer dented and chipped the thin swords of the Cyrenian as the two dueled. Among the waiting armies many of the men were sweating, mentally straining with their respective champions. On the field, Artair gave ground before the darting blades of the other man and waited for an opportunity to stop the furious assault. It came as Artimus dropped his right hand too low after it was parried away. Sliding to the side, he slammed his right-hand sword down on the blade, driving the point of it into the ground and shattering the weapon as it absorbed the shock of the blow. The Cyrenian backed away from the Sword Bearer and dropped the broken weapon to the ground.

"Join us, Artimus; we will beat your army together. Do not believe what you see, we will not lose today. We will get your wife back." the Helvetian promised as he tried to catch his breath.

The other man just shook his head. "No, Artair. If I join you, the message of my betrayal will reach Cyrene before I could stop it, and they would kill my wife. I cannot protect her. Either I die here on this field and you beat this army, or I must be victorious and find some other way to defeat the king. I'm sorry, Artair, but I have no other choice. They know me too well for me to allow you to win," Artimus said, his sword held ready in his hand.

"Answer me one question, then," Artair asked, warily watching the other man. "Is your wife's name Caelia?"

In the moment of hesitation that came after the question Artimus looked blankly at his adversary. While his mind was churning at the query, the Sword Bearer leapt at him, knocking the remaining blade from his hand and slapping his opponent on the side of the head with the flat of his sword. The general reeled, trying to regain his balance and his composure, as Artair scooped his broken weapon from the ground, stepped in close, and slammed its broken point into his stomach, the shattered tip breaking through his armor and stabbing into his middle. In the same motion, Artair brought the haft of his sword crashing up into the other man's jaw and then stepped away, pivoted, and swung his sword into the Cyrenian's chest. The blow knocked Artimus's already falling body backwards and ripped away his breastplate.

The final attack happened so quickly that most of those who watched would not have been able to say how it ended, but to the Cyrenian army, it seemed like it took several seconds for their General to hit the ground.

Artair fell to his knees beside his fallen opponent, raised both swords above his head and roared his defiance at the opposing army.

Utterly disbelieving, not a man moved. For a terse half-second, every eye was glued to the fallen leader and the blade protruding from his torso. Blood ran from the general's mouth and dripped from the wound on the side of his head.

Drake's frenzied yell ripped through the silence like the crack of a whip from the rear of the army.

"Attack, kill them all. Charge, you cowards!"

Chapter 48

The entire Cyrenian army reacted as a unit, charging forward with a shout of anger for the man who had now tossed the body of their leader over his shoulder and was running back toward his own lines. Every couple seconds, the barbarian turned in a circle as if to show off the body of his vanquished foe.

En masse, the soldiers broke ranks and sprinted, each striving to be the first to reach the retreating heathen. As if to mirror them, the Helvetian army charged forward with a yell of their own, and the valley shook with the shouts and rushing feet of the men of war.

In a matter of moments, less than fifty yards separated the two armies. After another couple of steps, Calum screamed a command and his men stumbled to a halt in front of the advancing force.

The attacking Cyrenians took heart at their action and ran harder. The first of the footmen were barely thirty yards from their target when the ground under their feet gave way and they vanished. The entire front line of soldiers disappeared as the camouflage covering the work of the villagers tore away with the weight of the charging men.

A deep trench, filled with a multitude of long, iron-tipped spikes, had been dug across the entire battlefield. More than twenty yards wide, the trench was a nearly impassable obstacle for the onrushing army.

As the first of their enemies fell into the trap, the militiamen each notched an arrow in their bows and fired at Calum's command, sending five thousand deadly shafts into the Cyrenian army at point-blank range. The enemy lines melted as men fell, pierced with the projectiles and shoved into the fatal trench.

Screams of dying and wounded men filled the air as the crush of the rushing army shoved more and more of their number to their deaths. Crossbowmen struggled to bring their weapons to bear in the crowd of humanity as body-length shields were handed up from the back of Calum's forces and held in place in front of each archer.

Confusion reigned in the Cyrenian ranks as volley after volley of arrows sliced through their numbers. The villagers had prepared and gathered tens of thousands of arrows for the battle, and without anyone to stop them, the militiamen kept up a steady storm of deadly arrows. The shocking sight of the pit and the devastating effect of the archers sent waves of chaos and fear through the soldiers.

The men in front who would have liked to retreat could not, due to the weight of their comrades who stood behind them, and the Helvetian archers kept a continuous stream of arrows pouring into them.

A group of captains finally regained control of a few units and lead them parallel to the deadly trench, intending to get around its corner and flank the other army.

From behind the archers, Artair blew a large horn, sending a booming note over the roar of battle. In response, twenty five hundred militiamen pushed themselves out of the ground amongst the trees that fringed the valley. Early that morning they had been partially buried there, and now rose from the dirt to attack the surprised Cyrenians.

Artair blew his horn again, twice in succession, and a multitude of shouts came from militiamen similarly stationed opposite their comrades on the other side of the valley.

The militiamen wore strange, multi-colored armor that proved impenetrable by the swords of their enemies. The dragons had given up

314

their armor to their killers, and now it was being used against their former masters. Until the slaughter of the dragons was completed, only the Sword Bearers had been able to wear dragon armor.

The Cyrenian army split in two to face the groups that had attacked them. The surprises were far from over, however, and men ran from the trees behind Calum's archers, pulling long planks, each a couple of feet wide and an entire tree-length long. The planks were set across the trench and several thousand men screamed across the improvised ramp to crash into the center of the disorganized army.

The screams of the dying were absorbed into the roar of battle as the two forces fought desperately. Thousands of swords clashed, arrows whistled, men yelled in rage and screamed in death.

Over it all, the horn sounded once more and a squad of five hundred unearthed themselves and attacked from behind the Cyrenian army. These were the Sword Bearers and their teams, a group filled with the resentment and aggression of a fifteen year war brought to a final battle.

The warriors attacked with the speed and ferocity of the dragons who had been their instructors. The Cyrenians melted from before them as the crimson-bladed weapons chopped down all before them.

Artair stood over Artimus's body and watched the battle unfold. Hit from every side, the Cyrenian army was confused and disorganized, but they still had vast advantage in numbers.

He exchanged a glance with Calum, who was directing the archers, and nodded. The battle was going according to plan, and the archers were inflicting a terrible toll on the enemy ranks. Several thousand men already lay pierced with arrows on the other side of the trench.

Then, from the middle of the massive army, a couple of men gained control of the nucleus of the Cyrenian fighting force and led them through their own ranks against the first group of soldiers who had appeared out of the woods. The militiamen fought like the dragons from whom they had stolen their armor, but the sheer numbers of their enemies soon began to push them back.

On the other side of the battlefield, increasing numbers of the Cyrenians began to surrender, dropping their swords and falling to the ground in front of their attackers.

Calum nodded to Artair and he raised the horn to his lips, blowing three consecutive blasts. The signal produced a shout from his forces, and the archers switched their fire to the side where the Cyrenians were pushing through.

Artair dropped the horn next to Artimus's body and ran along the trench toward the attacking soldiers. The militiamen were losing ground steadily, pushed back by the sheer numbers of their enemies. As they gained ground, more of the invaders joined their comrades in the push to turn the tide on the Helvetian archers.

Artair had covered half the distance to the end of the trench when the Cyrenians broke through the militiamen ranks and ran past the pit's open mouth.

The Sword Bearer didn't pause as he ran toward the oncoming army. Arrows whistled past him as the archers turned their full attention on the force that now threatened them. Behind him, Calum blew a long blast on the horn he had left behind, but he did not pay attention as he met the Cyrenian forces head-on.

As he ran, the original Sword Bearer pulled his newly acquired helmet from his head and held it in his right hand. The soldiers in the front recognized him, and some slowed down or tried to step away while others roared toward him.

Without slowing, Artair drew his arm back and threw his helmet at the onrushing horde. The heavy headpiece slammed one of the Cyrenians in the face, throwing the man back under the feet of his comrades. As his helmet left his hands, he pulled his swords from their scabbards.

The first man to reach him screamed as the blade tore into his torso, and the warrior spun past him to the next, ducking under the soldier's swinging sword as he thrust up into his chest. Without rising, he swung his weapons around the dying man's body and took another down as his blades sliced into the fellow's legs. Rising, Artair's swords slashed at two men as they passed and then buried themselves into the chest of another.

Through the haze of battle, the Sword Bearer heard yells and screams coming from his right, but he did not pause to wonder what was happening as another soldier ran at him, this one with a long steel lance.

Twisting, Artair's first sword knocked the lance point away a half second before his second blade split the soldier's helmet in two. The next man to come into his view was looking toward the trees at the back of the battlefield, and the Sword Bearer cut him down without a pause.

As his weapons came up, Artair realized that the Cyrenians were no longer attacking. He watched in amazement as the black-garbed soldiers began to retreat, running away from him. Perplexed, he finally glanced toward the sound that he had been hearing for the past few seconds.

In response to Calum's last horn blast, the villagers who had been waiting in the woods had charged the Cyrenians. Artair could see now why the soldiers were running away. Although there were only a few thousand of them, and none of them in the prime of life.

The villagers had spent the morning painting every piece of exposed skin on their bodies a multitude of colors. Demon-like and screaming, the civilians waved swords and spears. The effect on the attacking army was incredible.

The Cyrenians had been surprised a few too many times already, and this proved to be the last straw. The captains called for a retreat, but it was a useless order, as the soldiers had already begun running from their enemies.

The running troops met up with the ones still fighting on the other side of the trench and the movement became contagious. What was left of the Cyrenian army tore themselves from the battle and ran back up the valley from whence they came. The Helvetian forces chased them, ripping them down from behind.

As he ran, Artair glanced up toward the line of trees and saw a familiar figure standing with a sword in each hand.

King Drake screamed at the retreating soldiers as they roared up the valley toward him. The first couple of men who came too close fell to the tyrant's flashing blade, but the rest of the troops ignored their hysterical leader and ran for the safety of the caves. They knew that there would be repercussions for their retreat, but they could no longer face the Helvetians in that valley.

Artair lost sight of the leader when a Cyrenian soldier stopped and turned to face him. The Sword Bearer's first blow tore the weapon from the man's hand, and his second slid through the man's breastplate as if it had been made of cloth. As his adversary slid off his blade, Artair's eyes searched for the enemy king, but could not see him for the flood of black-coated soldiers that poured into the trees.

The Cyrenians did not stop or try to rally their forces until they reached the caves. Since all of them could not fit through at once, the bulk of the invaders were forced to turn and face their pursuers.

By this time, the Sword Bearers and the militiamen were in the front of the pursuing forces, and the Cyrenian army howled as their enemies sliced through their ranks.

Artair, accompanied by a few other Sword Bearers, slashed and cut their way through the crowds of their enemies, striving toward the only white contour of the army, the king's litter and his personal guards.

As they approached it, the soldiers they were fighting melted away from them, opening a passage to the king's entourage and its white-garbed protectors.

It was with these men that the Sword Bearers found their first real challenge of the day. Picked from the ranks of the soldiers for their loyalty and fighting ability, the king's personal guards fought like demons.

As he charged the group, Artair crossed blades with a large man armed with a long sword and a dagger. After their weapons crossed a couple of times, the Sword Bearer stuck the point of one blade into the guard's right hand, and followed with the other as the big man jerked back in reaction to the pain.

The red point slipped through the soldier's polished armor and sunk deep into his chest. Artair pulled his weapon free of his first victim's falling body in time to see another man running toward Calum from behind.

The Sword Bearer didn't notice the coming attack as he dueled with two of the guards, his red blade dancing in the sunlight. The threat to the warrior ended suddenly as the force of Artair's thrown sword knocked the man past Calum. He took advantage of the distraction and killed one of his opponents with a quick thrust.

Artair crossed blades with yet another enemy, and then jerked back as the shaft of an arrow materialized in the soldier's chest. Turning, he could see that the rest of his men were approaching, and the archers were already at work eliminating the Royal Guard.

In two quick steps, the warrior was at the side of the litter and, tearing away the covering cloth, exposed its contents. After only a glance, Artair turned away from the empty transport to fight with another guardsman.

Deep inside the caves, King Drake ran at the front of the retreating soldiers toward the safety of his homeland.

Chapter 49

Within six hours of the start of the battle, all the able Cyrenians had retreated through the tunnels. The dead and wounded of both sides covered the two battlefields, and the villagers were already working to bury the dead and care for the wounded. No one knew how many had died on either side, but the casualties had been much heavier on the side of the invaders.

The two original Sword Bearers immediately set their soldiers to work burying the dead and clearing the area directly in front of the caves. As a precautionary measure, the dead bodies of the invading soldiers were piled in the mouth of the tunnel, clogging the passage with their remains. Although they did not expect the Cyrenians to attack again so soon after such a defeat, they could not take the chance of being surprised if they tried.

After helping to set things in order, Artair left Calum and returned to the first battlefield. It was an eerie sight. Men lay dead across the entire valley, and the grass was torn up and shredded by the running feet of both armies. It was even worse as he neared the trench that had given them their first advantage.

When Calum had explained his plan to him he had had no idea how impressive and terrible it would turn out. Even walking past the trench ran a shiver down the Sword Bearer's spine, and looking down into it now nearly made him sick. The front lines of the attacking army had had no hope of surviving as the momentum and size of their force pushed them onto the long spikes at the bottom of the pit.

On the Cyrenian side of the trench the ground had become so covered with bodies that the combatants had been standing on them as they fought. The archers, directed by Calum, had done their job almost too well, decimating the enemy ranks with frightening efficiency. It had already been agreed that the trench would be filled in with enemy bodies, and then covered with dirt. There was no reason to try to pull the bodies off those terrible spikes.

As Artair approached Artimus's still-unconscious body, he could see that the villagers had, according to orders, bandaged his wounds and tied his hands together in front of him. After checking the gashes and the dressings placed on them, he heaved his adversary's body over his shoulder and laboriously carried him to his personal tent. Once there, he put him down on his own bed and then called for guards to be set around the enclosure. He doubted that his prisoner would wake up any time soon, but if he did, Artair wanted to be sure that he didn't get away.

As he was walking away from his tent, Caelia stopped him and, motioning toward the soldiers guarding the structure, asked, "Who do you have in there that's so dangerous?"

Blood covered the woman's hands and flecks of it lay on her clothes from working with the wounded.

"That is the general of the other army. That said, he's also the only reason we knew about the invasion. He's a friend and an enemy all at the same time." Artair answered.

"What are you going to do with him?" Caelia asked as the two walked in the direction of the battlefield.

"Well, that will depend on how much of him is enemy, and how much is friend. Would you like a look at him? You just might know him, he was a pretty well-known guy back in Cyrene," he offered.

322

She just shook her head. "There's no one from back there that I need to see, especially not any of the king's puppets." she retorted.

The Sword Bearer chuckled. "I wouldn't exactly call this man a puppet to anyone, though I did once, but that's okay if you don't want to see him." He waited just a moment, then said, "Hey, you say that your husband died, killed by King Drake, right?"

Caelia didn't answer and didn't look at him for several seconds. When she did it was with a hardness in her glance that Artair knew was to cover up the pain that came from the memory.

"Yes, he was killed by Drake. I told you that already, do you like reminding me of the fact?" she demanded.

The Sword Bearer took a step away from her. "No, why would I want to do that? I'm sure he was a good man. What was his name, anyway?" he probed further, hoping to get an answer before she stopped talking to him completely.

"Why do you care?" she asked, glaring at him. "He's dead and I don't want to talk about it, does that answer your questions?"

Caelia turned and walked away toward where the wounded were being cared for. Artair just looked after her, shaking his head in wonder and frustration. He would never understand women.

As soon as she was out of sight, he continued up over the hill to help in the aftermath of the battle.

Chapter 50

Artimus awoke in the early evening with a tremendous headache. As they had been ordered, the guards sent for Artair as soon as they heard the general begin to move around.

When the Sword Bearer stepped through the door of the tent, his prisoner was already sitting up in bed and seemed to be looking for a way to cut the ropes on his hands. When he saw Artair he tried to stand, but failed and sat back down on the bed. As the Helvetian approached, Artimus shut his eyes against the pain in his head.

"I told the men outside to send for me as soon as they heard that you were awake, because I knew that as soon as you woke up you'd be headed home--through my men if necessary. How do you feel?" Artair asked, and sat down in a chair next to the bed.

The wounded man opened one eye to glare at him. "I suspect I feel about as bad as I look. What happened?" the wounded general asked.

Before answering, the Sword Bearer pulled a small pouch out of his pocket and handed it to the other man, who eyed it suspiciously before taking it with his bound hands.

"Put that right inside your cheek and suck on it, it will help with your headache," Artair said.

Artimus raised an eyebrow at him and started to shake his head, but stopped with a wince. "After all the drugs I've snuck into you, do you really believe that I'm going to let you return the favor?" he asked.

Artair chuckled. "Artimus, I have no reason to want you unconscious. I want to talk to you. If I didn't, I would have killed you already." he answered.

The Cyrenian glanced down at the bandages on his stomach and looked at Artair questioningly. The other man held his gaze coolly. Finally, the general put the pouch into his mouth and immediately grimaced.

"Well, either this really is medicine, or you plan to kill me with the taste alone." Artimus said and shuddered.

"I guess we'll see in a few minutes, won't we?" Artair quipped and sat back in the chair.

"What happened?" the Cyrenian asked intently.

"You got knocked out in front of all your men and they attacked us. Drake himself sent them on a mass charge."

Artimus sucked in his breath.

"Yeah, it couldn't have gone any worse for them, or any better for us. They lost, and we drove them back into the tunnels. All in all, it was a very eventful day," Artair answered dryly.

Artimus glared at him. "I know the part about me getting knocked out, but I also know that your little band could not have beaten our army, so how did that happen?" he probed.

The Sword Bearer shrugged his shoulders and leaned forward. "Well, first of all, there was a trench dug across that battlefield with spikes at the bottom. The weight of one or two men did nothing, but as soon as your army hit it, the coverings broke and your men fell in. Second, there were a lot more of us there than you could see."

"When your men attacked, they ran at us en masse and without any organization. When they hit that trench they lost a lot of their comrades and two thousand of our archers opened up on them from close range."

"When they tried to get around the trench they met up with our militiamen who had buried themselves around the trees. For the sake of poetic justice, we made armor out of dragon skins and gave them to our soldiers. They tell me some of your men were just plain frustrated when they couldn't get their swords through that stuff. Somehow I can't feel any sympathy, though.

"Another group of militiamen was hiding in the trees on the other side, and they attacked as soon as the first group did. Then, another bunch of men, these all dragon fighters, hit them from behind. The story is a little bit longer than that, but it suffices to say that your army cut and ran clear back to the tunnels. I don't think they'll be back for a long time." Artair said, and watched Artimus for his reaction.

"Those fools, I told them not to cross that field. I knew there was something going on, but I wasn't sure what. I told them not to charge right before I went out to meet you." the general said and paused as the memory of the fight returned to him, and then he looked intently at the Sword Bearer.

"Artair, you asked me a question right before you attacked me the last time. You asked me if my wife's name was Caelia. Why did you say that?" The other man's eyes searched Artair's face.

The Sword Bearer just shrugged. "I needed to do something to distract you, and that was the name that came to mind. Was I right?" he asked.

The Cyrenian nodded slowly in response.

"Well, I'm sorry to get your hopes up, Artimus. The only Caelia I know is a widow and not too pleasant a person, either," Artair said.

The other man shook his head and waved a hand in dismissal. "Forget it, it's no problem. How many casualties were there?" he asked.

Artair winced visibly. "There were quite a few on your side, I'm afraid. At our last count, which is pretty close to done now, you lost over ten thousand men. We lost about two thousand," he said.

326

Artimus shook his head and whistled quietly. "Well, then, a lot of really good men died today, all for one man's insanity. Did you get Drake?" Artimus asked hopefully.

Artair shook his head. "No, I only caught sight of him once before he got away into the tunnels. He left his guards behind, and we thought he was in that litter of his, but he tricked us. Don't worry, though, he thinks you're dead so he'll have no reason to hold your wife any longer. After a little while we'll sneak back into Cyrene and find her for you. I don't think he will dare come back across the mountains again after the beating we gave him today. Just so long as your wife can learn our language, you two can live here with no problem. We'd like your help, actually, should they invade again," the Sword Bearer said, and was surprised at the look in Artimus's eyes as he finished speaking.

"Artair, you don't understand anything, do you? You think Drake won't attack again? You embarrassed him today, you fool. He'll be back, and this time with more soldiers and a better plan. He'll fight you right into the grave. He won't release my wife for any reason, because he has no sense of mercy or logic. He'll keep her wherever she is until she dies or he kills her. And me? You don't really know me. I didn't do all I did just to keep your people free. I did it to free mine." At the other man's quizzical look Artimus continued.

"I told you before that my countrymen were never going to be able to throw off Drake's rule because they feared him too much, and that he needed to fail first. Well, he failed today, and that's a start, but there's still no one there to take him out of power. We need to go back to Cyrene, get to the palace, and either kill him or at least take him prisoner. If we don't, neither of our peoples will ever be safe." Artimus stopped talking as the other man raised a hand to ask a question.

"Wait a moment, you're saying that 'we' need to go back. Now don't get me wrong, I'd love to see Drake fall, but I don't see how me being there would help matters. They all know me, and they all hate me. You could walk straight to the throne room as a conquering hero and shove a sword down his throat if you went alone," Artair said, but Artimus shook his head.

"You're right on most of that, but not everything. I could walk straight into the throne room, but I don't think that I could kill the king by myself," the Cyrenian concluded.

Artair stared at his companion with a confused look on his face. "You don't think you could...Artimus, after all he's done you don't think you would be able to kill that lunatic?" Artair sputtered.

"No, no you don't understand, of course I'd kill him if I could. You have to believe that." Artimus said defensively.

"Well, then why haven't you already? I know you've had the chance to," the Sword Bearer said and defiantly waited for an answer.

"I haven't because I can't, Artair, that's what you don't understand. A couple of years ago, my wife and I started a rebellion against him. Well, that might be the wrong way to put it. We started to start a rebellion against that lunatic. He found out and killed everyone he suspected might be helping us. He brought men to kidnap my wife and he and I fought. We dueled for over an hour, and I couldn't do anything against him. He's more than a decade older than I am, but he's a wizard with a sword. I think his insanity gives him strength."

"We fought until I collapsed from fatigue and loss of blood and then he shoved his sword through my shoulder to make me drop my weapon. I could hear my wife screaming as they hauled her away, but I was too tired to even move. He let me live, but he kept my wife hostage as insurance against any future actions I might take. It only made him appear stronger, showing that even someone as powerful as I was could do nothing against him.

"I know my abilities, and I know I can't beat him. I need your help. Together we can take him, but alone either one of us will die and he will have gained a victory that will lessen the effect of his defeat today." Artimus's voice was full of desperation.

Artair found it hard to believe that the old man he had taunted was good enough to beat the warrior in front of him, but he did not doubt the wounded man's honesty. Pulling a dagger from his belt, he leaned toward Artimus and motioned for him to hold out his hands so he could cut the ropes that held them bound. The wounded man rubbed his wrists and flexed his fingers as blood rushed back to them.

"That wound in your stomach isn't too serious, but it will need to heal before you'll be ready to travel or fight again. As soon as you've recuperated, we'll take Calum with us and finish what we started."

Artimus nodded in agreement, but then looked up from his hands. "Besides the fact that he's your friend, why do you want to take this Calum fellow?" the wounded swordsman asked.

Artair laughed out loud. "You mean, are you sure that he can take care of himself, or am I just taking him so that he won't be left behind again? You'll see." he said and Artimus nodded.

At that moment, someone knocked on the tent pole outside the door. Artair stood up, blocking the other man's view of the entrance.

"Come on in." he called, and a feminine hand pushed the flap aside as Caelia stepped through the opening. She was not smiling.

"Artair, about earlier…" she began.

"Oh, don't worry about that, I forgive you," he interrupted, and then grinned wickedly at the look on her face.

"You forgive me? You arrogant little…" Caelia sputtered, and Artair turned away from her to sit back down on the chair.

"See, Artimus, not very pleasant at all," he joked, but stopped when he saw the look on the general's face.

The wounded man's eyes were locked on the woman standing behind him, and he looked like someone had just punched him in the middle. Artair turned to look back at Caelia, and was surprised to see tears forming in her eyes. The hand that had flown to her lips was trembling.

The Helvetian glanced back and forth between the two for another second and then stood up. Walking toward the door of his tent, he paused next to the woman and, with a mischievous grin on his face, said, "Caelia, this is Artimus. Artimus, this is Caelia. I think I'll let you two get acquainted. I'll come back in a while." He backed out of the opening, leaving the couple alone in the small enclosure.

"I saw you die," Caelia said after a moment, breaking the silence.

"No, he did not kill me, but living without you these last two years was worse than death could ever be." Artimus answered, his voice cracking with emotion.

"Are you okay?" she asked, noticing the bandages for the first time.

Her husband nodded. "I'm better now than I have been for years," he responded, a smile growing on his face.

His wife smiled back, tears coursing down her cheeks. His wounds forgotten, Artimus crossed the room in three steps. As two years of frustration and loneliness melted from his memory, he took his wife into his arms and held her until long after she had stopped crying.

Chapter 51

When Artair relayed to Calum what Artimus had told him, the other Sword Bearer shook his head and looked at him questioningly.

"Artair, I'm ready to do anything to take this maniac down, both for our sakes and for the sake of everybody who has contact with him, but how do we know that this isn't just some scheme to get the two military leaders of our people back into his city? The pair of us would be quite a prize for someone scheming to get back into the good grace of the king he had just failed. Are you sure you can trust him?" Calum asked.

Artair paused for a few seconds before speaking. "You know, since all of this started, I haven't been able to tell who was playing games with whom. I haven't known who were the good guys and who were the bad guys, and the one time I decided to depend on someone I ended up being wrong about my assumption. So, I can't say that I 'know' too much, except for one thing. That is that if we don't break the reign of this king, he'll probably be back."

"You haven't seen what I have; they could easily return with another army in a month or so, and we would have to fight again. You know as well as I do that the next encounter will be a lot harder than the one today was. What he offers is a chance to end it once and for all. He needs our help and we need his. If we are wrong, we will both die. On the other hand, if we're right we'll solve the problem that has overshadowed our lives."

"What do you say, Calum, shall we take the chance?" Artair asked, his eyes probing into those of his friend.

The other man looked back for a moment and then sighed.

"It seems like we've spent our entire lives fighting this war, Artair, and I want nothing more than to see it end. All right, let's go, and we'll finish this if we can. As for the consequences we'll face if we're wrong, we've danced with death so much over the past fifteen years that I think he's probably given up on us." Calum quipped.

The two men laughed together and then separated to look after the duties of the night.

Chapter 52

One week after the battle, Artimus, Calum, and Artair headed back into the tunnels. The bodies had been cleared from the passage as soon as the Helvetians had set up defenses around the cave. Accompanying them were all the wounded Cyrenians who could walk. The warriors who still waited at the tunnels stood and waved farewell to their leaders as they disappeared into the darkness.

Caelia tried hard, but could not keep from crying as Artimus kissed her goodbye and walked into the cave. The time spent away from each other had only served to make them closer in the week they had had together as he recuperated.

Although she was sorry to see him go, and even more scared to have him go up against King Drake again, she had not tried to talk him out of it. She had known from the time she met him that he would be the one to take the tyrant from power; she just hoped that his destiny did not take him to his grave.

As soon as the group disappeared into the darkness of the passageway, Caelia headed back to camp where she had been helping with the wounded soldiers of both nations.

It was interesting for her to be with the Helvetians as they recovered from the battle. They had taken care of both their own wounded and the wounded enemies. Here she did not see the fear that she had become accustomed to among her own people.

Looking at them, she could understand why her husband and those with him were heading back to Cyrene--it was to put a stop to that fear once and for all.

*

Artimus showed no sign of pain as he walked, but Artair knew that the wound in his stomach had only barely healed over, and that in a violent conflict it would probably rip open again. He had tried to talk him into resting for another couple of days, but the Cyrenian could not be restrained any longer. He insisted that the more they waited, the harder it would be to get through to the king, and so they had agreed to leave before he was completely healed.

*

The trio left the wounded men behind soon after they entered the caves. The others would make it through just fine, but the three men's mission was more urgent, and they could no longer afford to be slowed down.

Several hours later, they spotted sunlight ahead, marking the approach of the opening to the Cyrenian side of the mountains. Artair stopped and checked his weapons as Calum did likewise. They had given Artimus a sword before entering the caves, but he left it in its scabbard and watched the Helvetians. He had more trust in his men's loyalties than they did.

When they were ready and all weapons had been put away, Artimus led the way toward the cave opening. Long before they reached the mouth, they could hear horns blowing, and as they reached open air they could see over five thousand men scrambling for weapons and heading for the passageway. The general stepped forward toward the army with Artair and Calum close on his heels. As soon as one man recognized him, they could hear Artimus's name spoken from person to person as the soldiers realized that their leader stood before them.

"Friends and comrades, I come at the beginning of a new day, a new era." The swordsman's words were lost to Artair and Calum because of the language barrier, but all of the soldiers listened with rapt attention.

"For years we have bowed to a man who, too long ago, lost his mind to power and bloodlust. As have the rest of you, I obeyed our king, but the time for that has passed. His time has passed. His leadership has only brought us fear, pain, and death. If we allow him to continue, that will be what he will bring us in the future as well.

"Let us through, join us, and we will end his reign of blood and terror. It is time, comrades, to dispel the fear we have bowed to for so many years. Join us, or remain slaves to a madman." Artimus's voice reached out to every soldier in the army as he began walking toward the front lines, his sword still in its sheath.

Artair and Calum walked behind him, heads up, adrenaline pumping.

As they neared the first line of soldiers Artimus did not slow but walked straight toward the unmoving mass of his countrymen. When only a step separated Artimus and the first man in line, the ranks split, clearing a path through the troops. The lines reformed behind the trio, and when they had passed through the entire army the men began marching behind them.

"What did you say back there?" Artair asked quietly as soon as he was sure he was not going to be attacked from behind.

"I told them that I convinced you two to surrender and that they should come with me to see your execution." Artimus said with a smile on his face.

The Sword Bearer glared at him and then shook his head when he saw the other man's smile.

"Oh, that's funny, he can fight and make jokes. Real good Artimus," Artair said with heavy sarcasm in his voice.

The general just chuckled while, behind him, Calum pulled his hand away from his sword handle.

They camped that night surrounded by the Cyrenian army, and they left again early the next morning. By mid-afternoon they stood looking out over Cyrene. Calum whistled softly as he took his first look at the sprawling city. Artimus glanced at him and chuckled.

"It's big and it's pretty alright, but by the end of the day it will be even better. By the end of this day it will be free," the general said, and led the way down the hill toward the massive gates.

The guards gathered at the portal as the general approached the walls.

"Open the gates, men, it's me," he said, looking up at the crowd above him.

"What are your intentions, Artimus?" one of the guards asked, a smile starting on his face.

His leader grinned up at him. "I intend to do what we should have done years ago, Jacob, nothing more."

The fellow grinned at the statement and nodded to someone below him. The gates swung slowly open to reveal several hundred soldiers. Sent to guard the entrance, they were now standing ready to receive orders from their returning general.

Artimus did not bother speaking, but headed off in the direction of the palace. The growing army followed him. The swordsman did not pause or speak until they made it to his house. Once there, he disappeared into the building and came back with his own sword at his belt.

The army followed the three men as they worked their way through the city. As they passed the crowds that gathered at the strange procession, people began to come out of houses and join themselves to the throng. By the time they made it to the palace, thousands of both soldiers and civilians had joined the general and his men.

The palace gates were open and Artimus walked through them without pausing. Covering the steps and overflowing onto the courtyard was the king's Royal Guard. The general stopped and looked at the group, nearly a hundred men in all, and smiled.

"It's all over, comrades. Step aside."

Chapter 53

None of them moved.

"There is an army behind me that could remove you from those steps, but I think we have had enough death in this palace over the past twenty years to last a dozen lifetimes. Step aside, join us, and we will end the reign of a man who should never have gained power in the first place. Think of who you are protecting, comrades. Your wives cry themselves to sleep at nights for fear of bearing children that will come under his rule, and you want to die for him? Let's end it, forever. Don't protect a maniac who does not care whether you live or die. Join us or do not, but his rule has ended. Choose whom you serve, for the time for indecision has passed."

No one in the courtyard moved for a couple seconds after Artimus's final statement. Finally, one man in the front of the group sheathed his sword and stepped forward. Walking up to the general, he stopped and looked into his eyes for several seconds, neither man blinking nor looking away. Then, the white-garbed swordsman nodded and walked past him. After taking two steps beyond the general, the former guard turned back toward his comrades and crossed his arms across his chest.

The sound of steel on steel was clear in the courtyard as several of the guards followed suit, sheathing their swords and joining their comrade in standing behind Artimus.

The trend continued until only three men remained, the ones standing at the very top of the stairs. The trio wore the white dragon symbol on the front of their armor. After a short pause, the three stepped back through the open doors of the palace and disappeared. Artair let out an exaggerated sigh of relief as he looked around at the guards. The action drew a glance from Artimus.

"You would not be so relieved if you knew who those three were. They have served Drake for years, and they are almost as dangerous as he is. Let's go," he said, and stepped forward.

The soldiers, obedient to an unspoken order, stayed where they had stopped when Artimus began speaking to the king's men. Twenty or so of the palace guard, on the other hand, began to follow the trio into the palace until the general stopped and turned to face them.

"This is no business for you, we will take care of it." he said.

The man who had first joined them shook his head.

"The King is yours, you can have him, but those three guards are our own, and as such they are our responsibility," he said, his voice incredibly deep.

After a moment's hesitation, Artimus nodded his acceptance and the guards followed them into the palace.

"Are you sure you can trust them?" Artair asked quietly.

"In fact, I'm fairly certain we cannot trust them, but right now trying to dissuade them from coming would be more dangerous than they might be," the Cyrenian answered, just as quietly.

Without hesitation, Artimus led them along the ornately decorated halls that led toward the throne room.

"How do you know where he is going to be?" Calum asked.

The general did not bother to look at him as he answered. "He will want to face us where he can feel the most powerful, you can be sure. That means the throne room."

As they turned the corner to the door that lead to their destination, the remaining three palace guards stepped from the doorway and aimed crossbows at the trio. As one, the three jumped back, away from the deadly weapons. As they leapt, they were pulled down from behind and their vision was filled with white as the guards behind them rushed toward their former comrades.

The crossbow bolts wounded two of their attackers, then the three guards dropped the weapons and drew their swords as the rest of the Cyrenians closed the distance between them. At the doorway, a vicious battle commenced, the three loyal guards fighting against their countrymen.

Artair and Calum jumped to their feet and started forward toward the fight, but Artimus stopped Artair and pulled him toward the throne room door. The battle between the guards and Calum raged behind them as they pushed forward.

The Cyrenian general paused only momentarily in front of the door and then shoved it inward. King Drake sat in an ornate throne at the opposite end of the room. The royal robes discarded, the king wore armor that showed a good deal of wear. A white dragon crest decorated the worn, but still serviceable, breastplate. A long sword lay in his lap and his head was down looking at the pale blade.

Even as they walked toward him, Drake showed no sign of even noticing their approach.

Their footsteps echoed in the massive room and each man ached to begin the battle. Adrenaline swirled like an angry wind in Artair's veins, and he itched to draw his swords. Artimus had locked eyes with the king when he finally looked up at the intruders, the crazed eyes of the king burning into his enemies.

"So, Artimus, in the end you prove to be both a traitor and a fool."

The king's voice was calm, but his eyes betrayed his madness.

The general stopped a few yards from the throne and Artair took several steps to each side, flanking him.

"You know," the king continued, "I don't understand you, Artimus. I gave you everything you needed. Power, prestige, everything. That wasn't enough for you, though, you wanted the throne. Now, you're going to try to take it with your barbarian friends. It won't work, you know that. You are no match for me, you never have been. The fact that you brought a couple of the savages with you will only delay your death, not prevent it."

"Do you really think that that army out there will stay loyal to you or to anything you've said when I walk out of this palace alive? No of course not, they'll scatter like sheep or bow to me as before, making some useless excuse. They will all die, of course, and without the leadership of these two the barbarian nation will fall to me in less than a month. You should have never crossed me, Artimus."

"I only wish that I could make Caelia watch you die, but don't worry about that. I'll tell her all about it later today before I begin killing her."

"You will do nothing to Caelia," Artimus hissed. "She is no longer in the stable of the Titans, you know that as well as I. We left her safe with the Helvetians only a couple of days ago. Your days of killing and hurting people are over, Drake. It's all over. Everything but your life has already ended, so don't make this too wordy."

"If you'd like to surrender we will not kill you, but I don't think you would be capable of it. Come then, Your Majesty, do your best and suffer your end." he yelled, and the tyrant left the throne in a blur of motion.

Steel clashed on steel as Artimus parried the king's first blow, followed by his second and third in quick succession. Artair attacked as his swords came clear of their sheaths, slashing toward the older man's back. Instead, Artimus had to duck as Drake slid out of the way and the deadly blades swung over the general's head.

Drake slapped the sword from Artimus's hand and thrust for his chest. Artair blocked the attack and tried for a killing thrust. It failed as Drake parried, and then kicked him in the stomach.

Artair stepped back, defending himself as he gasped for breath. Artimus attacked from the side, diverting the king's attention. He could not press his advantage, however, as the king's counterattack drove him back toward the wall. It was the best Artimus could do to keep the darting blade from his flesh.

Drake suddenly twisted away from his general as Artair's thrown sword sliced through the air where he had been a split second before. Before he knew it, the king was closing on him, the pale blade dancing. Their swords clashed twice, three times, and then Drake's sword slipped past the Sword Bearer's weapon and stabbed through his thigh. His leg buckling, Artair parried one more attack and then fell, trying to bring his sword around to stop the descending blade.

The king, on the other hand, had turned and was fighting desperately with Artimus. Behind the fighting pair, Artair pulled a tourniquet tight on his leg and tried to stand.

The general and his king fought furiously, neither giving ground nor gaining any advantage. Then the tyrant dropped to a crouch, slashed forward with his sword at his adversary's legs and, planting his weight on his free hand, kicked forward as Artimus parried the blow. The king's foot barely missed the moving blade and slammed into the swordsman's groin. Artimus grunted and stepped back.

The doors of the throne room crashed open, smashing against the walls and rebounding back. All three combatants turned to look at the same time.

"That is enough." Calum snapped, his tone similar to that of a father chastising bothersome children. "I have had my fill of this foolishness."

Drake stiffened slightly, pulling himself up to his full height and, while keeping an eye on both Artimus and Artair, turned to face Calum. "Who do you think you are, other than another man I must kill today?"

"Are you done playing?" Calum asked, ignoring the king's question. "Because if you are, we can end this now. I would rather see no more blood spilt today, so I would suggest you surrender. Live your life in prison, or you may die here and now."

Drake stared at Calum, incredulous. "Those are bold and also foolish words for one whose champion is lying over there bleeding and waiting for death. Who are you to think that you can defeat me so easily?"

Calum glanced at Artair, then looked back at Drake. "He is not our champion, Drake. He was the right man to fight Artimus, and Ragnal was our best dragon slayer, but I am the champion of Helveti. I am not your equal, I am your better."

"If you choose to fight, your last sensation other than pain will be embarrassment." Calum stated this last as a simple fact.

Drake snorted, then his face grew serious. "You will be known simply as one of the men I killed today, savage, and that is all."

The king attacked with his final word, not at Calum, but at Artimus, driving him back against the wall of the throne room. Then he turned to attack Calum as the Helvetian strode forward.

Their blades met once, then twice, and Drake stumbled backward, desperately defending against the powerful strokes of the Helvetian. He regained his composure, shifted his attack, and engaged again.

Drake continued to lose ground, moving back toward his own throne. Beads of sweat stood out on his forehead as he struggled to keep the ancient steel from his flesh.

Calum, on the other hand, moved forward as steadily as if going for an evening walk. The only part of his body that moved with any urgency was his sword arm.

Abruptly, Calum stopped advancing and stepped back from Drake.

"This is your last chance." Calum stated. "If you choose to continue, I will respect your choice."

Drake snarled at him, pulled a dagger from his waist with his free hand, and attacked, desperate to gain an advantage.

Calum pivoted by him, deflecting the king's momentum. The king tried to turn to face his enemy, but he was out of position and knew it. The ancient steel of the Helvetian champion slipped through the king's side armor. In, and back out again, and Calum stepped back from his enemy.

Drake clutched his side, staring at Calum with utter confusion on his face. He tried to draw breath, but couldn't. He looked around the throne room, desperate for some kind of help, but only saw his enemies, watching him with patient eyes.

He turned back to Calum, waiting for the next attack, but the Helvetian had already sheathed his sword and stood with his arms crossed, waiting. Enraged, Drake attacked him, swinging his sword, but then it stopped. Calum had seized his sword arm with one arm, easily stopping the attempt.

Drake's knees buckled, and he found himself kneeling at Calum's feet, staring up at him with eyes that refused to focus. He tried to lift his arm that held the dagger, but realized suddenly that he was no longer holding it.

He looked up in time to see Calum's kick coming. The Hellvetian's boot hit him in the middle of his breastplate, and he had the sinking sensation of falling. He landed on his back, sliding along the polished stone of his throne room.

The last thing he saw was Calum walking away, ignoring the king's final moments.

"See, I told you he can take care of himself." Artair said suddenly, breaking the silence. Artimus smiled apologetically.

Calum raised an eyebrow at the Cyrenian with a question in his eyes, and then they all laughed tiredly. The trio turned to look as one of the palace guards opened the door to the throne room and looked in at them.

"Is it over?" the guard asked tentatively.

Artimus nodded as he sheathed his sword and then he and Calum, taking the injured Sword Bearer between them, headed toward the door.

At the entrance, the palace guards waited, tending their wounded. As the three victorious swordsmen exited the throne room, all who were able to stand up rose to greet them.

"Is the king dead?" one of the white-garbed guards asked.

Artimus began to speak, but another of the guards interrupted him.

"No, the king stands before us." he said, and bowed slowly to Artimus, who stood with an unreadable expression on his face.

The rest of the guards followed suit until all of them bowed to the man who would now be their leader.

Motioning to Calum, Artair hobbled away from Artimus, leaning on his friend and grinning wickedly at their comrade.

"Well Artimus, it looks like your life just got complicated. Won't Caelia be proud?"

The two Helvetians laughed at their friend's obvious displeasure.

"Come, Artimus, there are thousands outside who still do not know whom they serve." Calum said, and motioned with his head down the hall.

The Cyrenian leader stepped up to take Artair's arm again as they started toward the exit. The palace guard fell in behind the trio as they hobbled along the hallway.

As the palace doors swung open a hush fell on the waiting multitude as they watched to see who would emerge. A thunderous cheer filled the palace grounds as they saw the three men step out of the grand structure.

"Go, greet your people Artimus, you are their king now whether you like it or not," Artair said. "They need a leader, one who is more concerned with life than death. If you remember how you got here, and why it was important, then you are that man," he concluded.

"I will never forget. See that you don't either," the swordsman responded, looking the Helvetian in the eye.

With a nod from his king, one of the guards stepped up to support the wounded warrior as Cyrene's new leader walked forward toward the cheers of his people.

Epilogue

Word was sent to Helveti, and to Caelia, telling of the death of King Drake and their victory. The new queen returned immediately to Cyrene to be with Artimus and to help Artair recover from his wound. Calum stayed in Cyrene until Artair was ready to travel, and then the two returned home.

Arrangements had been made that would allow for the slow integration of the two societies. No longer would the caves be seen as portals of evil, but as a passageway between allies.

Ragnal's hammer stayed where it had landed, waiting for it to choose another master. Most of the citizens of Cyrene had already tried to lift it, but without success. It was widely rumored that one of Ragnal's sons would be the most likely candidate.

The society and traditions of the Sword Bearers remained in place. Although the dragons had been destroyed, both peoples had learned that their societies would always have a need for men, and women, who were prepared to be guardians of peace and freedom. Or, if need be, to fight those who were foolish enough to bring war to their doorstep.

About the Author

Lance Conrad lives in Utah, surrounded by loving family who are endlessly patient with his many eccentricities. His passion for writing comes from the belief that there are great lessons to be learned as we struggle with our favorite characters in fiction. He spends his time reading, writing, building lasers, and searching out new additions to his impressive collection of gourmet vinegars.

Published works:

The Price of Creation (The Historian Tales)

The Price of Nobility (The Historian Tales)

The Weight of Swords (The Sword Bearer Chronicles)

Upcoming works in 2015:

The Price of Loyalty (The Historian Tales)

The Price of Redemption (The Historian Tales)

The Pawn's Advance (The Souless King)